Audrey Reimann was brought up ~~in~~ ~~Manchester~~ educated at the Macclesfield Grammar School for Girls. She and her husband now live in East Lothian.

Audrey has three children and is the proud grandmother of ten, and has been variously a bank clerk, a nurse, a teacher, and a foster mother to twenty-five. But, above all, Audrey is a storyteller. Recently, on Anne Robinson's BBC Two programme 'My Life in Books', comedian Sarah Millican named Audrey's novel *Flora's War* as one of her favourite books, saying: 'This is a book that will make you laugh and make you cry.'

Also by Audrey Reimann:

Flora's War

AUDREY REIMANN

The Runaway

EBURY
PRESS

1 3 5 7 9 10 8 6 4 2

Ebury Press, an imprint of Ebury Publishing
20 Vauxhall Bridge Road,
London SW1V 2SA

Penguin
Random House
UK

Ebury Press is part of the Penguin Random House group of companies
whose addresses can be found at global.penguinrandomhouse.com

First published in 1990 as *The Moses Child* by Corgi,
an imprint of Transworld Publishers
This edition published in 2017 by Ebury Press

www.penguin.co.uk

A CIP catalogue record for this book is available from the British Library

ISBN 9781785034893

Printed and bound in Great Britain by Clays Ltd, St Ives PLC

Penguin Random House is committed to a sustainable future for
our business, our readers and our planet. This book is made from
Forest Stewardship Council® certified paper.

PART ONE

A Fortunate Young Man

1875

Chapter One

It was the hottest day of a hot summer in 1875 and the ornamental lake in front of Suttonford House, one of the finest country houses in Cheshire, was as smooth as a sheet of glass in the midday August heat.

Sixteen-year-old Oliver Wainwright crawled through the hedge from the top field where the reapers worked and ran silently down the grassy slope to the water's edge at the far side of the lake.

He took cover behind a laurel bush near the reeds and lay looking down at the torn trousers and shapeless singlet, grey with age and careless washing, which barely covered his broad body. He was tall, over six feet, with black curly hair, startling blue eyes and a body grown strong and lithe from three years' work on the Suttonford estate.

His heart was no longer hammering with excitement and he began to roll up the ragged brown trousers while his eyes scanned the lake. There was a mallard, a little way out from the others, sliding over the smooth water, its metallic green feathers shining in the sun. Oliver felt in his pocket for the home-made catapult of hazel wood, slipped his feet quietly into the shallow water and narrowed his eyes in concentration.

He pulled silently on the leather sling, straining the rubber thongs to their tightest, letting the lead ball go whistling through the still air to crack into the skull of the unwary drake. The bird toppled sideways; so quick was its death that the reflex flutter of wings hardly disturbed the ducks that rooted in the shallow water at the lake's edge.

The soft, grey mud oozed between Oliver's bare toes as he waded out towards the mallard where it floated in deeper water. He would not be seen from the house. They would all be too busy preparing for this afternoon's garden party to worry about a duck.

'There he is!'

'Wainwright!'

Oliver turned sharply and saw Wilf Leach and one of the labourers running, crashing down the slope from the high wheat field. He could see the rage on Wilf's ugly face as the big man grunted, swore and stumbled, red-faced towards him.

'Get 'im! Hold 'im till I get there,' Wilf roared at the younger man. 'I'll teach 'im! He's been asking for a thrashing for weeks.'

Oliver dived smoothly into the green water, pushed his kill down the front of his singlet and struck out for the centre of the lake. Wilf Leach wouldn't come into the water after him, not after all the beer he'd drunk. Wilf must have seen him sneak away from the other field workers.

He pulled away from the lakeside swiftly until he was out of range of the sticks he heard dropping into the water behind him. Then he turned to look.

The two men were at the water's edge, shaking their fists and shouting. He couldn't hear them for the water in his ears but he knew that they'd hear him, all right. He put a hand up to his mouth to make his voice carry back to them.

'It'll take more than you, Wilf Leach, to thrash me! You may be going to marry Dolly, but I'll not obey you. You drunken animal!'

His heart was thumping, with anger more than effort, and he swam faster, towards the little island, which was off centre of the long, oval stretch of water. The island was twenty yards from the wide sweep of lawn, which ran down to the lake from Suttonford House. There was a wooden duck-house on the island, where the birds nested, and low trees for their roosting. He'd stay there until Will went back to the field.

Oliver swam until he could feel the muddy lake bed under his hands. He kept low in the water, crawled ashore and lay face down in the long grass. There was nobody to be seen on the lawn, though nearer the house he saw servants setting out painted iron tables and chairs under the elms and cypresses that flanked the three-storey limestone mansion of the Oldfield family. An open-sided marquee had been put up on the close-cut grass but it, the musicians' stands and the folding metal seats were unoccupied.

Dolly, his stepmother, would be busy in the kitchen at the big house until four o'clock so she'd not hear about his theft of the duck until Wilf came to their house tonight. Oliver rolled on to his back and closed his eyes against the hot sun.

He'd run away tonight. His mind had been made up for weeks. Dolly had set her cap for Wilf Leach, the crude, coarse farm manager Oliver hated. She didn't need him any longer. His only regret was for leaving Tommy, the eleven-year-old half-brother he loved. He'd speak to Tommy later and tell him not to be afraid. Dolly would protect her own son from Wilf's drunken rages.

Oliver had never called her 'Mother' though she was the only mother he'd ever known. His father had found Dolly in the nearby town of Middlefield at the end of a day's frantic search for a wet nurse and foster mother for Oliver, whose own mother had died in childbirth.

Dolly had been fourteen then and her own bastard child stillborn. Oliver learned to call her Dolly, as his father did, and it was too late to learn another name when his father married her, the year before Tommy was born.

The sun burned into his tanned face and broad shoulders. His singlet and trousers were dry and he could hear voices. He must have been asleep. Oliver rolled over again and opened his eyes.

In front of the house, ladies in bustled dresses, holding silk parasols to protect their complexions from the sun, were parading the wide sweep of lawn. Top-hatted men strolled with them or gathered in groups, drinking fruit cup. Oliver could clearly see one man lacing his with brandy from a flask. Their voices were raised to a certain pitch of refined excitement as they greeted Sir Philip and Lady Camilla Oldfield.

Oliver remembered Dolly telling them that Sir Philip's daughter, Laura Mawdesley, and her daughter, Florence, would be there. Florence's father had been killed a year ago, Dolly said, and they were coming back from London. Sir Philip was giving them a house in Middlefield. Dolly knew all about them.

Oliver accused her of kowtowing to them all the time. 'We're as good as them,' he told her. 'You don't have to talk about 'em as if they're bloody gods.' Oliver wouldn't kowtow to them. No, he'd never do that. His dad had never kowtowed, only been respectful. Well he'd not even be respectful, Oliver vowed. All the same, he wondered which one was Sir Philip's granddaughter, Florence.

There were four young girls at the water's edge, all unaware that they were being watched. One of them, the one he thought was the prettiest, turned round and, for a full minute, looked directly towards him. Oliver thought she had seen him but she turned away, her gold hair swinging lazily across slight shoulders that were alabaster white against her dress of pale yellow silk. He had never seen a girl as pretty as she was and he could have lain there all afternoon, watching her.

But he had to get away, unseen. Now that she'd looked away he'd crawl round to the other side of the island, drop into the water and swim for the far bank. Then he'd pull himself out of the water further down, under the overhanging trees at the water's edge, where the lake ended and the water funnelled over a weir, once again the river Hollin that fed the lake.

* * *

Florence had seen him. A dark-haired boy looked right into her eyes from where he lay on the island. He must be one of her grandfather's workers, hiding from his overseer.

She turned her head slowly so that he'd think she hadn't seen him. There was something arresting in the youthful arrogance of his strong features. She pretended to look into the distance so she'd not have to acknowledge his presence, but she saw him slide, long and sinewy into the water, and pull strongly across the lake with powerful arms. It made her feel like a conspirator, letting him go unchallenged.

She was troubled and a little ashamed of the thrill she'd felt at seeing, for the very first time, a young boy – no, he was assuredly a man – wearing so little. For in truth she had only once seen the unclothed body of another living soul and that had been a babe-in-arms.

She had seen statues, of course, in Paris and Rome; they had been informative. Once, when she'd disobeyed Mama and ventured into the servants' quarters in their London house she'd chanced on a group of housemaids admiring a naked baby that a disgraced servant girl who had come to beg for food had brought to the back kitchen door. Florence had insisted that the house staff fill the girl's bag with good food and she'd held the wriggling baby and tried to wrap him in his holey old shawl until the girl took him away.

She recovered her composure. 'Shall we go back to the marquee?' she asked her companions. 'Our mamas will be looking for us.'

Her voice, low-pitched yet clear, had not a trace of the north-country tones that touched the edges of the other girls' speech and it drew their attention at once.

'Do you think you will enjoy living in Cheshire?' The dark-haired girl whose name, Florence remembered, was Sylvia, spoke first as they crossed the lawn towards the gathering. 'Middlefield may seem small and dull after London society.'

'I saw very little of London society,' Florence told her. 'I'm only just out of the schoolroom. I shall enjoy living in Middlefield.'

Her natural gaiety and her eagerness to be liked by the girls who were to be her daily company made her reply with a little less than the truth. 'Indeed, I'm glad to leave the capital – and Mama's tiresome old friends.'

The Bell-Cooper girls giggled at this and Florence added hastily, 'What I mean is that they simply took no pleasure in anything.'

They had reached the tables where Mama, with a slight frown on her face, stood with Grandfather Oldfield and Uncle Bill. Mama's hand lifted: the signal that Florence was to go to her.

7

'There's Mama.' Florence raised her own hand almost imperceptibly in reply. 'I must join her. Shall we meet later?' She touched her new friends' hands in a delicate gesture of goodwill, which she hoped was neither too mannered nor too haughty. 'Let us sit together after tea.'

One of her faults, she well knew, was a tendency to 'climb the high horse' as her old nanny used to say. The other fault, she suspected, was a fierce determination to have her own way. On the good side she knew herself to be sensitive in the extreme to the feelings of others and aware at all times of the need to treat everyone with the utmost good manners. She simply couldn't bear to see anyone reduced to embarrassment or tears and often went to her room to weep when Mama turned cold contempt upon a servant, or a social inferior.

It was difficult, learning to be a lady when her impulses were to laugh out loud when amused or, as had happened only a few minutes ago, to stare rudely at a ragged, half-naked young man.

'Well, Florence? How do you like your new friends?' Uncle Bill's eyes twinkled, blue and lively under his bushy white eyebrows. 'Ye'll no be lonely. Eh, lassie?'

Florence laughed out loud. 'I'll no be lonely. Och aye,' she teased, trying to imitate Uncle Bill's deep Scottish accent.

She saw Grandfather flinch. Was it her laughter and mimicry that displeased him? Or was it Uncle Bill's presence? Sir Philip had never forgiven Uncle Bill for having no background. Mama had explained; Uncle Bill was rich, yes. But his money was made in the cotton mills of Middlefield. His money was from trade. Most of all, Florence knew, Uncle Bill had never been forgiven for running away with Grandmother's sister Lucy and marrying her when she was just sixteen.

Aunt Lucy and Grandmother were coming towards them now. Florence saw Uncle Bill's face break into a huge smile at their approach; saw Aunt Lucy's eyes flash with merriment in response and knew that, white-haired and old though they were, the old couple had never lost the love that had drawn them together so long ago.

Uncle Bill took hold of Aunt Lucy's hands. 'You look beautiful, Lucy,' he declared. 'It's a bonny gown.'

Mama's eyebrows lifted in disapproval. Public displays of feeling were never tolerated. But Aunt Lucy did look beautiful in a dress of fine lavender tussore. Mama herself, since they were out of mourning, wore only grey.

Grandmother – Lady Camilla Oldfield, small, birdlike and terrifying in her severity, wore indigo silk with a lace collar and a high, lace-trimmed hat of the same stuff. She appeared to be carved from stone, so set was her expression. 'How did you like the Bell-Cooper twins, Florence? And Sylvia Machin?' she was asking. 'Your mama says that you are to share lessons with them.'

'I like them very much,' Florence answered sweetly. 'It will be a great pleasure not to have a governess,' she added mischievously to see if Grandmother would delight, as Aunt Lucy had, in the facetious remark.

Grandmother remained severe. Grandfather, who had been approached by a footman, came to Grandmother's side and patted her shoulder. 'I have to attend to something, Camilla,' Florence heard him say. 'Servant trouble. No. Not you. I'll attend to it myself.'

Grandmother gave a brief nod. 'Come, Florence. Laura. We'll join the Davenports for tea.' She led the way with Florence and Mama following her across the crowded grass.

So Aunt Lucy and Uncle Bill were not expected to sit with them. Florence felt colour rush to her cheeks at the high-handed manner in which the snub to her darlings had been dealt and then relief when she heard, behind her, Aunt Lucy's tinkling laugh and Uncle Bill's hearty chuckle as the old couple turned their attention to the other guests.

Would she ever get used to the ways of Mama and the grandparents – to the assessing of people for their social standing before a friendly overture was made or returned? It had been easy in London. There, all she had to remember was never to go into the servants' quarters and to be welcoming, charming and polite to Mama's friends.

Here, in Cheshire, Grandfather dealt with the servants himself, yet held himself aloof from Uncle Bill and Aunt Lucy. She hoped that she would not do or say the wrong things this evening at the dinner. There was to be musical entertainment afterwards and Florence herself was to play her pianoforte piece. 'I shall simply observe the way things are done here,' Florence decided. 'I shall do things my own way as soon as I am able. Today is for enjoyment.'

* * *

Hollinbank, a settlement of squat, lime-washed cottages, was a mile from the big house. Oliver followed the river path on its meandering course until the Wainwrights' cottage came into view with Tommy, sitting on the step, waiting for him.

'Tommy!' Oliver saw the lad's face, so like his own, break into the mischievous grin that transformed his features from an expression of brooding to one of infectious gaiety.

'Where've yer been? I've been waiting for hours.' Tommy ran up to him and pulled the mallard from Oliver's hand. 'Have yer killed it today?'

'Aye. You don't think I found it dead, do you?' Oliver gave Tommy a playful clout across the head. 'I got it this afternoon, instead of working.'

'Ooh. Oliver. Wilf'll be mad. Does he know?'

'Aye.' Oliver laughed at his brother's worried face. 'Put the duck in't scullery. We'll walk down to the stones. I've summat to tell you.'

They walked, out of sight of the cottages, to the place where the riverbed was stony. They climbed a stile between stiff hawthorn bushes and slid down the grassy bank to where the river ran deeper, over green velvet stones that were leaden and polished from the passing of feet where they stood proud of the water. They plunged their bare feet into its cool depths and crossed to the other side where they sat watching the bright water.

'I'm leaving the estate, Tommy. I can't stop here,' Oliver told him. 'I don't want to leave you but I've got to go. I only stayed to help Dolly; to save us from the workhouse. She doesn't need me now she's got Wilf.'

Oliver saw the hurt in Tommy's face but he didn't know how to tell his brother kindly that eleven years of closeness were over. 'I don't know how she can do it,' he added bitterly. 'How can she want Wilf after being married to Dad?'

'When are yer going?' Tommy asked.

'Tonight.'

'Take me an' all.'

'I can't, Tommy. It's too dangerous. They'll come after you. But I'll come back for you one day. Get you away from Wilf.' Oliver wanted to console the youngster whose eyes were filled with pain at losing his big brother.

'She'll maybe not marry him,' Tommy said in a trembling voice.

Oliver sent a handful of pebbles skimming over the water, cracking sharply against the stepping stones. 'Hard to say. Meself ... she can do as she likes. I've had enough of her!'

'So've I, Oliver.' Tommy was near to tears.

'You can't have. She's your own ma. But she's not mine. I can go.'

'Suppose she sends Wilf after yer? He'll kill yer when he finds yer.'

'He'll not. He'll be glad I've gone.' Oliver spat out the words, hatred in every syllable. His blue eyes narrowed in concentration as he told Tommy. 'I'm going to run when they go upstairs. Wilf takes his clothes off and leaves them on the settle. We've seen him do that, haven't we?'

Tommy grinned weakly, recalling the night they sat on the stairs, not four feet from the gin-soaked pair, taking turns to squint through the cracked door, which opened into the living room.

'I'm going to creep down and take his britches and his boots.' Oliver's mouth twitched with pleasure at the thought of Wilf's face when he discovered the theft. 'The boots were Dad's anyway.'

'Oh, Oliver. Don't let 'im hear yer. Where are you headin' for?' Tommy looked taken aback with the effrontery of the plan and had lost his desolate look. 'I won't tell.'

11

'I know you won't. I'm going to Middlefield.' He gave a laugh of derision. 'Where the Mawdesleys are going to live.'

'Who's the Mawdesleys?' Tommy asked.

'Sir Philip's daughter and his granddaughter. The ones this big garden party's for.'

'They 'ave a garden party every year. Yer know they do.'

'Aye. But this time they're going on all night with it. Dolly says there's goin' to be a dinner and musical concert an' all. Then they're going to live in't biggest house in Middlefield.'

'What's wrong wi' that?' Tommy said. 'They can do what they want. It makes no difference to the likes of us.'

Oliver felt anger rising in him. 'They're no better than us, Tommy. Our dad's lying under tons of stone in their blasted quarry. And they're feasting and larking. It takes ten of us to serve every one of 'em. And they're not worth it.' He turned his head away and spat into the stream. 'I'm doin' no more of it.'

'Where will yer live?' Tommy's voice was shaking again.

'I'll get work in one of the mills and find a place to lodge. I've got four shillings hidden. Come on.' Oliver pulled his brother to his feet and together they crossed the stones and made for the path.

'Why won't you ask for a job at t'quarry? It were good enough for Dad. Old man Jessop's a good boss and they don't pay bad,' Tommy asked him as they went back to the house.

Tommy still didn't understand, after all the explanations. Oliver took his brother by the shoulders and turned him gently in the direction of the quarry.

'They'll not kill any more Wainwrights,' he said, his eyes hardening, his voice low and intense. He tightened his grip on Tommy's thin shoulder.

'We're as good as them, Tommy. Me mother worked right up to her time, on her knees in their damned kitchen. That's what killed her. It wasn't having me as killed her.'

He let go his hold. 'It's not just Jessop and Wilf. They're only lackeys. It's them – Sir Philip and Lady Oldfield and all like 'em. I'll never raise me cap to them again. Never!' He looked into

Tommy's face. 'I can't stop here, lad. You see that don't yer? The Oldfields can't take one generation after another and have 'em drop dead in their service. I'm not one to start a riot or set their workers against them. I want better for meself, like Dad did. Dad got to be quarry-master. We lived in the village in the quarry-master's house. When Dad died they threw us all out – Dolly, you and me. They gave us the cottage we live in so long as Dolly worked in their kitchens. You were a baby and I was five. Dolly was glad of the work and a roof over our heads. I don't hold with it; one man owning another; his house, the work of his hands. They'll never own me.'

Tommy didn't understand. He was only eleven. So Oliver went on, 'Dolly – I mean your ma – has always worked hard. She gives back a lot more to them, by way of her work. But I never felt like her real son. And I don't feel bad about leaving her. Not now she's got Wilf.'

Tommy was listening intently. Oliver put an arm about his shoulders. 'We're nearly home. Say nowt to your ma when I go. Tell them you were asleep when I went – if they ask.'

Tommy began to cry, jerking his chin in an effort to control his tears. 'Take me. Take me with yer,' he pleaded.

'Listen.' Oliver tightened his hand round his brother's shoulder. 'I'll do all right. I can work, I'm strong and I'm quick. And I'm clever. I'm cleverer than all of them. One day I'll have it all. You'll see. I'll have a proper home, with carpets and things and I'll come for you as soon as I can and I'll take you away with me. And we'll be rich, Tommy. Richer than the whole bloody lot of them put together.'

Chapter Two

Dolly Wainwright, assistant cook, red-haired and quick-tempered, stabbed at the lemon, over and over, put it inside the prepared goose and heaved a sigh of relief. She was a small, good-looking woman with fine, chiselled features, a sharp, sometimes waspish manner and a habit of scowling when she was upset or angry.

It was four o'clock in the afternoon and she'd been working in the kitchen of Suttonford House since five that morning. Not that she was the only one who was tired, of course, but there was only young Bessie in the kitchen with her at the moment. The others were all in the garden, waiting-on. They were run off their feet as well, but Dolly had not had a minute away from the heat of the stoves all day.

The results of her handiwork were spread out before her on the scrubbed deal table; a galantine of beef to be eaten cold, glistening on a dish of freshly pulled young lettuce. Tiny cold potatoes thinly coated in parsley butter were piled high on china plates. Crisp salads; a poached salmon, its pink flesh coated in a creamy sauce; fruit compotes of glowing late strawberries and ripe yellow peaches from the estate glasshouses; fruits she had preserved in syrups and brandy, thin almond fingers, macaroons, bread and cakes to last three days.

'What the hell can Sir Philip want with me, Bessie?' she asked the new kitchen maid. 'On a day like this, with his garden party goin' on. You'd think he'd have enough to do without sending for me in the middle of it.'

In their basement kitchen the heat was unbearable. The range had been lit since five o'clock that morning. The oak dresser was

14

almost bare of the piles of plates and dishes it normally held and the sounds of scurrying feet and the clattering of crockery in the side kitchen told of the fevered effort that four kitchen maids, ten housemaids and two footmen were making to serve the guests outside.

'With a bit of luck we'll not need to light the big fire tomorrow,' Dolly declared, before hooking a length of butter muslin from the rack high overhead in the old beams. 'If it's warm like this they'll not want hot food.'

She wet the cloth under the pump, then carefully, using upturned ewers as supports, draped it over her day's work. Taking the window pole, she fitted its brass hook into the top sash and pulled, letting a little more air into the stifling kitchen. Even the stone-flagged floor was warm. Dolly pumped water into the deep brick sink, her plump arm working the handle hard and fast.

Cold water gushed up from the well beneath the kitchen and she splashed her face, cupping the water in her strong, square hands, letting it run down her forearms. Then she ran wet fingers inside the tight, clinging collar of her grey working dress.

'Good job Jackson's in 'is pantry, eh, Bessie?' she said. The girl didn't answer. Dolly knew that Bessie would be shocked into silence by her offhand way of referring to the dignified old butler. 'He can't abide us washing at the sink. Silly old fool.' She laughed aloud. Bessie's eyes had flown to the door, afraid Mr Jackson might have overheard.

Dolly carried the goose on its iron skillet to the blackleaded range and placed it carefully in the big oven, adjusting the draught control so as not to let the fire get too hot.

'There! Take it out in an hour and put that 'erb stuffing inside. The lemon will have soaked up some of the grease by then, see? And mind yer don't break it up! Cook will be 'ere in a minute but Sir Philip wanted me to do the goose, particular.'

'He says no one can do them as good as I can!' she added with satisfaction as she pulled off the coarse blue apron, set her cap straight and made towards the door. 'I hope it's not our Oliver he wants to see me about.'

Dolly, of the sensuous hips, narrow waist and full breasts was, at thirty, becoming impatient with the toil that had been her life until now. She had rediscovered passion and shameless delight in the attentions of Wilf Leach and the reproaches and wilful contempt of him by her stepson, Oliver, and her own son, Tommy, angered her.

She knew they hated Wilf but they didn't understand how it was for a woman without a husband. Wilf might not be as good a man as Joe, their own father, had been. Wilf was a drinking man but he was better than none. He earned good money and could keep a woman happy in bed. And in time they would be given a farm manager's house in the village, once Wilf had married her.

'There's plenty as'd swap places wi' me to get a man and his wages,' she told them often enough. 'Believe me, there's a few women in the cottages as'd like to be in my shoes.'

Sir Philip Oldfield's office overlooked the kitchen garden at the back of the great house; a small room, one-third taken up by a big oak bench, piled high with heavy leather-bound ledgers and estate records.

Dolly saw the tall man with craggy features and greying fair hair as an aristocrat whose world was bounded by the stone wall, which enclosed his two-thousand-acre estate. He owned everything his stone boundary walls encompassed; Suttonford House, the farms and Suttonford village, the quarry where her husband's body still lay beneath a hundred tons of stone. Plus, rumour had it, Sir Philip owned most of the nearby town of Middlefield as well.

Normally the housekeeper or even Lady Oldfield attended to the domestic servants so it had to be something important for Sir Philip to send for her.

She stood before him, ginger curls springing out beneath her tightly drawn mobcap and her face pink and perspiring. Once, she had been told by the butler that she had a singularly disrespectful manner but since she did not know what the long words meant, believed she had been flattered. 'Did yer want me for summat?'

'Close the door, please,' he commanded.

16

Dolly ignored him and stood, head to one side, impatient to know the worst. 'It's not Oliver, is it? Has he been doin' summat? He's a wayward lad, sir. I can't do nothin' with 'im.' In Dolly's book attack was the best line of defence. She had practised the art for so long now that she knew no other way and found, in consequence, that she was seldom challenged.

Sir Philip looked down his aquiline nose at her. 'I am taking the unusual step, Mrs Wainwright, of speaking to you directly about your stepson's behaviour. I thought highly of his father. Joe Wainwright was killed on my estate. He was a good father and a fine man.'

Dolly's lips tightened into a hard line. She had no intention, five years later, of listening to hymns of praise to her dead husband. Soon she'd be Mrs Leach. It was time to forget the past. Life was for living and Wilf was bringing her to life again. She felt a thrill, anticipating the night ahead. 'What's he been up to, sir? He's too much for me. He is that!'

Sir Philip continued. 'He was seen by one of my workers, taking duck from the lake, here at Suttonford. I don't allow labourers or their families to come into the garden grounds. They must keep away from the house unless they are ordered to work here. If I send for him I shall have to punish him but I mean to let it pass this time. Does he work?'

'Yes, sir, but he ...'

'Here? For me?'

'On the farm, sir. But he won't take orders from Wilf Leach. That's the trouble. Me and Wilf's gettin' married soon but Oliver thinks he's the head of the house and he doesn't want Wilf in it. That's why he's behavin' bad.' She knew that Sir Philip saw plenty of wicked youths. They came before him twice a week at the bench. He'd not wish to see any of his own workers brought before the court.

'Send him to Mr Jessop in the quarry. Five o'clock sharp tomorrow morning. He can work where his father did.'

Sir Philip had seemingly done all he intended to do for Oliver. 'That will be all, Mrs Wainwright.'

'Do you still want me in the kitchen?' Dolly asked brazenly. Nobody else dared to speak to Sir Philip as she did. 'The new cook's here now but you was glad enough for me to do it when old Mrs Gunnel took bad.'

Sir Philip was losing patience. 'Mrs Wainwright, you are an exceptionally good cook. Had your manner matched your skill then you could have taken on Mrs Gunnel's job. You are the second cook. You are to work in the kitchen from five o'clock until four in the afternoon.'

He held the heavy door aside for her but Dolly, unused to courtesies, darted past him, almost breaking into a run as she descended the stair to the kitchen.

'I'm goin', Bessie. I'll catch 'im one!'

'Young Oliver?' Bessie asked.

'Yes. He'll cop it when I get back,' Dolly replied. She untied the mobcap and pushed it roughly into the pocket of her grey dress and folded the blue apron for tomorrow. It was clean on today and it would do another turn.

Dolly went out the back way, glancing quickly about her as she slipped through the gate into the kitchen garden. There was nobody about today, they were all at the front, but just to be sure she pretended to sit and rest for a moment while she edged nearer a small heap of carrots that lay on the end of a row. There was so much in the garden – so much went to waste it was wicked not to use it. She'd tell them so, if they caught her.

There were bunches of onions drying on a fencepost and she knew she could snatch a few of those as she went. The vegetables safely under her skirt, Dolly, well pleased with her haul, went on swift feet away from the distant sounds of music and voices, behind the glasshouses and onto the track that led to the cottage. She had a parcel of food for Wilf's baggin, which she'd also concealed under her skirt. He'd be working until it was dark and he'd be glad of a bite.

As soon as she unlatched the door she saw the duck. Oliver had been poaching then. She'd better not say anything to Wilf. Outside she could hear Oliver and Tommy rolling in the sun, armlocked in Tommy's impossible challenge to his idol.

She peered through the window and watched Oliver flatten her son on the ground, heard Tommy start to whine.

'Why don't yer let me win for once?' he pleaded.

'Because if I do, you'll take on someone bigger than yerself,' Oliver was laughing, 'and get a pasting for yer cheek.'

'Tell us what yer did then, our Oliver.' Tommy's high-pitched voice was muffled under his brother's chest. Dolly saw Oliver spreadeagle himself, laughing, over the lad, pinning his wrists to the baked hard ground.

'Then I hit him, Tommy. I hit Wilf Leach hard, right in the mouth. I broke what's left of his dirty brown teeth in his ugly mouth and I told him what he'd get if he came round our house again. I said to Wilf, "If you ever show yer face at our house again, Wilf Leach, me and Tommy'll string yer up from the rafters."'

'What did he say?' Tommy squeaked. 'You're a liar, aren't yer?' Tommy struggled and kicked, but could not dislodge Oliver.

'Aye. But I wish I had hit him.' Oliver stopped laughing and pushed himself up on to his knees. 'And if I don't go soon I'll probably kill him …'

Dolly heard him. She flung open the cottage door. 'Oliver! There you are, you lazy devil.' She could feel her face suffuse with anger as he came insolently towards her.

'I heard yer,' she said. 'Go where? You're not going anywhere.'

'I'm not stoppin' 'ere. I'll not live wi' you and Wilf Leach,' he answered her and she saw the defiance in his eyes.

'Yer will. And you'll have to change yer name. You and our Tommy. You can start calling yerselves Leach from now on, like I am.' That was the best way, just tell them to do it.

Oliver's eyes were full of scorn for her and she saw that his hands were clenched as if it was all he could do not to raise them against her. 'You can call yerself Strumpet for all I care,' he said. 'But I'll not answer to Leach … nor will Tommy. I'm leaving.'

'You've got to stop 'ere. You belong to the estate. Like we all do,' she told him. 'You have to work ...'

'They don't own me, woman!' He was shouting.

'They do!' She hesitated for a moment before adding, triumphantly, 'You're articled ... apprenticed ... and yer can't get away from that!'

'An apprentice? I'm an apprentice?'

'Stop shoutin',' she yelled.

'Apprentice what? Apprentice bloody slave?'

He'd got the better of her. Again. 'Get yerself up to t'farm,' she said, impatience with him rising above annoyance. 'Tell Wilf to bring some potatoes and milk if he can gerrit. And if you see Old Jessop tell 'im you're startin' work tomorrer at t'quarry. Sir Philip said so. Take Wilf's baggin with yer. And take our Tommy.'

She handed over the linen-wrapped parcel. 'Coom on. Be sharp.'

'What are yer feeding that great ugly beast for?' Oliver asked cheekily but he grabbed the parcel and ran. 'You don't send any baggin up when I'm in the fields,' he flung at her.

'No! And you don't earn enough to keep yerself in salt, never mind bloody baggin!' she called after them.

She raked the hearth and brought sticks and paper from a box under the settle. There were a few logs left, enough to finish the rabbit stew she'd started yesterday. When she had done, and the stew was bubbling over the fire, Dolly changed out of her working dress into a skirt of brown dyed calico and a blouse, pink silk and lace-trimmed. Apart from a feathered hat, the blouse was her best bit of finery, bought in a rummage sale for twopence. She boasted of its distinguished history, having once seen Lady Oldfield in something similar. Wilf would be back in an hour or so and she liked to look fetching.

Half an hour later she stood at the door, in her skirt and blouse, scowling, impatient for their return.

'Get some water, will yer?' she demanded of Oliver, lifting the pail from its shelf above the kitchen slab. 'Get a move on! And you, coom in, Tommy.'

Oliver took the iron-hooped pail to the pump, which was shared by all the cottages. She can't face the neighbours, he thought smugly. And no wonder when she goes around like a wanton woman. She's got nowt on under that skirt. Everyone can see right through it.

He took the water back to the cottage and placed it on the kitchen slab. The duck was hanging, plucked and drawn, at the open window.

Dolly stood at the door, arms folded in front of her waist, head cocked to one side in the battling attitude Oliver knew so well.

'I had to stand and take a tellin'-off from Sir Philip this afternoon – over you and yer bloody duck,' she said in her sharpest voice.

'You're glad enough to pluck it though, aren't yer?' Oliver replied caustically. 'You didn't chuck it out, did yer? Who told him? Wilf?'

'If he did, it's because he has to,' Dolly said. 'Sir Philip knows we're gettin' married – me and Wilf. He knows Wilf's responsible for us. So it's Wilf as'll get blamed for your nonsense,' she added with the air of one who has just put a miscreant in his place.

She was sticking up for Wilf again. Oliver's anger got the better of him. He grabbed her wrist and held it. 'I'd have looked after yer. You and our Tommy. I earn ten shillin' a week and I give you nine and six.'

'It doesn't alter the fact. Wilf's going to have to answer for us.'

'You can tell Wilf Leach that he's only answerable for his own bloody nonsense. Not mine,' he roared, bending until his face was close to hers. 'I only take what's there for the asking. Like wild duck and rabbits!' He gripped her wrist tight until he saw an answering anger in her eyes. She'd not let him know he was hurting her. Oliver loosened his hold but his mouth was a tight, hard line.

'I don't take anything that belongs to yer stinking Oldfield family,' he told her. 'They don't own what's wild and free. Ducks and rabbits come and go as they please. They don't have to kowtow!'

Dolly pulled her arm away and faced him, eyes blazing. 'You're just trying to make it harder for me, aren't yer,' she said, 'always making trouble. Yer can't stand it, can yer? Can't stand anyone else in charge?'

'There's nobody tells me what to do. Least of all Wilf Leach.' Oliver heard the fury in his own voice. 'How you can let him do what he wants with yer I'll never know.'

'Wilf wants to marry me. There's nobody else'll have us. The Oldfields put us out of the quarry-master's house when Joe died. They'd put us out of 'ere, soon as look, if I couldn't work. Wilf's going to look after me and you can't let him be. Can yer?'

'Marry you?' Oliver looked at her in disgust. 'He'll not marry you. He's promised half the silly widder wimmen in the village that he'll marry 'em.'

'You're a liar!' Dolly tried to push past him but Tommy was in the doorway to the living room, blocking her way.

'Don't marry Wilf, Ma. Find someone else,' he cried.

'Wilf's not a bad lot, son. I'll not let him do anything to you,' she said in a gentler voice. She went to the cupboard and brought out basins, placed them on the old stained table and began to ladle rabbit stew for them.

'Did you tell Old Jessop you'll start tomorrer?' Dolly asked as she sliced bread for them to dip in the bowls.

Oliver knew she was trying to change the subject. She half-believed all he'd said about Wilf's other women. He sighed and sat down. What did it matter? He'd be gone tomorrow. She could go to the devil any way she wanted. 'Aye. He said to be there sharp so I'll go to bed straight after me supper.' The lie came easily but he dared not look at Tommy as he spoke.

When they had eaten he climbed the steep spiral stair that led to Dolly's tiny attic room and the cubbyhole beyond, where he and Tommy slept. He gathered his few possessions into a roll, slipped outside, and hid them under a heap of dusty straw in the old stable, then went back into the cottage to wait.

At ten o'clock Oliver and Tommy lay in their corner on the heap of old clothes that served as a mattress. There was no window in the roof space and the place under the eaves that they shared was musty and airless in summer but damp and freezing in winter. They heard Wilf return, singing loud and tunelessly, swinging a sacking bag wildly as he tried to keep his balance on drink-weary legs.

'I'll take my belt to that Oliver. He's asking for a hiding, Dolly. I'll thrash the bugger to within an inch of 'is bloody life!' His words carried clearly up the stairs.

'Leave 'im, Wilf. Anyroad, he's starting work for Old Jessop in t'morning,' Dolly replied.

'Jessop's never seen 'im. Jessop would have told me if he'd taken 'im on. Look in the bag, woman!'

They heard him lurch against the stair door, heard the contents of the sack being spilt over the floor, heard Dolly set the milk can upright and squeal with delight. Oliver crept to the foot of the stairs and watched, through the cracked door.

'Here.' He saw Wilf pull Dolly towards him, gathering up her thin skirt in his dirt-engrained hands. The waistband tie came loose and he pulled clumsily at the fastenings on her blouse. His hands searched her body and he took her noisily and violently, standing against the stair door, his beard raking her neck, thrusting her hips repeatedly against the wood.

Oliver went back up to Tommy who lay, squeezing his eyes tight shut, his fists to his ears to blot out the sounds of Wilf's grunts and a strange high wailing that must surely come from his mother – and the terrible, rhythmic hammering.

The drinking started. Soon there would be angry voices. Every night followed the same pattern – Wilf enraged and bullying: Dolly placating and whining by turns until they staggered up the stairs to fall, too tired and drunk to do battle any longer, upon the rough wooden bed.

Chapter Three

Oliver waited until Wilf's grating snores masked Dolly's, then, lowering his head, he crept past the bed and edged his way downstairs to the living room that looked eerie in the pale light that bathed it. Wilf's breeches and boots were lying discarded on the settle.

He dressed quickly, his hands fumbling in their haste, and at last he was away, retracing his steps of the afternoon, now in brilliant moonlight and the air like wine, with only the gentlest of breezes, filling him with speed and energy.

He ran past the silent cottages at Hollinbank, along the whitened grass that bordered the path and up towards the high field where the stooks of wheat the men had made in the afternoon resembled groups of small people leaning together in talk. He ran through them swiftly and silently, along the top field to the hedge and down the long slope that led to the lake, back to where he been earlier in the day.

He paused at the lakeside and looked across the still, inky water to the big house. Lanterns were strung across the front of Suttonford House – bright yellow points of light hanging between the tall windows. On the wide semicircular sweep of gravel carriages waited to take the guests. Oliver heard light, happy voices. It was as if the lake amplified the sound for he heard the horses' hooves stamping impatiently, waiting their turn to move forward.

In the brightly lit entrance hall people were saying their farewells. Gloved hands waved from the darkened carriages as they pulled away and though Oliver could not see their faces from where he watched he wondered if she was there; the girl he had seen from the island.

He ran round the lake's perimeter, keeping to the trees and bushes, out of sight of the guests. He ran round the back of Suttonford House itself. He ran parallel to the two-mile gravel drive that extended from the manor to the highway and he crouched behind the hedge that bordered the road when the carriages passed by.

The last carriage passed within feet of him. And she was there; the girl he had seen earlier. She wore a dress of blue satin, cut low in the front and she was tiny, as aristocratic families are, not much above five feet, Oliver guessed.

She leaned out of the lowered window, her long fair hair fanned out about her shoulders and her voice when she spoke was musical and low. 'Mama. Do look. It's so beautiful. There's not a soul about.' The carriage rounded a bend and was gone from his sight but the impression remained for long afterwards of the loveliest girl Oliver had ever seen. He could have believed he had imagined her, were it not for the trundling wheels, crunching gravel and the rattling of harness he could hear through the trees.

* * *

Middlefield was a hilly market town between Manchester and the Derbyshire border. The three main streets met at the cobbled market square before the solid, four-square edifice of the Town Hall, which in turn was overshadowed by the Norman church of St Michael and All Angels. The church sat at the highest point of the town in a solemn churchyard, enclosed by a stone wall under which the steep, tortuous Wallgate led down to the cattle market and railway station below.

The three main streets, Rivergate, Wallgate and Churchgate, were busy thoroughfares, noisy with the passage of coaches and carts whose iron-clad wheels clanged against the stone setts and where the metal-on-metal screech of heavy brakes added to the din.

Oliver entered the town at dawn where the main road became Rivergate, beyond the bridge over the same river Hollin which meandered carelessly through the estate at Suttonford. By the time it reached Middlefield the river had become swollen from tributaries on the way and was a fast-flowing river that cut swiftly through the town, bringing with it the power to turn the machinery of the cotton mills lining its banks.

He felt excitement stirring within him at the clatter of heavy clogs on the little streets leading to the cotton mills. The mills lined the fortified walls of the Hollin and stood edge to edge with it, overpowering it and making it a dark rush of menacing waterway.

He found shops interspersed with taverns along the main street. There were entries – covered alleyways leading to flagged court-yards and damp workers' cottages and all were disgorging their occupants who, at six o'clock on this blue summer morning, appeared lively, even eager, to reach their workplaces.

Throwsters, spinners and weavers all made their way to the mills. Men shouted across the streets to each other, making ribald comments about the girls in bright cotton dresses who, in twos and threes, arms tucked into one another's, gave as good as they got, laughing and shrieking at the more outrageous remarks.

It was going to be another hot day. Oliver watched a farmer delivering milk from his cart, lugging the can through the alley-ways to the shared yards where old women brought jugs and basins to be filled. The man carried a long-handled measuring can under his arm and there was a second ladle on the side sill of the cart beside another churn. Oliver waited until the man disappeared from sight and, ignoring the protesting snorts of the horse, clam-bered over the side and drank deeply, ladling himself gill after gill of its creamy freshness.

He reached the market square and watched the stallholders set-ting up. He saw that the established ones got the best sites. The middlers took what came and casuals, men with laden ponies and donkeys, were given what was left. Latecomers had to find a space, clinging to the fringes, setting out their wares on the smooth brown cobblestones.

He walked around the stalls, enjoying the bustle, the air of purpose and the feeling he got, without his having any part of it, that there were rivalries and jealousies under the banter that passed between the traders. A man could start in business in a market he thought, if only he had something to sell.

A baker was laying out trays and Oliver led the man's horse to the yard behind The Bull for him in return for a couple of warm, sweet-smelling barm cakes.

'Here, lad! Want to earn a shilling?' A red-faced man from the oil and candle stall hailed him.

'No. I'm going to find lodgings. I'm new here.' Oliver replied, hoping that this would not be his only offer of work. 'I've nobbut a few bob but I'll find a place to live and come back up, eh? I'm looking for work.'

'There's a job going at The Pheasant on Rivergate. Leonard Billington's looking for a stable lad. You can handle a horse. Get a haircut and shave at the barber's and go for a wash. There's a tap behind the Town Hall. Come back when you're ready and I'll tell you where to go.'

'Ta. I'll be back in a while.' Oliver followed the man's pointing finger to the barber's shop. Inside, men sat on forms around the room, waiting their turns at the two chairs where the barbers worked, open razors skimming up and down the leather strops. Oliver felt the hot softness of the lathering brush on his chin and closed his eyes so as not to flinch when the razor stroked away the soap. He opened them to watch his hair being cut, falling on to his shoulders and prickling the back of his neck until finally it was combed and smoothed into a sleek, parted cap.

'That suit you, sir?' the young barber asked, holding aloft a mahogany-framed mirror, reflecting the shorn back of his head. Nobody had called him 'sir' before. Oliver could have lingered. He liked the mingled smells of hair pomade and bay rum, the gossip, smart talk and veiled hints.

He went back to the market place and crossed it to descend the bustling Rivergate where, outside The Pheasant, a line of men

27

waited. All were older than himself. 'Are you waiting for the job?' he asked a short man in a greasy top hat.

'Aye. Go to t'back of the line,' the man said sharply.

Oliver did as he was told and listened to the tales the men told him, of weeks without work. Some had not eaten for two days or more and all of them seemed ill-tempered and unfriendly. As he waited and listened the urgency to find work grew on him and when at last his turn came to go inside he wanted the job very badly.

It looked a busy place. A row of barrels, tapped and on their sides, lined the long, windowless wall of the dark tavern. Heavy tables with forms and stools were placed near the door and around the empty fireplace.

Oliver hoped the man would like him enough to take him on. His knees knocked as Mr Billington, a stout man in a hessian apron, looked him over. 'Can you handle horses? Drive a carriage and pair?' the man asked.

'Aye. I drove them on the farm. Big 'uns. Shires. And I ploughed and harrowed with them.' Oliver tried to make his voice sound confident.

Mr Billington wiped his hands on his damp apron and took in his appearance. 'What makes you think you'd be any better than the others I've seen? Why should I take you on?' he asked.

It was a strange question but Oliver answered him as honestly as he could. 'Well,' he said. 'I don't think you'll get another chance. I think I'll be taken on pretty quick.'

Mr Billington, who had seemed serious up until then, began to laugh though Oliver could not for the life of him see the humour in his answer. But he knew he'd made a good impression when the tavern-keeper said, 'You look strong. Big enough to handle the coach and harness the horses. You seem an honest country lad. They're often easier than town boys. D'you think you could get used to lighter horses and driving on the roads?'

Oliver had already marvelled at the drivers he had seen weaving in and out of the tangled network of narrow streets, passing one another on the steep Rivergate and backing laden carts down a precipitous Wallgate. Still, horses were only horses and he'd never let one get the better of him yet. 'Oh, aye. I'm not afraid of the roads. Will I get me dinner and somewhere to sleep?' Oliver asked.

'You'll have the groom's place. Back of the stables. Look after the horses, clean the stables and carriages and drive for anyone that wants you. Most bring their own drivers but we have a coach and pair. They'll pay you themselves for driving. A good groom can earn two or three shillings a day, easy.' He looked Oliver over. 'There's a morning suit and top hat should fit you. Ask Mrs Billington when you go round the back. Supper's at six. Breakfast at seven.'

He opened the door at the side of the counter. 'Albert!' he called. A tall, lanky youth, a little older than himself, Oliver guessed, appeared from the kitchen beyond.

'What is it, Dad?'

'Take this lad. What's yer name? Take Oliver round to the stables will you? Show him everything. He's our new stable lad.'

'Aye. Follow me.' Albert went ahead through the side door, which opened outwards onto the short driveway between Rivergate and the coach house and stables of The Pheasant. As soon as the door was closed behind him Mr Billington's son leaned casually against the doorpost, barring Oliver's way. 'Where are you from?' he asked. 'Country bumpkin are you, lad?'

He got no further. Oliver snatched his arm, turned it quickly behind the other's back and came forward until his face was level with Albert's.

'Don't talk like that to me, boy. You'll be sorry,' he snarled. He had no intention of letting Albert treat him like a servant. Even if he had to give the boss's son a black eye at the start it would put him right for later. Oliver wondered, fleetingly, if Mr Billington would send him packing but the question answered itself when he thought of Albert, who'd wait to beat him up every time they met if he didn't beat him now.

'You think you're a big man, do you?' Albert teased as he ducked under Oliver's arm. Soon the two were wrestling, each trying to pin the other down, rolling together, teeth gritted, each trying to overpower the other.

Oliver felt a thud, felt his teeth snap together as Albert's fist hit him in the jaw. His tongue was cut and he could taste his own salty blood. He threw himself forward, pitching into Albert with both fists but it appeared that he was not hurting his opponent. Albert was grinning, he was dodging most of the blows and Oliver was aiming wildly. Then he caught him one; a smart left to Albert's face and the smile was gone. He heard Albert gasp for breath and Oliver followed it with a lunge at the other ear.

Albert sidestepped and Oliver went headlong towards a stone water trough. Albert was on top of him now and Oliver gritted his teeth as he slowly forced him backwards, straining and grunting as the heavier town boy moved inch by painful inch into an upright position where Oliver could hook his leg around him and send him crashing to the ground.

Then Oliver was on top; kneeling on Albert's chest, trying to hold the position securely enough to aim a blow at Albert's nose but Albert turned under him and they were rolling again, the stone setts scraping their knuckles and cheeks.

The struggle might have continued had not a dray turned into the yard and an old driver wearing a striped hat shouted out to them, 'Come here. You two! Give us a hand to unload will yer?' as he pulled up the horses in front of the trough, 'and stop yer nonsense before you frighten the damn beasts out of their wits.'

Albert straightened up, breathless. 'Shall we call it even and shake hands?' he asked Oliver, who leaned, gasping for breath, against the far wall. The horses were between them, drinking thirstily. To continue the fight would mean either going outside onto the street or waiting until the dray was gone.

'Do you want to finish it later?' Oliver said, watching Albert's face in case this was a new trick.

'Shake hands. We'll be friends and not fight again.' Albert was out of breath too, but smiling.

Oliver hesitated for a second, but there was no sign of double-dealing from Albert, nothing but an open smile on his face.

He extended a hand, a hand as grazed and swollen as Albert's was. They grinned sheepishly at one another.

'We'd best help the drayman,' Albert said. 'He'll tell Dad if we don't and we'll both be for it.' They lifted the barrels onto the yard for the man then Albert picked up Oliver's bundle.

'I'll show you where the groom's place is. Come on!'

Behind the loose boxes was a room, not much bigger than a stable, with shoulder-high stone walls. Above them crude wooden panelling separated the horse's area from the groom's. The room contained a broken-backed chair, a slopstone and pail, a table, and in the corner, a palliasse to be filled with straw. There was plenty of sacking and even a torn blanket. There was a fireplace and the horses' heat to warm the place in winter. It would do him nicely.

Chapter Four

Florence could see the turrets of Balgone from the carriage window as they turned into the drive. It was quite her favourite house and though, in the months since she and Mama had come to Middlefield, Aunt Lucy had visited them, this was her first unaccompanied visit as a young woman.

She had wonderful memories of childhood when, during their summer and Christmas holidays at Suttonford, she'd be sent with her old nanny by carriage to Balgone. Nanny always spent the day in the company of Aunt Lucy's housekeeper and she, Florence and Aunt Lucy used to play together. Aunt Lucy always prepared for her coming. There were treasure hunts with rhyming clues hidden around the house and Aunt Lucy clapping her hands in delight when Florence solved them. There were winter afternoons spent toasting bread on long thin forks before a red fire, handing the pieces to a servant for buttering; and there were stories and kisses and Aunt Lucy holding her, looking into her eyes and saying, 'Oh, Angel-Child of Moon and Stars and All that in Them Shines,' and when she'd asked what it meant, Aunt Lucy always replied, 'It means that you are loved.'

She remembered praying that Aunt Lucy would be granted a baby of her own. She had asked God every night to send a baby to Aunt Lucy and every time she'd gone to Balgone she looked for God's gift but God had never given the baby to Aunt Lucy. Aunt Lucy said that having Florence to herself for a whole day at a time was almost as good. And today was her first grown-up call.

The carriage wheels crunched on the gravel, the morning sun that slanted between the firs that hid the house from the road glinting on granite and sandstone and lighting crocus and snow-drops on the grassy border.

On the step Aunt Lucy, dressed in green velvet, a picture of charm and sweetness, was waiting to greet her. Florence kissed her aunt and went ahead into the house. She gave her cloak and hat to the maid and took Aunt Lucy's hand in hers. 'Do you know, this is the first time I have ever been here alone, Aunt Lucy.'

'I know. How you are growing up, Angel-Child.' Aunt Lucy tucked Florence's hand into the crook of her arm as they entered the drawing room. 'Do you still like living in Middlefield?'

'I like it perfectly. Of course, I'm not allowed to walk in the town. But Mama and I pay calls on her friends and we go to Suttonford twice a week.' Florence sat down on the sofa and patted the folds of her skirt, blue wool with a matching bolero. 'Do you like my outfit?' she asked eagerly. It surely wasn't bad form to look for compliments from one's aunt. 'I chose it myself. Mama allows me to order my own clothes now that I'm almost fifteen.'

'You look lovely, darling. And your education?'

'Oh. Lessons with Sylvia Machin and the Bell-Cooper girls. Art and French at Sylvia's; the girls come to me in Churchgate for Latin and music.' She kept her mirth inside until Aunt Lucy's maid had left the room, then added with an irresistible urge to make Aunt Lucy laugh, 'Mama is trying to teach me to be an Oldfield between times.'

Aunt Lucy was laughing. 'And how, my darling, does an Oldfield behave?'

'With the utmost dignity,' she replied, lowering her eyelids droopily and imitating Mama's slow, drawling speech. 'I'm sure I'll never be a credit to poor Mama. I so want to run and sing and laugh ... all in the wrong places.'

Uncle Bill's footsteps sounded on the stairs and Florence turned to watch him come into the room; white-haired and fresh complex-ioned, lively blue eyes ablaze. 'How's my braw lass?' he said as she went into his arms.

She felt his prickly moustache tickle her cheek. 'Very weel ... thank ye!' she teased.

'And ye're happy to settle in Middlefield, are ye, Florence?' Uncle Bill asked. 'I'd have thought there was more excitement to be had in London for a young lassie growing up.'

'Mama wants to live in Middlefield. Her heart's always been here.' Then peals of laughter came from Florence as she told them. 'I think, too, that Mama and my grandparents are expecting me to marry young. They are going to occupy themselves in finding a suitable ... that is, rich ... young blade for me to wed when I'm of an age.'

'And you?' Aunt Lucy smiled. 'What do you think of their hopes?'

'Mama says there are so many dashing young men in Cheshire that I will be quite spoiled by their attentions. When I'm sixteen I'll be allowed to attend the Suttonford balls. Then I am to fall in love with the richest young man of them all.' She laughed again at the memory of Mama's oft repeated words. 'And we will all live at Suttonford happily ever after.'

'Couldn't you live at Suttonford now? And why must you marry a rich young blade to be happy-ever-after?' Uncle Bill asked.

'Grandfather says the Churchgate house is more suitable.' Florence began to laugh again, then added, 'Though I think he fears it will be too costly to educate me and entertain prospective suitors at Suttonford.'

Aunt Lucy dabbed her eyes to wipe away tears of laughter but Florence saw at once that her aunt's expression was not one of jollity.

'I hope you find a young man who will fulfil all your mama's plans for you, Florence,' she said quietly. 'I couldn't have married one of the young men Sir Philip thought right for me. I fell in love with Bill at our first meeting and there was never any doubt in my mind that it was right to marry him.'

Florence saw her aunt reach for Uncle Bill's hand as he said, 'Well, lassie. If you fall for one of the laddies they'd have you marry it will make them all happy. I hope you find what your aunt and I found.'

'What is love?' Florence asked softly. 'How did you know that you loved one another?'

34

'When it happens to you ... you'll know,' Aunt Lucy answered. 'There will be no need to ask.' She stood up and held out her hands. 'But since you are far too young to think about these things I suggest we go down to the morning room, take tea and chocolate cake and talk about what we will do with our lovely day.'

* * *

Every Wednesday Bill Grandison drove from Balgone to his mills and workshop in Middlefield. He stayed overnight at The Pheasant where he spent the evening working on his ledgers before his regular visits to his banker and lawyer on Thursdays. They looked after him well at The Pheasant, serving his supper in the family's own parlour and keeping the quietest bedroom for him.

It was no longer necessary for him to visit his mills. He was a rich man; there was more than enough money for himself and Lucy. Managers and accountants could do the work for him but he could never bring himself to release his hold on the businesses he had built against such odds. If he wished to he could spend his days driving Lucy on her weekly visits to her sister, Lady Camilla Oldfield, or pass his leisure hours in conversation with Sir Philip instead of with his stockbroker.

He chuckled to himself at the thought. The old baronet had spent forty years opposing him. Only during the last ten, when Sir Philip's fortunes had begun the decline a wiser man would have anticipated, had the old aristocrat begun to ask the advice and help of the brother-in-law whose company he had so long scorned.

No. Bill wouldn't join the sycophants at Suttonford, even in his old age. He preferred the company of young people. He liked to see the wheels turning; liked to watch the new young hopefuls trying to make their way in the world. He stood now at his bedroom window at The Pheasant, looking out over the stable yard, waiting for Mrs Billington to call him to supper, watching young Oliver lead the horses out through the gate in The Pheasant's high wall to the paddock the tavern shared with The Crown.

Since Oliver had come to The Pheasant last summer Bill had used the lad to drive him to his mills. He always chatted to the boy before he climbed into the carriage and again when Oliver helped him carry the heavy books from the mills' offices up to his room. The young man was polite and had made a name for himself for having the best-turned-out coach and pair in town.

Bill was pleased to see that his horses, as well as The Pheasant's own, were being turned out to graze overnight. Many a lad would simply have stabled them and avoided the hour's extra grooming time that the freedom of the paddock would entail.

He watched Oliver put them in the field and unfasten their leather halters. Then, out of the corner of his eye Bill saw her – Irene Wardle, the landlady of The Crown, tiptoeing stealthily alongside the wall that surrounded the paddock, out of Oliver's sight until she was a mere few yards from where he would soon come through the gate.

She was a handsome widow of thirty, dressed this spring evening in a black skirt and short red jacket. Bill stepped back into the shadows, not wanting to seem inquisitive yet unable to resist waiting to see if his suspicions would be confirmed.

Yes. She reached the gate at the same moment Oliver opened it and threw her hands up in the air as if startled. What an actress she was! The smile that had been hovering at the corners of Bill's mouth broke through as he watched with fascination while she smiled and fluttered her hands, making Oliver lean towards her to hear what she said.

Oliver wore high riding boots for working in the yard with trousers tucked inside. His blue shirt was open at the neck and rolled back at the sleeves, showing strong tanned forearms and hands, which he now held out to Mrs Wardle, steering her by the elbow away from the gate. The evening sun caught his black hair, lighting his face as he threw his head back to laugh at something she'd said, his hand pointing now to where the horses rolled in delight in the spring grass.

What a good-looking young man he was. He looked much older than the seventeen years Bill knew him to be and Bill wondered how Oliver would conduct himself, faced as he was with a woman hell-bent on seduction. For there was no doubt about her intentions. Irene Wardle was a woman of the world and had been looking for a man since her husband died two years ago.

Oliver was nodding to her now and taking his leave, coming into the yard and fastening the gate behind him. Bill saw Irene turn away and walk swiftly through the alleyway towards the side door of The Crown. He watched Oliver for a few more minutes until Mrs Billington tapped on his door.

'Your supper's ready, Mr Grandison,' she said.

Bill descended the winding staircase to the Billingtons' parlour, where Mrs Billington had lit a fire for him. The room was crowded with heavy furniture; hard-stuffed armchairs and a circular mahogany table. There were numerous large paintings on the walls and everything, mantelshelf, sideboard and windowsills, was hung with beaded and tasselled fringes.

At an ornate side-table beside the high fireplace Leonard Billington was setting a crystal decanter of Bill's favourite whisky and a jug of cold water. 'Would you think badly of me, Leonard,' Bill asked the big man, 'if I were to ask your stable lad to join my staff at Balgone?'

Leonard Billington did not reply for a moment. He considered his reply. 'I'll be sorry to lose him,' he said finally. 'But I suspected from the start that he'll not be satisfied with ostling. He's got a lot about him and I've nothing better for him here. What have you got for him?'

'I need someone for the Balgone stables. My old coachman hasn't done any driving for a year now and I want to retire him.'

'My Albert will miss him,' Leonard said. 'They've struck up a good friendship.'

'Where did you find him?' Bill asked. 'A youngster like that wasn't brought up on the streets.'

'He arrived one day last August,' Leonard said. 'He left his home on Suttonford estate. Wanted to "better himself", he said. Though I wouldn't say stable work was a step up in the world from working for Sir Philip Oldfield. Would you?'

'I would. I would indeed,' Bill replied. 'A big advance.'

'Do you know the Oldfields?'

'Oh, yes. I know them intimately, you might say.' Bill laughed heartily. 'Your young man has decidedly taken a step in the right direction.'

Ma Billington brought his supper to the table. She was a jolly, good-natured little woman who appeared to enjoy the ceaseless round of cooking and serving that being the landlord's wife entailed.

'What do you think of Oliver, Mrs Billington?' Bill asked as she fussed about, making sure the dishes were all within his reach.

Her round face broke into a beaming smile. 'Eeh, he's a grand lad. Him and Albert's got friendly and I'm right glad about it. Albert's steadied up a lot since Oliver came. He's often in with Albert. They've never had a cross word.'

As he ate his supper Bill wondered about the boy's reasons for leaving the estate. He decided not to mention, at first, that he was related to the Oldfield family. Time enough for him to find out when he worked at Balgone and drove Lucy to Suttonford. It would be interesting to hear what a young man of today found so unpalatable about living under the patronage of his brother-in-law.

After supper he went down to the stable yard and found Oliver cleaning brasses by the light of candles. He tapped on the wooden wall to attract his attention and noted the ready smile that came to the stable boy at his arrival.

'You seem to be a good lad with horses, Oliver. Have you thought about improving your station in life? Thought about bettering yourself?' he asked.

Oliver put down his cloth and stood up to speak. 'Yes. I've thought about it, sir.'

'I need a good man to take charge of my coach and horses; to live in the coach house at Balgone. Someone I can trust.'

It was a good offer, one any young lad would jump at but Bill found that he was not really surprised when Oliver refused it. The boy brushed the top of the chair with a duster and moved it towards him.

'I'm sorry, Mr Grandison, but I don't mean to spend me life working with horses,' he said slowly and Bill heard a genuine note of regret in his voice.

'What do you want?' he asked.

'I want to work for meself, sir. I'm saving money to start meself up in business and it wouldn't be right to take your job if I didn't mean to stay,' Oliver answered.

Bill sat down on the broken chair. 'You want to earn your own living do you? Not be any man's servant?' He saw that Oliver was serious but made a last attempt to divert him. 'I think you could succeed, but you could go a long way in a good master's house.'

'Mr Grandison, don't you see what's happening? Trains are taking people about. More ways of moving faster are coming all the time. The horse and carriage will be finished before I am. People are coming to the town every day ...' Oliver's face was alight with enthusiasm and Bill found himself responding to his youth and spirit.

Oliver went on, '... and the market men make a good living. I want to get a start in the market. There's always folks wanting to buy, far more than wants a ride in a carriage. It's not that I don't appreciate your offer.'

Bill was intrigued by the boy. Oliver reminded him of himself at that age; full of fire. 'Come up to the tavern when you've finished the harness,' he said at last. 'We'll talk about your ambitions. I'll advise you if I can.'

He went back to the tavern and asked Leonard to bring an extra glass. He had only been waiting for ten minutes when Oliver knocked at the parlour door. 'Come in.' Bill pointed to the armchair opposite his own when Oliver entered the room. 'Sit down. I'll pour a couple of drams. You've not signed the pledge or anything, have you?'

'No, sir. I quite like it,' Oliver said.

'Tell me all about yourself. Your ambitions – your plans for getting on in the world.' Bill handed the whisky to Oliver and seated himself.

Oliver leaned forward, eagerness written all over his countenance. 'I'd like to hear your story instead, sir. They say you made your own fortune. How did you do it?'

For a moment Bill was taken aback at the boy's directness then he began to laugh. 'Oh, laddie! You don't play with words, do you?' He took a white handkerchief from the pocket of his frockcoat and mopped his eyes. 'I didn't do it by asking rich men how they made their money. No, indeed. Have you any ideas yet?'

'Not yet. I thought I wanted to go into the mills but now I know I want to have me – I mean my – own business, no matter how small it is.'

'You didn't like working on the estate, I hear?'

'No. It wasn't the work. You don't belong to yourself. It's as if you're owned by others,' Oliver replied and Bill saw pride in the boy's face; pride as his had been; pride that would never allow him to comply with a system he resented.

'Were you treated badly?' he asked.

'No. Not me. Me mother died when I was born. She worked until a few hours before she had me. And she died,' Oliver said.

'And your father?'

'He was killed in the quarry six years ago. Dad told them – he told them it wasn't safe – but Sir Philip made him cut deeper, undermining all the time,' Oliver said.

Bill saw the quick filling of the young man's eyes. The loss of his father had affected him deeply. Bill remembered the talk about the accident at the time and wondered if he ought to tell Oliver now, that he was related to the family who had been responsible for his being fatherless. No. He didn't want to reopen old wounds; the moment passed and it was too late. He took the empty glass from Oliver and refilled it.

An impulse to help the eager youngster made him ask, 'Would you like to look round my mills, Oliver? I started with nothing, you know. It can still be done.'

'I'd like that, sir.' A smile of pleasure broke across the boy's strong features.

'Call me Bill. It makes me feel young.'

Bill had always been inward-looking but he was enjoying talking to this youngster. To his surprise he found himself telling Oliver about his own early years.

'Like you, I was brought up on an estate, Oliver; a Scottish estate called Balgone. I named my house after it. The countryside was not unlike Cheshire – soft, rolling land not far from Edinburgh.'

Oliver was listening with rapt attention.

'I was left an orphan, too. But I'd had an education and knew I could do better for myself than work on the land.'

'What brought you to Middlefield?'

'A lassie, Oliver. A lovely lassie I'd only seen once when she visited the estate. She was so beautiful … she still is,' he said. 'When I found out she lived in Cheshire I set out to follow her and win her.'

'Go on,' Oliver said.

'I hadn't a penny but I'd brought some tartans with me – a bagful. I'd saved my wages and I sold my few belongings and bought tartans in the borders on my walk south. And I took a stall here – and sold them all.'

Oliver, he could see, wanted more. The lad had poured him another dram to keep him talking. 'And then I bought silks with the money. And I sold those – and I sold them cheap.'

'Was it good luck? How did you know what to sell?' Oliver leaned forward, eager for more.

'It wasn't good luck. It was hard work – and good brains, for I had nothing else. I made a profit but I wasn't greedy. Week by week I built it up until I had enough to buy looms. There was an old mill, Hollin Mill, by the river. It had been a flour mill but the miller was gone and I discovered that it was owned by a wealthy man. I went to see him and asked him to lease it to me. He agreed and I asked an acquaintance to lend me money. I was sure I could do it, you see. We put the looms in and an engine and that was how it all came about.' Bill laughed at the memory. 'Then I bought another mill, for the money came in faster.'

'Did you see the girl again?' Oliver asked.

'I did that, laddie. She was related to the man I leased the mill from. I married her. We had to run away to Scotland to marry. Her brother-in-law – my brother-in-law he is now, didn't want her to marry me. And he had power, Oliver. He's a very powerful man.'

'Have you any children?' Oliver wanted to know.

'No. It's been a great sadness. But it's been the only one. We couldn't love each other more, even if we'd had all the children we'd have liked,' Bill replied. 'We have a great-niece though. What about you? Have you brothers and sisters? Did your father marry again?'

'I've a half-brother. His name's Tommy and I'm going to send for him as soon as I've got a place of me own and some money,' Oliver told him. 'And there's me stepmother. She's marrying a man we hate. She didn't need to do it. I'd have looked after them both.' A look of anger crossed Oliver's face when he spoke about his stepmother.

Bill wanted to know more. 'Are you disappointed in her?' he asked.

'I'm disgusted with her. She's behaving like a ... like a ...' He seemed reluctant to say what he felt about his stepmother's behaviour. 'She used to be a good woman. I never thought she'd throw herself at a man like Leach,' he added.

'Is he rich? This Leach?'

'No. He earns more than she does. He earns more and he steals a bit. She doesn't love him or anything. I'm sure she doesn't. She's fed up with being poor.' Oliver added fiercely, 'I'd have seen 'em right. I don't think a woman should marry a man she doesn't love. Do you?'

Bill chuckled. 'Would you marry a woman you didn't love, Oliver? If she could set you up in business? Give you your start?'

'No.'

'There's a woman who'd have you, you know. She's a good-looking woman. A lot of men would be glad to have her and her money,' Bill said, watching Oliver's face carefully. The look of pain at the mention of his stepmother had gone from the boy's face and Bill grinned as Oliver threw back his head and laughed.

'You're talking about Mrs Wardle?' he said.

'You've noticed?'

'Of course I have,' Oliver said. 'She's a nice woman. I like her but not to marry. I'd never take her – you know what I mean?'

Bill smiled. Oliver was trying to spare his feelings, not wanting to be thought coarse. 'Not even if she were worth a few thousand?' he teased.

'No.' Oliver's expression was serious again. He bent forward, the better to make his point. 'Making money, getting rich isn't the most important thing. I want the money so I can have the sort of home I want so I can ask the girl I want. I want the money for that, not the other way round. I won't take a rich woman just so's I can get started. But I do want to make me – my – own money,' he added. 'I suppose I want the challenge of it. Anyway, I'd have to feel a lot more for a woman than I do for Mrs Wardle before I'd – you know?'

'I know.' Bill smiled. 'I was the same. I wasn't cut out for flirtations.'

'Tell me how you met your wife. How did you find out she was related to this man? How did you come to meet up with her again and get married?'

'Why do you ask?'

'I saw a girl at Suttonford. The most beautiful girl I've ever seen. She's tiny and she's fair and even though I'll perhaps never see her again I can't forget her. When I marry I want a girl just like her.'

Bill was silenced for a moment. Could Oliver have seen Florence? 'When did you see her?' he asked gently.

'The day I left the estate. It was the day of the garden party. She was travelling back to Middlefield in a carriage with her mother.'

It must have been Florence. Bill thought it uncanny; there were so many similarities between himself and this young man. A strange feeling, almost a premonition, passed through him. He took their empty glasses and put them on the tray. He was tired now and he still had his figures to do. There were shares he wanted to buy and he must assess the likely return on them. 'We'll talk again next Wednesday,

Oliver. Come round the mills with me. I want you to think hard about your future before then. If I can help you, I'll do my best.'

'Good night, Bill.' Oliver put out his hand and Bill took it in his.

'Good night.'

* * *

The following Wednesday, a soft, warm April morning, Oliver waited with impatience for Bill's carriage to pull up in front of The Pheasant.

Albert had an attic bedroom overlooking the front of The Pheasant and Oliver stood at the window, dressed in the new suit of good blue cloth, which he kept in Albert's wardrobe. The expense had left him with only two guineas in savings but he was glad he had the suit. It made him appear older. He glanced at himself again in the wardrobe's long mirror. Yes. The high wing collar looked good. He'd tied his cravat loosely and had been to the barber's earlier for a haircut and shave.

He was pleased that he was changing. He'd been noting the ways and manners of men he admired and was no longer the country bumpkin that Albert had first encountered. He wanted to look right today.

The carriage turned up the hill and Oliver ran down the stairs to be on the doorstep at the moment Bill pulled up.

'Do you want to take the reins, Oliver?' Bill asked. 'Or would you rather sit inside? You look too handsome by half to do the driving today.'

Oliver laughed. 'You sit inside. I'll drive,' he said. He held on to the bridle while Bill climbed slowly down from the driver's seat, then Oliver leaped easily into it and steadied the horses until the old man was aboard.

He had to shout against the noise of other horses, carriages and carts, which were clattering and rumbling over the cobblestones.

'Which one first?' he called.

'Hollin Mill. The weaving shed,' Bill replied.

Chapter Five

The noise in the weaving shed was deafening. The air was filled with cotton dust and the wooden floor vibrated under the weight of the rattling iron looms; rows and rows of them.

Oliver had never imagined anything like this. The machinery rattled as the wooden shuttles flew between the close threads, clacking when they reached the sides. Heddle looms lifted and dropped between the whirring pass of the shuttles and the weavers and tacklers reached and pulled, their hands never still.

The weavers conversed by lip-reading. It was impossible to hear above the din. They talked while their fingers swiftly caught the occasional broken threads, twisting them into weavers' knots as the lengths of cloth steadily grew.

'Rosie!' Bill Grandison tapped the young forewoman on the shoulder. 'I'm going to the office. Show Oliver the machines. This is the young man who drives for me.'

Rosie nodded to Bill and went ahead of Oliver between the rows of looms.

Rosie.

She was tall; in her twenties, Oliver guessed, and she took him to each loom in turn, explaining the processes by leaning towards him, her mouth only inches from his ear. And he could not take his eyes off her. Her dark hair was drawn into a heavy plait to keep it from catching in the fast-flying shuttles as they crossed and re-crossed the warp threads. He found himself shaking, so conscious was he of her nearness, of the shining smoothness of her hair, the softness of her breath on his cheek and the feel of her skirt against his legs.

With an effort he made himself act normally. 'Are you in charge of all these people?' he asked her, mouthing the words carefully.

She had the most beautiful eyes of a soft, warm brown and when she smiled it was inviting and slow, so that for a moment it seemed as if the noise of the mill faded and he and she were the only people present. He wondered if she had felt it too.

'Yes,' she said. 'I've been the forewoman for a year.'

He watched the little creases that came in her cheeks when she smiled and he asked her to show him the rolls of woven cloth. 'Where do you store the woven cloth?' he asked.

She put a hand on his arm again. 'Follow me,' she said.

She walked ahead of him again, tall and slender with a sway to her hips and her head held high. They went down a short flight of wooden steps at the far end of the shed into a big, dark room where the bolts were stacked on slatted wooden shelves. Under the bottom shelves six large sacking bags lay open, filled with untidy pieces of cloth.

'What's that?' he asked.

'That's the waste,' she told him. 'The practice pieces and the ends; the pieces with faults.'

'What do you do with them?'

'We use them for rags. We clean the looms with them, wipe the oil off the machinery and send what's left over to the infirmary or the workhouse. They use them for floor cloths.'

Oliver felt a strange excitement in the pit of his stomach that had nothing to do with the beautiful young woman who stood beside him. If he could buy the ends, the practice pieces ... if he could bundle them up ... sell them in the market ... 'Couldn't they be sold?' he asked.

'If there are too many we get something from the ragman, but only if we deliver it to him. He gets it for nothing if he collects it,' Rosie replied.

'Do you have complete charge?' Oliver asked. 'Is there a manager? A man in control of the mill?'

She laughed, showing fine white teeth in the generous mouth. 'I can manage without a man,' she said. 'I was forewoman in a bigger place than this, before I came to Middlefield. It might seem a big mill to you but really it's quite small and easy to run.'

Oliver wanted to keep her there, talking to him. He wanted to watch her ever changing expressions.

'I'll get back now, Oliver,' she said at last. 'Mr Grandison will be waiting for me to give him the work reports. Look around the place for an hour, if you want. We'll be finished then.'

Oliver watched her from the open door of the storeroom as she went back through the weaving shed, stopping to speak to the weavers if they signalled to her, tall and graceful, confident and assured. Then he wandered the lines of looms, asking questions; standing to watch the processes until he had absorbed as much knowledge as he could take in on a first visit. He had a growing sense that this, this business of making and selling, was what he wanted for himself.

He made his way back to the office, a dark, partitioned corner of the mill, lit only by a small window, which opened into the weaving shed. Bill had the record cards and work books ready and he handed them to Oliver.

'What do you think of it then?' Bill asked him.

'I like it. I'd like to learn more about it,' Oliver told him.

'Put these in the carriage,' Bill said. 'I'll show you how I keep my records when we get back to The Pheasant.' They went together down the dusty wooden stairs and out into the sunny street.

Oliver placed the books on the floor of the carriage. 'Rosie knows all there is to know about weaving, doesn't she?' he said. He'd seen her deal quickly and fairly with an argument that had flared between two women. 'She keeps the place in order too,' he added, keeping Bill talking for a little longer before he unfastened the horses' reins from the post. He wanted to know more about Rosie and the work of the mill.

'Rosie's a good worker. I pay her well.' Bill told him. 'Her husband's a sick man and she has to work to keep them all; her husband and three little children.'

She was married. A wave of disappointment went through him. 'Is she a Middlefield woman?' Oliver asked. 'She doesn't talk like the others.'

'She was brought up in Bradford. She and her sister are orphans. She met Jim Hadfield when he went to their chapel to preach. He's a lot older than her; a good man and a moving speaker, by all accounts.' Bill said.

The sun was warm on their backs and Bill turned his face up to the sun, as if in no hurry to leave. Oliver dawdled over the reins, wanting to hear more. 'You don't need a man to look after the place when you're not there then? It must take a hardy woman to keep all those men and women in their place.'

'Rosie Hadfield runs the mill better than any man could. She's a clever lass. She's not at all hardy. She's high-strung, but you'd never think it, seeing her at work. Not a bad thing in a woman is a fine sensitivity.'

'Where to next?' Oliver asked as Bill climbed into the carriage.

'The spinning mill.'

There, too, Oliver found that long spools of cotton thread were wasted. Mistakes in the spinning led to the piling up of spools that could not be sold and he wondered if they would find willing buyers. Ideas now were spinning, like the very cotton, in his head. He'd wait until he'd seen the braid workshop before he spoke to Bill about them.

There it was much quieter. The braid looms were small and Oliver watched in fascination as reels spun fast. Shimmering silk threads in golds and crimson, purples and green seemed to hover in the air, unmoving. Yet they were transformed in front of his eyes into the intricately woven ribbons and braids that were carefully rolled, outside in, on the polished benches by girls with nimble fingers and sharp eyes.

'This is the expensive stuff, Oliver,' Bill told him. 'We can't have mistakes in the stuff we send out from here. The girls are looking for flaws.'

Oliver saw that they had cut off lengths of ribbon and braid and dropped them into baskets under the bench. Again came the excited feeling he'd felt at Hollin Mill. If only he could buy these wasted pieces he was sure it would be his start.

Bill Grandison called in at his banker and the lawyer's offices and at each stop Oliver helped carry the ledgers and boxes of papers back to the carriage. It was not yet the right time to talk. He'd wait until they returned to The Pheasant.

He carried books and boxes up to Bill's room before he stabled the horses and sat in the groom's place, thinking. Would Bill be angry, he wondered, if he told him that perhaps there was money to be made from Bill's own business? Would it imply that Bill was careless in not seeing it? Suppose it was an act of charity that made Bill send the waste material to the infirmary and the workhouse? There was only one way to find out. Oliver went into the tavern, ran up the stairs and tapped on Bill Grandison's door.

'Come in, Oliver.' Bill was expecting him. He was seated in front of the books, his eyes close to the pages. 'I'm finding it difficult to see these figures. I wonder if you'd mind helping me.'

'Bill,' Oliver blurted out, not in the business like manner he'd meant to use. 'I want to buy all your ends and practice pieces.' The words were coming as fast as his thoughts. 'I could sort them, put them in bundles and sell them in the market. I'm sure I could make a profit that way.'

Bill did not reply for a moment. He kept his eyes on the books in front of him, a frown of concentration making a deep line between bushy white eyebrows, though Oliver knew that he was considering his proposal. Oliver held his breath and watched for a change of expression on the old man's face.

Bill slowly straightened himself and looked at him. A smile spread across his face, turning up the pointed ends of his neat moustache, bringing a boyish sparkle to his faded blue eyes. 'I believe you could, Oliver,' he said. 'But you'd need more than I could supply if your bundles sold well.'

'I could ask at the other mills. I could go round to the managers and ask for their waste.' Oliver was gabbling the words in his eagerness. 'Do you think they'd sell to me?'

Bill raised a hand, as if to warn him to think a little more slowly, but he was smiling and Oliver suppressed his own excitement. 'I could take you to meet one or two mill-owners tomorrow and we'll see if you can do business with them,' he said. 'We'll go to Hollin Mill again. Rosie will let you have our ends. How much have you saved? You'll not be given credit the first time you buy.'

'I've two guineas. Will that buy enough to start myself off?'

'I'll sell you my waste and braid for one and a half guineas. That will give you some left over to pay for the stall,' Bill said. 'Now come and help me with my work. My eyes are not as sharp as they were.'

Oliver helped the old man with his books, adding the columns quickly, checking as he went along.

'Can you calculate, Oliver?'

Bill was testing him, giving him silly little sums. Oliver grinned happily to himself as he added and multiplied – twopence three farthings a yard for one weave – and there were twenty-nine yards, nine and a half inches on the bolt.

'It'd make more sense if you cut the nine and a half inches off, Bill. I'll buy the odd bits,' he joked.

'That's the way to do it.' Bill said. 'You'll have to do your sums quickly when you're doing business with the mill-owners. They will drive a hard bargain.'

'Do you think they'll trade with me?' Oliver asked. 'If they know I'm going to put the stuff on the market?'

'They'll trade. They'll try to get the better of you though. Offer them half of what you're prepared to pay. You can always raise your offer but you can't come down if they seem too eager to sell.'

'Will you advise me?' Oliver said. 'Can I ask for your judgement before I say a price?'

'No. You cannae, laddie. You're on your own when you haggle at the Middlefield mills. Watch their faces and offer low. Don't worry what they think about you. Just put your low offer down and judge for yourself how far you are off a deal.'

Oliver had the carriage ready early the following day. He wore his new suit again and awaited Bill's arrival in the yard where the horses stood, gleaming like new chestnuts from the polishing with a length of silk he kept for the purpose. He wanted to make the right impression on the mill-owners. Today would be his testing. He had to bargain with men who were used to making quick decisions. They'd have no time for anyone who wavered.

'Good morning, Wainwright,' Bill greeted him.

'Morning, sir,' Oliver replied. A quick thrill passed through him. Bill was treating him as if he were an equal. He was not going to give him any quarter. It was as if the great man expected him to be businesslike.

'Bring the boxes down, will you? Then we'll go to the mills of my rivals.'

Oliver stacked the boxes and ledgers inside the carriage and glanced at Bill's face before closing the door and climbing into the driver's seat. The old man said nothing more than 'Partington Weavers, please.'

Partington Weavers was larger than Hollin Mill and its office more imposing. Oliver and Bill were shown into a furnished inner room where Jack Partington, clean-shaven and soft-spoken, shook hands with them.

'To what do I owe the pleasure, Grandison?' he asked. He was a small, stout man with wiry brown hair.

'Oliver Wainwright, my young friend here, proposes to sell the waste from my mills. I've struck my own bargain with him. He wanted an introduction to make you an offer for your own pieces,' Bill announced.

Oliver saw a look of surprise cross the man's face. 'Are you selling it by weight?' he asked. 'How much are you asking?'

'Do you have much waste at Partington's?' Bill put in.

Bill had avoided any mention of price, Oliver noted, and he saw that Partington hesitated before answering, not wanting to give away too much information to a competitor.

'Yes. There's always waste, especially at our printing works. We sell the longer lengths of spoiled prints and woven checks, but there are always pieces the buyers won't take.' He looked at Oliver and said, 'Look at our waste. You can make me an offer when you've seen it.'

'I'll wait here, Partington, while you and Wainwright do your bargaining,' Bill said.

Oliver followed Jack Partington through the noisy weaving sheds, between lines of machinery to the storeroom where bolts of cloth were stacked to a great height. There was a small room beyond the store, half-filled with waste material; sacks of printed cotton ends, heaps of woven check pieces and plain-weave unbleached cottons. He picked up some of the pieces and found that the printed lengths, which measured three yards or more, were badly flawed. Some lengths had barely a yard usable. Some of the lengths would be useless, though a bundle of matching yard-long lengths would sell.

'Well, Wainwright?' Jack Partington said. 'How much for the lot?'

'Two guineas,' Oliver said. He felt a sinking feeling in his stomach as he spoke and wondered if the man would laugh in his face.

'Don't make me laugh. I can get more from the ragman,' Jack Partington replied. 'Five guineas.'

'Aye. But you'll have to get someone to load it all and cart it down there for you,' Oliver said boldly. 'That'll cost you a bob or two.'

'Have you seen how much there is, Wainwright?' Partington waved his hands at the sacks and heaps. There was hardly room for more, barely standing room for the two men.

'Aye. You'll be wanting it cleared out, won't you?' Oliver came back. 'So's you've room for more. You'll be glad to get shot of it, I should think.'

'Four and a half.' Jack Partington's mouth was starting to twitch.

'Three,' Oliver said and held his breath. The mill-owner's eyes narrowed. Had he been too greedy? Would Jack Partington tell him to leave?

'Three and a half. No less.' Jack Partington put his hand out to clinch the bargain. He was smiling.

Oliver shook the man's hand. 'I'll collect it on Monday and pay you then,' he said. Now, he knew, he'd have to sell Bill Grandison's stuff on Saturday or be shown up for a bad dealer. There were two more mill-owners to see that day as well and if they had as much as this he'd have to take a stall on every market for miles around and sell the stuff quick.

Bill didn't ask Oliver what he'd bought until they arrived back at the weaving shed of Hollin Mill and were seated in the little office.

'Now,' he said. 'Tell me what you've bought – how much you've promised to pay – and I'll tell you if you're able to strike a bargain.'

'Three and a half guineas. I told him I'd not pay more,' Oliver said. 'Anyway I haven't got more.' He'd been wanting to know, all the way back, if he'd done the right thing. Jack Partington had come to an agreement faster than Oliver had expected and it make him think he could have gone even lower, to three guineas.

Bill slapped the desk and roared with uncontrolled laughter. 'You've got the better of him. I thought I'd have to go back and talk the swindler round for you. Jack Partington's the biggest twister in Middlefield. You'll walk over the others if you can strike a bargain with Partington.'

'I'm glad to hear it,' Oliver replied. 'I couldn't have offered more. I've got to sell your stuff as it is, before I can pay him.'

Bill opened the door and called Rosie inside. 'Get one of the tacklers. He can help Oliver fill and carry the sacks, Rosie. He's going to buy all our waste and make himself a fortune in the market,' he said.

'I'll help him. It'll not take above half an hour,' she said.

He followed her to the dark storeroom and held the sacks as she pushed the loose ends of cloth into them. Their hands touched and he had to struggle with himself against the impulse to hold them and draw her close.

'Sorry,' she said quickly in a little shocked whisper and as she spoke she looked at him. Oliver knew again the quick surging of desire for her; could have sworn that the look in her eyes betrayed a like passion behind the calm oval beauty of her face.

He watched her bite her lips as she pressed the cloth down; caught a quick look from clear brown eyes as she worked, avoiding his hands as if they were fire. He felt the now familiar tightening sensation in his body that came when she was near.

They worked in silence. He could not bear to break the spell of her nearness with words until at last she stood straight. 'That's it all done,' she said.

He was still thinking about her when he stabled the horses. He'd not feel this way about Rosie Hadfield, he told himself, if he had a girl of his own.

He must find himself a girl. Surely any girl would do. He wanted one badly. He admired Albert who had one flirtation after another with the girls who went into the taverns. Oliver tried to copy his friend's free and easy way with them but had never managed to make the leap from bantering talk to a proper assignation.

Chapter Six

'Are you coming with me to The Crown or The Swan?' Albert asked, when he came down to the stables after supper. 'The girls from Paradise Street will be at The Swan.' He cast his eyes about the swept yard, the horses munching at their hay racks. 'You've finished up early,' he said.

'Aye. I've been with Mr Grandison all day,' Oliver replied. He was looking forward to Albert's reaction when he told his friend about his new enterprise. 'You go. I've a lot to do here. Anyway, you're better with girls than I am. I'm not much good at getting 'em interested.'

Albert leaned against the stable door in the lanky, casual way he had and which Oliver knew the girls found irresistible. 'You rush 'em,' he said. 'You want to watch what I do. I keep 'em wondering.'

'They never look at me when you're there,' Oliver said, without rancour. 'I don't know how you do it.'

'Course they look at you. You just have to practise. Tease 'em a bit. Let 'em think you're after another girl. That gets 'em roused.'

Oliver grinned. He knew his friend was thinking of the conquests he'd make tonight. Albert had the sort of look in his eye that brought the girls round. Albert's black hair, slicked back with the dressing he put on it, gleamed in the lamplight and his brown eyes danced at the prospect of taking one of the girls up to the paddock or behind the stables, later.

Oliver remembered that the village girls had just begun to be coquettish in his presence before he left Suttonford. He'd kissed most of them when he'd had the chance. But then, he'd known them well. It was different trying to get friendly with the girls who went into the taverns. Oliver suspected that, when he tried, he either held back too long or frightened them with his eagerness.

But tonight he didn't want to think about girls. He gave Albert a playful shove, making him lose his balance and land with a thump on the broken chair. 'Wake up! Stop dreaming about 'em,' he laughed. 'Go on your own. I'm not coming tonight.'

'Why not?' Albert looked disappointed.

'For one thing, I don't like the sort of girls who go in the taverns and for another' – he pointed towards an unused loose-box across the yard – 'take a look in that stable, Albert.'

Albert rose and crossed the yard, pushed open the half-door and held the lamp high as he peered into the dark stable. He turned to Oliver and looked at him in bewilderment.

'What's it all for?' he asked. 'Why do you want sacks of cloth?'

Oliver stood behind him. 'I'm setting up on the market. I'm going to sort this out into bundles and put tickets on them tonight. I can get plenty more, and better stuff, next week from the mills ... so long as I sell this first,' he said, trying to hide the excitement in his voice. 'Come here.'

They went back into the groom's place and Oliver pushed back the sleeves of the old jersey he wore for yard work and reached for a parcel beneath the table, opened it and showed Albert the contents. 'I've bought paper and Indian ink for the tickets. Will you ostle for me on Saturday, or get one of the lads from The Crown to do it? I'll give them a florin and all the money they get for driving.'

'How are you going to get the stuff up there? How can you be sure of a stall?' Albert asked.

'The market manager has to give me a stall once the regulars have got theirs. I found that out. It's the first one up there that gets it,' Oliver told him. 'I'm going to borrow the handcart from here and take it up early. I'll leave the cart in the yard behind the Town Hall.'

Albert took off his jacket and placed it on an empty hook. He undid the mother-of-pearl cufflinks he wore on what he called his 'wenching shirt', pushed back his sleeves and sighed. 'Never mind the girls,' he said. 'You'll not get this lot sorted out on your own. I'll help you.'

Oliver was touched by Albert's spontaneous offer of help. He knew Albert liked him and as for himself – well, it was as if they'd been friends all their lives. 'Thanks,' he said. 'I'll go to The Swan with you on Saturday night, after I've sold it.'

'You might be back here with it all,' Albert laughed, 'and you'll have bought yourself enough polishing cloths to last a lifetime.'

'I'll not.' Oliver couldn't contemplate failure. 'We'll make 'em cheap enough so they can't resist. And we'll tie ribbons and braid together so they'll have to buy a lot to get what they want.'

They bundled ribbon, cloth and braid all through the evening. Oliver thanked God that he had been quick at figures at school for now his brain worked faster than his hands.

Sheer cotton and cotton twill-weave went into the biggest bundles. 'They'll make pillowslips and bolster cases,' Oliver said. 'Put in enough to make half a dozen of each and enough twill for a small sheet. I'll sell them for two and six a bundle.'

Albert was starting to catch Oliver's enthusiasm. 'What's this stuff called?' he asked, holding a piece of cotton.

'Cambric. Put enough in to make a couple of petticoats or a pair of curtains. I'll sell them for a shilling.'

There was heavy cotton too. 'Give 'em enough for half a dozen cushion covers, Albert. One and ninepence a bundle. Then we'll start on the braid and ribbon.'

He made the bundles as cheap as he could, leaving a good margin of profit, trying to stop himself from counting and recounting the money he'd take if he sold them all. They had to work hard to finish the bundles on Friday night but by midnight it was done. He'd never have managed without Albert's help. Nor would he be able to sort and bundle all Partington's mill pieces by himself if he sold all this tomorrow.

'I'll fetch us a jug of ale each,' Albert said when at last the cart was piled with neatly tied and labelled bundles of cotton.

'Ta.' Oliver tied cord over the bundles, winding the ends round the axle bar to fasten it securely. At last he stood back. He was convinced that he would be fortunate, that all that remained to be done was to get through the next few hours.

Albert came back with the beer. 'If you sell it all, you'll be on your way,' he said as he handed the frothing pint jar to him.

'Aye.' Oliver drank deeply.

'Have you worked out how much you'll earn?'

'Aye. Near on eight pounds.'

'More than the pub takes in a week,' Albert said.

'Aye.'

'You'll not need to work here. If you're successful.'

'No.'

'You could move into lodgings. Rent a house, even.' There was a glum note in Albert's voice.

'I'll not do that,' Oliver said. He was tired now. He wanted to be alone for the last few hours of what he was sure was his old life, to think and to dream and plan. But Albert seemed to want reassurance, needed confirmation of their friendship.

'Look, Albert,' he explained. 'I'm not going to leave here. I've always wanted a home of me own ... a proper home. I've got a picture of it in me mind. But it's more than a rented house and I'll not get it yet. If I'm going to set up in work on me own I'll ask your dad if I can stop here ... take a room ... give up ostling. Anyroad, I'll know by tomorrow.'

Oliver hardly slept. He tossed and turned on the palliasse, thinking of the morning. He had to sell all the bundles. If he didn't? He'd promised to buy from Partington's. There'd be no money. But if he was successful he'd go to the other mills and buy burlap canvas for rug-hooking and velveteen for coats and suits ... Bill Grandison had promised to take him to Manchester for plush and Utrecht velvet and to Leek for printed Indian silks ... if he didn't fail. No, he wouldn't fail. He must try to remember the words he'd rehearsed, 'Ladies. Look at the pretty ribbons. Braid for your bonnets.' No, it was the other way round ... 'Ribbons for your bonnets.'

When dawn broke he dressed and pulled the loaded cart out of the coach shed. He'd brought bread and cheese down to his room the night before and he ate without appetite, for the tight knot of excitement in his stomach had dried his mouth.

It was cold. He looked anxiously at the little patch of sky he could see between the high sides of The Pheasant and the walls of the yard, fearful that rain might keep people away or ruin his cloth.

It was going to be dry. The clouds were high and light and there was a small breeze moving them along. The cart creaked and bumped over the cobblestone yard and the bigger setts of Rivergate but there was nobody else about so he kept to the centre of the narrow road.

'Oliver!'

Oliver looked behind him. He was being followed by Albert. He stopped and waited. 'You're out early,' he said.

'I waited up. To see you go,' Albert replied, then added in a rush of words, 'Oliver, can I come in with you? I've got a bit of money put by. It'll help you buy more. You don't need to tell me now. Only I didn't want to ask you afterwards – when you'll know if you're going to sell the stuff. I don't want you to think I'm only interested in the money. I'll come up with you today though and keep a look-out. See as no one pinches nowt.'

Oliver set down the cart, looked at his eager friend and considered. 'I'll be shouting, like the candle-maker does. I've got to be heard.' Albert showed no dismay at the prospect. 'Right! Come on! Let's see if we can get a stall.'

Albert grinned broadly and took a handle of the cart. It was easy going up the steep street with two pushing and they reached the market place to find the manager already there, putting up the wooden frames for the traders' stalls. They had to wait for an hour but they were lucky. They were the first in a line of casual sellers who came to the market occasionally. One of the regulars didn't turn up and they were allotted his stall, right by the gates of St Michael and All Angels, where people from both the Wallgate and Churchgate had to pass.

They set out the stall under the curious eyes of the other traders. There were no stalls selling remnants or ribbon and Oliver knew that they would be spared the spiteful tricks some stallholders used towards their rivals. He was no threat to the men who sold cloth by the yard.

He took loose ribbons and tied them to the corner posts where they would flutter gaily above the heads of the customers.

As soon as eight-thirty struck, Oliver went to the front of the stall. There were a few early shoppers about and he strode up and down, as the candle-maker and the baker did. He put his head high in the air and called out, 'Ladies! See the pretty ribbons and braid! Buy some for your bonnets. Only a few pence a bunch!'

Women approached the stall cautiously. Oliver saw them frown and pick up his bundles. Then they put them down again and walked away. They looked at him as if he were something strange and they scurried off, lifting their hems off the cobblestones, as if they were too busy to dawdle.

Why were they walking away? He wanted to ask them, 'Why didn't you buy, ma'm?', but he held back, pretending he hadn't seen their hesitation, striding up and down the length of his stall, now shouting, now holding his breath, waiting for the first sale. It appeared that they weren't sure. Had he made the prices too low? Or too high? He continued to call his wares. 'Three penny bunches of ribbon and braid. Fine cotton pieces at sixpence a bundle.'

The other stalls were busy now, people crushed between them, trying to attract the attention of the traders. If he didn't sell his goods when there were so many buyers about then he never would. He watched the women stop at the other stalls and open their purses. But they didn't stop at his and Oliver was starting to despair.

'Albert,' he almost wept, when above the noise of the market the church clock struck ten. An hour and a half had passed and the other stallholders were doing brisk trade. 'We haven't sold a thing. What can we do? Can't you charm them, like you do the girls in The Swan?'

Albert grinned. 'It looks as if I'll have to, doesn't it?' he said. 'Your shouting's not got 'em flocking.' He took the ribbons Oliver had been waving and placed them at the back of the counter.

'Go and get us a bun each,' he said, 'then sit quiet at the back.'

Oliver walked away from the stall and found the baker calling his wares, surrounded by eager buyers and he marvelled at the man's easy manner. He bought two Eccles cakes and, unable to face the deserted stall for a few minutes, he took his time returning, carefully noting the actions and words the others were using.

There appeared to be quite a crowd of people now in front of the church and Oliver had to push his way through to Albert. As he neared the stall his heart began to beat faster. Were all those women at his stall? Why were they laughing and smiling happily? What was going on?

He reached the front and now it was clear what the attraction was. Albert had a girl either side of him. He was holding a piece of gold braid against the hair of a blonde girl who was gazing into his eyes, transfixed.

'Look at the colour, ladies,' Albert teased. 'See how the hair reflects the gold of the ribbon. Oh, my goodness. There's not a rogue in the town could resist making eyes at a girl with gold ribbons on her bonnet.'

He was putting on his dandy voice, Oliver saw; the one he'd copied from the fancy-talkers who sometimes came to The Pheasant. And the women loved it. They were holding up bundles of braid, eager to buy, and the girls Albert had shamelessly flirted with stood near, waiting their turn to be complimented and noticed again.

'The linen pieces make fine samplers, ladies. And your sewing-maids can make pillowslips from those pieces,' Albert called to a pair of tired-looking women.

Oliver looked at the women in astonishment. They were flattered to be thought of as employers of sewing-maids. They bought a large bundle of cotton material each and exclaimed over their purchases in delight.

Albert caught his eye and jerked his head. 'Come over and take the money, will you?' he cried. 'We mustn't keep these lovely ladies too long. We'll be chased out of the market by their jealous husbands.'

Albert was obviously enjoying his new-found access to young women. Oliver watched with admiration the way he'd flirt with three or four at the same time, each girl leaving the stall believing that she alone was the object of his attentions. He didn't think he'd ever be able to draw a crowd of girls as Albert did, but he'd have to try.

He smiled at the girls who stood round Albert. He would never be able to match Albert's chatter but ... maybe if he gave them a flirtatious look? He glanced at a tall, dark-haired girl, over the head of the blonde one and saw that she had laughing eyes and was enjoying the exchange. He'd soon get the hang of it. But now he was too busy, selling the bundles, giving change, helping the matrons choose which purchase to make.

Halfway through the afternoon Oliver caught sight of Rosie Hadfield. She had a basket on her arm and was buying vegetables at the next stall. His body responded to the sight of her as it had to her nearness at the mill and he willed her to look his way but she moved on and when next he lifted his eyes she was gone.

There had not been a moment to spare since Albert started his chatter. It was four o'clock and the bundles were almost gone.

'Have we any more under the counter?' Albert asked.

'No. We've sold them all. Everything,' Oliver told him as he untied the ribbons and folded the empty sacks. 'I'll go and tell the market manager to keep me a stall for next Saturday,' he said. 'I'm going to get one on the Friday market as well. Your dad will find another stable lad easy enough. Do you want to come in with me?'

'Aye,' Albert said. 'But I've not got as much courage as you. I'll keep on as an apprentice for a bit yet. I'll come out on Saturdays though.'

'Do you know how much we've made?'

'No.'

'Have a guess.'

'Six pounds?'

'Seven pounds, thirteen and fourpence,' Oliver said. 'That should convince you that there's a living in it.' They took a handle each and pushed the empty cart back to The Pheasant.

'It was a lark, wasn't it?' Albert asked, a huge smile splitting his face. 'All those women round us.'

'I was afraid we'd sell nowt,' Oliver said. 'If you hadn't started them off I don't know what I'd have done.'

'Are you going to find stalls in the week then? Selling your Partington's pieces?' Albert asked.

'Aye,' Oliver assured him. 'I'm going to every market I can. I want to make enough to have me own mill and I mean to get it while I'm young.'

'You're confident,' Albert said.

'So should you be. Leave your job. We'll go to Stockport market next Tuesday and sell the stuff I'll fetch from Partington's.'

Oliver steered the cart into the stable yard of The Pheasant and set it by the wall. He leaned against it and grinned. 'It's neck or nothing for me now, Albert.'

Over supper Oliver asked Leonard Billington if he could live at The Pheasant as a paying guest. He'd take the worst room if he could have it cheap.

'You can have the attic room next to Albert's,' Leonard said. 'We can do without a stable-lad for now, as long as you'll drive for Mr Grandison on Wednesdays.'

'I will,' Oliver agreed.

'Do you think I should go in with Oliver, Dad?' Albert put in. 'I'd like to give up my apprentice work but I'm a bit wary.'

'Go in with Oliver if you want to,' Leonard Billington said firmly. 'You have to take your chances when they come, and better now than when you've responsibilities.'

'We'll borrow the horse cart on Monday if that's all right, Mr Billington?' Oliver asked. 'We'll pick up the stuff from Partington's and sort as much as we can for Tuesday in Stockport.'

Ma Billington brought plates of sausages and mashed potato to them and set them on the white-scrubbed table. 'Now, you see our

Albert doesn't get hisself mixed up with them cheeky girls as go up to t'Swan will yer, Oliver?' she demanded. 'I tell 'im to take a leaf off you and 'ave a bit of pride. Some of them girls! Really!'

'I'm all right, Ma.' Albert chided her. 'Stop yer fussin'.'

'If we sell up on Tuesday, Albert,' Oliver went on, 'I want to take two more lads on. There's three markets a week in Stockport and three here.'

'You're being a bit previous, aren't you?' Albert said.

Oliver roared with laughter at the expression. He'd not heard that one before. 'A bit previous?' he said. 'What's that supposed to mean?'

'It means you're counting your chickens too soon,' Albert replied. 'Maybe all as wants remnants has bought 'em this week. Maybe they'll have enough.'

'They'll not.' Oliver gulped down the ale Mr Billington had set down for them. 'They'll tell their friends and their friends'll want some an' all.' He wiped his mouth on his napkin. 'I'll buy proper stuff and rip it into lengths and let 'em think they're getting bargains, if I have to. They like buying it this way. It sets their brains working, thinking what they'll do with 'em.'

'Aye. They'll maybe find they can't do anything with 'em and what happens then?' Albert said.

'Course they'll buy,' Oliver countered quickly. 'D'you know how many dressmakers there are in this town? D'you know how many people have got sewing machines? They can't resist if they think they're getting something for nowt.'

'Will you be able to get as much as you want now, Oliver?' Leonard Billington asked.

'Yes. Mr Grandison's going to take me up to Nottingham. I can get lace there and folks'll buy that all right,' Oliver said. 'But I'll soon have sold all the ends. There's not enough faulty stuff to be had. There's money to be made, selling cloth. I saw what the others were selling and there's none can get the stuff I can. Bill Grandison will sell proper cloth to me and so will the other mill-owners, if I get rid of their waste an' all.'

Chapter Seven

Florence's fifteenth birthday party had been the best she could remember. There had been an afternoon tea party with her friends invited to Suttonford. Grandfather had been at his most hospitable and Grandmother smiling when she'd been introduced to the young people in Florence's circle of girlfriends. In the evening there had been dancing; not a real ball, those would come later, Mama said. But some of the good families in Cheshire had been invited: those with daughters and, more particularly, sons.

A military band, whose regiment was stationed in Chester, had played for them and Florence, in palest blue silk, her hair put up and ivory fan dangling from white-gloved wrist, had whirled to the waltz and cavorted in the gallop with the best young men the county could offer.

She and Mama were still full of the excitement of it late the following afternoon when they returned to Churchgate House. Mama was going to help her select patterns for her summer wardrobe as soon as she had dealt with the letters.

The curtains were drawn early and Florence was seated at Mama's desk under the brightest lamp. Mama sniffed in annoyance at something and Florence looked across the room at her. 'What is it?' she asked.

'You will have to decline this invitation yourself, Florence. The letter was addressed to you.'

'Really, Mama. You have no right to open my letters ...'

'I have every right, Florence. Invitations to a ball should not be sent to a young girl. It is incorrect and in very bad taste. It shows

65

that the sender does not know the proper course. Invitations should be addressed to a girl's mother or chaperone. Not to the girl herself.' She crossed the room and placed the card in front of Florence. 'Refuse it. And let me see your reply before you post it.'

Florence stared at the invitation. 'But, Mama. It's from Elsie Henshaw. She wants me to go to her birthday dance.' She looked up and saw that Mama's face was stony. 'Surely I don't have to refuse simply because the Henshaws don't know the right way to address an invitation.'

'You are being difficult, Florence,' Mama said. 'I don't wish to discuss it. You shall not go.'

'But – Mama! The Henshaws are a good family. You've met Elsie's mother. You spoke to her at dancing class. You were being charming ...'

'I was being polite, Florence.'

'But the ball is to be held in the Town Hall, Mama. Everyone will be there,' Florence pleaded. 'Uncle Bill and Aunt Lucy are going. Aunt Lucy has accepted her invitation.'

'The Henshaws are mill-owners. It is expected that Lucy and Bill will go.'

'Then surely ... You said yourself that Elsie had a winning way.'

Mama's voice rose ominously. 'Of course I did,' she snapped. 'But her background is unknown. She needs winning ways. These people are adventurers, Florence. Ill-bred and clumsy.'

Florence hated to upset Mama but was driven to argue with her. 'How can you say such things? The Henshaws are rich, they want nothing from us. They have a fine house and more servants than we have. Two carriages. Elsie wears gowns from London and Paris.'

'They are upstarts. You only need look at them. They are hoping to be accepted by us.'

Florence could not believe that Mama really meant what she was saying. 'How can you say so? How can you possibly look at people and know ... know at a glance what they are about?' she demanded.

'They are large and loud, like beasts of the field. In their dress and their manners they reveal themselves. The finery of their house

is a gross exaggeration of good taste and try as they will to ingratiate themselves their overtures must be discouraged.'

Florence wanted to cry. It was plain that Mama's mind was made
up. 'Will I ever be allowed to make my own friends?' she asked.

'You are expected to exercise restraint, Florence. For a girl in
your position ... It is intolerable that you ask for explanations.'

'What is my position?'

'You are Sir Philip Oldfield's granddaughter. You will remember that whenever good nature drives you into foolishness.'

'And what is expected of me?'

'It is expected that you will move in the right circles. That you
will uphold the family reputation. And that you will marry well.'

So that was it. She must be seen with the sort of people into
whose families she would marry. Her preferences were not to be
taken into account. If she mixed with the right people then she
would marry one of their sons. Did they hope, with her marriage,
to see the end of their financial troubles, for Suttonford could no
longer support the family's extravagant lifestyle?

She would not be used in this way. 'So now we have the truth of
it,' she said in a cold voice. 'I'm to marry well. To please whom?'

Mama was pale with anger. 'You are fifteen years old. You are
about to take your first steps into the adult world. You have been
allowed to put up your hair, to voice your opinion on matters that
don't concern a girl of your age ...'

'Mama! I have merely been allowed to choose my own clothes.
You have never sought my opinion.' Tears streamed down her face,
but inside a small reserve of spirit made her bold. 'And as for marriage, when I marry it will be to a man of my choosing. I will not
ask your opinion. Or Grandfather's.'

She fled from Mama and ran up the stairs to her own sitting room
where she threw herself onto the chaise longue at the window. Sobs
tore through her, making her shoulders and neck ache. Her life was
hateful to her. Why did Mama turn against her friends? Mama was
kindness itself underneath. Mama gave to the poor and helped support a mission in Africa. She encouraged Florence to read to the

children at Sunday school in Grandfather's village. So why didn't she see how hurt Elsie Henshaw would be if she refused the invitation? And it was to have been her very first ball.

* * *

Tuesday, Stockport market day, dawned warm and clear. Oliver and Albert had sorted and bundled all Monday afternoon and evening after collecting from Partington's and three other mills in Middlefield. They used a corner of the cart shed for storage and had improvised a table where they rolled the pieces of printed fabrics into big bundles and tied them with strips of cloth.

They had a wonderful assortment of taffetas and silks to sell as well as the printed cottons and they piled them onto the handcart.

Stockport was a bigger town than Middlefield and the market large. There were stalls selling cotton material by the yard, from bolts of cloth, which the traders laid out across their counters. It was easier to get a stall there but Oliver wondered whether or not the customers would buy as readily. The stalls were set out down the length of the main street, in the centre of the road and down either side. They had a good spot, in front of a busy tavern.

Their bundles made a brilliant splash of colour and hardly had they set out the stall than the customers came to buy. So busy were they that Albert had no need to use his charms, though Oliver saw that his friend caught the girls' eyes, winking and joking at every opportunity.

'Could I speak to you somewhere? Away from here?' A well-dressed man, tall and sandy-haired had come up to Oliver at the back of the stall. He had an accent Oliver recognised as cockney.

'Aye.' Oliver nudged Albert. 'Look after the stall, will you?' he said. 'I'll see what he wants.' The man led the way to the far end of the market, near the carters' stand.

'Fred Sheldon,' the man said, holding out his hand.

'Wainwright.' Oliver ignored the hand. 'What do you want?'

The man had an open sort of face. He didn't appear to be trying to warn him off, as Oliver had half-expected his competitors to do. He handed Oliver a printed card. 'My name and address.'

Oliver glanced quickly at the card but the name meant nothing to him. 'Well?' he said.

'I have a workshop, in London, making undergarments ... petti-coats, camisoles, bodices. I buy cottons and lawns.'

'Well?'

'The prints and taffetas on your stall are bought by sewing women. Ladies' gowns are made to order. They have to choose their patterns and wait until the dresses are made up.'

'Well?' Oliver asked. Why didn't the man say what was on his mind?

'In America they are making dresses in workshops. Putting them into shops. The women like to buy that way. I want to manufacture for them. But I can't spare the time to come north every week or so.'

Now Oliver had the same leaping ideas that his first visit to the mill had brought. He would be a go-between. He had access to the mills. For a percentage and his expenses he'd take samples of cloth to London. If Fred Sheldon was starting to manufacture in the American way then so would others.

'I'll do it,' he said quickly. 'Look around the stall. Choose the patterns you want. I'll tell you how much it will cost and send the stuff down to London.'

'What about future dealing?'

'I'll come to London in a month's time. I'll bring samples. Can you give me introductions to the shops?'

'Yes.'

'Choose your cloth then,' Oliver said grandly. 'I'll buy it tomor-row and have it sent.'

* * *

Bill Grandison always took a stroll through the market on Saturday afternoons and last week he had watched, from a distance, the two friends gathering a crowd of ladies round their stall. He smiled to himself, remembering his own early efforts.

Early the following Wednesday he pulled up outside The Pheasant, surprised and pleased to find Oliver, dressed in his blue suit, waiting at the front of the tavern, keeping a stand clear for the carriage. He climbed slowly from the driver's seat and stood in the warm sunshine. 'I thought you'd have found a market stall somewhere.' He handed the reins to Oliver and smiled. 'I didn't think you'd want to drive me now you're busy making your fortune.'

'I'd like to spend Wednesdays with you,' Oliver answered. 'If you don't object. Where to first?'

'Hollin Mill then back here. You want to go to Nottingham don't you? We'll take the train this afternoon.'

Bill smiled as Oliver leaped easily up to the driver's seat and called excitedly down to him, 'I'll wait until we're on the train to tell you all that's happened.'

When they arrived Bill saw that Rosie was in good spirits. She teased Oliver about his performance in the market last week, making him blush at her attentions. Oliver reminded Bill of himself at that age, unsure of his charms with the ladies. Well, the innocence would soon be gone, he was sure, and in the meantime it was nice to see a young man so full of life and good looks who was unaware of the impression he made.

Back at The Pheasant, Oliver proudly showed him the cart shed he and Albert Billington had cleared and the sack-loads of remnants they had bought from Jack Partington and the other two mills.

'So this is your warehouse, is it?' he joked. 'What a lot you've collected. How long will it take you to sell all your stock?'

'Not long,' Oliver said with an air of great assurance. 'These are the last of the remnants. I have to sell cloth by the yard. I've already started dealing with a Londoner. He wants me to buy for his manufactory. I've bought the cloth and sent it to London for him.'

They took the train to Nottingham in the afternoon and Oliver talked eagerly, the youngster's eyes intent on his face. 'They're building a station at Suttonford village, Oliver,' Bill said, pointing to the spot where labourers were digging the banks.

Oliver turned his head, as if to search amongst the faces of the workers for someone he knew but they were past the place now, steaming through the estate farms where men guided horses pulling great chain harrows over the fields.

Oliver's eyes were narrowed against the glare of the sun through the windows but he did not appear to recognise any of the men or boys and returned to the talk of the cloth he meant to buy, the amount he would be able to sell if all his hopes were realised.

Bill introduced him to three Nottingham manufacturers and watched shrewdly as the youngster paid cash for a considerable quantity of lace at the workshops. It seemed that Oliver had a good grasp of commercial dealing but he knew that he must caution him so when they returned to Middlefield he told Oliver to come up to his room after supper. He asked Leonard Billington to bring glasses and a decanter of whisky. He prepared for their talk, placing two large sheets of paper, ink and pens on the window desk.

Oliver's knock was not long in coming. The boy must have bolted his supper in his eagerness, for he stood in the doorway, changed into the old clothes he wore for bundling and loading his cart, a happy smile wreathing his face.

'Come in, Oliver. Sit down,' Bill said. 'I'm going to show you how to keep a check on your business. How to control your cash. You expect me to speak frankly, don't you?'

'Yes. Of course I do. I'm waiting to hear what you think about everything,' Oliver replied.

'How much have you taken in the markets?' Bill asked. 'I want you to write it down on the sheet of paper.'

Oliver looked puzzled but went willingly enough to the desk, dipped his pen in the inkwell and wrote in his firm hand. 'Saturday. £7 13s 4d.' He spoke the words as he wrote them. 'Tuesday £15. That's over twenty-two pounds.'

'How much capital has Albert put in?' Bill said.

71

'Eight pounds, eight and twopence. It was all his savings,' Oliver said eagerly.

'How much did the stuff cost?' Oliver wrote it down. 'Subtract,' Bill ordered.

Oliver did as he was told. 'But I ...' he started.

'Just a minute,' Bill said sternly. 'How much did the stalls cost? Write it down. And how much was the cloth you bought for the Londoner? Put that in.'

Oliver wrote. 'I still made a profit,' he said quickly.

'I know you did. How much would you have earned, if you'd stayed a stable lad? Write it down. And Albert's wages. And subtract them.'

The column of figures was getting longer. Oliver's pen scratched and a frown, Bill hoped not one of resentment, furrowed his brow. 'Subtract your train fares,' Bill said, 'and the amount you have to spend to restock to the same level.'

'Bill ...' Oliver looked up, as if he were prepared to argue with him.

Bill disregarded him and went on. 'Have you done that?'

'Aye.'

'And how much have you got in reserve?'

'Nothing,' Oliver replied. 'But I've bought more stock with it. I've bought stuff to sell to the London dealer and stuff to keep Albert and me going until next week.'

Bill picked up the sheet of calculations and glanced at it quickly. He knew what he would find and also knew that what he must say would be hard for Oliver to take. He spoke firmly. 'You mustn't bank on having one good day after another. You must only expand at the speed you can afford to go. You are not a gambler; not in a position to disregard common sense in business.'

He sat down beside Oliver at the desk and wrote quickly. He wrote out the sums clearly and handed the paper to Oliver. 'Look,' he said kindly. 'Always leave yourself some in reserve. It's exciting when you make a quick profit, I know. But it can go as easily as it came. Stick to these principles, Oliver. Never put all your money into stock. You could lose it overnight.'

Oliver looked at the figures. 'But I can sell it all, Bill. It will all be sold in two weeks,' he protested. 'And the man I told you about will take as much as I can get.'

'What if he doesn't?' Bill spoke sharply now. 'What if he's a villain? What if you and Albert sell nothing one week?'

'I wanted to take lads on and do all the markets I could,' Oliver replied. 'I thought I'd strike while the iron's hot. Make the most of it.'

Bill knew that Oliver had been shocked when he'd seen the result of his calculations. The boy's face had fallen when he saw that he'd ended with so little.

'Do you really think I should hold off?' Oliver spoke quietly now and Bill saw with relief that realisation was beginning to dawn in Oliver's mind.

'Sell the stuff you've bought, Oliver,' he said kindly. 'When you've enough money put aside to carry the business for four weeks without using each day's takings, you'll be in control, but not until then.'

He stood up and put a hand on Oliver's shoulder. 'Go canny, until you're on your feet. Always make sure you're out in front. Be prepared for a bad spell, for one will come, sooner or later, and you'll be able to ride it out. Somebody will have seen what you've done. You had a good idea, selling remnants, but you'll not be able to keep it to yourself. Soon there'll be others following you, copying you, making your takings fall away. That's when you'll need cash in hand, to take the lead again.'

'All right. I'll take your advice,' Oliver conceded.

'You've done well, though,' Bill said. He reached for the decanter and poured whiskies for them. 'We'll drink to your first success.'

'I was rushing at it, wasn't I?' Oliver said.

'Understandable. I felt the same.'

'Thanks,' Oliver said. 'You're right. I didn't really think it would be as easy as it was. I'll sell this lot before I buy more.'

'I'll advise you, if you wish,' Bill said. 'You can expand soon. Just see how it goes week by week and move on when the time's right.'

Oliver drank the whisky swiftly. 'Now shall I help you with your books?'

'Not tonight,' Bill replied. 'You've a lot of work to do. But next week I'll ask for your help. And I'll show you how you can make money on the stock market when you've so much that you wonder what to do with it all.'

Bill watched Oliver go down the winding stair. He was a sensible youngster. He'd go canny now. He'd hated pouring cold water on the boy's high spirits, but if Oliver was to succeed he'd have to pay attention to a wiser man.

Bill had been right to caution him. Two weeks passed before he received the money from the cloth he'd bought for Fred Sheldon and he'd paid for it in advance. He wouldn't do that again. But if Fred Sheldon kept his promise and introduced him to others, he'd subtract a percentage from the price of the cloth. Or ... his mind raced ... if he sold 100 guineas worth every two weeks that would be 30 guineas profit, less his expenses. He'd be able to take lads on to help Albert in the markets.

Then, months after their first, heady day in Middlefield market a newcomer opened a stall on the Thursday market in Stockport, selling remnants of cloth, and selling them cheaper than Oliver could buy.

Albert and the lad returned with the unsold bundles and a half-empty money bag and Oliver discovered that he could not tolerate opposition. He fretted and schemed. He'd drive the man out of business if only he knew where he bought. He'd stop him getting his hands on more stock. Stop the customers buying from the upstart. He waited with impatience for Bill to arrive on the following Wednesday.

'Look at this,' he said in the evening as they worked on first Oliver's then Hollin Mill's ledgers. 'Some jackanapes is taking my business. The man's made my profit drop by a quarter.'

'Then you'll have to do better, Oliver. You'll have to make your goods more attractive to the customers than his are,' Bill advised.

'What will that do?' Oliver's face was dark with anger at the effrontery of this newcomer, this stranger to the market. 'He'll simply make his cheaper and make my profits drop again. He can't be paying for them, or someone's giving the stuff to him.'

'Then he'll soon go out of business,' Bill said. 'There's room for both of you. Don't waste your energy in fighting him. Think of something that will put you in a stronger position.'

'Help me price this then, will you?' Oliver said as he pushed a bill of purchase for lace and ribbon towards the old man. 'Tell me what I should be charging so I'll get my customers back.'

He knew Bill was right and did his best to push down the desire for retaliation. 'I'll check your Sales and Bought Ledgers for you while you do it,' he said.

Oliver was cheered tonight though, when after half an hour's work he spotted a glaring error as he added columns of figures for his friend. 'I see you're getting three farthings a yard less for your twill-weave from this customer,' he said.

'Where?' Bill leaped over to Oliver's side, his keen blue eyes alert, not six inches from the paper. 'You're right, Oliver. You're quick, to spot that. I must be getting old, not seeing it myself.'

It was good to realise that Bill Grandison could make mistakes after all this time. 'What will you do about it?' Oliver asked, a slow grin spreading across his face at the sight of Bill's vexed old face.

'I'll send him short on the next few rolls,' Bill replied. 'I'll not be bested.'

The smile left Oliver's face and returned to Bill's when, minutes later, Bill pointed to a receipt. 'Why have you bought a bolt of pure silk?'

'I couldn't resist. It's a fair price and a good shade of green,' Oliver said airily.

'You're in this to make a profit, not to please your senses,' Bill told him crossly. 'No matter how much you like it, if you can't sell it fast then don't buy. You're not selling to the gentry, laddie. You're a market trader selling to the poor.'

The grin was back on Bill's face. The old man liked to put him in his place. 'You'll come to hate that silk, Oliver,' Bill prophesied. 'When they all handle it and nobody can afford to buy it, you'll begin to wonder where your brains were when you bought it,' he added.

Bill had a coachman now and Oliver sat inside the carriage with the old man on their Wednesday trips to visit the mill and workshop. Afterwards they often drove to a favourite inn near the cattle market and drank ale or porter with plates of beef and dumplings.

It was a popular stopping place and strangers often took them for father and son. This seemed to amuse Bill Grandison greatly and he did not trouble to correct the impression. They made a point, when they were dining, of not talking business but spoke of other things. Bill spoke about Lucy whom Oliver knew, in Bill's eyes, had never passed the age of twenty. She was still his girl and he spoke wistfully about their childless state and proudly about his early struggles and the opposition he had met from men he had bested.

He told Oliver too of the hostility he had met from Lucy's family towards their marriage. 'My brother-in-law would have done anything to stop us from marrying, Oliver. But he didn't think she'd defy him. He made good use of me though, afterwards. I had to do all his investing for him. The man thought money grew on trees and all he had to do was sit underneath and pick it up,' he added, cackling with laughter. 'He'll get the shock of his life if I die before him.'

It was September and Middlefield market square was carpeted in bronze, crisp leaves, which blew in from the sycamores and beeches that bordered the churchyard. They crunched underfoot in the little green space behind the Town Hall that was known to people of the town as Sparrow Park.

Oliver sat on an iron seat there, looking out over the ancient steps and cattle market. They had taken on two lads to help with the stalls but he liked to be here, in his favourite market place on Saturdays. He ate his bread and cheese and leaned against the back of the seat, thinking of his extraordinary good fortune. For now he had almost everything he wanted. He had a roof over his head, a good friend in Albert and he had Bill, a man he admired above all others, to help and advise him. He had a business of his own, he called no man master – and yet …

He sent lads or sometimes Albert to the Saturday market in Stockport because he liked to be in Middlefield when Rosie Hadfield came to the stalls. She stopped to speak to him and he found himself looking for her, warmth flooding through him at the sight of her slow smile, his nerves leaping at the touch of her hand on his arm and his head hazy from the lavender smell of her hair, which she wore pinned up, away from the mill.

He vowed to find himself a girl and stop acting like a lovesick boy, drawn to a woman so much older than himself and her with three children and a sick husband.

He'd go back to the stall in a minute. She might be there.

Chapter Eight

Mama was beginning to talk of their returning to London since she was so hard to please. Florençe knew that Mama hoped she would marry young. Was it to save the expense of launching her? Why could Mama and Grandfather not allow her to remain here, unmarried? In Mama's opinion a girl who had not made her choice by the age of seventeen, or at the latest eighteen, was wasting her charms.

It was Sunday, late in January, the sky was clear blue and the ground iron-hard under her winter boots as she walked to the village.

'My dear child,' Mama said yesterday. 'You have been in Middlefield for three and a half years. You have met the best the county can offer. Surely there is one amongst them ...? Florence! Pay attention.'

Florence recalled her reply. 'I am not going to fade, Mama, or grow old before your eyes. I shall not wither away, pining for a husband.' She had seen the shocked look in Mama's face but she had concluded that flippancy was her only defence against the relentless drive to 'marry her off' that Mama and Grandfather pursued.

'Then Grandfather must provide a season for you,' Mama had said. 'We will return to London. You shall come out.'

The road to Suttonford village, which Florence took every Sunday afternoon, was a well-beaten track between an avenue of firs, dusty in summer and a quagmire in spring and autumn. The village, less than a mile from the house, comprised twenty cottages, a farm manager's house and the quarry-master's place. There were stables for the farm horses, a shop and, a little way apart, Suttonford church and village school.

The Runaway

Every Sunday, after lunch, she left the family to their silly talk in the grand drawing room and went down to the schoolroom, behind the village church. She took the infants' class. Her hands were warm next to the soft fur of her muff but the cold air bit at her cheeks. She hoped there would be a fire or the children would freeze today. Their mamas were careless. Sometimes the poor mites had holes in their leggings and chapped and chilblained hands.

She ran through the hymn tune as she went, breath streaming out whitely between the words that were bouncing in her head in time with her quick feet. Playing the piano to their eager singing was the best part of Sundays.

Mama or Grandfather invariably waited for her when Sunday school was over. They liked to meet her, Florence suspected, so that the village children would not forget how to bob their curtseys.

'The children like to see us, Florence,' Mama said, only ten minutes ago, when Florence asked if she could return alone. She loved to be left to herself but hardly ever achieved the solitary state.

She crossed the frozen grass towards the little schoolroom with its tiny stained-glass windows. And there they were, waiting for her, six little angels, shivering under the shawls their mamas had pinned around their shoulders. 'Quickly, quickly, my pets,' Florence said as she opened the door. 'Let us sit by the fire.'

In her tapestry bag were six apples and a wooden box of chalks. She had been practising all week and could now outline very quickly a drawing of the African village.

'Me mammy's got a bilious 'tack, Miss Florence.' Connie Smith was tugging at Florence's coat.

'I'll send blue pills to her, Connie,' Florence consoled, 'after Sunday school. Now get the slates out of the cupboard and I'll sketch a picture of the mission. You can colour in.'

They were quickly settled. She would reward the best child with the chocolate she had slipped into her bag from Mama's box.

Florence watched them; their little heads bent down, eyes close to the slates, chalk squealing furiously as they worked.

Oh, how she loved Sunday. It was the only day of the week when Mama left her side for an afternoon; when pleasing Grandfather and Mama was no longer the sole reason for her existence.

This afternoon she would not have to be charming to the insipid young men whom Grandfather paraded before her at every turn. There were four at the house party this weekend: four spoiled, rich boys who had not a ha'porth of character between them. Why, oh why did they do it? She was not yet eighteen. It was not unnatural, though Mama said it was, that she should not want to wed young.

'I've finished, Miss Florence ...'

'So've I.'

'I finished before you.'

'Which is the best, Miss Florence?'

Florence took the slates onto her lap and pronounced Connie Smith's the best. Connie was a sweet girl and a clever child too. Perhaps she would grow up to be one of the higher servants. 'Stand beside the piano, children,' she said. 'We're going to sing our favourite hymn.'

It was dreadfully out of tune but if she struck the keys hard and jigged the tune a little the piano would make a good accompaniment to their joyful voices.

'Ready?'

> *Over the seas there are little brown children ...*
> *They haven't heard of our Saviour dear.*
> *Swift let the message fly over the water ...*
> *Telling the children that God is near ...*
> *Over the seas ... There are little brown children ...*
> *Nobody told them that God is near.*

Tomorrow there was to be skating on the frozen lake. Sylvia and the Bell-Cooper girls would be there. She hoped that the girls would be charming to the four young men and leave her free to skate by herself or with Uncle Bill.

* * *

Servants with besoms were sweeping the ice and following behind them housemaids and kitchen girls went with wide-headed brooms. Florence could hear their laughter as she crossed the frosted grass. Iron tables and chairs were ranged in front of the frozen lake, which was almost ready for the skaters, stark white against the snow-laden sky.

There were at least a hundred guests, Florence noted as she went, her skates gripping the snow, towards the bench where Sylvia sat. The scarlet coat with the deep band of fur at the hem made a vivid splash of colour against the whites and greens of snow and trees. She stood watching Sylvia Machin's maid struggling to lace her mistress's boots. 'Can you skate backwards, Sylvia?' Florence dropped down onto the seat beside her friend. 'Shall we go first? Will you lead?'

'Yes. I'll lead,' Sylvia said. 'What about the Hepworth brothers? Don't you want them to take us round?'

'Don't you find them tiresome?' Florence answered. 'I do.'

'John Hepworth has been ogling you all weekend.' Sylvia's dark hair fell across her face and as she tossed her head and pushed the loose strand back under the crown of her hat Florence saw the light of mischief in her eyes. 'I shall sport with him if you find him tiresome.' She laughed and held out her hands. 'Pull me to my feet and set me on the ice. It's a decade since I skated. I'm sure to fall at the poor boy's feet.'

Not far from the edge of the gravel path, towards the house, a chestnut burner had been lit. A barrel of chestnuts stood ready, the long-handled roasting pans propped against it. Guests were being served mulled wine from a china tureen above a charcoal burner on a trestle table where silver dishes piled with sweetmeats were set. Uncle Bill and Aunt Lucy stood nearby. Florence waved a gloved hand in their direction. They had seen her.

The cold air rushed against her face, bringing a stinging colour to her cheeks as she and Sylvia made the first cuts on the smooth, icy surface. They were being followed now, by the Hepworth brothers and the Bell-Cooper girls. Well, she'd leave Sylvia to their attentions as soon as they had circled the lake.

'Bother. My boots are loose.' Florence released Sylvia's hands. 'I'll go and fasten them.' She slid towards the lake's edge, steel on ice crunching into the rougher surface at the rim where she halted in front of Uncle Bill and Aunt Lucy. Sylvia, she saw, was already hand in hand with John Hepworth, her bright laughter and easy chatter floating back across the ice.

'Well, Florence. D'ye have a dancing card?' Uncle Bill said as soon as she straightened from tightening her bootlaces.

'I don't need one. When I want a partner, it shall be you,' she answered. 'You are by far the best skater here.'

Aunt Lucy, booted and clad top to toe in fur, held out her hands. 'Angel! Come, take your uncle onto the ice and I shall talk to your mama and Sir Philip. Bill cannot stop talking about the young man he has befriended. Indeed, he has spoken of nothing else for months.'

Aunt Lucy was smiling as she spoke, fondness and love for Uncle Bill in her every word and look. Florence kissed her cheek. 'I shall talk to him about myself then,' she teased. 'He shall listen to the outpourings of his once-favourite.'

Uncle Bill led her back onto the ice and took her hands. 'I cannae go as fast as I did, lassie,' he warned. 'We haven't had a winter like this for years. I'm a wee bit out of practice.'

'Oh, dearest. I simply wanted to be with you. I wanted to hear your words of wisdom,' Florence said. 'Let us go slowly around to the quiet side of the lake where we'll not be interrupted.' She held fast onto his hands and looked up into his dear old face. She must confide in Uncle Bill. He was the wisest person in the world and would advise her from his heart.

'What is it, lass?' he said.

'It's Mama. And Grandfather. They want me to marry.' They were out of the hearing of the other skaters now and Florence let the smile go from her face and looked into her uncle's eyes intently. 'It's dreadful. Every time I am taken anywhere a young man is presented.'

Uncle Bill wasn't smiling. He would never patronise her. Florence was encouraged. 'The young men are all perfectly acceptable. They will make wonderful husbands, I'm sure. But not for me.'

'Do you think you are too young, Florence? Is that what it is?'

'No. I want to marry. It's all I want – to marry and bring up my children – and to have time to help the needy. But I haven't met the right man yet. And someday I know I will.'

Uncle Bill had slowed to a halt at the far side of the lake. The sounds of merriment came faintly to them across the white expanse. 'Then you must wait until you find a man you can love, Florence,' he said.

'Do you think I am unnatural?' She saw with relief that he did not. He was smiling at her. 'Mama says I am wayward. Is it asking too much, to want more than this?' She waved her arm in the direction of the house. 'Am I ungrateful when I say I cannot accept a suitor on his acceptability to Mama and Grandfather?'

'I don't think so, Florence.' Uncle Bill was frowning in concentration. 'Your mama has your best interests at heart. But she and your grandfather are not the best judges of the man you must marry. You must stand firm. Tell them that you alone will choose.'

Having opened her heart, Florence could not stop herself. Tears prickled the backs of her eyes. She felt a lump in her throat as she added in a rush of words, 'I need to be loved, Uncle Bill. I need a man who will love me above all others. I will be a good wife to such a man. I couldn't take a man into my bed, Uncle Bill ... couldn't ... Oh, please don't despise me for saying these things. I do have deep feelings. Mama says I am capricious but I merely pretend to be so that they shall not see how afraid I am.'

Uncle Bill's eyes were sparkling with bright tears. He held her hand very tightly. 'Am I asking too much?' she pleaded.

Uncle Bill's voice sounded gruffer. 'No. Ye're not asking too much,' he said slowly. 'The young man I'm helping said very much the same thing. He's waiting until he meets the girl he wants. He'll not take a woman for her fortune, though there's one that wants him. And I admire him for it.'

'Perhaps your protégé will be more fortunate than I,' Florence said.

'Don't talk such nonsense, child. You're talking about the foundation of your life. Don't settle for less than you want. When you meet the right boy you'll have no doubts. And you must marry him, lass, whatever the cost to your mama and grandfather's hopes.'

'Thank you. Oh, thank you, darling.' Florence kissed his bristly old cheek, cold under her warm lips. 'Let us go back to the others now. Tell me about your young man as we go. I would so like to meet him.'

Uncle Bill moved stiffly to take her hands again and move forwards, towards the skaters in front of the house. 'I don't think that could be arranged. Florence. But I'll tell you that he's a remarkable youngster. While we're sleeping that boy will be pushing his handcart up cobbled, icy streets. He's always first into the market. He has to fight for all he earns.' Here Uncle Bill laughed. 'It's the truth. He often has a black eye, from footpads who try to set upon him and his partner to relieve them of their takings.'

They were approaching the others now. Voices could be clearly heard; delighted squeals from the girls, the raised tones of their elders as they exchanged pleasantries over the warm, spiced wines.

'He puts on his best clothes once a fortnight and journeys to London with samples of cloth. He never lets his customers down. He can bargain with the best of them, mill-owners as well. He could make a lot more money if he were a cheat but he's as straight as a die.'

Uncle Bill was so full of enthusiasm for this young man's progress that his cheeks were glowing with pride at the mention of his friend's successes. His hands were warmer now and his feet faster. 'He has a quality ... a character that I haven't met in years. He's good, Florence. He's honest and true. And if I'd had a son I'd have wanted him to be just like Oliver. And I wish you could see him, sweetheart. I wish you could.'

* * *

There had been a thaw at the end of January but the fastness of winter was upon them again, colder now than anyone could remember.

It was a bitter cold February morning. Bill Grandison had journeyed to The Pheasant as he always did and together Oliver and he were driven to the weaving shed at Hollin Mill, Oliver's thoughts far from the freezing cold of the streets he saw from the small carriage windows.

There was money in the bank now. He was making a good living from the market stalls, taking ten stalls a week and though Albert spent a lot of his own money on his many lady-friends Oliver had still not found a girl. He could attract a girl, could kiss even the plain and willing ones but his heart was not in it. Albert's ways were not for him. He went with Albert regularly to The Crown, to please his friend, but mostly he drank a few pints of beer, looked at the young women who clustered around Albert and dreamed of finding a girl like Rosie Hadfield.

He saw Rosie twice a week, once on Wednesdays at the mill where he plied her with questions about weaving and the management of a mill, and then on Saturday afternoons in the market where she lingered beside him for a few minutes.

And it was Wednesday and he'd see her again. The carriage bumped to a halt in front of the mill. Bill was quiet today. They'd hardly spoken a word, but sat facing one another in companionable silence through the brittle-cold morning.

* * *

Rosie pushed back the loose strands of her heavy, almost black hair. She bent her knee and stared at her reflection in the cracked mirror she'd hung on the old door of the mill's dry closet. Big brown eyes in a pale oval face looked back at her, a wide mouth with full lips, which she pursed and bit to redden them, and white and even teeth, which she rubbed with the inside corner of her clean apron to make them shine.

Then she sat down quickly on the long wooden seat and asked herself, as she did every day, why seeing Oliver Wainwright here, and in the market, made her act in this silly girl way.

Rosie loved her husband. Jim Hadfield was a good man who had met and married her eight years ago – and her a poor girl from the workhouse she'd been born into. He had been a mature man, a weaver of some forty years, an occasional preacher at revivalist meetings in the chapel that Rosie and her sister Agnes attended. Jim Hadfield went by train across Lancashire and Yorkshire at week-ends, preaching to unbelievers, bringing to the poor and ignorant the message of the Lord.

Before his lungs gave up Jim could move a congregation to tears or to public declarations of faith with one of his stirring ser-mons and Rosie and Agnes used to listen, enthralled. When Jim had asked to see her again after one of those meetings Rosie could hardly believe that a man of insight and eloquence, a lay preacher and scholar, had chosen her.

Jim had taught her much and she'd been a willing pupil at his scripture lessons but his touch had never roused in her more than a quick, involuntary response. They'd been taught at the workhouse and again at the chapel about sinful feelings that had to be quelled; about lusts that must be cast out before a pure life could be earned.

Rosie was glad she'd never been tempted to sample the sins of the flesh. Jim's caresses were respectful, given under the cover of darkness and the decency of a sheet. And that was as it should be. Why, then, did those very caresses disappoint her? Why did she long for something that Jim did not have to give? Was the touch she longed for one of the very sins of the flesh against which she had been warned?

Now if she'd been ten years younger when Oliver Wainwright came into her life she would have had to fight against the feelings his nearness brought to her. When Oliver came to the mill it was as if the lamps had suddenly been turned up bright. She could never ignore his presence when he stood beside her.

She left the little room and returned to the weaving shed. Soon, if she were not careful, the weavers would ask themselves why their forewoman put on her best skirt every Wednesday, why she appeared on edge as the time for Mr Grandison and Oliver's visit drew near. Weavers were never misled by words. They used other senses since their ears were redundant against the racket of the looms. Hollin Mill's weavers never misinterpreted any look or gesture, however concealed.

The familiar sensation of heightened awareness made her hands shake a little as she checked the cloth from one of the looms. Soon they'd be here and she would feel his eyes upon her across the weaving shed, making her aware of her every movement, disconcerting her, until her concentration went and she'd look up, to find his blue eyes holding hers, asking silent questions.

Her face broke into a smile at his arrival. He looked much older now than he had when he'd first come, as a young lad. He was twenty. Tall, loose-limbed and handsome, he had to duck his head to get through the low doorway. She waved her hand to attract his attention, then left the looms and followed Mr Grandison and Oliver into the little office. The boss looked pale today.

'Are you feeling well, Mr Grandison?' she asked. The old man normally had a good colour.

'Yes, thank you, Rosie,' he said. 'I'm getting old, you know. I always feel a bit weary towards the end of winter.'

Oliver had looked sharply at Mr Grandison when she'd spoken but he seemed reassured by the reply and turned his attention to her again. Those blue eyes, intently watching her face, the way his black hair curled, low on his neck, and his strong mouth and chin, sent the familiar trickling feeling down her spine.

Rosie drew herself straight. 'Be sure he gets a good hot toddy, Oliver, when you go for your dinner,' she said brightly as she tried to ignore the banging in her chest. She hoped they wouldn't see in her eyes her whirling confusion.

She had collected the record cards for Mr Grandison and handed them to Oliver. As if deliberately his hand strayed against hers as he took them from her. 'See you next week, then,' she managed to say before she left the little room and returned to the looms and the comforting, deadening noise of their clatter.

* * *

The frost had been harder overnight. The next morning was raw with a dull wind that crept around the corners of the yard. It had taken Bill Grandison's groom much longer than usual to harness the horses. The leather was stiff and unbending. The carriage was cold and Oliver stood with Bill in the windy yard until it was hitched.

Bill always left for the braid workshop and his lawyer's office at seven-thirty and it was now nearly eight o'clock. The old man's steps were slower than usual.

Had Oliver been older or wiser he might have seen that his friend was ill; he leaned so heavily on his arm as Oliver helped him to the carriage. The driver climbed up, took the reins and set off at a brisk trot up the steep street.

Oliver crossed the yard to the shed where the lad was piling bundles on to the cart, ready for market. He helped the boy for half an hour, working fast, feeling warmth come into his limbs as they worked. They'd set off soon. He pulled the watch from his waist-coat pocket; they'd better make haste.

There was a lot of noise in Rivergate, as carriages and carts trundled by; the sawdust that had been thrown over the frosty cobbles didn't quite deaden the sound of wood and iron but there was no mistaking the agitated hooves and the shouts of the groom as Bill Grandison's carriage rocked back into the yard.

'Come quick! I think the old man's dead!' Bill's driver shouted.

Oliver raced across the yard. He tugged at the door. Bill Grandison lay across the leather seat, his arms stiffly outstretched, and the pallor, the pinched nose, all should have told Oliver that help was too late. Oliver clambered into the cold carriage and lifted Bill gently, pulling him into a half-upright position so that the old man's head lay on his shoulder. He put his arms around Bill and held him close, trying to give him warmth. 'You're not dead, are you, Bill?' he whispered, rubbing his own glowing cheek against the cold, sunken face. 'You'll be all right in a minute, won't you?'

Then Oliver lowered Bill easily, so that the old man lay with his head in his lap, stroking Bill's face and the curly white hair, as if a coaxing touch would make the dear old eyes open. 'Speak to me,' he pleaded. 'Say you're not dead.'

Leonard Billington was at the open door of the carriage. 'We'd better get him inside, Oliver,' he said gently. 'Let go of him, lad. There's nothing you can do.'

It was as if something inside Oliver collapsed inwards, as if all the love, all the companionship that he had ever known had been crushed under the weight of this loss. He had never considered for a second that one day Bill would die. He'd never imagined his own life without Bill encouraging him, taking pride in his achievements, guiding him.

Oliver wept. He wept as he had not done for years. He wept for Bill Grandison and his Lucy; he wept for his father, his mother, young Tommy and lastly for himself. They tried to comfort him, bringing him hot toddy when they'd carried the body to the parlour where it would lie until the undertaker could be sent for and still the harsh, painful cries came, tearing at his throat, making his shoulders ache, causing his eyes to blur.

Finally, when at last he had to take leave of Bill, had to let them carry the wrapped body of the man he'd loved to the black, covered hearse that had been brought to the yard, Oliver's tears dried. He asked Bill's groom to take him to Balgone. He would tell the old man's widow himself.

They drove up the noisy Rivergate, through the crowded market and descended the gentle slope of busy Churchgate. Snow had begun to fall, muffling the sound of the iron-hooped wheels. Oliver rested against the brown leather upholstery as they climbed, away from the town, along the wide carriageway that led to Bill Grandison's home. His mind was numb, his eyes red and swollen and he hoped that the right words would come to him when the time came to tell her.

A high stone wall, two carved stone lions at the entrance, a sharp turn and the horse's hooves were making the first prints in the

snow-covered drive. Oliver made the driver keep the carriage waiting as he pulled the rope that hung beside the heavy door, barely
noticing the splendid high sash windows, the four turrets at each
corner of the roof and the grandeur of the house and gardens of
Balgone.

A maid in black, wearing a white lace apron and cap, opened the
door and hesitated, seeing her master's empty carriage, as if unsure
of what to do. 'I must see Mrs Grandison. Please take me to her at
once.' Oliver stepped into the wide, tiled entrance hall, dark and
rich with mahogany panelling and a warm Turkey carpet.

'Who shall I say is here?' the maid asked uncertainly.

'Oliver Wainwright. A friend of Mr Grandison's.'

The maid left for what seemed like an hour. When she
reappeared she held open a door on his right and announced,
'Oliver Wainwright, ma'm.'

Oliver entered the morning room. A white-haired old lady, tiny
and erect, stood before a tall oak fireplace where a newly lit fire
danced in the grate. 'Mrs Grandison?' The woman nodded but did
not hold out her hand. 'I'm Oliver Wainwright. A terrible thing
has happened. Terrible. Your husband, ma'm – Mr Grandison. He's
dead, ma'm! Dead! He died this morning in his carriage.'

Lucy Grandison leaned on her stick for support. 'Where is he?
My husband.'

'They've taken him to the undertaker's.'

'Take my arm. Take me to him.'

Oliver felt her frail weight on his arm as he helped her into the
carriage. His eyes were bright with tears as he faced her over the
narrow space that separated them on the journey back to town.

'I can't believe he's gone,' Oliver found himself saying, over
and over again. Then, as if he knew that he must try to be a friend
to the woman Bill loved, he squared his shoulders and said, 'If I
can be any help, any comfort to you, Mrs Grandison, I'd count it a
privilege to be asked.'

Together they entered the undertaker's premises and Lucy
Grandison kept Oliver beside her as she sat for an hour with her

husband, holding his waxen hand, tears coursing unchecked down the finely drawn cheeks. Then, with great courage and dignity, the old lady left, first thanking Oliver.

'My husband was very fond of you. I would like to see you again. I hope you will attend the funeral. I will have you informed of when it is to be.'

Later, Oliver sat at the fireside in Mrs Billington's parlour, his head in his hands, cold and weary.

'I've brought you a bowl of broth, Oliver.' Ma Billington spoke gently, as if he were the one who had died. She tucked a napkin around his knees and set the dish on a little round table in front of him, like a gift. 'There's a man waiting to see you, love. I said he must wait till you've eaten.'

'Ta.' Oliver gave her a weak smile. 'I'll be all right when I've had this. Who is he?'

'He's a lawyer. He mebbe wants Mr Grandison's books. I think they're up in his room.'

'I'll fetch them down and see him in here then,' Oliver said.

After he had eaten Oliver asked the man to come in. He was a tall, unhappy-looking man with bushy side-chops and a way of looking into the distance seconds after holding the eye of the person he was speaking to. It gave him a shifty air and Oliver did not like him.

'Oliver Wainwright?'

'Yes.'

'My name is Lloyd.' The man held out a cold, limp hand. 'I'm Mr Grandison's legal representative.' The man seated himself at the table and pushed back the thick cloth that Mrs Billington kept in place. He took from his leather document case a large brown envelope on which the seal had been broken and from this he extracted with his thin, blue fingers a folded piece of yellow parchment.

'My client ... should I say – my late client, William Hugh Grandison ... has bequeathed something to you. He added the bequest quite recently and since it is of an unusually generous nature I have enquired of Mrs Grandison if she wished to contest it.' The lawyer spoke in a monotone. 'She says it will stand. She asked me to inform you, before the official will-reading, of its content.'

He looked at Oliver briefly, then cast his eyes back to the paper and intoned in a voice as expressionless as his countenance, 'And to my dear friend, Oliver Wainwright, I leave the braid workshop and one hundred looms at Hollin Mill with the proviso that the sum hereinafter stated shall be paid to my niece and her daughter for life from the annual profit from the said mill and workshop. Should my dear friend wish to realise monies from the sale of the aforementioned mill then my niece and her daughter shall receive one-half of the proceeds of the sale, which is to be sold by my lawyer, Mr Cedric Lloyd, to the highest bidder.'

Oliver was stunned. He held on to the edge of the table and stared at Mr Lloyd.

'You have until after the funeral to give me your decision.' Mr Lloyd stood up. 'I cannot allow you to read the rest of the will. The family has not been informed of its contents. The will-reading will be held after the funeral at Mr Grandison's home.' He nodded formally to Oliver.

Oliver found his voice. 'Is it true? Did Mr Grandison really leave the business to me? What about his wife?'

'There is no need to concern yourself about Mrs Grandison's finances, Mr Wainwright. The mill and the workshop were not the only source of income for my client – my late client. Mrs Grandison agreed to the bequest when my client added it to his will.' He lifted his overcoat from the back of the chair and Oliver held it out for him. 'The funeral has been set for Monday, twelve o'clock at St Michael's church. Come to my office on Tuesday morning and I will give you the other details; the allowances and a statement of accounts. You will have to take up the running of the business immediately if you wish to continue with it. The formalities can be gone through at a later date.'

What a day it had been. What a terrible, awesome day. Albert was not yet home from the market and so much had happened. Oliver felt humbled by Bill Grandison's bequest. He was also bewildered and grateful. Though he could grasp the extent of his new-found wealth, for he had helped Bill with his books since the old man's eyes had begun to fail, he had never for a moment imagined that Bill wanted to go on helping him after his death.

Oliver vowed to himself that the inheritance that was going to change his life would never mean more to him than the man who had given it. He sat alone in the warm little parlour and tried to imagine what life held for him as the owner of a mill.

He would save his money to buy more looms. But he couldn't save for ever could he? Then he would look for a wife, buy a fine house and bring up his family in a proper manner as Bill would have wished him to do.

'You'll be a rich man soon,' Albert said as they counted the day's takings in the parlour after supper.

'And you.'

'I can't take any share in your mill or workshop. The old boy meant you to have them,' Albert told him firmly.

'Will you work for me then?' Oliver asked.

'Yes. We'll come to some arrangement. One that suits us both.' Albert tightened the cord on the last bag of copper. 'You'll not want to go to The Crown tonight? Those girls from Paradise Street might be there?'

'No. You go if you want to. I'm not much good at this alehouse courtin'.' Oliver packed the money bags into the leather portmanteau. He smiled at Albert. 'It's not that I don't want a girl. I've tried all your tricks; done all you told me to get them in the mood, but afterwards I feel disgusted with meself somehow. I'm on the lookout for a nice girl and I doubt if I'll find her in The Crown.'

'You're only twenty. What do you want to go looking for a courtship for?' Albert looked at him in dismay.

'Aye, well.' Oliver looked thoughtful. 'I'm mebbe old before my time. But I'll find meself a good 'un soon.'

Chapter Nine

Laura Mawdesley stared out across the park from the high drawing-room windows of Suttonford. In front of her the close-cut grass swept down to the lake where bare-branched trees waited in the sparkling frost of February sunshine for the earth to warm to life again. Laura loved her childhood home, even with the hand of winter on the land.

Her fair hair, upswept from her face, showed no sign of grey for her forty years and she still had the figure of a young girl. Erect and formal in manner, she gave the impression of a matron of supreme confidence, a haughty woman who expected deference from all who met her.

She and Florence spent most weekends at Suttonford. Her parents adored their granddaughter although, Laura knew, they found her dependence on them a financial burden. Such things were never spoken of openly. Oblique references were made to Uncle Bill's great wealth, which, since he had no heirs, would come to them eventually and revive the family fortunes.

And now it had happened. He was dead. Uncle Bill had been a vulgar, money-conscious character but he had always been kind to her and especially so to Florence. She hoped that he had made provision for them. He had given Laura an allowance for years. Perhaps he had not told Lucy about this money and she could never ask Aunt Lucy about it.

She'd hoped too that she had put away her black mourning clothes for a long time when the news came; not that she would need to wear them for longer than a month. It was not expected. Her

94

mother would wear black longer, out of respect for him. As for herself, a month of the hated black wouldn't hurt. Florence, of course, could wear dark grey. Florence was not yet eighteen and had already spent a year of her young life in mourning for her father.

Florence was fidgeting in the high-backed chair, her blonde hair caught on the buttons holding the plum-coloured velvet and she turned her head this way and that, trying to free it, making the chair squeak and annoying Laura. 'Florence! Do amuse yourself dear. It's a lovely day. Take a walk around the park while your grandmother and I talk,' she said with irritation. Florence was becoming rather touchy, Laura thought, as she watched her daughter flounce from the room in a pet.

Laura left the window and seated herself in the chair Florence had vacated, facing her mother who sat nearer to the blazing fire. 'I think I'll return to live with you and father once Florence is married,' she said. 'I hope we'll find a husband for her before she's twenty. I'll not live in town any longer than I have to.' She paused and looked hard at her mother. 'I hope we shall receive our allowance from Uncle Bill's estate,' she said.

Lady Oldfield, her white hair drawn back into a tight knot, looked severe.

Laura knew that her mother would be offended by the remark and was not surprised to hear her say, a shade stiffly, 'There was never an official arrangement. Nothing binding. Uncle Bill simply liked to help.' Her mother reached over and rang a bell beside the carved chimney piece. 'It really is too bad of you, Laura, to talk in this manner, even to me. Please say no more about it. I'm sure the arrangement will continue.'

A maid came in from the side room to receive her orders and Laura's face resumed its neutral expression. 'Ask Mrs Leach to prepare muffins and tea,' Lady Oldfield said. 'And tell Jackson to send Mr Lloyd up as soon as he arrives.'

Laura would not have her fears dismissed in this way even if Mother did find her outspokenness unseemly. 'Mother, will you ask Mr Lloyd about our allowances?' she persisted.

'I'll do no such thing. At a time like this!' She waved her hand to stop Laura from rising from the chair. 'Sit down!' she commanded. 'Uncle Bill said he'd take care of you and Florence after dear Geoffrey died. He will not have neglected to provide for you.'

It seemed that her mother wanted to reminisce about the old man. Laura sighed quietly and prepared to give her attention to the story she had heard so many times.

'He was a handsome man, Laura. But so different from the young men my sister and I were used to. He was well educated. Even the poorest children in Scotland receive an education, you know. But he had no social graces and if he had not met Lucy I don't think he would ever have acquired them.'

Laura tried to retain the look of interest on her face as her mother continued. 'I think he despised our sort. He had no respect for anyone who didn't work, though he came to see, finally, that not everyone was blessed with his ability. Lucy will be well provided for but your father will not be able to control his investments so well without Bill's help, and your father was one of his most implacable opponents until Bill and Lucy were married.'

'I expect he'll leave everything to Aunt Lucy and we'll have nothing until she's gone,' Laura said with an air of pessimism. 'I hope he remembered our allowances.'

She was spared her mother's rebuke by the butler's knock. 'Mr Lloyd, ma'm,' he announced.

* * *

There was a boy, fishing in the lake, far from the area the labourers were allowed to use. He was going to brazen it out. Impudent lad! Florence had walked right round the lake and her feet were cold. She was wearing soft kid boots designed for indoors and the frost and damp had stained them. 'Hoi! What are you doing here?' she called imperiously, tossing back her head, and hoping that he'd be afraid of her.

He did not look up. 'Fishin'.'

'You'll not catch anything at this time of the year. Ought you to be working?'

'Aye.'

He looked her way. Blue eyes, dark curly hair and a bold way with him; a defiant air that Florence would not tolerate. 'Well. Explain yourself!'

'Not to you, I won't.'

Florence put her straight little nose high in the air and turned sharply on her heel; but he was away, running like the wind, his wild laughter ringing out behind him, the sound of it still cutting through the thin air for seconds after the sound of his feet died away.

She tightened the neck of her blue velour cloak, pushed her hands into the muff of black fur and walked smartly back to Suttonford Manor.

A carriage waited by the wide steps leading to the door. Florence watched from behind the great oak as Mr Lloyd, the lawyer, descended the steps, his wide bushy side-chops incongruous under the black top hat that covered his thinning hair. He'd be here to talk about Uncle Bill's death. Aunt Lucy had urged Florence to be brave and not to grieve as Uncle Bill would not have wanted her to be distressed by his passing,

She loitered outside and then, the cold making her face smart, returned to the drawing room where she could hear, two yards from the door, the voice of her mother who was clearly agitated. 'Who is this Oliver Wainwright?' Mama was saying.

Florence saw that her mother still gave the appearance of composure but the high pitch of anxiety was in her voice. 'This upstart! Has anyone heard of him before today?'

Gran answered, 'Lucy says he's a young man Uncle Bill thought well of. I'll have no more of this ingratitude from you, Laura! Florence is here. Please don't alarm her.'

'Do tell me. Mother? Gran?' Florence could not contain herself.

'Your Uncle Bill has left everything to a young man he hardly knows. Heaven knows what is to become of us!' Mama dabbed at her eyes with a lace handkerchief and collapsed on to the sofa.

Lady Oldfield answered Florence while glancing disdainfully at Mama. 'Your uncle has left only a part of his estate to the young man he admired. The mill and the workshop are to be his, as are the obligations he honoured; your allowance, your mother's annuity. We don't know about the rest. The young man may wish to sell, of course, and in that case a large proportion of the money comes straight to you.'

'He'll not sell. I know he won't.' Mama's voice had taken on a whining note of self-pity. 'Uncle Bill said the boy was like himself. Just mark my words! He'll prosper!'

* * *

Carriages lined up at the gate of the icy, damp cemetery behind St Michael and All Angels, waiting to take mourners to Balgone. Oliver stood alone at the graveside. He had been taken aback to see the Oldfield family in full attendance. Even the dissipated son, Godfrey, heir to the estate, had come from his London home. Sir Philip Oldfield had read a lesson and Lucy Grandison, at the front of the church, had been supported by him and Lady Oldfield. It was quite plain that the two old ladies were sisters and that Bill Grandison had been related to the family by marriage.

So Bill's brother-in-law, the man who had been so firmly set against the young Bill Grandison, had been Sir Philip Oldfield! Oliver knew now why Bill had told him so little about his family life. It would have amused him to picture Oliver's reaction when he finally found out.

Oliver sensed the Oldfields watching him. Their eyes were constantly turning in his direction, making him feel uncomfortable. They had the advantage of him. They'd known he'd be there and yet none of them had so much as lifted a hand to greet him. If these were the manners of the aristocracy, he could teach them a thing or two.

He moved his numb fingers inside the leather gloves, remembering not to put his hands in the pockets of the black overcoat of

Mr Billington's. He decided not to look at them but turned his attention to the yawning grave. One of the flat stones of the churchyard had been lifted and the black earth lay heaped beside it. The Oldfield family were buried in the little churchyard at Suttonford village.

Oliver tried to picture Bill's face but could only capture a memory of his chuckle and the quick mind of the man who had come to seem like a father to him. He wondered if Bill were watching him now from some heavenly vantage point. He could imagine him enjoying the scene, waiting to see what his protégé would make of a meeting with the family he had despised. The thought gave Oliver strength.

The coffin was lowered into the grave. Oliver watched Lucy Grandison, upright and dignified, standing unsupported while the priest intoned, 'Ashes to ashes ... Dust to dust.'

He kept behind the other mourners when they left the churchyard until the family were gone and Oliver found that he was in the last carriage to make its way through the crowded market square. Men doffed their caps in respect as the cortege passed. Occasionally one would recognise the young market trader and not believe his eyes.

At Balgone their coats were taken by a servant and he saw with relief that he was correctly dressed, in black trousers and long coat.

Lucy Grandison came forward and took his arm. 'Come with me, Oliver,' she said, steering him through the little mob of mourners. The Oldfields didn't speak to him.

Lucy led him into the morning room to where a girl sat alone at the window. Oliver recognised her before she turned her head; the girl he had last seen on his flight from Suttonford. She extended a delicate hand to him and smiled.

'Florence, this is Oliver Wainwright, the young man your uncle so admired.' Lucy turned to Oliver. 'I would like you to tell my niece all you can of your association with Bill. Florence was very fond of her uncle.'

Close to, she was smaller than he remembered. Dark lashes fringed her wide grey eyes. The radiant blondeness of her hair, caught at the nape of her slender neck with a black velvet bow, struck him as it had done in the moonlight on the night he ran away. She wore a plain dress of grey moiré silk, as dark as charcoal, with a close-fitting bodice that was demurely pin-tucked. Her tiny waist, owing nothing to corsetry, was encircled by the same black velvet she wore in her hair.

'How do you do, Mr Wainwright.' Florence held out her hand towards the chair facing hers. 'Please sit down and tell me how you came to know my uncle so well.'

Her voice was musical and low. It had the cultured tone that marked the landed people he remembered from his childhood at Suttonford. He had heard her speak on the night he'd left the estate and even then the sound had stirred him, not as those other voices did, with feelings of contempt, but with a longing to hear more.

'Your uncle was a friend to me, Miss Mawdesley. In the three years I knew him I grew to love and respect him,' he replied. 'I'm sure you will find his loss a great burden.' He was aware of the heads turned in their direction; aware of the hostility of the Oldfields, but most of all he was acutely conscious of the enchanting girl before him.

Her face broke into a smile. 'Call me Florence,' she said. 'And please let me call you Oliver.'

'It may not please your family,' he warned her, 'but of course you must call me Oliver.' He grinned at her and added, '... Florence.'

Her eyes sparkled as they held his and Oliver was bewitched.

'Come with me, Oliver. I'll take you into the hall and drawing room and show you the portraits of Uncle Bill when he was a young man.' Florence led the way through the groups of mourners, touching an arm here, inclining her head there, tiny and exquisite. Oliver felt clumsy and yet protective next to her and he followed, shaking hands when introduced and saying 'How do you do,' to which, he noted, replies were neither given nor expected. He was aware, as Florence appeared not to be, that her family were disinclined to shake his hand.

At last they reached Sir Philip who stood with his back to the fireplace. The close-set grey eyes, the long hooked nose in his thin face, were familiar to Oliver. His condescending look today was joined with an air of mockery, as if he knew the measure of Oliver and found it no threat.

Oliver's eyes were on the same level as Sir Philip's. It was the first time they had met on neutral territory and he knew, the moment the old baronet put out his hand, the same sense of being in the presence of an opponent that Bill must have felt years ago.

'Wainwright, isn't it?' Sir Philip said before Florence could begin the introduction.

'Yes. How d'you do, Oldfield?' Oliver put his own hand out and watched Sir Philip's face to see his reaction to the insult. He had enjoyed calling him Oldfield, as if he were a common man. It was not as if he didn't know better. Oliver knew perfectly well that the man had a right to be given his title. By not doing so he knew it was clear to Sir Philip that he had no respect for his authority.

Sir Philip drew his breath sharply. His eyes hardened momentarily and he withdrew his hand.

Oliver turned away, satisfied. Now Sir Philip would know that he could no longer act as if Oliver were still a servant of the Suttonford estate. He could make what he liked of it.

Florence had gone ahead of him. She had not heard the exchange but was waiting for him to catch up with her, under the portrait in the hall. He followed her to the upstairs drawing room after they had looked at the painting. She climbed the wide stair ahead of him, turning to smile when she reached the top.

Oliver had never seen a room as fine as this. He had seen only the servants' quarters and the kitchen at Suttonford. The high ceiling and cornice were decorated in fine plasterwork; acanthus leaves, rosettes and vines intertwined, with the pattern repeated on the pale, silky wallpaper.

Opposite the door a wide bay window with shallow sills revealed a spectacular view of the garden, its rose beds and walkways, and beyond, the whole of Middlefield with the hills in the far distance. A fire blazed in a white marble fireplace over which a gilt mirror reflected the long wall where the second portrait hung.

'This is a lovely room, Oliver. Quite my favourite. I loved coming here to talk to Uncle Bill.' She took him by the arm to the

101

portrait and together they searched the face for traces of the man they had known.

'It's a beautiful house, Florence. I mean to have just such a house when I'm a rich man,' he told her. They stood together at the window, watching the grooms and drivers who had gathered together behind the stables, stamping their feet to keep warm, their breath clouds of vapour when they spoke. He could feel the silence of the room, was conscious of the beauty of the girl beside him and as he looked at her, knew again the feeling that had overcome him on his run for freedom, more than three years before.

She turned her grey eyes, large and expressive, upon him and he saw, momentarily, the determined girl that dwelt under her fragile exterior.

'Oliver,' she said and her little soft hand was over his. 'Please say you'll call on us. I don't want to wait until you're a rich man to be invited to your house. You shall come to Churchgate; number twenty-three, in two weeks' time. I insist. I'll tell Mama you're expected and you can tell me how you mean to proceed now you have your own mill.'

She led the way back to the mourners who had moved to the dining room where tea and sandwiches were being served at small tables placed around the walls.

Oliver was shown to the table where Mr Lloyd sat. 'You know the contents of the will, Mr Wainwright. If you wish to leave before it is read I am sure the family will understand and be grateful to you. Please come to my office tomorrow. There are documents to sign and I'll explain the legal necessities to you.'

A rage – was it in reaction to the Oldfield family's ignoring his presence? – rose in Oliver. How dared they treat him in this manner? It was as if he didn't exist. If Florence hadn't spoken to him he would have been cold-shouldered by all but Lucy Grandison. They had not so much as nodded in his direction, yet they were well aware of him.

Did they think they could pass over the matter of his inheritance? Did they imagine that Bill wouldn't have wished him to attend? No.

They had no regard either for Bill or for himself. Bill, and now he, were mere sources of income and not to be treated as anything more.

They were in for a shock.

He rose to his feet. His voice was hard and indomitable. 'I'll not leave.' They were all listening. Not a knife or teaspoon clattered. It was as if the very walls held their breath. 'I wish to hear the will-reading,' he stated in a clear, strong voice. 'I shall stay.' He saw the shocked looks on the faces that were now turned in his direction. 'With the bequest I have inherited obligations. I'll hear you out.'

He sat down, half-expecting to be asked to go but it appeared that he had trounced them. The family returned to their tea-drinking, to all outward appearances as if nothing had been said. Oliver caught Florence's eyes over the head of Mr Lloyd. They were shining with admiration.

The mourners dispersed. Only family, the servants who had an interest in the will and a few other beneficiaries had been asked to remain. They assembled around the oval mahogany table. Lamps had been lit, for dusk came early, and the heavy curtains of blue velour pulled across the window.

Florence and her mother sat in the centre of the long side, Godfrey Oldfield, an elderly bachelor, beside them. Sir Philip and Lady Oldfield sat with Lucy Grandison at the foot, or was it the head of the table? Oliver could not be sure. He had been placed two seats down from Mr Lloyd at the other end.

The lawyer opened his case and placed a sheaf of yellowed parchment before him. He glanced around the table, as if to assure himself that everyone was present and began to read:

'To my dear wife, Lucy, I leave my entire estate with the exception of the bequests as set out in the following pages.

'To my head gardener, George Peck, the sum of £50. To the under gardener, John Culshaw, the sum of £30.

'To the housekeeper, Mrs Bostock, the sum of £50. To each of the four parlourmaids, the sum of £30.

Mr Lloyd droned on, reciting the small bequests to his faithful servants. Bill had been generous, remembering all who had served him well. There was not one who received less than £30 and Oliver saw the delight that crossed their faces as their names were mentioned.

'And to my forewoman, Mrs Rosalind Hadfield, the sum of £50, for good and faithful service …

Oliver was pleased that Bill had remembered Rosie. Fifty pounds would be a sizeable sum to her. He didn't think she knew about it yet and he looked forward to seeing her surprise when he told her.

'My niece Laura Mawdesley and her daughter Florence are to receive an allowance of £2,000 annually from the profits of Hollin Mill, in the form of an allowance of £800 per annum to Florence Mawdesley and £1,200 per annum to Laura Mawdesley, to be administered by my dear friend, Oliver Wainwright. Should Oliver Wainwright wish to dispose of his interest in the said mill then a trust is to be executed, from the sale, for the said allowances to continue.

Oliver saw, first, a look of relief on Laura Mawdesley's face, which was followed by another look, of displeasure, at the mention of his name. She had not wanted to have any dealings with him, he could tell. She evidently had no further interest in the will for she excused herself and Florence and they left the room.

There followed his own bequest, which Oliver had looked forward to hearing again. So, it was true! Lloyd had not been playing a trick. He was to inherit the weaving shed and the braid workshop. The spinning mill had been leased so the machinery was to be sold and the proceeds were to go into the estate.

Outside, beyond the blue curtain, Oliver heard carriage wheels crunching on the gravel, heard the melodic tones of Florence's voice speaking softly to her mother as they left Balgone.

'To my brother and sister-in-law, Sir Philip and Lady Camilla Oldfield,'

Oliver saw Sir Philip's eyes flick over to the speaker. Not a muscle betrayed any expectations he might have but Oliver had sensed the impatience with which he'd been waiting.

'I leave 20,000 shares in the railway company, the income from which is to be used to improve, first, the houses of the estate's employees and afterwards, the school and church of Suttonford village. Should the beneficiaries wish to dispose of these shares, the sum so raised shall be used for this purpose and no other.'

Oliver knew with what delight Bill would have added this last and final bequest. He would not have wanted to snub the Oldfields outright, yet he had not been able to bring himself to benefit them; to think of his money at last being spent to support their way of life.

Chairs were being pushed back. Lloyd continued to intone,

'Signed and dated this fourteenth day of December, in the year eighteen hundred and seventy-eight.'

Oliver said farewell to Lucy Grandison. 'Please visit me, soon, Oliver,' she said as he took his leave. 'Bill spoke often of your many qualities. I should like to enjoy your company, as he did.'

Oliver walked from Balgone to The Pheasant, glad of the clean, cold air, glad to be away from the oppressive presence of Sir Philip Oldfield, whom he knew now to be his implacable enemy. He thought clearly and deeply about the skirmishes he was sure lay ahead. Sir Philip would do all he could to discredit or ruin him and there was a lot that a man of such wealth and power could do.

Oliver knew also that he looked forward to his first brush with the old baronet. It would be more enjoyable to tangle with Sir Philip than it was to do business with the other mill-owners. Sir

Philip, of course, would be at a disadvantage since he would have to work through an agent. It would not do for him, a gentleman and a Justice of the Peace, to be seen to do his own dirty work.

'I wonder who will strike the first blow for him.' Oliver laughed aloud at the thought and broke into a joyful run. 'I'll not let him have your money, Bill,' he shouted to the dark, empty sky.

Chapter Ten

Florence lay in bed at nine o'clock, having excused herself to Mama, declaring that she felt quite drained from the solemn day.

She had ordered a fire to be lit and she tossed and turned, a prey to wild fancies she believed were peculiarly her own. Sometimes at night she would discard her fine lawn nightdress and lie naked between the linen sheets, imagining herself carried away by a faceless, nameless man. Then, unable to resist, she would submit to and endure the state of voluptuous torture these longings brought.

She knew she should feel shame for her wicked thoughts but she did not, and tonight, full of unfulfilled passion, she at last had a face to put to her sweet tormentor and she burned with the desire to see and touch Oliver Wainwright.

She went back through the day, minute by minute. She had been sitting alone, in the window seat at Balgone, not wanting to engage in insincere conversations with the family, who all professed to be stricken at the death of poor Uncle Bill, yet were dry-eyed and on their worst behaviour. As the carriages arrived she had noticed the tall young man in a greatcoat several sizes too large, who arrived last and alone.

Aunt Lucy had brought him to meet her. Oliver Wainwright, Aunt Lucy had said. What a strong name it was ... Oliver ... Oliver. She had seen that he was ill at ease, seen that he was uncomfortable in the company of her family.

He'd talked about Uncle Bill in a voice that was deep, with a pronounced local accent, and the sound of it sent a thrill through her senses. His face had been strangely familiar. She had seen those dark good looks before, and recently.

She had been taught to put good manners above all and she had determined that the family should not disdain his company because they begrudged him his inheritance. Grandfather had pointedly ignored him, Grandmother had acted as if he were invisible and Mama at the very moment they were speaking had been flashing warning looks towards her. The poor young man must have been feeling dreadful.

She had said something about Aunt Lucy's loss, in a well-bred sort of way, she remembered. Then she'd known that she was being stiff and formal, and impulsively she'd placed her hand over his and asked permission to use his Christian name.

He had relaxed at once and his features, which had seemed grim and brooding in his discomfort, softened, breaking into the most engaging smile Florence had ever seen.

Perhaps he was married? No, he wasn't married. Aunt Lucy told her that he lived at The Pheasant. A married man wouldn't live at a tavern. Perhaps he had a lady-friend? What if he loved someone? No. He didn't love anyone. She was sure he'd not have looked at her the way he had if he loved another. He had deep blue eyes and they had never left her face. She just knew he didn't love another. He couldn't have let his eyes burn into her as they had, if he loved another.

Mama had called him a 'common creature of the market place' and taken her away from him, before they'd had a chance to speak again. How could she say that? One only had to look at his well-cut features. Such faces surely weren't given to common creatures. And wasn't there something exciting about a man who had no pretty manners? Oliver had a rough, masculine voice, which was much to be preferred to the teasing, silly tones of all the other young men she'd met.

Suppose she never saw him again? He hadn't replied when she asked him to call. Florence sat bolt upright in the bed, her hair dishevelled, grey eyes wide with alarm, her naked body translucent in the flickering firelight. She had to see him again.

She experienced a feeling of panic at the prospect of never seeing him, her heart pounded, heat flooded into her face; she, who had so far rebuffed the overtures of every young man she had met, rose from her bed and by candlelight composed a letter.

Finally she slept, delighting in the thought that she had at last found a man of character, unashamed that she'd made the first advance. She had invited him to call on her a week next Wednesday at three o'clock.

Mama did not come down to breakfast that morning so Florence had no opportunity, until after the letter had been posted, to speak to her mother about the invitation. When she did so in the afternoon she was astonished at Mama's reaction. She had never seen Mama so angry.

'To think that you, my own daughter, should ask this ... low creature to call upon us. What possessed you?' Mama said.

'Since Mr Wainwright is going to provide a fair part of our means of support, Mama, it's only right and just that we should welcome him,' Florence replied.

'There is nothing just or right about defying me, Florence.' Mama's voice was shrill. She seemed to have forgotten her own strictures about not letting the servants hear. 'You will never see him again. Do you hear me? You will write and tell him that he is not welcome in my house.'

Since Uncle Bill's death, tears had been very near to the surface and now Florence could not hold them back. 'You are being hateful, Mama,' she cried. 'Uncle Bill meant Oliver to have the inheritance. You are all behaving as if he had no right to it.' Tears were streaming down her face. She had never spoken so rudely to Mama before and the fury in her mother's face at the outburst added to her anguish. But it was not right that the family should treat Oliver so.

'He had no right to it.' Mama's voice became cold again. 'He must have preyed upon a sick old man. That money, those mills belong to the family. They were Oldfield family property.'

'Then why doesn't Aunt Lucy ask him to return them? They were Uncle Bill's. To do with as he liked. And he didn't want you to have them,' Florence shouted. 'I hope you are punished for your vile greed!' She ran from the room, blinded by tears, almost flooring a startled maid in the hallway. She lifted her rustling grey skirt and fled upstairs to her bedroom where she turned the key in the lock. Then Florence threw herself, face down, on the silk quilt, sobs of anger and frustration shaking her slight body until the afternoon light began to fade and she had no breath left for crying.

She turned over and lay on her back. The tears had subsided and left her numb-faced and clear-headed. The events of the previous day had not faded from her mind. She remembered them as sharply as if she were reliving them. She would see Oliver again. If it meant forcing herself into deceit then so be it.

She would go downstairs and apologise to Mama. She would allay Mama's fears about her intention to see Oliver, even as she was working out the details of the plan that was taking shape in her mind.

Florence rinsed a facecloth in the cold water jug and pressed it to her eyes and her cheeks. Her looking glass reflected back her white face as she brushed her pale silk hair into place. She seldom had so much as a cross word with Mama so it should be easy to persuade Mama of her contrition.

The lamps had been lit when she re-entered the drawing room. Mama was seated at her desk, a glass of brandy to hand. Poor Mama must have been under severe strain. It was the second time in as many days that she had needed the sustenance of strong spirit.

'I'm sorry, Mama,' Florence said as she closed the door behind her. 'It was wicked of me to speak as I did.'

A look of relief crossed Mama's face. 'We've both been hasty, Florence,' she said. 'Let us put it behind us now.'

'Do you remember the girl I met at Miss Fern's dancing lessons, Mama? Edith Clayton.' Florence sat beside her mother at the desk.

'The pretty girl with auburn hair?'

'Yes. I want to ask her to tea. Instead of Oliver. Do you mind?'

'She's not really our sort, Florence. Isn't she an innkeeper's daughter?'

'Oh, Mama. Don't be tiresome. There is nobody else I want to see. You said yourself that she dances well and has been well brought up.' Florence affected her most persuasive tone. 'You surely cannot object to my making a friend of her. The Swan is the largest coaching inn in Cheshire. The Claytons live in the big house next door to it – a bigger house than this. Mr and Mrs Clayton are staunch church members.'

Florence saw that her mother was softening. 'Why, Mama, the Dean himself has asked Edith, as well as me, to take a class at St Michael's Sunday school. You were pleased that I'd been singled out, weren't you?' She took Mama's hands in her own and closed her warm fingers around Mama's cold ones.

'I thought you didn't want to take a class. You told me that you preferred to spend the weekends at Suttonford.' Mama was smiling as she spoke and Florence knew that agreement was not far away.

'I shall do as the Dean asks, Mama, if Edith will take a class too. I'll feel too exposed to scrutiny to do it by myself,' she said.

'When will you start?' Mama asked.

'This Sunday. I'll take a class on Sunday afternoon. I'll ask Edith to tea on Thursday.' Florence pulled gently at her mother's hands. 'Come. Sit by the fire with me. You are cold, Mama.'

'I'd prefer to go to Suttonford on Sunday, but if I must, I'll remain here.'

Florence had not thought of this possibility. Her plans would be ruined if Mama remained here. 'You go, Mama. I'll come back here after church and be quite content to wait for your return,' she said firmly.

'Very well. Ask your friend to tea and I'll speak to the Dean for you.'

Florence said a silent prayer of thanks. All that remained was for her to persuade Edith to accompany her on a visit to The Pheasant on Sunday afternoon.

* * *

The entrance hall at Suttonford House had been designed and built a century before by Italian craftsmen, from white marble and rosewood. Two curved staircases of marble, to the right and left of a central atrium, flanked a square Roman bath and fountain. Water played constantly from a gilded torch in the raised hand of a cherub and was fed to the fountain by an underground system of lead pipes – copied from ancient Rome.

Around the panelled walls, behind the white marble columns, which supported the upper floor, doors opened onto reception rooms and corridors. On the floor above, beyond the white balustrade, were the drawing rooms, private sitting rooms and ballroom. Here, on rosewood panelling between the doors, hung the family portraits and from this upper landing two polished staircases led to the topmost floor.

The panelling was again repeated on this floor and the hall was lit, above it, from a dome of etched and stained glass, which spanned the central area of the house and was itself surrounded by painted frescoes and ceiling panels.

To the right of the entrance hall, behind one of the columns, was an open corridor. This long passageway, oak-lined and hung with antlers and sporting trophies, could not be seen from the classical entrance and led to the offices and kitchens of the big house.

Sir Philip Oldfield's study, overlooking the front of the house, was a warm, book-lined room with a high fireplace in which a log fire burned. Here, two days after the funeral of his brother-in-law, were gathered Sir Philip, Lady Oldfield, Laura Mawdesley and Mr Lloyd.

Sir Philip stood with his back to the fire, impatience in every line of his face, his grey eyes cold and calculating. 'We stand to lose if Wainwright can't be stopped,' he announced. 'Have you any suggestions as to how we set about it?'

Lady Oldfield glanced at the others. 'I don't think we can stop him,' she said in a matter-of-fact way. 'He'll not give up his inheritance. Can't we buy him out?'

'Well, Lloyd? Can we?' Sir Philip demanded.

'There's no money for that kind of purchase.' Lloyd pulled at his side whiskers thoughtfully. He was seated at the desk where four open ledgers lay before him. 'There'd be money if you sold the railway stock, but any income from the sale would have to be used for the purpose of improving the cottages. It's all here, in the will.'

Laura leaned forward in the leather armchair. 'Do you think I might have a small glass of brandy, Father? I think I'll die from anxiety.' She pulled a lace handkerchief from beneath the neat cuffs of her black dress and touched her forehead with it. 'I must receive my allowance. Florence and I cannot continue without it. She must make a good marriage.'

Sir Philip handed to Laura a small glass of cognac from the decanter he kept on a side-table. 'The money must be found, Lloyd. Sell some land. Offer Wainwright as little as you need. But get that mill.'

He returned to stand in front of the fire. 'I own the property. I cannot allow one of my own servants control over family income. The mill belongs to us. Grandison must have been out of his mind.'

Lloyd drummed on the table with thin fingers. 'Oliver Wainwright is no longer a servant. As for the bequest, there is nothing to be done, even if Grandison was of unsound mind. His widow is the one to institute proceedings, not the minor beneficiaries.'

'Then get her to contest it, Lloyd.'

'She means it to stand,' Lloyd said.

Sir Philip's face, normally a cool mask of neutrality, blanched at the lawyer's words. His teeth were tightly clenched. 'He was a servant. He insulted me. Keep my name out of it, but get that property.' He left the study. His family were annoying him with their acceptance of Oliver Wainwright's good fortune. Lloyd was half-hearted in his support. Grandison had always been an awkward fellow. He ought to have expected something like this from Grandison, he told himself. It might seem foolish, irrational even, to Lloyd but the family name was at stake. It was preposterous. Laura, the dear girl, understood.

'Blast the man,' he cursed. 'My ancestors would have gone to war for less.' Opposite the door was another, leading to the kitchen stairs and the little estate office. He opened the office door and hit the desk with his closed fist. 'I'll not give up. I'll ruin that arrogant devil.'

He remembered the look on Wainwright's face when he'd delivered the insult. 'How dared he call me Oldfield and stand his ground?' he asked himself, whipping up his anger still more. 'He'll be glad to sell the mill by the time I've done.'

He rang the servants' bell. A footman answered the summons. 'Find Leach and bring him here,' Sir Philip ordered. He considered, while he waited, dismissing Wainwright's stepmother and her son from the estate but remembered, finally, that she was now the mistress, if not the wife, of Leach and had recently borne him a child.

No. Her cooking skills would be missed. Servants were ten a penny but a good cook was beyond price. Her loyalties now lay with Leach. He recalled the last meeting he'd had with the woman; remembered her saying that the boy was beyond her capabilities. Oliver Wainwright had been her stepson and she'd be glad to see him go. She'd not owe Oliver Wainwright any allegiance.

From the window Sir Philip saw Wilf Leach swaggering up to the house. The man was dirty and often the worse for drink but he could make the labourers work. He also knew Wilf Leach to be dishonest, but not clever enough to rise above petty pilfering. The man would co-operate. 'Enter,' he called when he heard the obsequious tapping on the office door.

'You wanted me?' Wilf Leach asked.

'Yes. Come in, Leach.' Sir Philip pointed to a stool at the far end of the bench. 'Sit. You have friends in the town? In Middlefield?' he asked.

'Yes, sir.'

'Do you know any of the weavers at Hollin Mill?'

'I know some.'

'Are you in their confidence?'

Wilf Leach looked puzzled. Sir Philip decided against discretion. It was wasted on Leach. 'Oliver Wainwright is now the owner of Hollin Mill,' he said. 'I want it.' Leach's loose jaw dropped. So the news had not flown round the estate as speedily as Sir Philip had imagined.

'Set up a meeting with the men who work for Wainwright. Offer them three and six a day each, to be paid daily, for their refusing to work for him. Suggest that Wainwright is going to reduce their wages. Tell them that he has plans to increase the hours they work.' At last a look of recognition was crossing Leach's sly face.

'I want them to strike, Leach. I want them to think that Wainwright is out to break them. My name must be kept out of this. I want the workers to believe that their new boss is lying when he protests his innocence,' Sir Philip told him. 'I want that mill out of Wainwright's hands. It belongs to the Oldfield family, not to one of our servants. I'm going to run it myself.'

Leach was leering at him as if waiting for something. Sir Philip unlocked a safe that was set into the wall behind him. He withdrew a small leather bag and counted out twenty sovereigns, which he put into a cloth purse. 'Pay them with this,' he ordered. 'Keep two for yourself and there will be much more when you've broken Wainwright. Report back.'

Wilf Leach extended a filthy hand into which Sir Philip dropped the bag. 'Remember, if you are caught you will take the consequences. Not I.'

'Wainwright won't catch me.' Wilf licked his lips as if in glee at the prospect of avenging himself on the antagonist he'd long wanted to score over. 'I'll enjoy his downfall.'

* * *

Oliver walked to his mill two days after the funeral. It was his first visit as the new owner and he savoured every moment of the walk, ignoring the clamour and clangour of Rivergate, concentrating his mind on his future plans. He would keep the stalls until the output of the mills was such that the income from the market was insignificant. Albert and the lads would take care of the selling for the present.

He'd spent the day before in serious thought. There were opportunities for increasing the yardage. The weavers would be glad of a chance to earn more money if he started a system of longer hours of work and of staggering the shifts. Rosie would help with the details. If everything went according to his plans then within six months he could look for bigger premises, take on more looms.

Other questions had still to be answered. He'd puzzled long and hard, well into the nights that had followed his meeting with Florence when he'd known again the longing that the sight of her, over three years ago, had roused in him. She'd looked at him as if she too were overwhelmed by their meeting. The Oldfield family would keep them from meeting again, come hell or high water. His chances of seeing her alone were naught.

Oliver also knew now that he would never find it easy, as Albert did, to take his pleasures where they were offered. He was a complicated creature, even to himself, and he wondered how it was that a man could see the heart-stopping beauty of a girl like Florence and want to hold her sweetness to himself, and at the same time feel the powerful desire of a man for a woman that he felt when he was near Rosie Hadfield.

How could he be attracted to the two women he could never hope to marry? He must put these thoughts behind him. He went through the narrow lane that separated Hollin Mill from the cotton-spinners next door and stood in front of his mill, enjoying a moment of pride. Then he opened the outer door and ran up the dusty stairs to the office where Rosie waited for him, brown eyes glowing and a blush on the creamy skin of her face as she held out her hands to him.

'Did you know that the mill is mine, Rosie?' he asked when the door was closed. He'd seen the heads of the weavers turn all the way along the lines of looms and knew, of course, that she knew.

'Yes,' she said. 'I'm glad, Oliver. I'm glad it hasn't gone to anyone else. Did you know that Mr Grandison left me fifty pounds?'

'Yes. I was at the will-reading. What will you do with it?' he asked her.

'I'll try to find a better house to rent. One where the damp won't go for Jim's chest,' she said. 'Are you going to make changes?'

'Yes,' he told her. 'I want to put up the production. I'll start the system the bigger mills use, of longer hours, staggered shifts. There's plenty of demand for our cloth.'

He was still holding one of her hands and felt her pull it gently from his grasp. 'I'll tell the weavers,' she said, 'when you've told me how we'll operate the new system.'

'Help me with the details, Rosie.' Oliver placed two chairs side by side at the desk and motioned her to sit. 'There's more I want to do. The property's leased from a Manchester trading company. I only own the looms. I mean to find a bigger place, get more looms and make us the biggest weavers in Middlefield.'

'There's bigger places going up further along the river, Oliver. One of those would do you proud,' she said. 'Will you keep us all on?' she laughed. 'When you get to be a man of means?'

She had a low, throaty laugh. Oliver had never heard her laugh out loud before. Again, he had the sense that the noise of the weaving shed faded and only he and this warm, inviting woman existed. 'I'll need you, Rosie,' he replied, and there was no answering jest in his voice. 'I'll need you more than ever.'

She stopped laughing. She appeared to have taken fright at the intensity of his words. 'I'll help you with this work,' she said quietly. 'Then I must get back to the weavers.'

She turned her attention to the papers he'd brought, working silently, averting her eyes from his when she asked for an explanation of the new proposals. Oliver felt, as he always did, near her, an almost irresistible urge to take hold of her, so he forced his attention away from her to the record cards and the pile of letters that had arrived for the new mill-owner.

Rosie returned to the looms as soon as her work was done. Once or twice he stopped work to look through the dust-clouded glass of the office window, to the weavers and the reverberating clatter of the looms and to Rosie as she walked the lines and at the lengthening rolls of his cloth. He left, for the braid workshop, at twelve.

When he returned to The Pheasant at six o'clock in the evening Oliver found three letters on his window desk. One, he knew, was from Mr Lloyd. He knew the lawyer's handwriting and was not surprised that the man wanted him to call into the office at his earliest opportunity. The other two he saved until Lloyd's had been read. He studied the envelopes carefully, delaying the moment when he would open them. They were both written in feminine handwriting and he chose first the one in a careful copperplate, which, he suspected was from Florence.

He slit the envelope and took out a single sheet of pretty, deckle-edged vellum with Florence's signature at the foot of the page.

Dear Oliver, Mama has asked me to invite you to take tea with us, a week from Wednesday. Please come to twenty-three, Churchgate at three o'clock when we will renew our acquaintance. Florence Mawdesley

Oliver read it through twice, incredulously. He knew without doubt that Mrs Mawdesley hoped never again to offend her eyes with the sight of him. And yet she had invited him to tea? No, of course she hadn't! Florence had asked him on her own account.

He had not been mistaken then, in thinking that she wanted to know him. A great rush of pleasure swept over him at the thought. He grinned and pocketed the letter. He'd certainly go to Churchgate next Wednesday, but he did not believe for a minute that he'd be met at the door by Mrs Mawdesley.

The second letter was from Lucy Grandison, asking him to call in two weeks' time. Oliver wrote an acceptance at once.

The next morning, Thursday, he walked to the lawyer's office. 'You wanted to see me, Mr Lloyd?' he asked as the man came forward to usher him into his inner office.

'Be seated, please.' Lloyd pointed to the only chair in the over-crowded room that was not taken up with heaps of papers.

Oliver saw that the man was trying to be pleasant, trying to ingratiate himself. His smile was far worse than the normal dry, humourless cast of his face. Oliver wondered, not for the first time, how the old man had been able to do business, to trust Mr Lloyd.

'I have a client, Mr Wainwright, who approached me recently with an offer to buy Hollin Mill,' he began.

'It's not for sale,' Oliver interrupted.

'Quite. Er – quite.' The smile went from Lloyd's face. He leaned across the desk and spoke earnestly. 'It was an excellent offer. Almost a foolish one, you might say. The man would pay five thousand.' He said the words slowly, with an air of conspiracy.

Oliver pushed back his chair and stood up. 'Who made this offer? Sir Philip Oldfield?'

'No! Heavens, no!' Lloyd replied. 'I am, however, obliged to withhold the name of the purchaser.'

'The prospective purchaser, don't you mean?' Oliver said coldly. He reached the office door and turned to face Lloyd. 'Tell your man that I'll not sell. Ever.'

This encounter with Lloyd had angered Oliver more than he had shown to the lawyer. The man was underhanded. There was only one man who would want the mill and that was Sir Philip. The offer had Oldfield's stamp all over it.

Oliver fumed as he covered the half-mile to Hollin Mill. If Sir Philip couldn't get the property by fair means, then he'd have no scruples about using foul ones.

Rosie, too, did not seem to be her normal, calm self. She seemed harassed but relieved to see him. 'Anything wrong?' he asked after she closed the office door to cut down the level of noise. 'You look worried.'

'Four men haven't come in, Oliver,' she said. 'It looks like trouble.'

'What sort of trouble? Anything suspicious about four absentees?' he asked. 'They could be ill.'

'We never have four ill at once,' Rosie replied. 'They can't afford to be off work. They're all married men.'

'Has it happened before?' Oliver asked.

'Once. Four came out on the first day, six the second and ten the next. They were union men. They demanded more money.'

'What did Bill Grandison do about it?' Oliver asked.

'He sat it out. He said if he paid up whenever they demanded it, they'd do it again a year later.'

'How long were they out?'

'Four months.'

'Well I can't afford to lose four months' production. We must take on replacements. If they don't come back tomorrow we'll sack them.'

'If you sack them you'll have more out.'

'We'll get others,' Oliver declared angrily. 'I'll not be dictated to by my own workers.'

'Oliver,' Rose said reasonably, 'don't you see? It's not that easy to get good weavers. They're skilled people. If it was a spinning mill or a dye works, it'd be different.'

'What do you suggest, then?' he replied.

'Let's wait and see. Let's see what happens tomorrow.' She opened the door to go back to the weaving shed. 'Will you be here tomorrow?'

'Yes. I'm going to do the Middlefield market on Saturdays with my partner but after that I'll be giving all my time to the mills.'

'It's not going to be easy is it?' Rosie smiled her gentle smile at him.

'No. But I learn fast. I'm not going to lose my first battle,' he told her. 'I was offered a lot of money for the mill this morning. But I'm not selling. And I'm not going to be tricked into giving up.'

Rosie went back to the looms and left him to sit at the desk and ponder on the turn that events had taken. His money would come from constant, profitable running of the mill. He could not afford to fund a strike from his own savings. He could afford to lose one week's production and no more. After a week he would be asking the goodwill of suppliers with whom he had never as yet had dealings on his own account. He'd also have to let down the customers he supplied. And that was unthinkable. He must get the weavers back.

He returned to The Pheasant again at six o'clock. Leonard Billington nodded to him as he entered through the tavern. 'There's a visitor to see you, Oliver,' he said. 'He's in the parlour.'

Oliver went through to the back of the tavern and pushed open the parlour door. There, his back to the fire, an impudent look on his face, stood Tommy.

Chapter Eleven

'I left home, our Oliver. Yer said yer'd coom for me when you got a place,' he said accusingly. 'They say in the village that you've got a lot of money.'

'Do they?' Oliver grinned at his brother and put an arm around his shoulder. 'They have too much to say in the village, then, don't they?'

'Don't send me back. I won't go. I'm fifteen. I can work. Let me work for you, Oliver. Please!'

There was a lot Oliver wanted to know before he could decide what to do with Tommy. 'Have you been working on the farm?'

'Aye. I did the same as you did. I worked with the horses and in the fields,' Tommy said. 'I've been working for Old Jessop an' all. Doing a bit of labouring, but he can't put me and Wilf together so that weren't much use.' Tommy was trying to look knowing and wise but was succeeding only in grimacing.

'Tell me everything that's happened since I left,' Oliver said. He sat down with Tommy at the supper table and asked Mrs Billington to bring them food. Albert had eaten and gone to The Crown so there would be no interruptions. 'Is Wilf a good husband to your ma?' he asked.

'No. He knocks her about something awful. He gave her a black eye last week and when I hit him he told me to leave. It was worth it though. I nearly broke his nose.' Tommy's attractive smile broke through when he delivered this piece of information.

Mrs Billington brought steaming bowls of chicken broth with bread, roast beef and pickles. Tommy ate ravenously. 'He's got another woman an' all. Him and Ma fight about her.'

Oliver could have told Dolly all about Wilf's other woman. He still felt angry at the thought of Wilf in his dad's shoes. He studied his half-brother while the boy was talking. Tommy was thin. His bony wrists stuck out of the tight sleeves of his high-buttoned brown jacket. He wore old boots, too small for his feet that made him stand awkwardly. He had grown, almost as tall as himself, Oliver saw, and he had a wily manner he'd not had before, constantly looking over his shoulder as if he were afraid of being caught.

'Isn't Leach in charge of the farm?'

'No. He's in charge of a gang of Irishmen. Sir Philip owns ships, Wilf says. He sends Wilf to Liverpool to get them unloaded proper. Wilf helps himself to a lot and sells it about the place. It's a wonder Sir Philip hasn't caught him at it. Ma says if he doesn't stop seeing that woman she'll tell Sir Philip. Then they fight again. Real fighting, Oliver. With fists.'

They talked far into the night, after asking Leonard if Tommy could have the job as stable lad. Finally, Oliver walked him down to his old quarters, his arm about Tommy's shoulders. 'You'll be all right here, Tommy. Good night, lad. It's good to have you with me at last.'

* * *

There were signs of spring on Friday. The sun was weakly warm and the soft wind fresh and sweet. It brought a scent into town of the clean mountain air blowing down from the Pennine Hills. It was a day of promise, of new life and fresh starts.

Yet there were ten men out at Hollin Mill. Rosie told Oliver that she had asked every weaver in the place if they knew the reason behind their absences but for once the workers kept the answer to themselves.

'All I can discover,' she said when he arrived early at Hollin Mill, 'is that a man has been talking to them, talking about the new arrangements. They don't like it. I can see they're worried.'

Oliver was unconvinced. 'How can a man have talked about it?' he replied. 'I only mentioned it to you yesterday, yet they were out.'

'I know,' Rosie said. 'Who can it be?' I've said nothing to anyone.'

'Keep asking. Someone will tell you before the day's out,' Oliver said. He was angry and anxious and found himself speaking roughly to her. 'If you can't get anything from them then at least make a list of the men who are out. Get their addresses and I'll talk to them at their homes.'

'I'll do what I can, Oliver,' she said, 'but they don't like it if the boss comes to the door. It's something you can't do.'

He saw that she was upset at his tone of voice. Her face, normally pale, had two bright spots of colour on her cheeks and her lips were pressed together tightly. He was annoyed with himself for losing his temper with her but was unable to stop. 'It may be one of the things nobody else does, but I'll damn well do it. I'll get to the bottom of this. I'm going to the braid shop. Have the list ready for me on Monday.'

He left the mill in a hurry, angry because he was powerless to find the cause of this sudden reversal. He'd wait only until Monday before taking action himself, no matter what Rosie advised. She might know all there was to know about running a mill from the inside but when outside forces threatened he would have to deal with things in his way.

And all the time, a warning voice was telling him that this was, indeed, the first move of Sir Philip Oldfield's against him. But he knew that the baronet would not stoop to coming out in the open and speaking to his weavers in person. There had to be another, or others, involved.

There was no insurrection at the braid shop. The braid shop brought a steady income for little effort but here the materials were expensive, and skill and a high degree of supervision were necessary. Oliver preferred the fast, noisy world of cotton weaving to the more artistic one of colour and pattern that was the lifeblood of the braid shop. Still, the business here could do more. He determined to look for bigger contracts for the braid and expand here too.

He spent the afternoon at The Pheasant, preparing rolls of cloth for Middlefield market for the following day and overseeing Tommy in his new position as groom and stable lad. His mind was not entirely occupied with worries about the future of the mill. There were other, sweet, exciting thoughts that intruded throughout the day and again on the Saturday when he and Albert took the stall in Middlefield market.

Oliver's eyes searched the crowd, finding a tiny waist that brought Florence to mind, a pert figure, a laugh here, a head of blonde hair there and all the time wondering if she really was as lovely as he remembered her. For, since they had met, Oliver had felt a strange weakness – a weakness of affection that even the imagining of Florence brought. Her face swam before his eyes when he closed them.

Albert told him to stop daydreaming and attend to the customers. Still he found himself unable to concentrate, letting his mind wander to the prospect of seeing her again on Wednesday at three.

He had already spent a good deal of time since the funeral studying the windows of the drapers' shops. He had visited a tailor and bought himself two fine silk shirts. His clothes now seemed to be nothing but serviceable and he began to set about making himself, as he thought, into a more acceptable suitor.

'Pay attention, Oliver!' Albert was saying. 'You've just sold two yards of twill at half price.'

Oliver brought himself out of his reverie and apologised. 'Sorry! I don't know what I'm doing. My mind's on other things.' He smiled at Albert. 'I don't know how you manage it, Albert,' he said wryly, almost to himself so that the women around the stall wouldn't hear him.

'Manage what?'

'Keeping yourself above it all. You can like a girl and not get tangled up with her,' he replied.

Three women were holding out bundles of cloth. Oliver took one and Albert, smiling at both of the others in turn, served them, to their evident appreciation. 'Don't tell me you've been smitten, Oliver,' he teased when the customers left the stall and there was a temporary lull. 'I don't believe it! Is this what all the absent-minded stuff's about?'

'Aye. I think I've taken a tumble, Albert,' Oliver told him, trying to make it sound like a jest.

'Who for?' Albert's face was a study in eagerness to know.

'Oldfield's blasted granddaughter. That's who!' Oliver confessed.

Albert whistled slowly, drawing out the sound. 'You make it hard for yourself, don't you?' he said finally. 'Of all the girls in this town, you have to go for the one right out of your reach.'

'I think she likes me,' Oliver replied. 'She's asked me round for tea.'

'I thought it was the other one ... the woman from the mill that gave you palpitations,' Albert said.

'Aye. She does an' all,' Oliver replied, smiling at last at the absurdity of his revelations. 'I'll have to get myself someone that's available and willing and forget both of them.'

'Come to The Crown tonight,' Albert breezed. 'There's plenty there.'

'All right.' Oliver forced himself not to think either of Rosie or Florence for the rest of the afternoon. He'd have a few pints of beer, at the very least, tonight and see if there was a girl who'd do, at The Crown.

* * *

Mama had departed, at last, for Suttonford. Florence couldn't remember a Sunday morning that had dragged so, a sermon that had lasted so long or a wait for Mama's carriage that had seemed so eternal.

Florence blew a kiss towards the rear of Mama's carriage then she tripped, like a weightless creature, back into the tall town house and up the carpeted stairs to her room, to lie triumphant on her bed. Everything was going so easily, she told herself with glee. All that remained was to give the silly maid, whom Mama had engaged in her personal service, the afternoon to herself and to prepare for her visit to The Pheasant.

She rang the silver bell on her desk. A plain-faced young servant, Florence's new maid, answered the call. The girl, hardly older than herself, stood in the doorway, a simple soul who appeared to have no ideas of her own but simply accepted whatever was proposed. Florence made her most agreeable face.

'Lily, dear,' she said. 'Would you like to visit your family this afternoon?'

'Madam told me that you'd need me today, Miss Florence,' Lily said.

'But I don't, dear Lily. You shall visit your family. My friend Miss Clayton will be here within the hour and I shall have no need of your attentions.'

The girl looked doubtful and Florence added quickly and in a sharper tone. 'If we are to be content, Lily, then only by pleasing me will we achieve understanding. I do not need your services for the remainder of the day. See that you are back here before eight o'clock.' She lifted her hand in a gesture of dismissal and saw that the girl would not disobey.

'And, Lily,' she said before the maid left the room, 'say nothing to Mama – to Mrs Mawdesley – about this.'

Florence's clothes were already laid out. She would wear her velvet suit of a dark chocolate brown with a matching hat that looked well against her hair. The ensemble had been made by a good London outfitter and depended for its provocative lines on the excellence of the cut. Nobody in Middlefield made clothes as well as this. The jacket nipped in her tiny waist, making her hips appear wider. The understated bustle was perfect for her small build and, Florence decided, with Mama's pearl neckband, which she'd put on after church, she would look her absolute best.

Her stomach turned somersaults at the thought of seeing Oliver again. How lucky she was that Edith had agreed to accompany her. She had not told Edith the real reason for her boldness, of course. She had told her new friend that the poor young man had been ostracised by her family and that she felt it incumbent upon her to make amends, but to do so without Mama's knowledge.

Florence heard the front doorbell ring and the housekeeper, Mrs Booth, invite Edith to wait in the drawing room. She went to the landing and leaned over the wide, flat banister.

'Edith. Come up. Do,' she called and smiled encouragingly at Mrs Booth. Mrs Booth was an angel who silently, Florence knew, always took her part. Florence watched Edith climb the stairs. Her new friend was quite the prettiest girl she had met in Middlefield. Edith had auburn hair, luxuriant and glossy, which she wore pinned up in a positive sculpture of waves and curls. She had eyes that were neither hazel nor green but rather a combination of the two, and lips that were naturally full and red. But what Florence admired most about her was her air of complete assurance. Edith was never at a loss, she was sure. Edith would never find herself having to resort to deceit or connivance to get her own way. But Edith was never opposed. And deception was so deliciously thrilling.

'Do you think these things are suitable for Sunday school, Florence?' Edith asked, whirling around in front of Florence's pier glass, her skirt of moss green swinging in a wide circle beneath the darker green jacket.

'Very suitable, Edith. You haven't forgotten that we are going to pay a call at The Pheasant afterwards, have you?' Florence placed the brown hat on top of her shining hair. 'Can you put the pins in for me?' she asked, handing two pearl-tipped hatpins to Edith.

Edith tucked a strand of the golden hair under the band of Florence's hat and placed a pin securely across the back, then criss-crossed the other when the tilt of the hat was at its most fashionable angle. 'You're on edge, I can tell. Haven't you rehearsed your lesson?' she asked.

'Yes. I'm prepared for Sunday school. It's the idea of walking into a tavern that excites me. Mama would die of shame,' Florence blurted out.

She had not meant to hurt Edith and as soon as the words were out, she regretted them. 'I didn't mean that there was anything shameful about taverns – or inns, Edith,' she finished, her face pink and apologetic.

'I don't mind,' Edith said with a good-humoured smile. 'I've never even been inside the tavern of The Swan, though I've seen the back rooms, of course.' She patted Florence's hair. 'There! You look far too pretty to be a teacher. Even a Sunday-school teacher. Are we ready?'

They walked the few yards across the quiet market square to St Michael and All Angels. The classes, for the children of the poor, were well attended and the girls were despatched each to a separate schoolroom at the back of the church, where they told Bible stories and led the children in singing for an hour.

As the time of her visit drew near, Florence dared not contemplate the enormity of her deception. It was not only Mama who would be outraged if this were ever to come to their ears. Grandfather would be incensed and Florence was aware of the lengths to which Grandfather would go to see that it never happened again.

She held onto Edith's arm as they left the church and made their way down Rivergate, her heart banging in her ribs so loud she was sure Edith would hear. Edith went ahead and pushed open the door to the tavern. 'May we speak to Mr Oliver Wainwright, please?' she said to a large, apron-clad man.

Florence dared not glance at the men who sat at the tables or leaned against the wet counter, afraid that she might even recognise one. Suppose one were a tradesman known to the family? Would he tell? Her hands were weak and her knees trembled as she followed Edith and the large man through the door at the back and into a tiny parlour.

'I'll send him down to you, miss,' the man was saying. He left the room and they heard his heavy footsteps on the wooden stair beyond the door. 'Oliver!' they heard him call. 'There's two young ladies to see yer.'

There were heavy footfalls on the stairs, the sounds of at least two men. Florence's eyes were enormous and round as she saw the china door handle turn. She took a deep breath to prevent herself from fainting as she looked, at last, up at the great height, deep into the watchful eyes of Oliver Wainwright.

'How do you do, Oliver.' To Florence's surprise her voice was normal. 'We haven't inconvenienced you, I hope.' She held out her hand and felt the warm clasp of his, enclosing her own. 'May I present Edith? My friend, Edith Clayton.'

'How do you do, Edith,' Oliver replied and his voice was just as she remembered it, plain and manly. 'My friend, Albert Billington. Albert – Edith Clayton and Florence Mawdesley.'

He didn't even seem surprised, just pleased that she was here. 'I've come to say that I'm not to have your company on Wednesday, Oliver,' Florence said. 'Mama won't hear of it, I'm afraid. I had to see you ... I had to tell you ...'

He didn't appear to be put out by her explanation. He was smiling. 'I never expected she would, Florence.' He grinned. 'But I'm just as pleased to see you here.'

Albert had led Edith to a seat by the parlour window and was deep in conversation with her. Florence so admired Edith's poise. 'Are you?' she asked weakly. He led her to a chair near the fire and Florence found that her nervousness was disappearing. Oliver had a wonderful effect on her.

'Tell me what you've done since I last saw you,' he said. 'I've thought about you often.'

It was impossible not to respond to his smile and her nervousness fell away as she answered. 'Very little,' she told him truthfully. 'I'm taking a Sunday-school class at St Michael's but since Mama has three more weeks of mourning for Uncle Bill our social life has been curtailed.'

'I'm taking Edith up to Ma's sitting room, Oliver,' Albert was saying. 'She says her mother knows Ma.'

Oliver began smiling happily, as if he was glad that they were being left alone together. Edith still kept her composed expression, Florence saw. Edith gave her an encouraging, wide smile as she followed the nice-looking friend of Oliver's out of the parlour and closed the door on them.

'What have you been doing?' she asked him. 'You are going to keep the mill, aren't you?'

'Yes.' His face took on a serious look for a moment and he added after a moment's pause, 'Some of the men haven't come in to work since I became the owner. I have to get them to return, and soon.'

'Oh,' Florence told him airily, 'that will be Grandfather's doing. He's raging about the mill going to you.' She put her hand on his arm and laughed softly at the quick look of displeasure that crossed his face at her words. 'Don't let us talk about Grandfather, Oliver. Let us talk about you. Do you live here with your parents?'

'My parents are dead. I have a room here; the one your uncle used to have. I was brought up on your grandfather's estate. Did you know that?'

'No. But I saw a young man recently at Suttonford, who bears an uncommon resemblance to you.'

'Tommy. My half-brother. He used to live in one of the cottages at Hollinbank.'

'By himself?'

'No, with my stepmother, Dolly Leach. Tommy's mother. My mother died when I was born. My father was the quarry-master. He was killed at Suttonford,' Oliver said. 'My stepmother's in service there. Does that make any difference to you?'

'Not in the least, though I imagine it has made a difference to you,' Florence said, glad, so glad that they were chatting normally, as if it were an ordinary social occasion. 'Was she kind? Your stepmother?'

Oliver considered his reply for a moment as if he had often asked himself the same question. 'She wasn't cruel but I knew she liked Tommy best. She's well able to look after herself and care for children but she came to see me as a nuisance.'

131

'I can't imagine how dreadful it must be to have no mother. Do you know, Oliver, that I have not been parted from my mama for a single day?'

'Have you finished your education? What will you do now?'

'Mama wants me to go to a young ladies' establishment, here or in London. Then I am to have a "coming out" ball in London, be presented to the Queen and then, I suppose, I'll marry.' She looked into his face as she spoke, hoping to see some sign that he wished her to stay.

'Is that what you want, Florence?' he asked. 'Do you want to be paraded before a line of young men, hoping to catch the eye of one?'

She felt the disdain in his voice. Of course she didn't want that. 'No. I want a man I can love and respect and I think I'll find him here, in Middlefield.' She felt bolder. It was as if his own forthrightness had conveyed itself to her. 'I'll refuse to go to London. Shall you marry?'

'When I find a girl like you, yes.' His eyes never left hers.

The shivering feeling she'd had at their first meeting returned in force. She blushed, chiding herself for bringing the conversation to this point. But she had never been taught the niceties of flirtation. 'Will I see you again?' she asked softly.

He reached for her hand. 'Yes,' he said. 'But if I cannot see you at Churchgate, then where?'

'If Edith will come with me I could come again, next Sunday afternoon,' she told him. She had thought no further ahead than today and her mind began to race through all the possibilities.

'And if Edith won't?' Oliver still had hold of her hand and she felt the tightening of his fingers on hers.

'I shall come alone,' she said without so much as a blush. She knew now that he was sincere. He would not think ill of her for her immodesty. She freed her hand from his. 'We have been here for an hour, Oliver. Will you find Edith and tell her it's time to leave?' She did not want to leave, to wait a whole week to see him again, but unless Mama was reassured by her quiet demeanour then Mama would not leave her again. Not a hint of an adventure must come to Mama's ears.

'Would you like me to call a carriage?' Oliver asked, when Edith and Albert returned to the parlour.

'I think it would be better if we walked, alone,' Florence told him. She put out her gloved hand, which he took eagerly.

Albert was holding Edith's hand rather longer than necessary, Florence noticed, but soon they were saying polite farewells and she and Edith slipped, unnoticed, into the Sunday quietness of Rivergate.

'Oliver has asked me to see him next Sunday afternoon,' Florence told Edith when they reached the market place. 'Shall you come too?'

'Do we have to conceal it from your mama?' Edith said. 'I shall see Albert before then. He has asked me to supper on Tuesday, with a companion. I thought you might wish to come.'

'If only I could, Edith,' Florence said in a yearning voice. Then the rash impulse, the impulse that might lead to uncovering her defiance of Mama, reasserted itself. 'I will. I will go with you. I must see Oliver again,' she promised. For now she knew herself to be passionately in love and unable to stop herself in her headstrong desire to be loved in return.

Chapter Twelve

On Monday, twenty men were out; a quarter of the weavers. Oliver stared at the silent looms, at the faces of the men and women who were working. He went into his office and found Rosie waiting for him.

Her beautiful eyes were troubled, as if she expected an angry outburst and Oliver put a hand on her shoulder to comfort her. 'I'm sorry I spoke as I did on Friday,' he said.

'It doesn't matter,' she said. 'I've spent the weekend asking around. All I've learned is that it's a man and he's paying them three and sixpence a day to stop out. An ugly man with horrible teeth, by all accounts.' She smiled hesitantly. 'Not that it matters what he looks like, does it?'

Realisation came to Oliver in a flash. In jest Florence had given him the true picture. 'Of course!' he bellowed, 'Sir Philip Oldfield's behind it, and I know who he'll be using. He'll have sent an old enemy of mine; Wilf Leach. It's the only person he could use.'

'He's calling another meeting tonight, Oliver. Eight o'clock in the mill yard.'

'Good.' Oliver let out a long sigh. 'I'll be there.' He could not keep the look of glee from his face. 'We'll have them back at work tomorrow.'

'How are you going to do it?' she asked. 'Will you call the police in?'

'No. There's a new law – the Conspiracy and Protection of Property Act, which I think makes Oldfield's plot a criminal one but I haven't time to find a new lawyer and verify it. I'm not sure of my ground and I don't trust Lloyd. Anyway' – he smiled at her

134

to calm her fears – 'Wilf Leach is a fool. He thinks he's a clever trickster but all he has is a big mouth and a strong body – and I'll stop both of them for him tonight.'

'Do you want me to come along?' Rosie asked.

'What for?'

'You might need me to talk to them. If you see Wilf Leach off they might still need persuading. They trust me.'

'Right. I'll go down to the yard and wait for Oldfield's lackey. You come down later when I send for you.'

Rosie smiled her slow, warm smile. 'You can last out more than a week, you know. The money comes in faster than it goes out. If you want to sit it out you can, easily. They'll come back of their own accord when their money runs out.'

'I don't want to run the mill that way, Rosie. I want them to be rewarded for hard work, for good production, not just because they can't afford to stay at home,' he said. 'They'll be better off working my way.'

His eagerness always transferred itself to her. She seemed to be lit from within when he took her hands, as now he did, to emphasise his words. 'If we can keep ahead, as we are doing, if we can outrun the competition when trade is falling off around us, think how well we'll do in better times,' he said.

'You're going to do well, Oliver,' she said, and there was admiration in her eyes. 'Once this trouble's over and they're back you'll forge ahead of the other mills.'

Oliver smelled again the faint lavender of her hair, sensed the magnetic force that drew him. Her nearness was arousing him again. He released her hands and went to look through the dusty window at the busy looms.

Why, he asked himself, should she do this to me? Yesterday I almost had Florence in my arms; sweet, charming Florence, the girl I love. Yet this woman, this woman who belongs to another man, slips into my dreams every night and disturbs my working day. He took a deep breath. 'You'd better get back to the weaving shed,' he said.

He could not concentrate on the calculations he had to make. He added the columns of figures six times and got a different total at every attempt. It didn't matter. There was more than a week's supply of cloth and spun cotton. He could hold out for a month but he wanted to justify Bill's faith in him. He had to make the mill an even bigger success than it had been under the old man. It would take more than Wilf Leach to stop him, even with Oldfield behind him.

He returned at six to The Pheasant, to supper with Albert and all the while the bubble of excitement grew inside him at the prospect of the coming clash with Wilf Leach. He refused a second helping of brown stew and had no appetite for the batter pudding.

'What's up?' Albert asked. 'Lovesick?'

Oliver laughed, a deep, throaty chuckle. 'No. I'm fighting tonight, not philandering. What about you? Are you going to The Crown?'

'No.'

Albert sounded weary. Oliver looked at him in mock concern. 'Sickening for something, are you?' he asked.

'Aye,' Albert said. 'Same as you, I suppose. I've had me mind on Edith Clayton all day long.' He left the supper table quickly and Oliver heard his feet clumping on the wooden staircase to his attic room.

A great grin spread over Oliver's face. 'Serve him right,' he muttered happily. 'I hope she keeps him guessing.'

An hour later and under cover of darkness Oliver crossed Rivergate and entered one of the alleyways that led down to the mills. He could not risk being seen by Wilf Leach, who, he was sure, would be fortifying himself in one of the many taverns along the street.

When he crossed the river and reached the mill there was no sign of Wilf or the striking men. They would have to come into the yard through the high wooden gates that opened into the passageway between Hollin Mill and the spinners next door. Oliver reached the yard through the back entrance of the mill and waited, well back in the shadows.

They came quietly, the men who had been at work that day, twelve of them. They stood in three small groups at the far side of the yard from Oliver, subdued, waiting for the man who had paid their workmates to stay at home. There were low murmurings from these men but Oliver could not catch the words. He saw, however, that they were being joined by some of the men who had not been in to work.

The church clock, high above the river, struck eight and as if he had been called on to perform, Wilf Leach arrived on the second stroke, swaggering and unsteady on his feet. He closed the wooden gates behind him and raised his hands.

'Is everyone here?' he called into the gloom.

One by one they gathered around him until they formed a semicircle and Oliver could no longer pick out the figure of Leach but he heard his unmistakable rough voice.

'You know why I'm paying yer, don't yer?' he called over the heads of the men. 'It's so yer'll stop out till that bugger Wainwright gives up. He can't keep going if you all keep away. There's a better man as wants to buy the place. He'll pay yer more for shorter hours if you help him get the mill. Wainwright's too young to know what he's about. Yer don't want a bloody boy in charge of the mill, do yer?'

'No. No.'

Oliver's mood changed. He had been prepared to let Leach talk for a while, to hand out the money and then to challenge him when the men were ready to disperse. Now, anger rose in him while he commenced his slow approach around the edge of the wall.

He was within ten feet of Leach before one of the men saw him. Oliver moved out of the shadow of the high brick wall and saw Leach, who was as tall as himself, over the heads of the men who were now looking from one to the other of them in anticipation of an enjoyable encounter. Oliver knew there was no risk of the men taking Wilf's or even his part. They were spectators. It would be as good as a night's cockfighting to them.

'You're on my property, Leach,' he bellowed.

137

A look of surprise on Wilf's face was instantly followed by a snort and a sneer.

Oliver's fists were like iron, curled tight as he pushed aside the men who stood between him and his old opponent. He stopped in front of him. 'Get out of my yard,' he roared, 'before I lay you out.'

Wilf quickly stuffed the money bag into the pocket of his loose brown overcoat and raised his fists to Oliver, bending his knees, the better to throw his weight behind his punches. He lunged for Oliver's head but Oliver moved to the left and sent his right fist cracking into the side of Leach's face, stopping Leach's forward momentum.

Leach shook his head slowly. His loose lips were wet and strung with saliva. He sucked in his breath and turned, wild as a bull that had been prodded too hard. 'I'll kill you,' he snarled as he lifted his arms again.

Oliver moved in closer and brought his left fist, then his right up under Wilf's guard, thudding into the man's rough, unshaven chin. 'You haven't got the strength, Leach,' he jeered. 'You're too old and too drunk.'

Oliver felt Leach's fist thud into his eye, felt the skin split and the warm trickle of blood slide down his face towards his earlobe. He brushed it away with his sleeve and returned the blow.

The men had fallen back. He could hear, behind him, growling encouragement for him. 'Come on, Wainwright,' he heard one man say. 'Come on. Give it to him.'

He felt a fist contact with his ear, a sharp pain shooting through to the back of his throat, making him cough. He also heard others join in the murmuring that came from the darkness behind him.

'Come on, Wainwright,' they called, louder now.

Oliver went for Wilf, intent now on stopping him before he took another blow. He threw his right fist at Wilf's eye, felt him reel against the blow, followed with his left to Wilf's ear and immediately came back with his right and his left. Leach staggered backwards and a final burst from Oliver had him on the cobbles, face down. 'Had enough?' Oliver knelt on Leach's back, pressing his knees cruelly either side of his spine.

'Stop!' Wilf screamed, but he was beyond moving. 'Enough, I've had enough!'

Oliver pulled him to his feet, holding the man's wrists behind his back. He wrenched the belt from Leach's overcoat and twisted it fast, binding it tight until it cut into Leach's flesh. He pushed Leach forward until he faced the men. 'Now. Tell them, Leach! Tell them who put you up to it,' he shouted. 'Come on, men. Listen to your bloody paymaster.'

They came slowly, reluctantly, and made a half circle around Oliver and Leach. Then he pulled the belt tighter, jerking Leach backwards, making him yell. 'Oldfield. Sir Philip Oldfield. He wants to wreck yer bloody mill. He wants you out.'

'And what is he going to do with it, when I've been put out. Leach?' he called over the bent back. 'Speak up. Tell my good weavers. Tell them loud and clear. Is he going to keep paying them three and sixpence a day to stop out?'

'No. He's going to run it himself,' came the muffled reply.

'Personally?' Oliver shouted. 'Speak up. They can't hear you.' He tugged again at the wrists.

'No.' Wilf's voice was strong. Angry rumblings came from the crowd of men. 'He'll get a manager in.'

'And will the new manager pay more money and for shorter hours, Leach?' He threw his voice as far as he could, out to the back row of men. 'Surely not. My men aren't fools. They know I won't cheat 'em. Does he care about the mill? Does he?' Oliver went on, tugging and pulling to keep Wilf's disclosures coming freely. 'What's it to Oldfield? He'll close it down. Tell them! Tell them!'

'Stop it, damn yer. You'll break my bloody arms,' Wilf squealed.

Oliver let go of his arms and Wilf fell backwards towards the gate, where he half-lay, panting and groaning.

Oliver stood over him. 'Three and sixpence a day, per man ...' he sneered '... and how many men, and how many days does that add up to? Eh, Leach? You could make yourself a tidy packet if you let your master think you were having some success, couldn't you?' He took the money bag from Wilf's pocket and emptied the contents onto the yard. The men, behind, were silent as the silver coins went clinking, scattering over the yard. 'I'd be inclined to get a bit for myself, if I were you. It's not worth it, just to get beaten up, is it?'

Oliver turned to face the men. 'Do you want a bloody fop runnin' the mill?' he called out, strong in voice, to move them. 'Does Sir Philip Oldfield know anything about mills? Eh?'

There was a chorus of 'No', from half of the men and Oliver shouted louder, throwing his voice out towards the back of the throng. 'All Oldfield's good for is riding a horse. Who do you want in charge, eh? Me or a blasted aristocrat?'

'You. You.' More were calling back to him.

'Do you want a boss who'd steal a man's inheritance? Who knows nowt about a working life? Eh?'

'No! No!' They were roaring in unison now.

'Then be back at work tomorrow. All of you,' Oliver shouted. He spoke to the men at the front. 'Will someone run inside and tell your forewoman to come down?' he said. 'Mrs Hadfield will tell you about the new system. You'll all benefit if you come back to work.'

One of the men crossed the yard to the back door to call for Rosie. 'What's going to 'appen to them as came out?' a voice called from the back of the bunch.

'No hard feelings,' Oliver promised. 'A new system. A new start.' He walked towards them. 'Make way!' he demanded. 'And – someone pick that bugger up and throw him off my premises!'

He felt no pain from his cut eye; nothing but a great swelling feeling of triumph as he made his way up the stairs to the washroom. Rosie's face wore a horrified expression when his bloody figure passed her on the stairs. She could handle the weavers. They'd be back tomorrow.

* * *

For a month Florence had been coming to The Pheasant on Sunday afternoons and twice she'd come with Edith to supper on a Tuesday, though the evening visits demanded a massive deception of her mama and were fraught with the danger of discovery.

On Sunday afternoons they stayed for an hour, Albert and Edith going to his ma's sitting room where, Albert told Oliver, they talked. Oliver was glad. It meant that he was alone with Florence once a week for an hour.

Today she wore a silk dress of deep rose with dark ruby insets at the neck and wrists. Her hair was taken back with a silk ribbon, which caught and held it demurely in place, a cascade of brightness spilling from beneath its folds.

Florence delighted him. Oliver found her easy to talk to. They exchanged confidences effortlessly, all the while excited by the other's nearness. Now, sitting beside her, he knew that the girl he had first seen when he was sixteen was the girl he wanted to spend the rest of his life loving.

'You visit Aunt Lucy, she tells me,' Florence said provocatively. 'I think I may start to call on her by myself, instead of in Mama's company.'

The thought that soon their hour would be over and there would be another empty week until he saw her again made him despondent. He took her little hand in his. 'We can't meet at your aunt's house,' he told her gravely. 'Your mama will find out and Aunt Lucy will be blamed.'

She must have been dreading the hour of her departure too for all at once the bright smile that hardly left her face when she was with him faded and she turned enormous grey eyes upon him and Oliver saw that they were brimming with tears.

'I can't wait a whole week to see you again,' she whispered, her voice full of choking sadness. She averted her eyes and began to dab them with the most ridiculous slip of cotton and lace Oliver had ever seen.

He had never attempted any intimacy with her in the weeks that had gone before but he could not keep himself in check now. He lifted her to her feet and put his arms around her, touched the tears that were falling, rolling, down her lovely face. 'I can't wait either,' he said softly, pulling her in towards his chest. She lifted her arms and placed her hands at the back of his neck. Oliver felt her fingers threading in and out of his hair as he began to kiss her gently and he tasted the sweetness of her mouth.

'Do you love me, Florence?' He held her close, his eyes searching her face as he asked the question. He could feel her heart, through the silk, a strong, steady thudding against his chest. He had never seen, never held anything as beautiful in his life. Her heart-shaped face was turned up to his, her lips were parted and red from their kiss and he was having to restrain himself from covering her face, her neck and her white bosom with hungry, eager kisses.

'More than anything, Oliver. I love you more than I have ever loved anyone in my life before,' she said.

'I want to marry you,' he told her. He kissed her again and felt the answering passion in her response. 'I can't wait.'

He couldn't bear to let her go. He was filled with resolution. Her mother would see that he'd be worthy of Florence. She'd allow him to call; let them meet openly. 'I'll speak to your mother,' he said. 'I'll come to the house tomorrow.'

'Oh, no. We can't tell Mama.' Her breath was coming short and fast and she pulled down his head so that their open mouths met again.

But their hour was slipping away. As they kissed so hungrily they heard the footsteps of Albert and Edith outside the parlour door and they wrenched apart and tried to compose themselves.

Each week it was becoming harder to see her go, hard to watch the little figure depart secretly when all Oliver wanted was to take her proudly by the hand and proclaim his love to the world.

When Florence and Edith had gone Oliver returned to the parlour and sat by the fireplace. He must be allowed to marry her. He was ready, now, for marriage and Florence would be the perfect wife. He had always wanted a home, a wife and children. He wanted Florence to be the mother of his children.

He saw it as if it had already come to pass, his house and Florence at its centre – lovely, loving Florence. They would have a lot of children and she would be kindness and sweetness to them; the kind of mother he and Tommy had never known. She would teach them by example to be as she was, happy and good, and they would be like her with exquisite manners and low, musical voices that made your toes curl with delight, listening. All his own dreams, all his promises to Tommy would come about.

He'd asked her if there was much to learn, for he knew nothing of keeping house. 'There's lots to learn, Oliver,' she'd replied airily. He smiled to himself, remembering the eagerness with which she'd added, 'I practically run the house by myself, at present. Mama leaves it all to me.'

'I could show you how to cook,' he'd told her.

'I'm sure I'd find a good cook, Oliver,' she'd said. 'The cook at Churchgate would come with me ... Mama would never live there alone. She'd go to Suttonford.'

He could afford a house and a cook and a maid ... and a couple of servants. It took his breath away to contemplate what he could afford. It would take everything he had to start them up but the mill profits would pay for all that.

Albert came in, disturbing his dreams. 'I want to marry Florence,' Oliver blurted out. 'They'll never let her go, of course, the Oldfields.'

'They'll maybe come round, in time. When you've got more money than they have,' Albert tried to console him.

'I want her now. I've got enough money to get married. We could rent a nice house and pay for a cook and a maid,' Oliver told him. 'There's enough coming in to set us up.'

'You can't expect a girl like Florence to live in a little house, with a cook and a maid,' Albert said in his practical way. 'Look at the house she lives in. There must be twenty rooms in their house and at least eight servants. She couldn't run a house.'

'She can learn. She says she wants to learn.'

Albert put a hand on his shoulder. 'Be sensible. The Oldfields'll lock her up if they know you've been seeing her. You've got what they thought was their mill. They're not going to let you walk off with their daughter.'

'Then what can we do?'

'You'll have to wait. You'll have to tell Florence that you can meet secretly but you can't marry her yet.'

A new wave of despondency swept over Oliver. Was Albert right? And why should he have doubts when he knew that Florence was the girl he wanted? He was sure of his love for her. Was it impossible to make the Oldfields agree to a betrothal?

'I don't want any supper tonight, Albert,' he said. 'I'm going to my room.'

He had been in his room for less than an hour when he heard a carriage draw up outside The Pheasant, heard Ma Billington running up the stairs on her fat little legs and stop outside his door.

'Oliver! Oliver!' he heard her whisper hoarsely as she pummelled on the door. 'Your young lady's downstairs.'

Oliver was galvanised into action. He pulled on the jacket he'd thrown over a chair and raced down, taking the stairs two at a time, heart pounding. He flung open the parlour door. Florence stood on the hearth mat, a diminutive figure in a coat of green velveteen and pale fur cape and hat. 'Mama knows. She says she will disown me, Oliver, unless I swear never to see you again.' Tears coursed down her cheeks as she spoke. She took another scrap of lace from under her cape and attempted to stem the tide of her tears with it. 'I've brought my clothes. I'm going to stay with you.'

Oliver could not bear to see her like this, tearful and afraid. He held out his arms and she came to him. He wiped the tears from her eyes with his own large white handkerchief then, turning her face up to his, his mouth came down on hers, gently at first, then with a passion that was flaming within him. His hands found the buttons of her cape, of her coat.

She shrugged them off, still clinging to him. His mouth was on her neck and her throat and his hands were sliding across her slender back. She made no move to stop him but began to shake violently when they came to rest on her breasts. Her fingers raked through his hair as she pulled his head down against their round fullness and he felt her trembling need of him as she whispered his name against his ear.

He lifted his eyes to hers and gently straightened, holding her close. He was shaking too. He wanted to take her to himself, to love and protect her and he had to fight this driving desire for her.

They faced one another and Oliver picked up the damp strands of hair that clung to her forehead and replaced them tenderly. 'We must control ourselves, Florence, until we're married. I'll take you home and speak to your mother. Wait here for me. I'll get my coat,' he said, ignoring her tearful protests.

She waited for him in the hot little parlour until he came down, dressed in his new overcoat with the beaver collar. He was ready to face her mother. They walked the half-mile to Churchgate, Florence halting to plead with him every ten yards of the route.

'Don't speak to Mama, Oliver. Please,' she begged.

He held firmly on to her hand and made no reply.

'Take me away, Oliver.' She spoke fast, gasping for breath. 'Just take me ... Please! Uncle Bill and Aunt Lucy ran away to Scotland. He married Aunt Lucy when she was only sixteen,' she cried. 'Please, Oliver, take me to Scotland. I don't care what people say.'

Oliver took her in his arms in the middle of the market place. 'We'll not be ashamed to marry, Florence. I'm good enough for you, we both know that. But I have to make my living here, I have to succeed here and I couldn't do that with the town against me.'

'Don't you see, Oliver? They'll never let us marry. My grandfather will do anything, anything at all, no matter how wicked, to prevent me from going against him.'

Oliver's face was grimly intent as he rang the doorbell of the house.

Laura opened it herself. She must have been waiting for him. Oliver was determined to be reasonable and polite yet insistent with her.

'Come in, Mr Wainwright. Florence, please leave us, will you? I wish to speak to the young man alone.' Her tone was icy and controlled and Florence obeyed her without a word.

Laura Mawdesley went ahead of him and held open the drawing-room door. As soon as he was in the room she snapped the door shut and turned to face him. Her eyes, he saw, were steel.

'Mr Wainwright, my daughter is a foolish child. She is not yet eighteen years of age and fancies herself in love with you.'

Oliver drew breath to speak. He wanted to stop her there and tell her that their love was not mere fancy but she continued without pause. 'I can see what draws her to you. You are a handsome young man. But you are not the right man for Florence. She would soon be heartbroken to find herself married to a man of so little refinement.'

She raised her hand to silence him when he began to answer her and the diatribe continued unabated. Her voice was raised and her glinting eyes were cold and contemptuous. 'You are a fortunate and clever young man but you must look to your own class for a partner. You cannot hope to marry so far above yourself. Be respectful of my wishes and allow me to know what is best for my daughter.'

She made to move towards the door, to signal his dismissal. 'And now you must leave. I shall speak to Florence and assure her that, painful though they are, these feelings will pass. Good day, Mr Wainwright.'

At last she'd stopped. The injustice of her attack on him pained him but his temper had been rising. He looked down at the cold-hearted woman who professed only to care for her daughter's welfare and the control he had exercised in the face of her assault made him feel he had aged since he came into the room only minutes before.

'I've listened to you, madam. Now you'll hear what I have to say,' he began. 'I love Florence and she returns my feelings. Your anger won't stop that. And when I marry her I'll give her everything she needs for her happiness.'

Laura Mawdesley caught her breath sharply at his words and Oliver found that his voice was rising. 'You imagine you know what is in her best interests but you know nothing. Florence would never be happy with the sort of man you'd choose for her,' he continued. 'I pity her and you if you try to force your will on her.'

Laura raised her hand as if to slap him and Oliver's anger came to the surface. He towered above Mrs Mawdesley.

'Don't imagine for one minute that I'm not worthy of your daughter, or that our marriage would bring shame on your family. I'll never be the kind of man you envisaged for Florence but, by God, I am a man and soon I'll be a man of means. But I'll never, never be the kind of man you're used to. You'll never get me to do your bidding with a wave of your hand.'

He stepped back and reached for his coat.

He left.

He saw himself out of the house and walked the quiet streets. And again doubts assailed him. He asked himself if Laura was right. Would Florence regret marrying him? Then he remembered her sweetness and was comforted. He wandered for an hour about the narrow back alleys that meandered like a crazy tangled web behind Rivergate, heard the cries and shouts of children, watched a drunkard reel from doorway to doorway and tried to put from himself all thoughts of Florence and their love and to consider her interests above his own.

Chapter Thirteen

There was no word from Florence for two days after the confrontation Oliver had had with her mother, then on the third day he found three letters at breakfast, addressed to him at The Pheasant.

He knew Lucy Grandison's and Florence's handwriting. The third must be from Laura Mawdesley. He slit it open quickly and read.

Dear Mr Wainwright,

I am leaving Middlefield with Florence immediately. We shall close the house and live in London for a few years. I hope that you prosper and that you find for yourself a good young woman. Our acquaintance will not be renewed but I wish to thank you for continuing my uncle's financial obligation towards myself and my dear daughter.

Laura Mawdesley

The letter from Florence, in her careful copperplate, said:

Dearest Oliver,

I will always love you and shall never forget our moments together. You may not want to wait for me but until I hear from your own lips that you do not then I live in hope that I will return to you in Middlefield.

I shall write to you at The Pheasant and beg you to reply as I cannot survive without knowing how you feel towards me.

Florence

The letter slipped to the table. He had known that he would lose her. For two days he had thought of little else but their love for one another and recognition had come to him that he must wait. He did not believe that her mother was right, nor did he think he would change but he saw that Florence might. He must give her these years of freedom. She was young and she must have a chance to reflect on what might be a girlish fancy. He could not write to her at Churchgate but would give his reply to Lucy Grandison who, he was sure, would forward it to Florence. He took pen and paper and began to write:

Dearest Florence,

Please do not think ill of me when I tell you that I shall not write to you when you are away. Be assured that in my heart the place that you occupy can never be filled by another. I shall not forget you, my sweet girl, but I ask you to try to forget me. If we meet again, and we may never meet, your wiser self will tell you if our affection was lasting.

Please be happy during your exile in London. You deserve all the joy and happiness that the coming years can afford you.

Oliver

He sealed the envelope quickly, before he could re-read his words and change them. He put the letter into his pocket and immediately opened the one from Lucy Grandison. She wanted him to call on her, the following week. Oliver wrote her a letter of acceptance.

On the appointed day he bought spring flowers and walked to Balgone. The sun shone that afternoon and Oliver wore a soft grey suit, to please the loveliest old lady he had ever met.

She greeted him warmly. 'I'm not receiving yet, Oliver, so there are no other guests but I'm glad you've come.' They sat in her elegant drawing room and she rang for tea. 'Are you managing all right at the mill? There's a friend of Bill's who can advise you if you have any problems.'

Lucy had the poise and assurance of a woman of breeding without the snobbishness that so affected the other members of the Oldfield family, and Oliver enjoyed her company.

'Everything is going well at the mill, Mrs Grandison. The weavers are working in relays – a sort of rotation – to keep up with the orders we're getting,' he told her.

He smiled happily. 'Mr Lloyd's attending to the lease and so on.' He thought it might be indelicate to talk of the allowances so he walked over to the window and looked out over the newly dug gardens.

The rocky mountain tops shone brilliantly in the slanting rays of the afternoon sun. The dense forest on the lower slopes of Shuttleston Hill appeared to be etched in fine lines against the whiteness beyond and the river Hollin flashed quickly here and there as it moved towards the edge of Middlefield and the people whose life it had supported for so long. The town, often suffocated with a pall of yellow smoke, was sharp and detailed. Horses and carts moved slowly in apparent silence up the steep streets towards Middlefield or trotted easily down from the town.

'What a magnificent view you have. You can see the whole of Middlefield and the hills beyond,' Oliver said.

'It is a great comfort to me but let's not talk about the view. Come, sit beside me.' She patted the seat and Oliver stretched his long legs out in the warmth of the fire and relaxed against the comfortable sofa, but only for a minute. Lucy came straight to the point.

'You are forbidden to see Florence again, I hear?'

Oliver reacted instantly to the mention of Florence. His blue eyes narrowed and his mouth set in a tense line.

'No, Oliver. Don't be angry with me for speaking. If Florence were my daughter I'd be happy for her to marry the young man she loved. But she's not mine and I must warn you to tread carefully. Don't set her grandfather against you. He's a powerful man and accustomed to getting his own way.' She spoke slowly and there was no mistaking her warning.

'I have a letter for Florence,' Oliver said quietly. 'Will you send it to her? I have told her that she must forget me.' He tried not to let his feelings show in his face as he added, 'I've not come to this decision because of Sir Philip. I'm not afraid of him. He can't do anything to harm me now.'

'Did you know that your mill building is owned by Sir Philip?' Lucy asked gently.

Oliver was shocked. He felt the old grip of anger in his insides at the thought. 'No,' he said, 'I didn't know. I was told it belonged to a Manchester trading company. I pay my rent, my lease money to them.'

'As long as you never default, never pay even a day late, he can't do anything to you,' she told him.

'The Manchester Trading Company belongs to Sir Philip, then?' Oliver echoed his earlier words.

'Yes, my dear. He never sold it to Bill. But once we were married my husband had no more to fear from Sir Philip.'

'So he'll not sell to me, either?' Oliver said softly. Sir Philip had tried to hide his ownership of the mill. He was a cunning devil. He'd not changed one whit from the young opponent Bill had had to contend with so long ago. 'Say nothing, Mrs Grandison. Thank you for warning me. I'll find other premises soon and move my machinery. I'll not be beholden to Suttonford estate.'

Oliver had much to think about on the walk back. Lloyd was still working in Sir Philip's interests, not his own. His mind was rapidly taking in all the implications.

He enjoyed a battle. Outwitting his opponents gave him a sharpening, a heightening of his intellect that simple moneymaking did not. But until now he had always known who his opponent was, another market trader or a salesman who wanted to get the better of him. Now he had to face the fact that he was still under the patronage of the Oldfield family. Lloyd could deliberately delay his next payment of rent and the mill would be seized by the Oldfields.

'I must keep my head,' he told himself. 'I vowed I'd not work under the system that killed my mother and father but there's a year or more to run on the lease – time to find different premises.'

There was time, if he made haste, to get to the lawyer's office before he called in at the mill.

The lawyer ushered him into his gloomy room where around the walls deed boxes were stacked, topped by string-tied bundles of documents in brown envelopes. Ledgers and law books filled the alcoves beside the fireplace in front of which was placed a large mahogany table cluttered with inkstand, blotters and sealing wax in dusty profusion.

'What can I do for you, Mr Wainwright?' Lloyd asked.

'I want to look at the lease of the mill,' Oliver said. 'Get the papers out for me.' He watched Lloyd's face for any sign of suspicion but the man had never yet shown a simple emotion on his mask of a face and it remained expressionless as he handed to Oliver the long envelope containing the lease. No mention was made on it of Sir Philip Oldfield's position behind the Manchester Trading Company and Oliver saw that the last instalment of rent had been paid promptly, and another was due in two weeks' time.

'I want to buy the mill,' he announced finally. 'Give me the address of the Manchester Trading Company and I'll go and see the board.' Oliver looked the lawyer straight in the eye. He could not buy the mill, even if it were offered, but only subterfuge would make Lloyd reveal his hand.

Mr Lloyd drew back his lips thoughtfully. He appeared to be considering his reply. 'They may not wish to sell the property. I'll write to them and make enquiries if you wish.'

'No. I'll go tomorrow. Give me the address.' Oliver only intended to push so far.

'The company has always made it plain that its only interest is in leasing the property, Mr Wainwright. All I can do is to put your request into writing.'

'Do that then, Mr Lloyd,' Oliver replied drily. 'In the meantime please hand over all the papers you have relating to me and my business.'

There was not even an eyebrow lifted at the demand. Lloyd was probably glad to be shot of him, Oliver decided. He took his papers and left Mr Lloyd's office. Within the hour he had found a new lawyer and had time enough to go to the mill before dark.

He ran down Rivergate and was rewarded by seeing Rosie's face break into a smile at his arrival. They sat in the dusty little office together, discussing the day's problems, checking the records of cloth sent to the dye works, heads almost touching as they studied the figures.

Oliver was conscious, as he always was, of the scent of her clothes, her long, slender fingers and the way she rested her chin on them when she concentrated. The sweet, loving feelings he had for Florence and which had sustained him through the trials of the last weeks, were vanquished, swamped now by the desire that rose in him in Rosie's company.

'Rosie. I want to talk to you about the mill. Away from here where we can talk undisturbed. Can you come to The Pheasant this evening?' he asked her.

'No. Of course I can't.' Rosie's dark eyebrows, silky as feathers, lifted in amusement. 'Only a ... a fast woman ... would go to a tavern on her own.' She smiled as she said it, as if she didn't want to embarrass him.

'Forgive me. I wasn't thinking.' Oliver saw, with a little shock, that Rosie was defending her reputation. 'We'll talk here then. I want to move the business. I'm going to see about the new factories. I think they'll be ready by this time next year.'

'Come to my house tonight if you like, Oliver, and I'll help you all I can. Jim's got a wise head on him too. He was a weaver, you know. Come at eight o'clock when the girls are in bed.' She found a piece of paper and wrote down for him the name of her street.

But he had known for months where her house was. He remembered the nights, before Florence had come into his life, when he used to take an evening stroll, as he told Albert, and his feet had always led him past the house where Rosie lived.

It was the first in a short row of neat terraced cottages, all with whitened steps and windows hung with heavy net. Oliver arrived promptly at eight and tapped lightly with the well-polished brass clapper.

Rosie opened the door. She was wearing a soft skirt and a pretty blouse and her hair, no longer plaited, was pinned on top of her head. She was holding aloft a tallow candle in an enamelled holder. Three small children in cotton nightdresses clung shyly to their mother's skirt.

'Come in, Oliver.' She held wide the door. 'Come and meet Jim.'

The door from the street opened directly into the living room where an oil lamp cast a pool of light in the centre of the table. The smell of damp reminded Oliver of the cottages at Hollinbank. No amount of washing, warming or airing ever got rid of the smell that seeped through and eventually rotted the worn linoleum covering the flagstone cottage floors.

Rosie had made colourful rag rugs and placed them over the ridges, the largest being set in front of the fireplace where, lost in the embrace of a huge wooden armchair, sat the shrunken, blanket-clad figure of Jim Hadfield.

Jim Hadfield was much older than Oliver had pictured him. He was a tiny, shrivelled figure with sunken eyes in a face with an unnaturally high colour. He held out his hand. 'Pleased to meet yer. Sit down, Mr Wainwright. Rosie's going to make a pot of tea for us when she's taken the children upstairs.' It was a long speech for him and he began to cough the tight, wheezing cough of a man with chronic chest disease.

Oliver sat opposite him in the neat little room, sparsely furnished but homely and comfortable. For all the smell of damp it was a well-kept house and Rosie obviously took pride in it. Above their heads a washing line, filled with freshly laundered clothes, was stretched. On the table a white cloth was laid with cups and saucers for their tea and in the hearth a black iron kettle with a string-wrapped handle jiggled merrily on its trivet. Pride of place above the mantelshelf was given to a picture of Queen Victoria, resplendent in jewels and silk, gazing down remotely on the humble abode of one of her subjects.

Oliver shook Jim's outstretched hand. 'I'm glad to meet you, Jim,' he said. He placed his coat over the back of a chair and they chatted politely until Rosie returned and poured the tea. He noticed that her hands were trembling. She had to still the cup in the saucer with her left hand as she passed it to him. He looked at her over the cup and saw that his presence was disturbing to her.

She pulled up a low stool and sat between them, looking from one to the other as they talked about cotton and cotton mills and Jim's long years as a weaver. And the nearness of Rosie set Oliver's pulses thundering.

He told himself that his heart was given to Florence, that Rosie had never given him reason to harbour this violent passion for her and with a great effort of will he forced himself to remember the reason he'd come.

'I'm going to take on a bigger place, Rosie.' He glanced at Jim. 'You don't mind my calling your wife by her first name, do you, Jim? Good. Don't say anything yet,' he continued, animated now, 'especially at the mill. Will you be able to control it if I take on as many looms again?' He leaned towards her, watching her face with the reflected flames dancing in her warm brown eyes, now lighting up with pleasure at the prospect he laid before her.

'Yes,' she replied with excitement tingeing her voice. 'I could easily run it for you.' She had little creases at the corners of her mouth and they deepened and disappeared as she talked.

'Would you be prepared to move house? Nearer the new mills? What about you, Jim? Would you move?' he asked them.

'It'd be better for all of us if Rosie were nearer to her work and if the new house were a dry one,' Jim replied.

Oliver loved the way her hair grew to a point at the back of her neck. When she turned her head it made a knot tighten inside him and he wanted to slide his hands into the upswept dark locks, to loosen the pins and see how she looked with her hair falling about her shoulders.

'What about weavers?' he asked her, but his mind was no longer on the new factory, or the weavers. His thoughts were of her, of her wide lovely mouth, the long oval of her face and the outline of her breasts under the soft woollen blouse.

'It's not so far. You'd get them out there if you paid them a bit more, the good ones. It's only about a mile and a half from here. You might have a job getting the looms out of the mill. Maybe you should buy new and sell the old ones with the property.'

Her eyes never left his face as she spoke. Her pupils were very large, making Oliver feel as he looked into them that he was being drawn inside her. It was as if she were telling him something, inviting him to draw closer. Oliver moved, to back away from the heat of the fire and slowly and quite deliberately he let his leg lie next to hers, to see if she would flinch and he watched intently for her reaction.

She paused, momentarily, as if shocked or startled but it was for a mere second, before she continued to talk. And she did not move away from the contact.

Jim was growing weary. 'I'll go to bed, love,' he said, touching Rosie's arm as if to remind her, gently, of his presence. 'No, don't fuss, lass. I can manage on me own.' He pulled himself to his feet on thin, spindly legs, and slowly and painfully made his way, bent almost double, to the stair door. Rosie jumped to her feet to take his elbow and help him.

'Had I better leave?' Oliver asked, rising to his feet.

Jim turned painfully. 'No. Stay on a little while, Oliver,' he said kindly, 'Rosie's enjoying herself. It's not often she has good company and a chance to forget her troubles. Perhaps you'll come again?'

Rosie looked at him as Jim spoke and Oliver saw the look of fear and yearning in her eyes that he had seen so often before. He knew its significance at last.

'I will. I most certainly will,' Oliver said as Rosie led her husband upstairs, lighting his way with the lamp.

Oliver stood in the firelight, back to the fire, waiting for her to return, his pulses racing for her. He had been studying her face, her mannerisms, the movements of her body all evening. He knew now that she felt it too; the desire for each other that their every look had betrayed. Every nerve in his body was stretched, waiting for her.

Oliver heard her upstairs, surefooted and unhurried. Did she love Jim? Did they still kiss? No, he could not picture her in a passionate embrace with a sick man. She respected her husband and loved him kindly but Rosie had repressed her strongest feelings. He understood that. His emotions were too powerful to be frittered in casual encounters.

He need no longer look for answers to the questions that tormented him in her presence at the mill. The fire in his blood, the look in her eyes were answer enough. He knew with absolute certainty that she would be his tonight. He knew that she wanted him. The time for restraint had passed.

It was almost five minutes before she came back into the room and closed the door quietly behind her. She did not look directly at him but went, tall and nervous, towards the door that led to the scullery. He moved quickly to her side, so that their bodies were touching, silently took the lamp from her hands, dimmed it and set it on the table.

'He tires easily,' she said in a halting voice. 'I'll make another pot of tea.'

He caught her wrist as she moved away and drew her around, making her face him. Her eyes were dark and shiny in the moving firelight and her warm, sweet breath came fast on his cheek as he pulled her close. There was no need to speak. He held her gaze steadily and saw, reflected in her eyes, the same desperate need that was in his own and in an instant his arms were around her and his mouth crushing down on hers, igniting the passions they had so long held back.

157

Like the pull of a magnet his tongue was drawn into her sweet, soft mouth as she clung, helplessly, to him. He knew that she had never been kissed in this way before, that her head was swimming, her body was softening under his touch, melting into his. His breath was coming fast and deep and when they pulled apart momentarily she drew breath quickly and sought his mouth again.

Oh, God, it was true. His beautiful Rosie wanted him. He felt a surge of exultation, a wonderful sense of power in his own body as he felt her hands, under his jacket, toying with his silk shirt, teasing it out where it met the waistband; felt her slender fingers touching his belly, and her arms sliding around his bare, muscular back.

His hands were no longer inexpert. He found the buttons of her blouse and, still with his mouth on hers, he gently and quickly released them, exposing her heavy, full breasts.

Rosie caught her breath sharply as his searching mouth found her dark, rigid nipples and she began to writhe in his arms. 'Oliver,' she cried, 'Love me.' Her hands were on his skin, in his hair, digging into his flesh. She was moaning softly as he kissed her neck and held her full, warm breasts in his cupped hands.

'I want you,' he said, his voice sounding harsh and insistent in his ears. With one hand he loosened her hair and felt it tumble, thick and silky, about her bare shoulders.

He heard her murmuring his name while her strong fingers were pushing back the stiff material at his waist, unfastening the rigid buttonholes, at last freeing the hardness of him from the constraints of the cloth.

He found the button that held her skirt. It came away easily and he slid the material down over her wide, flat hips. Then he stood and held her at arms' length, marvelling at the beauty of her naked flesh, the long slim legs so finely muscled, her dark body hair against the creamy skin.

Oliver pushed away the last of his clothes and stood before her, proud of his strength. Then her arms were around him and her mouth was on his naked body exciting him beyond endurance.

He moved his hands over her legs, inside her slim, silken thighs. She was like hot mercury and she moaned as his fingers slid, moving inside her. There were faint silver streaks from childbearing in the soft centre of her and he buried his face, in an agony of hunger for her, in her warm, soft flesh, feeling her ready for him as she slowly sank to the rug.

'Oh, God, you're beautiful,' he groaned.

It had never been this way before and Oliver wanted to sink into the softness of her, to crush her warm, pliant body into himself.

She wound her legs around him when he went into her; she gave quick little cries, which he stifled with his kisses. Their long, supple bodies moved together. He could feel the pressure of her thighs pulling him in. He felt the heat of the fire on the side of his taut, urgent body; saw the tiny beads of perspiration that had sprung along Rosie's top lip, watched with delight as her gasping matched the fast, torn breaths that were coming from him.

She was digging her nails into his back, sinking her teeth gently into his broad shoulder, calling out for him softly and he held himself back until, at last, she drew in her breath sharply in abandonment and he let himself go in simultaneous, shattering release with her; his own sounds strange to his ears and hers subsiding.

At last they rested, still entwined, his head heavy on her breast, his eyes closed as she gently stroked his hair.

He lifted himself to his elbow and looked down at her, awed by the perfect harmony they had discovered. She lay, white and lovely, her breath coming easily, her hands playing with his shoulders and his broad, powerful chest.

'Rosie?' She lay beneath him, dark hair loose and tousled. 'This will happen again. I'll not be able to stop myself from wanting you. Do you want it to go on?'

If she had stopped him then, he knew, it might still not be too late. He could have pulled himself back from the well of an all-consuming love.

'Yes. Oh, yes!' she whispered, moving under his weight, seeking his embrace again.

He stayed with her, there on the hearthrug, until four in the morning. Then he slipped from her house like a silent shadow. He met no one as he walked through Churchgate, though he heard the echo of his footsteps from the cellars beneath the stone setts. He thought wonderingly of Rosie, her sensuality, the white beauty of her flesh and the discovery in himself of a hunger only she could appease.

He sat, silent, at the window of his room at The Pheasant watching dawn lighten the sky beyond the tower of St Michael and All Angels. Less than twenty-four hours ago he had set out for Balgone, his heart full of romantic love for Florence but the day had brought another love, a powerful love that had nothing of romance in it and which even at that moment was beginning to stir within him again.

Of Jim he thought only dismissively. Jim would live at the most for another year. He was not taking anything away from Jim.

He turned his thoughts to practical matters and brought a square, brass-bound box to the table as soon as there was light enough to see. The bank books showed a fine balance and already, Oliver knew, the profit from the mill would make him a wealthy man. He'd put Tommy at the Stockport market soon, selling braid and ribbon bundles, as he had done. Let him start at the bottom and learn the business.

He had a hearty appetite for breakfast and did not wait for Albert before starting to eat. Albert joined him at the table and Oliver asked, 'Are you still struck on Edith Clayton?'

'Aye.' Albert grinned happily. 'Who are you courting, then? You weren't home last night. Yesterday you were pining for Florence.'

'I can't pine for ever, can I?' Oliver told his friend. 'Florence'll never come back to Middlefield, her mother will see to that.' He helped himself to more bread and said under his breath, 'And I've found myself a real woman at last.'

After breakfast Oliver walked to the riverside site and reserved one of the new factories. He told the architect that it was to be called Wainwright and Billington's and he ordered that the name be built into the front, in lighter-coloured brick. He had a year's grace.

Time to raise the money, which he meant to do without loans from outside sources. He would not lease or rent the premises; it was essential that he own it.

The new working system at Hollin Mill had doubled production in the few weeks it had been in operation. He would have enough to pay outright for the new place if Hollin Mill continued to flourish. He would buy new looms to fill the large working space, on a short-term loan if necessary.

A new street was being added to the town, running parallel with Churchgate and facing the playing fields of an ancient boys' public school. It was near to the new factories. Rosie would find it easy to get to work from here.

A terrace of Accrington-brick houses was nearly finished. They had iron railings around the front gardens and high-walled yards at the back with access to these yards from the alleyways behind Churchgate.

Inside were a hall, two rooms and a scullery downstairs and three bedrooms and an attic above. Impulsively, and with his need for Rosie driving him on, Oliver found the site foreman and by midday he had rented one, paying six months' rent in advance.

When he reached the mill Rosie was busy but she smiled her slow, warm smile and it seemed to Oliver that she was more beautiful than she'd been only hours before. He called her into the office, closed the door behind them and took her into his arms, hungrily.

'Not here, Oliver.' She pushed him away gently. 'Tonight, at the house. But after nine o'clock, when they are all in bed.'

'Rosie, I want you now.' Oliver gritted his teeth in mock anger and she smiled the playful smile of a teasing lover and sat with him at the desk where they could be seen, but not heard, by the weavers.

'The new factory will be ready next year,' he told her, 'and I've rented a house for you – a bigger house, where I can see you without starting the tongues wagging. Tell Jim I need you to move nearer the new place. Tell him the rent is no more than you are paying for yours.'

161

He had surprised her. She hesitated and he became more persuasive. 'It's got gas jets, Rosie – and a modern kitchen range with a tap for hot water. Tell Jim that.'

'I'm twenty-eight,' Rosie reminded him sharply. 'I'm not a young woman any longer. You're twenty. You'll get tired of me. How can I leave my cottage and move to a new house where we can see more of one another, for a brief love affair?'

Oliver was made cross by her lack of faith in him. He pressed her hand hard on to the desk, making her look at him; making her see the fierce light in his eyes. 'I'll never be tired of you. I'm not that sort of man. It won't be a brief affair, Rosie. I know we can't marry. But trust me.'

She capitulated before the week was out and moved her family to the new house. And Oliver came to her every night, after dark. He left The Pheasant at ten, strolled around the town and slipped, unnoticed, through alleys that led to Rosie's back yard.

Chapter Fourteen

It had been a satisfying year. Oliver had a firm grip on the reins of his business. The mill's profits had been even higher than he had anticipated, the new factory was almost complete and the money to pay for it was earning him a decent interest.

Oliver was comfortable at The Pheasant. There was no advantage to be gained from moving. He had the best room and was treated as one of the family. His only concern was for Tommy.

Tommy was working in the markets, going out on his own, or with a lad and always he returned from his day in Stockport market, a job he did on his own, with little money in the bag. Tales of losses were offered glibly. A thief had snatched some bundles of braid, a pickpocket had stolen two sovereigns or Tommy had fallen and so spoiled some goods that they had thrown away.

It was late summer, evening time and Albert and Oliver were preparing Tommy's stock for the following day when Albert voiced his misgivings.

'I hope Tommy's takings aren't short tomorrow,' he said sternly. 'He should have mastered it by now.'

'He's had some bad luck lately.' Oliver sprang to Tommy's defence.

'I know you want to help him, Oliver, but do you know he's spending a lot of money in the tavern? More than he should from his wages?'

Oliver could not admit to Albert that he, too, had suspected Tommy's honesty. 'He gambles on the cards,' he explained, 'puts wagers on with the runners. He's young. I'll speak to him. I'll make him see sense. I'm going to Nottingham tomorrow but I'll check his takings when I get back and if there's a difference I'll deal with him. I'm sure he'll not cheat us.'

Early the next day Oliver helped Tommy carry the bags to the station. Together they wound their way down the steep incline of Wallgate, behind the church, to the railway station.

They could barely speak for the noise of carts and horses' hooves clattering over the cobblestones.

'We'll check the stuff when you get back, Tommy. It's no good if we're running a stall for no profit,' Oliver warned him gruffly, hoping the boy would be deterred if he knew that he must explain himself before the day was out.

Oliver had had the same thoughts as Albert, had harboured the same suspicions, but he'd put such questions out of his mind. Tommy wouldn't let him down. Tommy was learning; he'd always copied his brother. Surely he wouldn't cheat them? There was a good living to be had in the markets and Tommy was welcome to share in it.

Tommy's train was in. There was no time to give him a second warning but Oliver helped put the bags in the luggage compartment and saw him settled into a seat.

He felt a responsibility, a sense of guilt, about Tommy. He had not taken his brother under his wing as he'd meant to do; not guided him. Perhaps, he thought, I ought to have spent more time in his company. But there had been Rosie and the demands of the business; hours of idleness were a thing of the past.

Perhaps he should take Tommy away from the markets into the mill where he could keep a more watchful eye on him.

Oliver caught the train to Nottingham after Tommy had gone. The journey took him past the station of Suttonford and thence across the hills and moorland of Derbyshire. Would Tommy have been happier here, he wondered? Town life had temptations unknown in the villages.

From the carriage windows he saw men in the fields walking behind heavy horses and it felt a lifetime since he'd been one of them. He knew in himself how much he had changed. He was not as hot-headed, more in control of himself.

Lucy Grandison, on his fortnightly visits to Balgone, had helped to urbanise him. He leaned back against the train carriage's upholstery and closed his eyes, smiling to himself as he remembered the brash character he had been when first they'd met.

Subtly, by example, she had civilised him. She had invited her friends to meet him and had taught him the manners of the drawing room. She had let him escort her and with the utmost tact shown him how polite society was conducted. And as ever he had been quick to learn. Now he could disport himself well in both worlds; his world of trading where manners were a hindrance and their world, the snobbish society of the upper classes where traders were held in contempt.

He did not think he would ever settle a score with his fists again. He opened his eyes and gazed out on the fields and forests. Through the familiar landscapes, steam high above the carriages, the train gathered speed between stations on the descent into Nottingham.

He bought lace for the stalls and finished early after checking that his purchases were loaded on to the train he caught to return.

Back in Middlefield Oliver saw his parcels safely on to the carrier's cart. It was a fine, warm day and he ran up the Wallgate to loosen his legs and strode confidently across the market place.

'Mr Wainwright?' Oliver turned at the sound of his name and saw that a constable had come from the police office and was hailing him. 'Can you come inside for a few minutes?' the man said. 'The sergeant wants to see you.'

The burly young copper had a different air from the tone of bantering joviality he normally used. Oliver re-crossed the square and entered the tiny waiting room. The place was dark and dirty. It was a great inconvenience, being hindered like this. Oliver wanted to go to the mill before the last relay came in. He was also annoyed by the curt manner of the young policeman.

The elderly sergeant came to the door of his office and motioned him inside in silence. As soon as the door was closed the officer unlocked a cupboard and brought a wooden box to the table. It held a collection of jewellery, some of it good, heavy stuff, other pieces ordinary. There were two gold watches, an emerald and pearl ring and a necklace of garnets set in gold. The rest were no more than trinkets and glass beads.

'Have you seen these before, Mr Wainwright?' the sergeant asked. He was watching Oliver closely and his manner was formal.

Oliver knew that the man expected him to confess to knowledge of their theft, for theft it must be. 'No,' he said calmly. 'Why are you asking me?' Inside he was seething. The man had no reason to think of him as dishonest. Why should he be under suspicion of stealing?

'They were taken from the pawnbroker's back room last night. A man answering your description was seen running from the shop after dark. The bag was hidden in a place I'm not prepared to disclose to you. I must ask for an account of your movements.'

A man answering his description? Tommy? For God's sake. Tommy wouldn't be involved in anything like this, surely? Oliver managed to control the expression on his face, to convey dignity with innocence. 'If you come with me to The Pheasant, sergeant, I can prove to you that I spent last night in the company of my partner, Albert Billington. We use one of the storerooms to prepare stock for the next day's work. Mr and Mrs Billington will tell you so.' He stood up to leave.

'Do you know why the goods were pawned in your name?' the sergeant asked. 'Do you use the services of the pawnbroker?'

'No. And I never will! I can't tell you anything about the stuff. There must be other Wainwrights in the town. The man could have used a false name,' Oliver replied but his heart sank as he spoke the words of indignation. If Tommy was on the road to crime then it must be because he, Oliver, had not protected him well enough, not taught him honesty.

The sergeant put the jewellery away and opened the door for him. 'There were other articles in the hiding place, Wainwright. Our men will be watching to see if the thief returns.'

Oliver ran to The Pheasant. It was a long time since he had felt such anger. He ran up the stairs from the yard behind the kitchen, his feet noisy on the narrow, unpolished flight. Their stockroom, at the top of the house, was the attic he had once used; an ill-lit place with one tiny window.

Oliver opened the chests, checking their contents. All were half-empty. Some had been packed with newspaper under the tissue, making the boxes appear full. He was livid. How could he? How could Tommy do this? They'd trusted him. They had to trust, there was no other way of working together. And now the lad was in trouble; not only with them but with the police. He must put a stop to his cheating and put Tommy beyond the reach of the law.

He thundered down to the kitchen where Ma Billington and the kitchen maid were peeling potatoes for the supper. A pot of beef stew simmered on the range, ready for customers and family alike. The two women jumped in alarm as Oliver, his face hard and set, asked, 'Did you know Tommy was stealing?'

'Ee, Oliver!' Ma Billington was evidently glad that she could tell him at last. 'He's a bad 'un, that brother of yours. I'm right sorry to tell you so. We have to watch him all the time in case he makes off wi' owt. It's right you should know. I said to Leonard, "It's not fair Oliver and our Albert working their tripes out for that wicked little devil to take it all."'

'Thanks, Mrs Billington. I'll see there's no more of it. I'll give him what he deserves when I catch him,' Oliver said grimly. 'Tell Albert when he comes in not to wait up for me. I may be late but it could be tomorrow. Don't worry. Say nothing to the police if they come. Tell them I'll call in and see them on my way back. Just tell them that I was here last night.'

He made his way back to the station the long way round, not passing the market or police office and waited, pacing the dusty platform, backwards and forwards, mouth set and grim, all his fine manners forgotten, hands eager to get his brother in their grip, to shake and strike him.

The train arrived in a cloud of steam, which rebounded off the glazed canopy above the station, temporarily obscuring the faces of the passengers who alighted. Tommy was there. It would be obvious from Oliver's face that he'd been caught out.

Tommy stood by the bags, defiance in the posture of his wiry body. 'Well?' His voice was mocking. 'I suppose you've found out about my bad deeds?'

Oliver sent him sprawling with a quick blow from his right hand. 'Get up!' he barked, his eyes blazing with rage. 'And get up quick and come with me quietly if you want your bloody face saving.'

Tommy struggled to his feet, diving off to the left of his brother. Oliver put out his foot and sent the boy to the ground. This time Oliver took him by the collar and wrenched him to his feet, Tommy's face level with his own, his feet off the ground.

'Before I kill you, lad, do as I say. Follow me. Don't try any bloody tricks.'

The stout, uniformed stationmaster hurried towards them. 'I'll have no brawling on my station,' he said officiously.

'Move over!' Oliver pushed the little man aside and led Tommy into the booking hall. 'Deliver these bags to The Pheasant,' he told the station boy. 'There's an extra sixpence for you if you take them now. Tell Albert Billington I'll be back in a day or two.'

He rapped on the glass. 'Two tickets to Manchester. One single, one return.'

There was a train due and they were seated and steaming through the industrial heart of Lancashire within the hour. Oliver did not look out of the windows at the narrow streets, shiny black railway arches, rows of houses and muddy alleyways. He sat, grimly determined, watching Tommy.

The streets gave way to city warehouses and factories and soon they halted at London Road station. Tommy had sat sulking and soundless throughout the journey, and was now reluctant to alight and follow Oliver. And again Oliver, tight-lipped, dragged Tommy from his seat, almost ripping his thin coat sleeve. 'Keep going. We're not there yet.'

Down the long approach slope, with its iron handrail separating foot passengers from horse wagons, they hurried. Oliver headed through the crowded city centre to the other, bigger Exchange station.

'A single and a return to Liverpool,' he demanded.

'What are we going to Liverpool for? Can't we talk?' Tommy said at last. 'Is the single ticket for me?'

The train to Liverpool was crowded but Oliver kept Tommy firmly by his side. As it drew to a halt he grabbed his brother again, as if to thwart any attempt on his part to escape, and drew him to a line of hackney carriages. 'Take us to the docks.' He pushed Tommy ahead of him and they sat in the comfort of the leather upholstery.

'Now, our Tommy. Now I'm going to tell you what's to become of you.' Oliver faced his brother. 'You're going to join the navy! You're going to live for a while with the big, tough men you like. You want to be a man, don't you? You want to gamble and cheat? Well, you'll not stop me from doing what I want to do and I won't stop you either.'

Tommy still had a defiant look about him and Oliver shook him roughly before continuing in a voice as hard as iron. 'If you return to Middlefield you'll be arrested. The police have got the stuff you stole and your mates are going to think you told on them when they're picked up tonight.'

'I never—' Tommy started to protest.

'Shut your mouth. Before I do it for you,' Oliver said. He knew when Tommy was lying. 'You know how serious this is. You're no fool.'

Tommy looked repentant for the first time as Oliver returned to the subject. 'So you won't dare show your miserable little face in Middlefield,' he told him. 'But you'll learn all about cheating if you want to. You'll learn about it from men who've been at it a lot longer than you! And you'll learn about other things. Like being trusted by your mates. When you're out there at sea with a hard day's work under your belt and, if that's what you want, nothing but a black eye to show for it, you'll soon learn what trust means. It might make a man of you, Tommy. I can't.'

It took two days, two hungry days of passing from navy offices to merchant navy companies, army recruiting offices and finally to an Australian shipping office before Tommy was taken on, as a deckhand. He was sixteen and had no documents to prove to anybody who he was.

The Australian emigration official didn't care about documents. 'You look strong and healthy enough,' he declared, 'and you'll work your passage out. What does a birth certificate matter? Apply for one when you get out there; nothing easier.'

Oliver gave Tommy twenty sovereigns, out of pity. He told him he was forgiven and to be sure to write. He saw Tommy on to the ship, saw the wretched little space the boy would have to sleep in, met the rough crew he'd have to learn to live with. He choked back a sudden urge to take Tommy by the arm and hide him somewhere, where the police wouldn't find him. He was losing the brother he loved, his last link with the father he'd loved; a Wainwright.

Then he hugged Tommy, thanked the Australian and returned to Middlefield to assess his losses and lie in the arms of Rosie.

* * *

Lucy was supervising the packing of her trunk. The maid folded her clothes, layering them with tissue paper. She would have a month in London with Laura and Florence before the Oldfields went to visit them. A letter had arrived that very morning from Florence and Lucy took it to her sitting room to read it again.

The Runaway

Dearest Aunt,

The house is convenient and comfortable and far enough away from Uncle Godfrey for us to be able to avoid his company. Godfrey's friends, as you know, are not acceptable to Mama who is throwing herself into an endless round of bustle in order to get me on everybody's list.

This morning I have fittings for the coming-out dress and three ball gowns. I have chosen my headdress. It has white ostrich feathers that sit at the back of my head. It makes me look tall and imposing.

I do want to do Mama proud but so often I find I want to laugh at the wrong moments. But I expect I shall be too nervous when I'm presented to do anything other than follow the rules.

I have met some interesting people and some so appalling that I cannot describe their stupidity without exaggeration. I envy and admire the girls I see at St Thomas's Hospital when we take alms. They must think of us as empty-headed and trivial.

Dearest Aunt, I find the whole business of being presented and entering a society I never wish to join a complete waste of time and effort. And it is all to find me a husband. How can I tell Mama that I shall never find a husband here?

I long to be in Middlefield. I cannot bear to think that Oliver may forget me.

You tell me that he is in good health and is changing into an assured and respected businessman but you do not tell me what I want to hear. Does he ask about me? When he escorts you to the theatre does he ever wish I were there too?

Mama will not hear of our returning to Middlefield for another year at least but I am so longing to see you.

Please bring me news of Oliver.

Love, Florence

Lucy sighed. It seemed to be an unspoken rule that she and Oliver never spoke about Florence. They talked about everything else but she would not be able to tell Florence what she wanted to hear.

* * *

They had been lovers for over a year and their need of one another had not diminished, but had rather been fuelled by the necessity of working together during daylight hours, not daring to acknowledge their passion until they were alone.

As their second spring gave way to warm, scented summer and the summer to a golden autumn Rosie's fears grew. She was trapped by the power of her love but she knew they could not continue in this way for ever. She knew that he loved her. He was not a man who needed the reassurance of frequent conquests, neither was dalliance in his make-up. He seemed not to notice the charms of other girls. There were comely girls by the score in Middlefield; girls who threw bold looks at him and yet he appeared not to see them.

But when Rosie was alone with her thoughts she was assailed with fears and guilt. If this love that she felt was in reality the lust of the scriptures, then the sermonisers had need to fear its sweeping hold.

And what of the other face of love; the tenderness when their bodies were sated, the hopes for the lover's happiness, the sharing of secrets no others could know? Was this sinful too? Could it be that the chapel wanted to keep from its members all knowledge of earthly love?

She saw little evidence of earthly love on the faces she saw around her on Sundays when she stood in the pew. She could not imagine any of them doing as she had done and if they discovered her secret, she knew, they would shun her, cast her out, shame her and Jim.

At the chapel Rosie prayed to be delivered from her passion for her lover; to regain the calm spirit that was hers before she had consented to be Oliver's mistress. But she was torn. She was torn between her need for Oliver's love and her duty to her husband and children. These tormenting thoughts did not come to her when he was near but she could not share these fears with Oliver. He had shown a new side of his character to her since they had become lovers. He had shown an intolerant, possessive side of his nature and seemed impatient with the need for secrecy.

And what if it were no longer a secret? Already people knew. She counted them daily and the list seemed to grow. There was Albert, and therefore Edith. Rosie herself had confided in her sister, Agnes. Agnes had visited earlier in the summer and she and Oliver could not keep apart for her sister's month-long stay.

Rosie was sure that most of the weavers knew. Weavers had no need for words. They could communicate by a lift of the eyebrow. A look passing between their forewoman and the mill-owner would be interpreted accurately.

It was a warm August night and she waited for him, slipping quietly from the room where Jim lay in broken sleep through the hours of darkness, tiptoeing into the back bedroom where her three girls slept soundly, watching for him from behind the white cotton curtains, standing back from the window, every pulse in her body keeping pace with her hammering heart; waiting for him to swing into her little back yard from the alley.

She came to him in her nightgown and they lay together on a bedspread she had placed on the floor of her parlour and tonight she told him of her fears. She told him of her fear that their affair was no longer secret, but he laughed at her. Oliver would not admit to complications in what was to him the simple fact of their love.

'Does it matter?' he teased her, sliding his hands under the folds of her nightgown, drawing her to him. 'Who cares if they know? It's only for Jim's sake that I'm being so careful.'

'But you must come back to earth, love. We have to live like this. Oh, Lord, I wish I could stop loving you now,' Rosie replied.

When he kissed her, her fears were forgotten. Their lovemaking was wild and abandoned. When they were together nothing mattered but the desires they inflamed in each other. But there was another question that needed an answer, and after they had made love and he lay beside her, spent and content, Rosie brought herself to whisper it.

'What about your promise to Florence?'

It was almost dark but she saw the clouding in Oliver's eyes as he sat up and leaned his elbows on his strong, bare thighs.

'Who told you about Florence?' His voice was controlled and suddenly distant.

Rosie clasped her arms around her knees. Her hair fell forward and concealed her face. 'I've known about her from the beginning,' she said in a breaking voice. 'It was all over the mill. All the weavers spoke about her and how you wanted to marry her.'

She had filled the hearth with late cabbage roses and their heady scent filled the little room, making her feel faint.

'It was true. I did. But I don't want to marry her now. I want to marry you and I can't.' He spoke quietly and did not look at her but stared with unseeing eyes at the floral curtains. 'You've told me about you and Jim. How you met and why you married. I know you were happy enough until I came along ...'

There was a long silence before he continued. 'That's how it was with me and Florence. I thought I'd found the girl I loved but it was nothing like the love I have for you. What I felt for Florence was romantic, youthful affection, not love.'

There was another pause before he continued, speaking slowly and carefully as if he were repeating his deepest thoughts. 'I never knew a man and woman could be so close; so close that a part of them seems to be missing when they're not together.'

He dropped his eyes to his hands, where they clenched his knees. 'I've never had a proper home, Rosie. I've always wanted one; a home with a wife and my children glad to see me; a happy house where it doesn't matter what goes on outside because you have everything in the world that you love right there beside you.'

He took one of the roses and began, absent-mindedly, to crush the crimson petals in his strong fingers. 'It sounds a strange thing for a man to say, doesn't it? It's unusual for a man to admit he wants a home and babies. More like a girl's dreams, really.'

Then he placed an arm gently around her and lifted her chin. And he saw that she was crying. 'I've got money now. I've enough to buy the new factory. I've enough to live on and I expect I'll make more and more.' He looked deep into her troubled eyes. 'But my ambitions don't lie there, Rosie. Making money's a game. It's a game I'm good at. But I can't make a home on my own.'

He kissed the tears on her cheeks and pulled her hard towards him and there was a hot and painful knot in her throat, full of sobs that she could not release until he left her. Her hair lay across her bare shoulders and she hid her face from him as he told her, 'I'm in this just as deep as you are, love. I want a home and I want you in it. And, God help me, I've got to wait for Jim to die before I can have it. I can't let you go.'

* * *

Sir Philip Oldfield had made two attempts to discredit Oliver during the year. On the first occasion he had given, through an agent, an order for such a great quantity of woven twill that Oliver had suspected the old baronet's hand. It had been easy to make enquiries and find that the order was a hoax and a crude attempt to run Oliver, through Hollin Mill, into serious debt.

On the second occasion Sir Philip, hiding his identity behind the Manchester Trading Company, had offered to sell the freehold of the mill but at such a high figure that Oliver wondered if the man was in his right mind.

'I don't believe he thinks the mill's worth that,' Oliver said when he showed the letter to Albert. 'The old devil's either deranged or he's in trouble.'

They were counting the market takings after a busy Saturday's trading. 'Do you think he's losing money?' Albert replied. 'I'd have thought the Oldfields had plenty.'

'Bill Grandison used to advise him. He reckoned that Oldfield had no head for investment,' Oliver said. 'I've been putting a bit away; buying here and there myself and I've bought a lot that has come from the Suttonford estate.' A great grin of satisfaction spread across his face. 'He doesn't know I've been buying from him, of course. I've not used my own name.'

'Can't he find out?' Albert asked.

'No. But if he keeps selling and I can buy, I'll own him in the end,' Oliver replied. 'And when I do, I'll laugh in his bloody face.'

'Maybe his son will take over. What's his name? Gilbert?' Albert asked.

'No. Godfrey. Godfrey Oldfield, a bigger fool than his father.' Oliver placed the linen cash bags into the leather case. 'The fellow's a drunkard. He's debauched. His father'll outlive him. They think he'll marry and keep the family name going but the fellow can't raise an eyelid, let alone anything else.'

'Not like us, eh?' Albert bragged.

Oliver threw back his head and laughed. 'God, no. Not like us.'

'You'll be seeing Mrs Hadfield tonight then?' Albert said.

'Yes. What about you? Are you going to The Crown?'

Albert grinned. 'Where's that?' he asked.

The following day, to Oliver's surprise, Dolly appeared at The Pheasant.

Chapter Fifteen

She had not changed. She still had the scowling, sharp-eyed look he remembered. Her clothes were more stylish than a country woman's normal wear but they were cheap and gaudy and had probably been worn out by someone else before Dolly acquired them.

On that September morning she sported an emerald-green dress in limp satin, its dark trimmings frayed and faded. A flattened green pancake of a bonnet sat awkwardly atop her wiry hair. Oliver no longer felt anger towards her. Instead he saw that she cut a comical figure as she stepped clumsily down from the cab that had brought her from the station.

Oliver was outside The Pheasant when she arrived. 'Where's our Tommy?' she barked as soon as she saw Oliver. 'Tell 'im to coom out 'ere. I want to talk to 'im and you an' all.'

'Come inside, Dolly. We'll talk in the parlour. I'll tell you all about Tommy when we get in.' He knew she was capable of making an exhibition of herself, and of him, here in the middle of the Rivergate.

He wouldn't tell her all about Tommy. For one thing, he knew she'd swear that Tommy had never given anyone a minute's trouble in his life before he left her tender care. And for another, he wanted Dolly to be proud of her son. Tommy would be all right when he'd grown up a little.

He guided her through to the parlour and seated her on one of the plush chairs. Oliver sat and stretched his legs lazily. He leaned back in his chair and told her about Tommy.

'You know what a lad our Tommy was for adventure, Dolly?' he began. 'This town didn't have enough for him. So he went to

Liverpool and joined a ship to Australia. He hasn't gone penniless, though. He'd a bit of money by him. If he's any sense he'll set himself up.'

Dolly seemed pleased to think that her faith in Tommy's abilities had been vindicated and she seemed satisfied when Oliver said that the boy had money with him.

Mrs Billington popped her head around the parlour door. 'Are you all right in here, Oliver? Shall I light the fire for you?' Her kind face beamed a welcome as she waited to be introduced to the mother that Tommy and Oliver had spoken of.

To Oliver's amusement and embarrassment Dolly adopted the air of lady of the manor.

'No, my good woman. We'll ring when we want you,' she intoned in a strange nasal voice, at the same time raising her reddened hand imperiously, pointing towards the door.

Oliver winked at Ma Billington who immediately saw the funny side of Dolly's behaviour. She barely suppressed a snort of laughter as she bobbed a little curtsey to Dolly before leaving them to their talk.

'We was talking about you and our Tommy, wasn't we?' Dolly went on, this time in her normal, rasping tone. 'That's right! I look after you both all your lives, wear my fingers to the bone for yer. And as soon as you could put a bit of money my way, you "ups and off". Both of yer!' She settled back into the armchair and cocked her head to one side. 'You want to know what's going on, don't yer?'

Oliver hoped it was not going to take her all day to get round to telling him some trifling piece of Suttonford gossip. 'It depends on what it is, Dolly,' he told her. 'I don't lie awake at night wondering what's going on at Suttonford.'

She sniffed, disdainfully. 'Well, what I've got to tell yer, you'll not get for nowt. I'm not coomin' all this way and going 'ome empty-handed. No, I'm not!' She looked sharply at Oliver. 'I don't know why I should come and help you out. Why I should tell yer that someone's goin' to smash yer ruddy business for yer! Not for nothing! No!'

'What's up, Dolly?' Oliver sat up straight, interested now. Dolly wouldn't have come all this way for nothing. 'If you've something to tell me that's worth listening to I'll give you a half sovereign.' He rattled the gold coins in his pocket, to whet her appetite.

Dolly patted her hat with a work-worn hand, flicked at an imaginary speck of dust on her skirt and looked at her stepson slyly. 'Two sovereigns!' she demanded.

'Tell me first,' Oliver said, then added with a trace of sarcasm, 'Would you like some tea, or maybe a drop of gin before you start?'

He called Ma Billington back and repeated, 'Tea or gin, Dolly?'

'Gin, please. And tea after.' She leaned confidentially towards Oliver. 'In my kitchen – I'm second cook now, you know – there's a flue as needs brushing out every week. Sometimes Bessie leaves the plate off it. She forgets to put it back, like, and when it's off you can hear every word they say in the office above ... Sir Philip Oldfield's office!' she added dramatically.

'Did I tell yer about Wilf?' she said. 'About 'im getting thick with Sir Philip. Well, he is. Wilf does things, he does underhand deceitful things when Sir Philip orders him to. And sometimes when 'e doesn't.' She broke off as the door opened and Ma Billington brought in a tray of tea and a glass of gin. Dolly sipped genteelly. As soon as they were alone again she continued eagerly.

'Yesterday, he says to Wilf, "You know my mill in Middlefield? The one as Holiver Wainwright uses?" Well, as soon as I heard your name, Oliver, I put me ear to the flue. "I want you to go down there next Thursday and smash it all up. I'll pay yer well," he says. "Do it at night. I 'ave a key to the door in me desk. Smash them up well, Wilf, and I'll reward you 'andsomely," he says.'

Oliver felt the hairs on the back of his neck begin to prickle. Sir Philip was determined, then, to have a last attempt to ruin him before he left the mill for the new factory. Next Thursday! That left him only four days. His thoughts were racing so much that he hardly listened as Dolly continued her tale.

'So. Tip the police off. Get them down there and they'll arrest Wilf and you'll save yer machines!' Dolly went on, a smile on her face. 'I can just see it! Wilf locked up and that slut from the village tearing her hair,' she finished.

Oliver leaped to his feet, so grateful to her that he slapped her across the shoulder as if she were a man. 'Dolly Leach!' he declared. 'You're a clever woman! Three sovereigns is what that little bit of news is worth.'

He brought a leather pouch from his pocket and counted the gleaming sovereigns, letting them drop with an inviting 'clink' into her bag.

Her face was flushed with excitement as she drained the glass. Already a plan was forming in his mind. He gave Dolly his arm and led her towards the door. 'Don't let anyone know you've been here. Get the next train back.' The coach was in the yard and he called to the new boy. 'Take this lady to the station will you?'

Dolly settled herself, smiling smugly but clutching the bag as if she might be set upon and robbed at any moment.

'Don't spend it all on Wilf!' Oliver warned. She sniffed in disgust at the mention of Wilf's name and attempted a haughty look.

When the coach had rolled away Oliver looked for Albert.

'Get the looms at Hollin Mill insured tomorrow. Insure them as high as you can will you? I'll put some of the stuff we'll need at the new factory in the storeroom here!' He slapped Albert on the shoulder and grinned.

'Don't look so worried. I know what I'm doing. And arrange for a night out at The Swan on Thursday for you, me, Herbert Clayton and the police inspector. They've been wanting a game of poker with us for weeks!'

The four men were to meet in The Swan at eight o'clock that night: Herbert Clayton, Edith's father, a young-looking, florid man of around forty; Inspector Dale; Albert; and himself.

Oliver watched Inspector Dale stride across the market square from the police office in the narrow lane between the Town Hall and the church. 'Everything all right?' he asked when the inspector reached his side.

'Aye. There's only a handful of thieves. They're locked in the cells. They'll be dealt with severely by Sir Philip Oldfield on Monday. They'll not trouble Middlefield for a year or two.'

They drank a couple of pints of beer in the public bar where an old woman picked out a tune at the piano. The air was thick with smoke from tobacco pipes and the old woman's fingers moved desultorily. Customers were barely listening so early in the evening. Later the playing would become louder as the old one became tipsy and the patrons, working men and a few women who cared nothing for their reputations, stood up to sing sentimental, popular songs. Yet another glass of port would be placed on top of the piano for Ma Burkitt who could keep the tune going with her right hand while the left took the elixir of life to her purple lips to be drained in seconds.

'Shall we go up now?' Herbert Clayton asked.

'Aye. Lead the way.' Oliver bought more beers and carried them up to the room overlooking the square, where a games table had been placed for them in front of the window.

Oliver was enjoying himself. His mind was never so sharp as when it was being challenged and tonight the challenge was to concentrate on the game and not let the others suspect that his imagination was elsewhere. By two o'clock in the morning Oliver had won two guineas, Albert had won four and the older men were hoping to make up their losses, when at last it came; a knock on the door.

A burly constable stood in the doorway. 'There's been trouble ... an intruder, sir. Down at Hollin Mill. A man's gone berserk and smashed the place up. He must have had help. There's a lot of damage done. We've arrested one man. He was in the water, must have left the mill by a window over the river. But he denies it, sir. Says he fell in the Hollin after he'd drunk too much. Says he was making his way home to Suttonford village and lost his way. Name of Leach. Not from Middlefield, sir.'

They went to see for themselves, carrying oil lamps through pitch-black, moonless streets to where the inky waters of the Hollin surged alongside the narrow pathway bordering the mill.

181

'Oh, God!' Albert was stunned by the scene revealed in the dim lamplight. He leaned weakly against the splintered door jamb. 'We've lost everything. The man's mad.'

Oliver had not told his partner about the plot. He knew that Albert's genuine distress would be plain to the onlookers. Inside, the machines looked grotesque, twisted and smashed. Wooden frames were shattered, cast-iron loom sides were snapped in two. Even the heddles and shuttles were broken, torn from the cloth in a tangle of threads that were strewn over the ruined machinery.

'I am sorry, lads,' Inspector Dale said. 'If we've got the right man he'll be dealt with good and proper. Sir Philip Oldfield's on the bench on Monday. Are you insured?'

'Aye. But it's the lost production, Inspector. It'll take us a while to recover from this,' Oliver replied in sorrowful tones, bringing from the inspector a sympathetic pat of friendship.

Oliver was delighted. Wilf, in his usual inept fashion, had smashed up the great steam engines which worked the looms, and these belonged to Sir Philip Oldfield's company. It would cost him a pretty penny to put the place back into working order if he wanted to let it again.

'There's money enough in compensation to buy twice as many machines,' Oliver told Albert, 'and more modern ones at that. Our old machines need one man to two looms. The new ones have got self-acting temples to control the tension. We'll need fewer skilled men to work them. They'll work faster and weave wider cloth.'

'Make 'em an offer for the broken ones,' Albert said. 'We can cobble together twenty new looms from the parts that are undamaged.'

Sir Philip Oldfield found Wilf Leach not guilty on the following Monday morning. He was, he said, one of his own workers and had been seen in a tavern by three witnesses at the time of the incident. The man was drunk and had taken a wrong turning home on the night in question.

After listening to the case in the magistrates' court the two friends went to The Swan where Herbert Clayton was waiting to hear the judgment. He set beers before them at the long bar and commiserated with them.

'Disgraceful, that's what it was. Letting that rascal free to commit another crime. What are you looking so pleased about, Oliver?'

Oliver could not conceal his delight. 'We're on our way now, Albert!' he rejoiced. 'Sir Philip Oldfield's given us the chance. Wainwright and Billington will be the biggest name in cotton in the whole country. Now we can give up the market stalls and concentrate on weaving cloth.'

'You knew what he was up to all along, you crafty devil,' Albert replied, though there was admiration in his look as he gave Oliver a push, sending beer splashing over their shoes. 'Anyone else would have gone ruddy bankrupt!'

The new factory was ready to move into but first there were three weeks, three empty late-summer weeks, before the new machinery arrived and could be installed. Oliver could not remember when he last had a day, let alone three weeks, of idleness.

He decided to take Rosie to the seaside.

* * *

On the pretext of clearing up the devastation at the mill Rosie joined Oliver every day and they planned their holiday by the sea. 'I've never seen the sea,' she told him. 'I came here from Bradford when I got married and I've never been anywhere else.'

'Wait till you see it, love. Big and blue and endless.' He embraced her there amongst the debris of the weaving shed. 'And the shops. Big shops, Rosie, with things you could only dream of. We'll walk arm in arm and everyone'll say "What a handsome couple they make. I wonder who they are?" Will you be able to get away?' he added anxiously.

'Yes. I've written to Jim's parents and sent them money for the train. They want to come and see Jim and the children, and the new house.' Rosie smiled. 'They're not so fussy about seeing me. They always thought I'd too much of a mind of my own. They think I'm going to stay with my sister Agnes.'

'Albert's given me the address of a house near the sea. The woman takes in guests. We're booked in as Mr and Mrs Wainwright,' Oliver told her as he held her hard up against his chest. 'Oh, God, Rosie, I wish it were true.'

'It'll never be true,' she whispered. 'Suppose they find out we're not married?' She was full of fear at the enormity of the plan.

'Nobody knows us there. How could they find out?' Oliver could not contemplate anything upsetting the arrangements he had made with such care. 'Nobody will know. We'll travel to Manchester separately. I'll get an early train and meet you off yours.'

Rosie packed her best dress, a blue shantung with a small bustle, which a dressmaker had made for her. She put in her good skirt, three silk blouses and a velvet shoulder cape. She wore a mauve hat, large brimmed and heavy with silk flowers and velvet ribbon. The sun warmed her back, early in the morning, as she carried her bag down Wallgate, feeling the edges of the stones through her thin-soled shoes.

She would have blushed to tell the lies she had ready in case anyone stopped her. She was glad she saw no one she knew as she reached the station unseen, out of breath and flushed from the effort of leaning backwards to compensate for the weight of the heavy bag on the hill.

'A single ticket to Manchester, please,' she asked of the clerk behind the tiny arched opening.

'Off on holiday, then, Mrs Hadfield?' The man lived in the next street.

They were a respectable family and Rosie felt that he must see right through her lies as she replied. 'It's my sister in Yorkshire ... she wants me to stay with her for a couple of weeks.' Her face reddened as the man gave her a ticket.

Oliver was waiting on the platform in Manchester and her heart gave its usual lurch when she saw him, head and shoulders above the other passengers, searching the crowd until his eyes lit upon her.

The Southport train was almost full. Oliver had bought first-class tickets for them. They sat at opposite sides of the compartment, by the window. Rosie studied Oliver as they steamed across the green Lancashire plain. He was even more handsome than when she had first met him and she marvelled at his continuing love for her. The five years since his arrival in Middlefield had brought changes. He was still occasionally impetuous and boyish but this side of his character was less evident than his sharp intelligence and swift mastery of the world of business.

It was going to be wonderful to have him to herself for two whole weeks. The new factory would take his attention when they returned. The speed with which he and his partner had moved to wrest advantage from potential ruin had drawn admiration from all the mill-owners and clever businessmen in Middlefield. The same men who had cautioned the young marketeers and foretold disaster were now beginning to talk of Oliver's astuteness.

Cold fear clutched her when she imagined life without him. Soon she must tell him that she carried his child, but not yet. Soon she would thicken more noticeably; already her breasts were becoming fuller. Oliver's method of prevention was the oldest in the world but there had been times, many times, when nothing but completion would do. They would have their holiday, their two weeks of carefree enjoyment before they faced the problem of her pregnancy. There was no place for an abandoned woman, if Jim turned her out, and there was every chance that he would, since the baby could not have been his.

'Soon be there, Mrs Wainwright,' Oliver said, catching her eye and bringing a smile to her wide mouth. 'Wait till you see the sea, eh?'

With brakes scraping and steam shooting upwards as the pressure released the train drew to a halt and they alighted from the stuffy carriage into a different world.

Southport was flat, its streets wide, tree-lined avenues where well-shod residents of the splendid houses strolled the neatly tiled pavements. The air was clean with a faint tang of the sea on its breath as it rustled through the branches of the sycamore, beech and horse-chestnut trees the town had in abundance.

Flowers bloomed in neat beds and borders at every turn. Scarlet geraniums hung in profusion from wrought-iron brackets under deep glass canopies above the heads of the people who walked beneath them. These shoppers needed never fear to alight from their carriages even in inclement weather.

The town was full of life. Lord Street, the main boulevard, had elegant shops and fashionable restaurants along the mile and a half of its length and the clients of these establishments desired as much to be seen as to see the fine displays of expensive wares artistically arranged for them.

Rosie gripped the side of the open carriage with her left hand and held Oliver's hand tight with her right. She had never seen a town like this. They turned into Lord Street from London Square where a line of hire carriages moved slowly forwards to pick up passengers, empty carriages joining the back of the line at the same time, in easy-moving harmony.

'Middlefield square would fit into this twice over.' She clutched Oliver's hand. 'Look! Over there – the wheel chairs for hire. Oh! See here – the trams. Look at the people on top holding parasols.' She turned to face Oliver as the carriage, out of the slow-moving procession that had left the station, began to bowl along smoothly, unlike the jolting and lurching of carriages in hilly, narrow Middlefield.

'I can see for miles. Oliver. The roads go on for ever. Ooh, look at the dresses. How beautiful the women are!'

Oliver was relaxed against the upholstery. He had been here before, with Albert and Edith, and could point out, with a proprietorial air, the places she might overlook in her excitement.

'We'll be passing the Winter Gardens on our right soon, Rosie. Here we are,' he told her. 'I've asked the driver to stop for a minute.'

The horses seemed to know exactly what was expected of them. They drew up in front of the imposing entrance without so much as a twitch of the reins.

Chapter Sixteen

Sign boards proclaimed at the entrance, where three sets of double doors opened to receive the public, that inside could be found, 'The Wonders of The Aquarium. The Finest in the World, Containing Europe's Biggest Alligator, Sharks, Sturgeon, Octopods and many varieties of Shells. Conservatory and Theatre, Concert Room with Concerts Twice Daily, Outdoor Firework Displays and Refreshment Room.'

'I'll take you there tomorrow. You'll like the aquarium,' Oliver promised.

They climbed back into the carriage and the driver turned the horses up the gentle rise towards the promenade and Rosie's first sight of the sea. The tide was out and people walked the tight-ridged sand, carefree and barefoot in the warmth of the afternoon sun.

'What are those contraptions, Oliver?' Rosie pointed to five or six long, wheeled sand yachts whose owners were unfurling the high sails. 'Oh! Look. That must be the pier!'

They read the announcement at the entrance, telling the times of sailings from the pier head to Bangor and Beaumaris, Jarrow and the Isle of Man.

'Shall we go on a trip, Oliver?' Rosie asked eagerly. She could not contain her excitement.

'Aye. We'll do everything, love. First we'll find the house, and unpack.' The carriage drew up before a tall house of shiny red brick. A short flight of steps, under a portico with cream-plastered columns, led to the heavy front door and stained-glass windows of the porch.

It was a mansion. Rosie's knees were knocking with fear. She had never spent a whole night with Oliver. Not in a bed. Suppose the woman discovered that they were not married and ordered them to leave? She could have turned and fled.

Oliver prised the bag from her white-knuckled grasp. 'Don't worry, love. I'll do the talking.' He gave her a quick hug before the door opened and they were welcomed into the wide hall of a comfortable guest house by a jolly little woman of around sixty years.

'Mr and Mrs Wainwright? Did you have a good journey?' She led the way up the carpeted stairs and down a long passage to a room overlooking the quiet street. 'We take one family at a time, so you are the only guests. If you want anything, just knock at the door downstairs – the one next to the dining room.' She beamed at them. 'Dinner's at six. It gives people time to get out for a concert. Shall I put a pot of tea out for you?'

'No, thank you. We'll unpack and rest before dinner.' Oliver was on his own ground. He was used to hotel living.

The room was spacious. Red and cream roses were arranged in a glass bowl on the high, mirrored dressing table and the carpet was patterned with the same colours against a deep blue background. At the two windows, which reached almost from floor to ceiling, fresh white lawn curtains gave privacy while heavy blue tapestry ones were hung from brass poles and fastened to the wall with silk tassels. A large bed faced the window, piled with soft pillows over a fringed counterpane. Brass bed knobs shone from energetic polishings and the whole room reflected back at them from two ornate mirrored wardrobes.

Oliver put their bags beside a marble-topped washstand. 'This will do us nicely,' he told the woman. The moment the door closed behind the old dear Rosie fell backwards on to the bed.

'Phew! What an ordeal!' She pulled off her hat and hung it from the brass knob of the bedhead. 'Does she suspect we're not married?'

'Of course she doesn't.' He was teasing her, laughing at her fears. 'You're timid, aren't you, Rosie? Under that serene face you're all turbulent emotions.'

She loved it when he looked at her that way, the quick spark of fire, the light in his eyes, one minute teasing, the next taking her in his arms.

'Come on, lass,' he said. 'Take your coat off.'

Rosie smiled her long, slow smile. She stretched out in mock languor against the cream counterpane. 'You take it off,' she invited. He undressed and she watched him, wide-eyed, as he placed his clothes over the bedside chair and went to the window to untie the cords that held the curtains. There was no self-consciousness in his actions. To Rosie, who had been taught to think of nakedness and sin as synonymous, his joy in his powerful body was a revelation. Her own modesty seemed to her a foolish denial of her femininity and an affront to his open pleasure in her.

He sat beside her on the bed as, leaning on one supportive elbow, he began to unbutton her clothes with deft hands; hands practised in the art of bringing her to the brink of expectation and need as they moved expertly over her body.

'What if ...?' she started to ask, but his mouth silenced her protests in deep kisses that brooked no questions. He freed her arms from the loosened blouse and she dug her fingers into the firm muscles of his back, her taut nipples pressing into his chest.

He tugged at the restricting band of her skirt with unusual impatience and dropped it to the floor. Later they would make love slowly; now they were in a state of urgency that the tensions of the day had heightened.

'I love you, Rosie Hadfield,' he said, between kisses. 'I want you – you beautiful, sensuous woman. You respond to my every touch, don't you?'

His mouth left her lips and moved hungrily, searchingly towards her breast, pulling invisible strings inside her, making her moan with longing.

He raised himself above her, watching her face, aware of the strength of her need, tantalising her with delay, in command of his body. She lay still, luminous eyes half-closed, strands of dark hair straying over her face, every nerve in her body reaching out to him.

'Now?' he asked.

'Oh yes ... Oh ... quickly,' she whispered urgently, and the pull of her arms brought him into her, carrying them higher and faster with every movement, until, locked into each other's responses, one body obeyed the demands of the other.

They would never forget the holiday. For two weeks they walked in the streets together, rode horse-drawn trams to parks and gardens that were only minutes away from the town centre. Rosie learned to swim at the public baths in the Ladies Plunge Pool while Oliver read the papers in the reading room or played billiards with strangers in the games room. They paddled in the sea, took a steamer to Liverpool and even ventured on to the ice of the Glaciarium.

Midweek, they went to Sampson's photographic studio. Provided the weather was bright, they were told, appointments were made between the hours of 10.30 and one o'clock. The photographer posed them in his sunlit yard beside an ornamental Greek urn, against a backcloth of lurid mountains. Rosie let her hair down for the picture and the photographer draped her shoulders in a fringed shawl and gave her a bouquet of roses to hold.

They made love in the afternoons and again before dinner. They made love before breakfast and quite often in the early hours of the morning when fishermen's carts woke them as they rattled by on their way to the shrimping grounds. It was going to be hard to part when the time came and as the second week drew to its end a frenzy seemed to overtake them. A frenzy that owed much to the need to return to their individual lives again where they must hide their need for one another.

As the day of departure drew near Rosie began to dread the return to Middlefield. She had pretended to herself that they were a married couple, that they would never live separate lives again. She knew that Oliver was starting to miss Middlefield and wanted to be back in the world he knew, of business dealings, of setting up the new factory. He was not a man who could easily cope with leisure. Even on this holiday he had kept up with the movements of the stock market.

They went for a last drive around the town Rosie felt she wanted to live in for ever, before arriving at the station on the last day. She was silent as the train steamed towards Manchester. A dread of facing Jim and the girls descended on her. They would be waiting to hear about her holiday with Agnes and she was not a practised liar.

Oliver saw her on to the train to Middlefield. 'I'll spend an hour or two in Manchester, love. I'll catch a later train so nobody will see us together.'

Oliver reached Middlefield at eight o'clock that evening. He had spent three useful hours in Manchester with some cotton brokers and was hoping to spend an hour with Albert.

Outside the station, on the little rise where the cattle market joins Wallgate, Mr and Mrs Hadfield held on to Rosie. 'That's him, isn't it?' the old man said as Oliver came towards them. 'Don't start pretending you don't know!' He shook Rosie roughly.

'Hey, you! Wainwright!' Wesley Hadfield's voice rang out above the noise of departing passengers.

Oliver stopped in his tracks. 'Rosie? What are you doing here?' he said.

'Don't look surprised. You only saw her a few hours ago,' the old man snarled. 'Just you come up to t'house. You've got some explaining to do.' He let go of Rosie's arm and set off up the hill, bent almost double but covering the ground with a speed that would have done credit to a far younger man. His wife, cloaked and hooded, kept pace beside him.

Oliver turned to Rosie. 'What is it, love?' He saw her tear-stained face. 'What's happened?'

'Come to the house with me, Oliver.' She could scarcely speak for the choking sobs that racked her. Oliver put his arm protectively around her shoulders.

'I'll come with you,' he assured her. 'What's going on, love?' His heart missed a beat. Surely nothing had happened to Jim or her children?

'Come on! Get a move on!' The old man halted, only moving on when he saw that they were coming towards him.

Rosie could barely speak audibly. 'They – they've found out, Oliver. Agnes came to Middlefield to see me and I'd said I was with her. They've sent Jim and the children to Bradford. Now they say I've got to go.'

Oliver held her, half-carried her to the house. There were questions he must ask her and she was almost hysterical. How dared these people speak to her as they were doing?

Old Mrs Hadfield slammed the front door and stalked ahead of them. The living room was almost empty of furniture. Ash spilled out on to the cold hearth. Rosie's high brass fender had gone. A wooden chair and small cupboard were all that was left in the room she had furnished so lovingly.

Wesley Hadfield's face was distorted with rage. He stood with his back to the fireplace. 'What have you to say for yourself?' His voice was harsh with age, though powerful with anger. 'Bringing a respectable family down to the level of the gutter! Taking your cheap pleasure from a cheap woman and leaving her poor husband and children to suffer!'

'Rosie's no cheap woman, old man! Hold your tongue!' Oliver, tight-lipped and angry, made a move towards Rosie who sat, crumpled in the chair, clutching the cupboard as wracking sobs tore through her.

The old man leaped between them and raised his stick to stop Oliver from going to her. 'You have made her cheap! The wrath of the Lord will be upon you!' His eyes were wild. 'If I were a young man I'd horsewhip you.'

The old woman stood, stony-faced, beside her husband. 'And her expecting a bastard child! Did you think my Jim would bring it up as his own? Did you think a decent man would shelter a child brought forth in sin? Did you?' She filled herself out with God-fearing indignation. 'She's not fit to breathe the Good Lord's air!'

There was silence.

'How did you find out?' Rosie whispered.

'Agnes told us. We held her hand on the Bible and made her tell us the truth. We knew you were with him – the man who led you from the paths of righteousness,' Wesley Hadfield shouted.

'Rosie? Is it true? A child?' Oliver saw the answer in her eyes.

'And the sins of the father shall be upon the children. Unto the third and fourth generation!' the old man screamed. 'And the Lord said "Vengeance is mine".'

Rosie's sobs were tearing at her. 'Stop! Stop!' she begged.

A terrible anger came over Oliver. 'Quiet!' he ordered, in deceptively calm tones. He stood head and shoulders above the bitter old man. 'I'll not hear another word against the woman I love. None of you is fit to tie her shoelaces. Rosie has worked all her married life for her children and your sick son and she's been a damned good wife and mother. Little thanks she's had! You'll not speak to her like that.'

He pulled Rosie gently to her feet. 'How long have you had to listen to this? These ranting bigots? I wish I'd been here when they started their self-righteous bloody humbug.'

The old man was apoplectic. 'That's the way you treat your elders, is it? You think you can do as you like because you've got a bit of money? Well, you'll not buy me and mine!' He moved to set about Oliver with his walking stick. Rosie screamed and ran towards the scullery door.

Oliver caught the stick. He wrenched it from the old man's hand and raised it. 'Get out of my house! Yes, my house!' he roared. 'I'll give you one hour to pack your things and go. You can sit on the station all night. There's a train out at five o'clock. See you're on it!'

The old man was not prepared to challenge him for, with a cry of bitter rage, he turned and went from the room. His wife swept after him.

Oliver went to the scullery. He had silenced the old couple and they would be gone within the hour. Rosie was clutching the edge of the sink, retching sounds coming from her as she leaned over its edge. 'Come with me,' he ordered. 'Put your coat on and come down to The Pheasant. We'll talk there.' He grabbed her by the hand and led her towards the front door. 'Come on, lass. Wipe your eyes. We've a lot of talking to do.'

By the time they reached The Pheasant Rosie had regained control of herself but Oliver heard, all the way along Rivergate, the quick, catching breathing of a woman in distress. They sat in his room at The Pheasant. Oliver went down for hot punch and was grateful to the Billingtons for saying no word of disapproval to him.

'I can't stay in this town, Oliver. Scandal will do us both a lot of harm.' Rosie sipped the punch, ashen-faced, leaning against his shoulder. 'You're not angry about the baby?'

'No.' Oliver slipped an arm around her waist. 'I'm not angry. I can't believe it though. Me! A father!'

'Let me go back to the house. I can't stay here all night,' she said.

Hand in hand they walked through the dark streets to the house Oliver had rented for Rosie. They cared nothing for their reputations that night. The Hadfields were gone. They had left her a bed and little else.

'We'll look for a place in Southport shall we? For you and the baby. I'll come over at weekends.' Oliver held her in his arms. 'We can't be married yet but we can live together as if we were. It will be all right, Rosie. We'll have a proper home.'

He left her in the early hours of the morning, when he was sure that the Hadfields would not return. She was his. At last she was his.

* * *

Oliver chose the house. He hated little houses. The quarry-master's house he'd lived in until he was eleven had not been large. When Dad had been killed, Dolly, he and Tommy had been thrown out of there and given the tiny cottage at Hollinbank; a tiny cottage with one room and scullery downstairs and one bedroom and a cubbyhole above.

Now he found and bought a house in a prosperous locality where the houses were large, built for stylish family living. The red bricks shone as if they had been polished, making a perfect background to the plaster of the ornamental window lintels and sills. The front gardens were short with walls to the street of the same red brick. Cream paint on the triangular coping stones finished off the walls at shoulder height. Herbaceous and wooded gardens at the back gave privacy and a feeling of the country in the heart of town.

Oliver's house had bay windows to all the rooms at the front. The attics had little bays. Inside the double front doors a tiled entrance porch opened on to the hall where stained glass cast a warm glow over the wide staircase.

Golden oak doors, perfect in their proportions, opened to reveal three fine reception rooms with marble fireplaces and elaborate cornices. Six bedrooms opened off the wide landing and a concealed staircase led to two pretty attic rooms.

Downstairs, at the end of a narrow passageway, were the more modestly appointed servants' rooms and a large, square kitchen where ovens were set into a steel fireplace and a modern gas range was installed. Beside the kitchen was a pantry, shelved in cool slate and, next to that, a door to the back stairs and servants' quarters.

Outside was a veritable warren of outhouses and a long flight of stone steps with iron balustrades leading down to the garden.

'Isn't it a wonderful house?' he asked Rosie, his face a picture of satisfaction. 'It's what I've always wanted. I only wish I could come home to you every night. We'll have more children, Rosie. We'll have at least six ... and you'll have servants to help you. I'll find you a cook and a housemaid to start with.'

He took her in his arms and there was an edge of demand as well as affection in his tone as he told her: 'You can forget all about your old life. You'll be known as my wife.'

Rosie refused to have more than one servant. Later, she said, when she was more used to giving orders she would consider taking more, but, 'Why,' she asked, 'should one woman, living alone, need more than one extra pair of hands?' Besides, they would surely not be furnishing the whole house immediately.

In this she was wrong.

Oliver took the train to Southport early on Friday afternoons, arriving before the shops were closed, giving him more time to choose his furniture. He delighted in his home though he could spend no more than two days each week there. He would have been happy for them to brazen it out together and buy a house in Middlefield but now that their first child was due he would not have accusing fingers pointed at his family.

He'd marry Rosie as soon as she was free and, meanwhile, there was the excitement of making a home. He ordered the large pieces of furniture from a cabinetmaker; wardrobes, chests of drawers and tallboys. He bought washstands and china washing sets. He bought a mahogany dining suite with a table, which he opened out for the fun of it, placing leaf after leaf into the space revealed, still not overcrowding the dining room with its splendidly ornate sideboard and two matching sets of chairs with hard-stuffed tapestry seats.

He told Rosie to order anything she fancied and she made a tentative purchase here and there but upbraided him for spending half the weekend in shopping for china, silver, curtains and covers.

Oliver ordered the nursery to be painted in blue and he bought an expensive picture frieze. A safety guard for the fire was made to his own design and cradle and cot, cupboard and clothes awaited the little one.

And he loved it. He loved seeing the house take shape. He stood at the doors of the rooms he had furnished, pleased with his choices. He made Rosie stand by the windows and the fireplaces to complete the picture as he gazed in satisfaction.

He also bought the layette. Horse-drawn vans arrived daily, bringing long cardboard boxes filled with clothes; nightdresses in fine cotton, a dozen at a time, each separated from its neighbour by layers of tissue paper. A dozen lace caps, a dozen day dresses, a dozen petticoats, two dozen lambswool vests, two dozen cotton undervests – more came by every delivery.

He chose the perambulator with the utmost care and it took pride of place in the nursery, splendidly coach-built, with enamelled black and gold paintwork and noiseless rubber tyres on the elegant spoke wheels.

Rosie remonstrated, 'We don't need all this for one baby, Oliver,' as the pile of parcels mounted for him to unpack at weekends and place carefully into the empty chests of drawers in the nursery.

'Nonsense! Our child will have everything of the best,' he repeated, when she raised an objection. 'You never knew your parents. I had only a father, and him only until I was eleven. Our son will have a proper home, with a mother and father. He'll have everything I ever wanted.'

Chapter Seventeen

Oliver told no one the reason for his weekend absences from Middlefield. He had expected a lot of gossip to be abroad over the hasty departure of the Hadfield family from the town but it appeared that no one had heard of the events that had led to Rosie's disappearance.

It was better that they did not know, he decided. This way, his child would have a proper upbringing and Rosie, when she felt able, would join the congregation of one of the chapels, since chapel-going had been such a big part of her life until now. Oliver professed to be just as mystified as everybody who had known the family. He determined to keep it a secret, even from Albert. When asked by Albert if he too planned to buy a home of his own, he replied that he was content to remain at The Pheasant.

It wouldn't be the same at The Pheasant when Albert was married but he'd keep his evenings occupied, studying the stock market.

Albert and Edith were planning a June wedding and the first bricks had been laid on the house they were building on the hill below Balgone. Oliver took as much interest in it as they did and on his visits to Lucy Grandison he always stopped to watch the work progressing.

Oliver called on her, one afternoon in late November.

She seemed frailer, not quite as quick on her feet as she had been but he knew she looked forward to his visits and referred to him in fun as 'My gentleman caller'.

'What a lucky woman I am to have the attentions of such a handsome young man, at my age!' she said. They stood together at the window of the drawing room, watching a gardener raking leaves into a damp heap and Oliver pointed out to Lucy the site of Albert's house.

'The wedding's in June,' he told her, 'and I'm to be Albert's best man.'

A log fire crackled in the grate and a stack of hot buttered muffins waited under a linen napkin on a side-table where tea and cakes were set for them.

'Did you know that Florence is returning to Cheshire?' Lucy said with what appeared to Oliver to be studied unconcern.

'I didn't know,' he replied. He could match her now for composure, though the news, to his dismay, had unsettled him. 'Will they live in Churchgate as before?' he asked in an even voice.

'Yes. Mrs Mawdesley doesn't enjoy living in London and Florence wishes to return.' Lucy poured tea. 'Will you be at The Pheasant for Christmas, Oliver?'

'No. I'm spending Christmas in Southport. I have friends there,' Oliver replied. 'I spend the weekends with them. And you, Mrs Grandison? Will you be at Suttonford?' he asked.

'Yes. But I don't go until Christmas Eve. Will you come to Balgone on the Wednesday before Christmas? I have a little gift for you.'

'Of course I will.' Oliver changed the subject quickly to talk of the new factory. 'Albert is coming in as a full partner, after the wedding,' he told Lucy. 'The Claytons are giving Edith a marriage settlement. We'll buy the factory next to ours.'

'You've done well,' Lucy said. 'Does that mean that you'll not have complete control?'

'Of the factory, no. But I'm going to take out my original investment – Bill's gift to me,' he told her. 'And with that and the braid workshop income I'm going to do as he did and invest.'

'Would you like to see Bill's investment diaries, Oliver?' Lucy asked him. 'I still have them. It may help you, especially as he kept a record of the market prices along with them.'

'I would.' Oliver knew how much it would assist him, to see the way the old man had dealt. Bill had taught him how to buy. 'But I'm going to buy local stock, as far as possible. I want to buy land.'

'Sir Philip is going to sell off some of the estate land soon, I hear,' Lucy said. Oliver looked at her sharply. Was she hinting that he should buy it?

'Well, he certainly wouldn't sell it to me,' he replied with a laugh.

'Come, come, Oliver,' she said. 'Let us not talk of sordid things, like money.' She laughed lightly. 'Tell me all about your partner's wedding.'

* * *

In the music room at Suttonford, Florence, in a dress of yellow silk, deep bustled and trimmed in satin ribbon, sat next to Aunt Lucy. Grandfather had taken it upon himself, since her return, to fill her days and most of her evenings with social diversion.

This afternoon she looked around at the guests who sat on gilt chairs waiting for the musicians to arrive, and felt she would scream if she had to sit here for a whole hour, listening and politely applauding.

'Aunt Lucy,' she whispered. Aunt Lucy looked at her enquiringly.

'Come with me to the library, will you?' Florence mouthed the words so that she should not be overheard. She saw assent in Aunt Lucy's smile, rose and made her excuses as she edged along the row to the door, smiling apologetically, pretending not to see Mama's frown of annoyance.

It was cold in the hall and Florence hurried on white, high-heeled slippers that tapped against the marble floor of the hall. She opened the library door, leaving it ajar for Aunt Lucy and went to warm her hands at the big log fire.

'Don't you want to hear the music, Florence?' Aunt Lucy closed the door and joined her in front of the flames. 'I thought you liked concerts.'

'I do,' Florence said. 'But I couldn't wait a whole hour to talk to you.' She turned her grey eyes, expressive and questioning, onto Aunt Lucy. 'Have you asked him?' she said.

'Yes. He will come to Balgone next Wednesday,' Lucy told her. 'I hope he doesn't blame me for such a small deceit. I've not told him that you'll be there.'

'How is he?'

'He is much changed, Florence,' Lucy told her. 'He is no longer the gauche boy you knew. He is a man; a man of great assurance and charm.'

'Does he look the same?' Florence asked eagerly. 'Is he as handsome?'

Lucy sighed and gave Florence a smile of understanding. 'He's more so. Are you sure you want to see him?'

'I want to see him,' Florence said firmly. 'Does he have an attachment, Aunt Lucy?'

'As far as I know there is no woman in his life but he has never confided in me on these matters,' Lucy told her kindly. 'You're not much changed, darling, are you? You have spent nearly two years away and yet you still have a fondness for Oliver.'

'I am changed, Aunt Lucy,' she said. 'I can manage a household, arrange flowers, engage a cook, entertain my husband's friends, when I have a husband, of course. I can dance and I can sing – oh, and I can be flirtatious without giving offence. Don't you think those are desirable accomplishments, Aunt Lucy?'

'I do, dear,' Aunt Lucy said, 'but where are you going to use them?'

'On Oliver, my dear, sweet aunt. And you are going to be my accomplice,' Florence said emphatically. 'I've warned Mama that I intend to see him again.' She lifted a delicate hand to push a strand of her spun-gold hair back into the fashionable upswept style she now adopted. 'She believes I no longer care for him, of course,' she added. 'And Mama is not herself. She has to take brandy to calm her nerves. She says she despairs of me; says she cannot go on much longer trying to make a match for me.'

'Your grandfather is intent on finding a young man of good family for you, Florence. He has high standards.' Aunt Lucy was not smiling. A frown of worry had settled on her face. 'Your mama told him that you'd have none of the dashing young men you met in London. You must marry.'

'Grandfather is intent on finding a young man of good income for me, Aunt. He is not in the least concerned about either my happiness or his lofty standards,' Florence replied.

'And you?'

'I, my darling,' she said, 'am intent on marrying Oliver Wainwright.'

* * *

Oliver was taken completely off guard when he called at Balgone with Lucy's Christmas gift. He was shown into the drawing room by the maid and had taken his usual position by the window when the door opened and the girl he had put into a secret compartment of his mind stood before him.

For a moment or two neither spoke. He took in her poised and elegant appearance at a glance. 'Florence. How lovely to see you again.' He clasped her hand warmly and, astonished, saw that he had forgotten how beautiful she was. She wore a dress of green velvet, which made a perfect background for her translucent skin and the dazzling glory of her hair. He looked at the golden-haired girl he once wanted so desperately; he thought with love of Rosie and his child so near to birth, and kept himself aloof from the least intimacy with Florence.

'You are changed, Oliver. You have the air of a man of purpose!' She spoke the words lightly and the warmth of her smile took away any sting of reproach he might have detected.

He had known, since Lucy had mentioned her homecoming, that he would see her and he had asked himself how they would act, face to face, after so long. He knew that he loved only Rosie; but he had often reflected on the speed with which she replaced Florence in his heart. Had Florence, too, given up all thoughts of him?

Now he was relieved that their first words had been spoken. She had not thrown herself into his arms with tears and words of love. How ridiculous of him to have imagined she might.

'And how does a Man of Purpose look, Florence?' he teased. 'Do I have the light of ambition in my eye?' He widened his eyes in jest and the embarrassment of their first encounter after so long was gone.

* * *

Rosie had never had so much time to herself. Her earliest memories were of work; work in the workhouse that even the children shared and work before marriage and since. There had only been the lying-in week after each girl was born, when she'd lain, rigid as an Egyptian mummy, bound from chest to thigh with bolster cases pinned tightly round her body. The old women said it put everything back in place after the birth.

It wasn't going to be like that, this time. This time it would be proper linen binders and her breasts bound too, if she didn't suckle.

Oliver was like a child. He came only at weekends – and when he was with her he played at 'house', just as she and Agnes used to do when they were little – changing round the furniture and setting out the cupboards. Then he left her alone, from Sunday night until Friday; alone with nothing to do but wait – and think. And she wasn't used to being alone. She couldn't sleep, alone. Every night, when she lay alone she awoke at two o'clock. The girl, Iris, slept, the town slept, only Rosie was awake, needing Oliver and the comfort of his arms.

She had started to build a good fire so that it would be in, glowing and reassuring, when she woke. But the bedroom had a tiny fireplace and often the fire went out. It was then that she heard the voice. It never came when Oliver was there or when she was talking to the girl, Iris. At first she used to place her hands over her ears and blot out the sound. Lately she'd been listening.

Her head ached and her eyes burned in the night. She would awaken with a start at the sound of the voice. The voice spoke into her ear. She could tell the direction it came from but when she stared, terrified, into the dark room, there was nothing. And sometimes the voice spoke right inside her head, waking her with its booming tone. 'Go home to your husband and children, Rosie,' it said, louder and louder until she felt her head would burst if she didn't reply.

But how? How to reply to a voice?

There were some exercise books in the house and she wrote down her replies, working by the light of candles. She wrote the replies and she copied the questions. 'Why have you left your husband and children? Sin no more, Rosie,' the voice said.

Rosie wrote the answers, breathing fast and wild, putting the words on paper until her hand lost its grip on the pencil or the questions came faster than she could answer them and then she would cry as if in pain, her tears splashing onto the paper. But still she didn't sleep.

When morning came she was tired and she found herself following Iris around, helping. One day Iris found her wandering upstairs, a shovelful of cinders in her hand, looking for the back door. Iris had laughed about it and assured her that her mam took 'funny turns' when she was expecting, but Rosie knew it was a punishment.

The baby would come in February. Oliver would be with her for a week at Christmas. Perhaps the voice would tire of her and go away.

It was late on Christmas Eve when Oliver arrived at Chapel Street station in Southport. Last-minute buyers filled the crowded shops and he waited his turn in Boothroyd and Rimmer where he bought Rosie a heavy velour cloak, deep purple, trimmed in silver-grey squirrel. It was large enough to conceal her considerable size and handsome enough to be worn later.

He was impatient to see her. Since she had come to him he found himself more strongly devoted to her. Her every need was anticipated by him; he could not bear to see a troubled look in her eyes. He strode as fast as he could through the busy throng and soon was running down the gaslit streets he knew so well to the house where everything that he loved was waiting.

She had left a lamp in the hall and in its glow he saw that she had placed sprigs of holly along the top of the ornate mirror above the half-moon table. There was a new runner on the shiny floorboards and in the drawing room a fire danced in the high marble fireplace throwing gleaming glances off the polished brass fender and reflecting warmly onto the red plush of the armchairs.

Rosie was in the kitchen, up to her elbows in flour, pressing cut circles of pastry into patty tins and filling them from a stoneware jar of mincemeat. There was flour on her nose and in her hair and by reason of her size she was obliged to stand back from the table. She pushed a floury hand into the small of her back and straightened. Her smile was as warm as ever but to Oliver she appeared weary.

'Why are you doing that, love?' he asked gently. 'You don't need to do the cooking yourself. Where's Iris?'

'I let her go home to her family. She's very young you know, only thirteen. It's the first time she's been away from home at Christmas and I think they'll be glad to see her.' She looked apologetic. 'You don't mind, do you, Oliver? She's coming back the day after tomorrow and we can do without her for one day. Her mother has just had a baby. I gave her some food to take home with her. They haven't got much.'

'You're too soft-hearted, Rosie,' he chided. 'I love you for it but you must remember that I'm paying her to help you; not the other way round.'

'I know. I can't get used to having someone work for me. I feel awful when Iris is rushing about, filling coal scuttles and carrying pails of water and I'm sitting there, watching.'

She put the tin in the oven and washed the sticky board before taking off her pinafore and wiping the flour from her face.

'How's my son doing?' Oliver put a hand on her round, swollen belly. 'He's taking up a lot of space.' He felt the child moving under his touch and kissed Rosie's floury cheek.

She pushed him away, smiling. 'You're sure it's going to be a boy, aren't you?' she asked. 'I've only made girls up to now.' A shadow crossed her face. 'I hope my girls are going to have a happy Christmas without me.' Her eyes filled with tears. 'I've sent them three beautiful dolls and a picture book each. I sent them to Agnes to be sure the girls get them. The Hadfields let them see my sister.'

He did not want to be reminded of Rosie's children. They were well cared for, she knew they were, and he did not want to talk about them. 'You're not still worrying about them, are you?' he asked and there was an edge of annoyance in his voice. She had been talking a lot about Jim and the girls lately. He believed that she should pour all her love and all her heart into him and the child she carried for him. 'I thought you'd put all that behind you and wanted to live as my wife?'

'I'm not your wife, though, am I? I never can be. There's to be no more talk of divorce.'

He had upset her and was instantly contrite. He covered her mouth in kisses. 'I love you, love you,' he told her fiercely. 'I don't want you to think about anyone else.'

She pulled herself from his embrace. 'I miss you so much when you aren't here,' she said tearfully. 'Go into the sitting room, Oliver. I'll come in when these mince pies are done.' The Christmas season had been a trial for her. She found herself thinking of the girls, of Jim.

The voice came intermittently. Some nights she slept but she did not feel rested. Her mind was in a turmoil. It was as if her own voice came from afar off. She heard quite clearly what people said, around her, yet she was not always able to reply.

* * *

There were only three weeks to go. Soon the nurse would take up residence and the doctor had been told when to expect a call. Rosie found her thoughts turning away from the present. Agnes wrote, secretly, telling her that the girls were well and that Jim's health had improved. Agnes said they missed her and Rosie began to long to see them again, to be a family once more.

In her mind a terrible plan was forming and she found herself unable to stop from daily working out the details. Letters flew swiftly between Yorkshire and Southport. Agnes was a tower of strength. Agnes would help. Jim was pining for her. The children were refusing food. She would go to them as soon as the baby was born. She would refuse to suckle the child, then she would be able to forget it had ever been born. She would tell Iris to find a wet nurse for the infant.

She'd write a letter of explanation to Oliver. She'd wrap up the exercise books for him and then he'd understand, when he read, what the voice had been saying. He'd never forgive her.

She was unable to face him with the truth ... the truth ... in truth she'd made a dreadful mistake. God would punish her and the children if she didn't repent. Wesley Hadfield's words came back to her, 'The sins of the father shall be upon the children', he had quoted, and she was ashamed. But didn't Wesley himself preach in chapel? And didn't he say that the Lord forgives those who truly repent of their sins?

'Oh, Lord, forgive me!' Rosie prayed, muttering the words to herself when there was no one around to hear.

Her labour pains started, two days early, in the middle of the night, only hours after Oliver had left the house to return to Middlefield. The midwife Oliver had engaged was in residence, sleeping in an attic bedroom. Rosie roused Iris and told her to call Nurse Allenby down.

It was going to come quicker than the others, Rosie knew. Already the cramping waves of pain were coming fast and long. She pulled her knees up, rubbing the soles of her feet on the bottom sheet, gripping the iron bar she could feel underneath the mattress's edge. Iris and the nurse would soon be there. Iris was a sensible girl. There were twelve children in her family and Iris was the eldest. Where was the woman? How long did it take her to get dressed and downstairs?

Rosie heard them, coming down the stairs, their voices a long way off. It was a dream, an awful, painful dream. She heard them talking at the foot of the bed. 'I was with me mam when she had our Kenneth,' Iris was telling Nurse Allenby. 'There's always someone expectin' at our house.'

'Is everything to hand, girl?' Nurse Allenby asked. 'The binders? The napkin and the shawl?'

'Yes. There's new clothes. Everything new. I hope Madam lets me help with the baby. I hope she doesn't get a nursemaid.'

Rosie twisted the sheets, almost tearing them. A hand touched her forehead and she heard the nurse say, 'They're coming good and strong, Mrs Wainwright. It's good, my dear. Good.'

'Mrs Wainwright asked me to find a wet nurse,' Iris was saying in a faraway voice. 'I found one but I told Madam what me mam says. She says it's nice, feeding babies. Like a little bird, filling itself up. I could show Mrs Wainwright how to do it, like me mam does.'

The nurse was pulling the sheet out of Rosie's hand. 'Get the clean towels. Now, Iris. Hurry, girl. The baby's coming.'

It would soon be over. She could catch the train to Bradford – Bradford.

'All right, my dear?' the nurse was saying. 'It's coming. I can see baby's head.' Rosie gritted her teeth, held her breath, grunted against the effort, grasped the woman's apron. 'It's coming too quick, Mrs Wainwright. Too quick for a first baby.' The nurse's strong arms were pressing into her. 'Right, mother. One more push ... Good ... Nearly there ... And again ... Push.'

Rosie fell back, panting for breath. 'I can't! I can't, oh ... No ...' she heard herself wailing before another, final surge of pain took her.

'Here we are, love. Here comes your baby!' Nurse Allenby was cupping the baby's head in her capable hands as the little slippery body eased out of her.

It was over. It was done.

'It's a boy, Mrs Wainwright. A fine, healthy boy. Oh! What a little beauty. He's a big 'un!'

The baby's cries rent the air. The afterbirth slid away from her. It was all over. Rosie turned her face to the wall.

Nurse Allenby didn't like the look of the mother. The woman was clearly in a fever. She lay there, white-faced, two spots of flaming colour in her cheeks. She wondered whether to send the girl, Iris, for the doctor. No, the girl was a simpleton. She'd sponge her patient down and get a drop of quinine for her in the morning.

Nurse Allenby knew how long first babies took to bring into the world. No, this mother had had at least one child before. And Mrs Wainwright wouldn't look at the baby. The mother had turned her face to the wall when she handed it to her. She'd refused to hold it. It was not as if it had been a difficult birth. It had been quick and easy.

Nurse Allenby tucked the sheets round Rosie. 'You, sleep, dear. I'll take baby into my room. He won't need milk for hours.'

Rosie left the house at seven o'clock that morning after creeping into the nurse's room where the child slept peacefully. She would not pick him up. She stroked his dark, downy hair and he stirred. She'd call him Oliver. He would have to be Oliver Hadfield, since she couldn't put his father's name on the birth certificate.

'Oliver Hadfield,' she whispered. 'I can't take you with me. You belong to your father.'

Her bag had been packed for a week. She took with her all the letters she had received from Bradford, so that she could not be traced. She wrote a letter to Oliver and left it with the three exercise books full of her rambling thoughts.

She felt light and cold and wonderfully free as she made her way to the station. Unless guilt came to torture her, she thought, her mind would be calm. She was doing what was right. The voice would cease.

There wasn't a train until ten and she was afraid of being found, if they sent out to search for her. She bought her ticket and left the station. There was time to call in at the registry office before the train left.

Chapter Eighteen

Oliver let himself in on Friday night and found Iris standing before him in the hall.

'She's gone, sir! I didn't have your address. The midwife left the next morning. I couldn't reach you. She left the baby behind. I took him to Mrs Marsden's. She's the wet nurse. Five shillings a week, sir. She's nursing him until she knows what you want to do with him. Me mam said she'll take him in for you, if you want.' The words came out in a rush as if she'd been dreading telling him.

'What are you saying, girl?' Oliver shook her by the shoulder. 'Is this some kind of a joke? Answer me!'

Iris faced him, trembling. 'Mrs Wainwright had her baby last Sunday, after you left. The baby's at Mrs Marsden's. She's the wet nurse. Madam told me to ask her. Madam left the house the next morning and I don't know where she's gone. I knew she hadn't gone to you or you'd have brought her back.'

A feeling of cold fear washed over him. Could it be true? Would the girl lie over a thing like this? He released her shoulder and raced up the stairs. Their bedroom was empty. 'Rosie!' he called out, over and over. 'Rosie! Where are you?' He crashed from room to room. 'She must be here.'

There was no trace of her. The wardrobe held only his clothes. Her brushes were gone, where they'd lain beside his. He couldn't believe it. Now he came down the stairs, heavily: bewildered.

'Sit down, sir,' Iris was saying. 'It's not my fault. You won't tell me to go, will you? She's not in the house. Here's the parcel she left.'

A fire blazed in the drawing room. Oliver took the parcel and sat with it, turning it over in his hands, not wanting to know what it might contain. Iris made coffee and brought it to him and when she left the room he slowly opened the parcel and took out a letter from inside.

'Oliver, my love,' she had started, in her untidy handwriting. 'You'll never forgive me. It's hard to write this. God wants me to go back to my husband and children. I must repent of my sins. I am a wicked woman but Jim has forgiven me. Voices talk to me in the night and then they talk to me when there's nobody else around. The Voice says I am a sinner. "Go home to your children and sin no more", I hear it over and over, louder and louder and the Voice will not go away until I leave you. The Voice will not follow me to Yorkshire. Please don't try to find me. I'm not going to live in Bradford. Agnes has found us a house on the moors, where Jim will get better.'

He opened up the parcel and found the exercise books. They were pages of scribblings. She had underlined the Voice every time she wrote it; her handwriting almost indecipherable. The book dropped from his fingers. They were the scribblings of madness. Rosie had gone mad and he had not even known.

His thoughts went back to her, to her sleeplessness, her tears, her turning away from his kisses. He'd imagined it was normal behaviour for women in her condition. Women spoke of strange cravings they had, out-of-character demands they made at these times. And he'd done nothing, waiting for it to pass.

And now she was gone. All that he loved was gone from him. It was not anger he felt now but a terrible, cold loneliness. How could he go on, without Rosie? Who would he live for? How could it end like this; his love for Rosie and their love for the child? Hadn't she wanted the child? Had he been blind?

Finally he rang for Iris. 'Take me to see the child,' he said.

He followed Iris through the cold dark streets, past the big houses and down smaller roads. They turned into a street of mean houses, cramped and close. Iris stopped and nodded to him. Oliver rapped on the door.

A big woman, plain and unwelcoming, showed him in. 'Your baby's in here,' she said, opening a door into a small, unheated room to the right of the front door. She went on, grumbling in rough tones, 'It's about time someone came to see him, the poor mite. Is the mother dead or something? Why did she send him with a house-maid? Why hasn't she come for him? And I haven't been paid yet.'

By the wall stood a high-sided wooden cot and the woman reached inside, lifted out a long white bundle and placed it, heavy, in his arms. She left the room.

Oliver gazed at the little scrap of humanity, the tiny face of his son, lost in a welter of nightdress, woollens and shawl.

'How could your mother leave you, little one?' he whispered. 'Oh, my God. How am I going to bring you up?'

The baby opened his eyes and stared, unblinking, into the eyes of his father and in that moment, as he looked, a new emotion burst into bloom in Oliver, a feeling he had never experienced; a fierce protectiveness that was religious in its intensity. He would never let any harm come to this child; his child. He would defend it with his life.

Tears sprang to his eyes and splashed onto the tiny face. He took a corner of the flannel nightgown and wiped both their faces. How could she have left her baby? Rosie wasn't impulsive, she hadn't left on a whim, and Oliver knew with a sudden, cold certainty that she would never come back. Unless, he thought, she came back for the child.

He held his son to his cheek, felt the snuffling of the baby's face against his own. This feeling, the strongest he had ever had in his life, had shaken him with its power. He was a father. Was he alone in feeling this? Every minute, somewhere in the world, fatherhood came to some man, so why had nobody told him it would be like this? And now that he knew this emotion, this overpowering love for his son ... his own ... his flesh and blood, he must make plans for the future.

He placed the child carefully in the cot and slipped from the room. There was a table in the tiny hallway and he put two gold sovereigns on it, for the baby's milk. Then he left the house, and went back to the home he had created for Rosie and was now to be his son's. He sat by the fire, alone, thinking deeply and more seriously than he had ever done.

'What choices have I?' he asked himself. Then, as if to answer, 'I could take the child to Middlefield ... engage a nanny and a governess ... sell this house and buy a house in Middlefield.'

But what would this mean for the child ... to be brought up by a succession of paid helpers ... to have no proper home ... to be stigmatised as the illegitimate son of a marketeer? No. His son must have better than that.

He could marry. But he knew, with the thought, that he could not take a woman to himself for any other reason than that he loved her. And what if Rosie came back for her son? What if she tried to claim him? She had every right, since the child was illegitimate. Had his love for Rosie turned to bitterness? No. But he could not bear to lose the child as well.

He discovered that he could not contemplate the idea that the child might be returned to his mother. If the child had been of their marriage then he, as the father, would have absolute rights. Mothers, legitimately married women, had no rights over their children, he knew that. But Rosie was not his lawful wife.

Fear came to him at the thought that he could lose his son. He must make it impossible for Rosie to claim him. If she returned for the child he must be sure that she would not be believed in her assertion that she was his mother. So – who knew that she was the mother? Iris knew.

Iris's silence would have to be bought. The midwife knew, but she had flown, back to Manchester, the day after the birth, afraid she would be blamed for Rosie's desertion. Rosie had no friends here. She had never left the house. No doctor had been called.

He must find a woman who would care for the child as her own, here in the house where he was born. His son must have a normal life, the proper home that he, his father, had never known.

There was only one woman who could do it, only one woman with so little to lose that she would gladly leave her old life behind.

Only one woman who, in spite of her shortcomings, had absolute loyalty. There was only one woman who bore the name of Wainwright. Dolly.

Leach had never married his stepmother. Dolly's name was still, legally, Wainwright. If she would register his son as her own – live here in Southport – then he, Oliver, would come at weekends as he did now – they could conceal from everyone the fact that the child was not Dolly's.

His son would have a birth certificate with the name of Wainwright upon it. The child must never know that he, Oliver, was his father. He would assume the role of the child's older brother.

Wasn't there a story in the Bible about a child who was cared for by his own mother, but who knew her as his nursemaid? His son would be cared for by his father and know him as his brother. It had been done before. He thought the biblical child was Moses.

He went into the hall for his coat. There was just enough time to catch his trains and be in Middlefield before anyone had missed him.

* * *

Suttonford station, constructed since he had left the estate nearly five years before, was deserted but for a uniformed man who collected the tickets at the gate. There was no sign of Wilf in the little goods yard and Oliver made his way to Hollinbank unobserved.

A bitter wind blew across the bare fields he had last crossed in the heat of August. Now he kept to the path where ice glazed the brown, stagnant water lying in deep-rutted cart tracks. Snow had fallen overnight in a thin layer and drifts settled into the margins of the winding lane.

Smoke billowed from the chimney above the familiar cottage. He hoped to find her alone. Had Wilf Leach left the estate? He'd seen him often, in Middlefield, drunk in drunken company. Sir Philip Oldfield didn't give his workers time or money for that kind of living.

What would she think of his proposition? He knew that Dolly would 'keep her counsel' even if she refused to help him. She had never been a gossip and he knew his secret would be safe with her.

He thought it strange that nobody was working on the land. Even in the worst of winter weather there were jobs to be done, gamekeepers ferreting, men cutting wood, the gravel drive to be raked daily. Sir Philip kept them all busy when he was in residence. Perhaps the family was away. Oliver ran the mile to the cottage. The fewer the people who saw him, the fewer the questions asked. He was gasping for breath by the time he reached the house.

'What brings you here?' Dolly said, the moment he opened the door. 'It's got to be summat serious. You'll not be paying a social call.' She carried on shovelling ash from under the fire, making no pretence of being pleased to see him. A tiny girl played at the table with a heap of clothes pegs, humming to herself, not turning her head to look at Oliver directly but peering sideways from under the mop of ginger curls she had inherited from her mother.

'Where's Wilf?' Oliver closed the door behind him and looked around the room that had once been his home. It was even shabbier and smaller than he remembered. The paint was a dingy yellow where it still clung to the rough plaster walls; the unvarnished furniture was marked and cracked. Dolly had never shown interest in home-making, but it was clean and the child looked well fed and healthy. 'Is he still working for Sir Philip?' he asked.

'No. He lives in Middlefield with that harlot from the village.'

'Stop shovelling ash, Dolly. Sit down and listen to me.' He took off his overcoat and warmed his hands at the fire, smacking them together and turning them in the heat. The child began to cry.

'It's all right, Lizzie. It's only your Uncle Oliver!' Dolly picked her up and held her over one hip. 'Or is it your big brother? I don't know how you're related to him.' She set the child down in front of the fire.

'We're not related at all,' Oliver said. 'She hasn't got a drop of Wainwright blood in her. And neither have you.'

'Well, what does that make me then? I married your father before our Tommy was born. He's not a bastard!' Dolly said defensively. 'I'm not going to stand here and be insulted. And if you and our Tommy are brothers you must be related to me – at least related by marriage!'

'Sit down, Dolly, I've something to tell you.' He'd get straight to the point. They could be arguing for hours about relationships. Dolly couldn't work these things out for herself. He sat down heavily on the wooden settle and stretched his legs towards the fire.

'I've got a son, Dolly. A baby son, not a week old and no one to care for him.' It was going to take an effort to ask her what had to be asked. 'I know you're not my mother but you are family. And family's better than strangers. I want you to look after him!'

'Like father, like son, then, is it? Where is she? The mother? Is she dead?' Her voice was as sharp as ever.

'No. She's gone back to her husband. Left the baby with me.' Oliver would not tell her more. Dolly need not know everything.

Dolly placed her child back at the table. 'You want to bring him here then?' she asked casually, as if it were an everyday occurrence.

'No.' Oliver tried to judge from her tone of voice how she'd taken the news and if she would accept his plan. If he'd been dealing with a trader, a businessman, he could strike a bargain. But Dolly? Women? Women never jumped in the expected direction, though she had everything to gain from it.

'What do you want?' Her arms were folded like a washerwoman's as she waited.

'I want you to live in Southport. I have a house there. A house much better than anything you'll ever get for yourself. I'll pay for everything. You need have no worry about that. I'll put money in the bank for you. A year's money at a time and enough for you to pay for a maid and a woman for the rough work.' He spoke in a low, earnest voice and saw that she had taken him seriously.

'Me? Me with a house and a maid?' Dolly was taken aback for once. 'Me? In another woman's house?'

'It's not another woman's. You'll be in charge.'

'What if she comes back? What happens then?'

'She'll not come back. The hardest part for her was leaving us in the first place,' he said bitterly. 'She's abandoned my child and she'll never see him again. I'll have him registered in the name of Wainwright as soon as I've got a name for him and that'll settle that. She's lost all rights. She can't claim him if you'll agree to my plan.'

Oliver looked now at the child who had jumped from the chair and played on the peg rug at her mother's feet. He wondered at the ways of women. He did not understand how Rosie, so gentle and loving, could desert her child, yet Dolly, hard and calculating Dolly, could care so well for her own and even care adequately for another woman's.

He looked down at the rosy-cheeked child whose vibrant colouring was the more noticeable against her drab dress. There was not a trace of her father's coarseness in her and it was hard to imagine Wilf having had any part in her procreation.

'But I'll not have Wilf Leach in my house,' he insisted. 'You'd have to go back to your old name. Call yourself Dolly Wainwright again. You see, Dolly, I'd have to ask you to register the child in your name, as if he were yours.' He looked intently at his stepmother. 'We'd be breaking the law, claiming that you were his mother, but I want to keep him. He'll never know I'm his father. He must think he's yours. You aren't married to Leach, are you?'

'I'm still Dolly Wainwright,' she replied quietly, as if confessing a guilty secret. 'Wilf never did marry me. I called myself Mrs Leach to stop the neighbours talking.'

'Then the child is Elizabeth Wainwright?'

'Yes.'

'Has she got a birth certificate?'

'Yes.'

'With just your name and hers?'

Dolly appeared to hesitate for a moment; she was holding something back.

'Well?'

'I put your father's name on the birth certificate. I didn't want her to be illegitimate. I didn't want her ever to know that Wilf Leach is her father. I shouldn't have done it. I was scared they'd find out but nothing happened. Nobody asked. She's got Joe's name on her birth certificate, same as you and our Tommy. He wouldn't have minded, Joe wouldn't. He was a good man.'

Oliver interrupted her, 'Show me the birth certificate.'

She went to the wooden settle and lifted the lid. It was here she kept her treasured belongings. She took out a long envelope and handed it over. Inside were her marriage certificate, his father's death certificate and, next to it, to his amazement, a certificate of birth.

'Elizabeth Wainwright,' he read. 'Mother: Dorothea Amy Wainwright. Cook. Father: Joseph Edward Wainwright. Quarrier.' It was signed by the registrar, dated and stamped.

'They didn't ask?' he said, looking hard at Dolly. 'Didn't they check? Did nobody ask to see the father? Did you take the baby with you?'

'No. I just went in, told them lies—' she confessed. 'I went in in me best clothes, so they wouldn't recognise me, just in case. But there was nobody there that knew me. I was going to run for it if they challenged me.' She managed to look crestfallen and defiant at the same time.

'Then you can do it again, Dolly,' he spoke sharply. 'We'll put him down as yours and Dad's. He'll be legitimate and when the children grow up and ask questions we can tell them Dad died just before he was born.'

She got to her feet and looked down at Oliver as she said, in her normal aggressive way, 'You're not in a position to do all the demanding, are yer? It's your kid as needs a mother!'

She went to the window and looked out. Oliver waited for her to speak. From his side it appeared a good solution for both of them. He asked himself what she had here; an empty life, no man, only her poor wage to keep herself and her child. She had no protection if illness struck.

Yet she was an obstinate woman and he could not be sure of her response; not until she agreed. Then he'd be sure. There was great loyalty in Dolly that would be brought to defend all she had charge of. But would she do it? She was a good-looking woman. Perhaps she hoped to marry again. 'Could you live without Wilf? Live respectably and not find another man?' he asked her.

'I'd not need a man. Not if I had enough money. I'll be glad if I never see Wilf Leach,' she replied, still with her back to him. 'I never want to hear the name of Leach again.'

She turned and walked towards the fire where she leaned against the mantelshelf, her head cocked to one side in the mannerism he knew so well. He didn't think she'd refuse the offer. There were no signs of prosperity in her clothing or the furnishings of the room, but it was impossible to know what would sway Dolly. Her expression gave no clue to her thoughts.

'I'll settle two hundred pounds on each of them, yours and mine, and we'll tell them it came from Dad,' he said. 'It will be good for him to have a companion as he's growing up, like I had in Tommy. I'll never treat my child better than yours. Elizabeth will be a big sister to him.'

'You're asking a lot. You want me to put a lie on the birth certificate for you; bring the child up. What if you get married?'

'Dolly! For God's sake don't talk rubbish. I'll never marry.'

He had to do something, offer her something now to sway her. 'If you do this for me we'll have it all made legal. The house and all that will be yours. Yes, yours! In your name! I'll have the child brought up the way I want and, in that, you must do as I say. He's my son. I'll come to the house as often as I can. But I don't want you to tell a soul here, at Suttonford. No word must get about. As far as they'll be concerned Dolly Leach and Lizzie Leach will have gone.'

There was a moment's pause before he repeated, 'Dolly and Lizzie Leach will have left the estate and no one will know where they have gone.' She was hesitating. 'You'll be the widow of Joe Wainwright; Mrs Dorothea Wainwright and her daughter, Elizabeth

Wainwright. In Southport nobody will ever know you as anything else,' he told her.

He saw that she was nearly there and pushed her, as he did with the men he dealt with. 'Well? Will you do it? I have to have an answer before my train leaves.'

'I'll do it,' she said at last. 'I'll pack our stuff up and you can carry it to the station with you. Me and Lizzie'll be at The Pheasant tomorrow morning.' The old sly look crossed her face. 'You'd better give me some money for the train – and a carriage from the station. Lizzie can't walk all that way in the cold.'

'What about the Oldfields? You can't tell them where you're going.' The last piece in the jigsaw had not yet been placed. Oliver would not have his son's existence revealed to the Oldfield family, or have them trace Dolly.

'Haven't you heard?' Dolly looked surprised. 'Sir Philip Oldfield was thrown from his horse last week when he was out with the hunt. The village has never stopped talking about it. He's in a wheelchair. Crippled. They say he'll never walk again. They won't be wanting three cooks any more. I don't think there'll be much entertaining done at Suttonford.'

* * *

Oliver sent Dolly to the registry office in Southport, to put Dorothea Amy Wainwright down as the mother's name and Joseph Edward Wainwright as the father. It proved just as easy here as it had been in Middlefield to give false information. Nobody asked to see the baby.

He would think of him as his Moses child, but Oliver called him Edward, after his own father and Cromwell to link his son's name to his. 'Edward Cromwell Wainwright,' he read proudly when she returned with the certificate. 'Don't start calling him Teddy. That's my first rule. Push him out every day in the baby carriage; rain or snow. And make sure that the Marsden woman is feeding him well. I won't have her child fed first and Edward last.'

His bag was packed for his return to Middlefield. There were a few last-minute instructions to be given before he went back to his old life. At the moment he was not needed here. In a month he'd come over to see that all was well with his son.

'Buy some clothes for yourself and Lizzie. There's a woman in the next street who sells hats. Get yourself a hat or two and some for Lizzie. You're not in the country now. In Tulketh Street there's a registry office for servants. Go down there tomorrow. Engage a woman for the washing. You've got Iris to help you with the children. You'll do the cooking yourself. There's money in the bank for you and you can spend a bit getting yourself smartened up. There are good dressmakers in the town. You'll find their names in the paper.'

This advice, he knew, would be taken with alacrity. Dolly already had fallen in love with the town and to his great amusement had begun to give herself airs, to talk of how she would run 'her' household. He pulled on his leather gloves, pushed one hand deep into the pocket of his overcoat, lifted the bag and inclined his head towards the door so she'd open it for him.

'If you have to get a message to me, go to the station and give a letter to the stationmaster. He'll see I get it the same day. If there's nothing to worry about don't bother me. I'll be back in a few weeks' time.' If he ran, he could be at the station in five minutes.

'Oh yes! Anything else?' Dolly asked with a fair attempt at sarcasm. He knew she wanted to show him that she was in charge. 'Surely there's something more I can be doing in my spare time?'

He turned as he reached the gate. The old temptation, the old habit he'd had of having the last word with his stepmother suddenly and mischievously reasserted itself. His parting words to her, which he delivered with a cheeky grin were, 'Aye. You could maybe learn to act like a lady! I'll pay for your lessons!'

If it hadn't been for the fact that the neighbours might hear, Dolly would have thought of a good rejoinder. This time she was

221

going to be looked up to and respected, not looked down on like she'd been in the village. Neither would she be at everyone's beck and call.

She was still a good-looking woman and, if she did as he asked, she could make more of her life than she'd done so far. A child or two wouldn't take all her time. Mrs Dorothea Wainwright she'd be known as. 'Dolly' was too common a name for a woman with a house of her own, a maid and a woman to do the rough stuff. She'd never dreamed he had a house like this. He must be doing well.

She'd been round the town, looking at the shops. There was money in the bank to spend and plenty to spend it on. Edward was a contented baby and she was going to 'bring him up proper', just as she had with Oliver and Tommy, only this time she'd have help. She'd make sure she got good help too; none of them lazy creatures the big house had tolerated.

'By gum, Lizzie,' she said to the bewildered child. 'I wonder who she was. Who Edward's mother was? She was either daft or had plenty of her own money to leave all this behind. She must have been one of the la-di-dah women he likes so much.'

Chapter Nineteen

They drew up the partnership deeds two months before Albert's wedding. Now Wainwright and Billington was jointly owned, and Oliver could use his inheritance to purchase shares and property.

First, he dealt with the allowances to Laura Mawdesley and Florence. He was generous. The fund he set up for them would bring in a lot more than the thousand a year Bill had provided under the terms of the will. The Mawdesleys would benefit from his astuteness to the tune of an extra five hundred pounds a year. It need not be administered by him as it had previously been. Correspondence between their lawyers and annual signing would no longer be necessary. It would save Laura Mawdesley any embarrassment she might feel.

It suited Oliver to continue living at The Pheasant. It gave him more time to study the movements of the stock market and plan his investments. He gambled on the exchange occasionally, trusting his hunches, finding they seldom let him down. He purchased under several names. It was quite legitimate and ensured that a seller was unaware of the buying power of the purchaser.

Sir Philip Oldfield was selling. Shares in the Manchester Trading Company came on to the open market and Oliver bought. Land on the Suttonford estate, near to Middlefield, came into his hands.

'You make money faster than anyone I know,' Albert told him over supper one evening, a few weeks before his and Edith's wedding. 'You make it. I spend it! What drives you on? Do you think you'll stop and start enjoying yourself when you've got enough?'

It was a warm May evening. They were going to eat supper in the parlour and then sit outdoors on the bench in the stable yard. Edith had sent strict instructions that their presence was unwelcome. She had last-minute things to see to.

'I don't have any inclination to stop, Albert. I just like to watch it growing. I'm sure I'll spend it when the time comes but now … Well, there's nowt to spend it on.'

Mrs Billington cleared away the plates and they took tankards and a jug of ale into the sunlit stable yard. They sat on the bench, closed their eyes and leaned against the high stone wall, letting the sun warm their faces.

'How many guests will there be at the wedding? I've never made a speech before,' Oliver said lazily. 'Can I write it down and read it out or do I have to memorise it?'

He was making light of it but privately thought that he'd need a stiff drink or two before facing what promised to be an assembly of all the local families of importance.

'You'd best memorise it.' Albert poured ale into their tankards and handed one to Oliver. 'Did you know Florence Mawdesley and her mother have accepted their invitations?'

Oliver's tankard clattered to the ground. 'How've you got them to come?'

Albert looked momentarily surprised by his reaction then could barely conceal his enjoyment at Oliver's discomfiture. 'What are you getting alarmed about?' he said. 'I thought you'd given up any aspirations towards Florence.'

'Are you pulling my leg?' Oliver said. His eyes narrowed as he tried to ascertain if Albert was mocking him. No, he was telling the truth. No doubt at all. They could almost read one another's thoughts. 'I didn't think they were that friendly.'

'Oh, aye. The Claytons are big noises in the church. Edith's dad's the treasurer of the parochial church council and her mother's the leader of the Mothers' Union.'

Oliver still did not see why these revelations should have any bearing on the fact that the Mawdesleys were coming to the wedding.

Albert continued proudly, 'Edith and Florence taught Sunday school and had singing lessons at the same place. I suppose the Mawdesleys couldn't really refuse without upsetting half the ruddy congregation.'

'Oh, I see.' Oliver thought privately that nothing would induce Laura Mawdesley to accept an invitation if she knew he'd be there. 'Tell Mrs Mawdesley that I'm to be best man,' he said, 'and I'll wager they don't turn up.'

* * *

Laura wheeled her father down to the lake. Sunlight dappled the water through the branches of the trees and a slight breeze stirred it, further out, towards the little island.

Laura sighed as she pulled the long handle, securing the brake on his wheelchair. 'I love Suttonford, Papa,' she said. 'I want to come home.' She adjusted the shawl over her father's lifeless legs. 'Are you comfortable?'

'Yes.' He scanned the lake. 'I see everything differently from this angle, though I prefer the view from a saddle.'

'You've been so brave, Papa.' Laura sounded melancholy.

'You haven't brought me here simply to look at the lake, Laura,' he said impatiently. 'My legs may be useless but my mind hasn't followed suit. What is it?'

'I can't pay the servants' salaries, Papa,' Laura said. 'And I owe the tradesmen money.'

'How much do you need?'

'Three hundred pounds,' she confessed.

'I sold land and some stocks last week.' He smiled thinly and patted her hand where it lay on the basketwork arm. 'Don't excite yourself. You shall have it.'

'Oh, Papa.' Laura sniffed delicately into a handkerchief. 'You're so good. It won't be for long. I'll leave Churchgate and come home to you and mother when Florence is settled.'

'Has she found a suitor?' Sir Philip asked sharply. 'She's twenty, isn't she? If she waits much longer nobody will have her. It's time she was married.'

'Oh, Papa. You've no idea how impossible she is.' Laura recovered fast from her mood of self-abnegation. Now she glared out over the lake and spoke of her dissatisfaction. 'Half the young men in the county seek her favour. She behaves as if they were idiots.'

She turned to face Sir Philip and her face was pink with annoyance. 'Since that dreadful time after Uncle Bill died she's never so much as looked twice at a man.'

Sir Philip eyed her inquisitively. 'What dreadful time?'

There was a pause before Laura went on. 'I never told you, Papa. You would have been so angry.'

'Well?' Sir Philip appeared to be losing patience with her. 'Tell me now. I assume she developed a passion for someone unsuitable. Who was it?'

She ground the heel of her shoe into the short grass. 'It was Oliver Wainwright!' she said. 'She had a girlish fancy for him. It was dreadful.' Sir Philip clenched his hands tightly but Laura did not notice this sign of his anger and went on, self-pitying. 'The child practically swooned every time she heard his name. He encouraged her. She met him in secret. It was awful! She told me that they were going to elope – that he'd asked her to marry him. She declared undying love for him. Oh, it was too distressing.'

'And now?'

'It's all over,' Laura said emphatically. 'I'm sure of it. She has met him once or twice at Balgone. She never speaks of him. It has gone – her affection for him.' She looked imploringly at Sir Philip. 'But where will we find a husband for her when she's so impossible to please?'

'I'll give it some thought.' Sir Philip slapped angrily at a fly that had alighted on the shawl. 'Let's move from here. Push me to the yard, Laura. I'll take a look at the horses.'

He inspected his stable and demanded that he be returned to the house in time for an appointment he had made with the lawyer.

'Take me to the study,' Sir Philip told Laura. 'I have business to discuss.'

She wheeled him to the study and left him there.

'Well, Lloyd,' he began as soon as Laura had departed. 'Did you find out? Who's buying my land?' Lloyd pulled at his side whiskers and looked uncomfortable. Sir Philip was impatient. 'Well? I know it's the same buyer as before. There's no hesitation. No quibbling about price. The man just buys if it belongs to the estate.'

Lloyd's eyes left Sir Philip's face. He looked, as usual, slightly to the right of his ear. 'It's Wainwright,' he said flatly.

Sir Philip drew in his breath sharply. 'I suspected it,' he said at last, 'but where's the money coming from? The mills can't be bringing in that kind of profit.' He looked hard at the lawyer. 'Can they, Lloyd? It makes my blood boil to think of it.'

'He's gone into partnership with his friend, Billington. Wainwright has taken his original investment, the amount he inherited – out of the mill.' Lloyd's glance rested for a few seconds on Sir Philip's face. 'It seems he's intent upon it. Slowly but surely he's buying you up,' he declared.

'Why, Lloyd?'

'Old scores?' Lloyd asked shrewdly.

'Nonsense!' Sir Philip replied sharply. 'I've done no more than any man would do to protect his property.'

'There's something else. Something I ought not to tell you, but I think it may have some implication for you when you come to make provision for after your death.'

'Well?'

'Lucy Grandison has changed her will. She is leaving her house and an annuity to Laura. She's leaving half her estate to Florence.'

Here he paused, as if afraid that the news would be too much for the old baronet. 'The rest goes to Oliver Wainwright,' he said.

'Christ!'

Lloyd had never heard Sir Philip blaspheme. He looked at him anxiously. 'There's no possibility of her changing her mind, Sir Philip. I have no influence over her. I couldn't use it if I had.'

'We must get it back, Lloyd. At all costs we must get my property back.' Sir Philip's face was pale and set. A muscle moved at the corner of his mouth, pulling it sideways in a stiff grimace.

Lloyd went on tonelessly, 'So you must make provision for Florence. She will inherit Suttonford. Godfrey ... I'm afraid ...'

'I know, Lloyd,' Sir Philip interrupted him angrily. 'My son is a wastrel. Florence is the one I must consider. My granddaughter must marry.'

'You must look to her to make a good match, Sir Philip,' Lloyd said. 'She must marry a man of means.'

'She'll marry well, Lloyd,' Sir Philip said coldly. 'I'll see to it that the estate is in competent hands before I die.'

* * *

Laura was alone in her sitting room. She poured a large measure of brandy and steadied herself against the chiffonier. How had it happened? When had events taken the disastrous turn they had? Had they remained in London for another year she would have found a suitor for Florence. Sir Philip and the Wainwright creature were to blame. Father must take responsibility for the outcome; first for refusing to renew their tenure on the house in Belgravia and properly fund Florence's debut, and second for allowing that upstart Wainwright to have access to her.

If Father had had Florence's welfare at heart he'd have refused them this Middlefield house; he'd have insisted on their living at Suttonford and he'd have made her marry a boy of good family.

Remembering yesterday's scene with her father Laura dabbed her brow with the cuff of her sleeve and rapidly drained the glass.

'There's nothing for it, Laura,' Sir Philip had told her when Lloyd had gone and they were alone. His face, normally tender in her presence, had taken on the hard expression she knew so well. No amount of cajoling would get him to change his mind. Florence took after her grandfather in his inflexibility.

'How can you, Papa?' she'd protested. 'Do you have no feeling for me – or for Florence? She cannot marry a vile, low-born peasant.'

'Oliver Wainwright hardly fits your description. He is of low birth but he has risen above it.'

'Six years ago, Papa, he was a farm labourer. One of your own workers,' she'd snapped in anger. 'It is not enough that Lucy has given him a superficial air of gentility and that he has a little money!'

'He has a lot of money, Laura. And most of it is rightfully ours. Wainwright has enough to save the estate and maintain our standards.' Her father had risen to her own fury. 'And, what is more, he wants to be custodian of Suttonford. He's bought every parcel of land I've sold and every wretched hovel on it. He'll not tire of it. If he wants Florence for a wife you will see to it that she welcomes him. Without Wainwright's money we are done for.'

Laura rallied. 'He may not wish to marry Florence. A man of his type would prefer a coarser woman. An actress or ...'

'Enough, Laura! Speak to Florence. Tell her that Wainwright is welcome to call.'

* * *

Albert's wedding day dawned clear and hot. It was set to be a real 'scorcher' Oliver thought when he opened his eyes and found that his head ached from too much wine the night before. There were dozens of little Billingtons from all over the country staying at The Pheasant and it seemed to Oliver that they were all running around outside his door.

He groaned as he heard Leonard Billington calling, 'Oliver! Albert! Come on, you two. Breakfast's ready.' He was going to make the most of his role today. Oliver dragged himself from bed. 'The barber'll be here in a minute. I want you two done first,' Leonard added, noisily.

The wedding was set for midday and as the hour drew near Albert and Oliver left The Pheasant and walked together up Rivergate to the little park behind the Town Hall. Sparrow Park was hardly a park, just a few square yards of grass, five or six trees and a bench seat. But the view was spectacular, so high above the cattle market. Trains pulled out of the station and disappeared in a cloud of steam through the tunnel, only to reappear a mile away, like toys crossing the Cheshire plain.

'Nervous?' Oliver asked.

'A bit. I'll be all right when the church part's over. How about you?'

'I'll be happy when the speech is over!' Oliver put an arm around Albert's shoulders for a second. They had never been demonstrative; there was no need for declarations of friendship and support between them. It was there and they knew it. He gave Albert a shove and grinned. 'Come on! Let's get round to the church,' he said. 'The bells are starting up.'

A crowd had gathered in the market place to watch the wedding parties arrive and the bells were pealing out joyfully above their heads as they entered the church and took their seats.

Murmurings behind them grew in volume as guests entered the pews. Oliver turned his head and saw that the church was full. Florence and her mother were seated at the opposite side of the aisle, a little further back. She wore a dress of pale blue satin, gathered into her waist, bustled and trimmed in white pleated silk. She caught his eye and smiled.

Heavy doors were being pulled back, and the congregation fell silent as the organist swelled the background music in the waiting church to a resounding anthem. Oliver and Albert turned to watch the bride approach on her father's arm.

Edith's auburn hair was taken up under a circle of pale yellow roses. A veil of cream lace fell around her shoulders. Her dress was made of filmy white silk, with pearls at the high neckline and the deep point in front of her tiny waist.

Albert, normally debonair, seemed about to be overcome by the momentous occasion and Oliver had to grip his elbow and steer him forward to stand beside his bride.

Oliver was acutely conscious of the presence of Florence and her mother all through the ceremony. He wanted to turn around, to catch her eyes on him as Albert and Edith made their vows.

He gave the bridesmaid his arm as they followed the bride and groom out into the sunlight. Now, as he passed Florence he gave a self-conscious smile. It was a feature of her beauty, he thought, that her grey eyes reflected the colour of her clothes, so that today her eyes were like the summer sky outside. He could not help but think back to the days of his innocence when he had had the effrontery to demand that they be allowed to marry. Did she remember it? Was she thinking, as he was, that Albert and Edith might never have met but for them?

The crowd in the market square made a pathway for the wedding group as they crossed the square to The Swan, calling out good wishes to the couple as they covered the few yards to Edith's old home.

A wedding breakfast was set in the marquee tent behind the house and there Mr and Mrs Clayton and the Billingtons received their guests with Albert and Edith relaxed and happy beside them.

Oliver drank three glasses of champagne as the toasts were being drunk. He had rehearsed his speech so many times that, his agitation calmed by the champagne, he simply stood up and recited it without a tremor.

Now, at last, his duties were over and he could mingle with the guests. Most of the town's dignitaries were there, many of Middlefield's wealthy merchant families had been invited and Oliver moved easily amongst them, respected and accepted in their midst.

To his surprise Laura Mawdesley appeared quite unconcerned to find Oliver in attendance as Albert's best man. She spoke to him as though they had never had even a difference of opinion. 'Your friend and his bride make a lovely couple, Mr Wainwright,' she said as Oliver approached their table.

'They do. Will you be at the ball this evening?' he replied in his most formal manner.

'Yes. I expect you to ask Florence and me to dance,' Laura said.

What was the woman saying? Her eyes still held their look of cold dislike for him and yet her manner was almost flirtatious. Oliver didn't let a trace of the astonishment he felt at her response appear in his face as he smiled back and nodded his head in acquiescence. Had the sun and the wine so affected her? Was she so sure that no danger remained in allowing himself and Florence to meet socially? He glanced at Florence and saw that she was blushing.

'Mama. Let us go and speak to Mr and Mrs Clayton.' Florence sounded agitated. 'We have barely had a word with them the whole afternoon. Excuse us, Oliver.'

* * *

The windows of the Town Hall were opened wide to let the cool evening air into the ballroom. A courtroom and the debating chambers were being used by guests who did not want to join the youngsters in dancing and the talk was loud and unrestrained since champagne was still being served.

Oliver found Florence and her mother in the mayor's parlour, a panelled room next to the ballroom where the highest-ranked guests were assembled. Florence had changed for the dancing into a dress of white organza and Laura, elegant and cool in grey silk, chatted to the mayor.

'Florence. Here you are!' Oliver said, feigning surprise as if he had come across them by accident. 'Are you and your mother going to join us in the ballroom? I've come to claim my dance.'

'Mama! I'm going to the ballroom with Oliver.' Florence tapped her mother discreetly on the elbow and took his arm.

It gave Oliver a feeling of pride, escorting her, surely the prettiest girl there. They were making sets for the eightsome reel and he led her on to the floor. Her eyes were sparkling with happiness. She was light and life in his hands when they touched. He had never seen her look so lovely and all at once he wanted to take her by the hand and run, run away into the warm summer night that waited, balmy, beyond the gently billowing curtains.

They sat out the next dance; too warm from their exertions in the reel. Oliver took her hand as they left the floor and did not release it. She kept her hand perfectly still in his, not speaking or looking at him. Her face grew pink as he watched her and he began to ask himself if she could ... if she would ... after all this time ...? He could not be sure but he knew that he had started to hope for her presence at Lucy's, to feel a quick tug inside himself when he looked at her and a sweep of desire when their eyes met.

He let go of her hand when her mother came to sit beside them on the red velvet bench. 'Florence, dear. You promised Mr Hiddlesworth that you'd save a dance for him. Here he is to claim you!'

Florence seemed put out by her mother's assumption that she would prefer to dance with the fat little mayor but she took his hand, threw Oliver a look of despair and set off with the delighted man to the music of the polka.

'I wanted to speak to you alone, Mr Wainwright, and this would seem to be our opportunity.' Her speech was very slightly slurred but she conveyed to Oliver the impression of having measured her words. There were women who frequented The Pheasant and whose first step on the road to utter inebriation was this not-quite focused look and the hint of loss of control of their speech. Oliver had seen it before, but never in a woman of high position.

'My father, Sir Philip Oldfield, as I am sure you know, wishes you to call on him. You are to go on Tuesday of next week to Suttonford Manor at half-past two if that is a convenient hour for you.' Mrs Mawdesley looked past him, towards a group of guests nearby, whether to avoid his eyes and the astonishment she would have seen there, or because she did not want to be overheard, Oliver could not guess. 'Please say nothing to Florence of this. She will be at Churchgate with me when you go.'

'Do you know the reason behind the invitation, Mrs Mawdesley? Do you know why Sir Philip wants to see me? Should I take my lawyer along?' Oliver could not resist the jibe although he was aware that it was wasted on Laura who could have known nothing of her father's past intrigues. He was on his guard again. This time he'd be ready.

'Yes. I know what he wants and I don't think you'll be in need of legal advice. Please see him. He is an old man and afraid that his time is running out.' Laura fumbled in her tiny evening bag for the scrap of lace with which she touched the corners of her eyes. Oliver felt sorry for her. He had nothing to fear from the Oldfield family after all this time. His business was flourishing and could not be harmed by any scheme they could devise for his downfall.

'I'll see him,' he said.

The dancers returned and Oliver stood up. 'Florence, will you come with me? Albert and Edith are leaving soon and I'd like to see them off.'

They waited on the steps of the Town Hall for Albert and his bride to come outside and climb into the waiting coach.

There was still light enough for the newly-weds not to need lanterns on their drive and the couple believed that they were slipping away unobserved. But just the same, handfuls of rose petals were thrown into the coach.

'Quickly, Florence. Let's slip into the park for a moment or two. Nobody will know we've gone.' Oliver tugged at her hand and before she could consider it they were running towards the little patch of grass and trees behind the hall. A wall ran along the edge of the park and they leaned over it, watching the road that Albert and Edith would take and the outline of the church against the setting sun.

'What a lovely night.' Florence drew back from the wall and leaned against the great horse chestnut tree. 'It's so cool here.'

Oliver took her hands in his, pulled her towards him and under the rustling canopy of leaves he kissed her. Her hair smelled of perfume and he buried his face in it, crushing her into his chest and holding her there as if he were afraid to let her go. His mouth found hers again and there was passion as well as sweetness in her response; a response that was all too brief as she pushed him away with gentle hands.

'Come. Let us return to the dance,' she said. 'We cannot be seen here, like a pair of street urchins.' She walked ahead of him until they reached the market square and the set of her told him his advances would not be welcome if they were offered inappropriately.

'Florence?' Oliver caught up with her and walked by her side. 'Do you think you could consider ...?' There was a look in her eyes, which lasted only for a second, and it told Oliver that all was not lost. But before she could reply they were met by Laura and the jolly Mr Hiddlesworth.

'We were just waving to Albert and Edith, Mama. Their coach passed right under the wall. Did you think we were gone?' She had no compunction in telling the lie, Oliver noticed. 'Is our carriage here already? Oh, pity!'

She turned to Oliver and extended a polite hand. 'Thank you so much for escorting me, Oliver. I am sure to see you soon at Aunt Lucy's. Good night.'

It was all there, Oliver recognised; the imperiousness; the cool control of the aristocracy; the swift change from sweet acquiescence to haughty superiority. She had not shown this side of her nature to him before.

'Phew,' Oliver whistled as he ascended the steps to the Town Hall and the remaining guests. 'I like her the better for it. I believe I do!'

Chapter Twenty

The coach was not being used on Tuesday and Oliver decided to go to Suttonford in style. As soon as the driver turned in through the wide-open gates the horses were able to lengthen their stride, away from the busy main road, and Oliver was exhilarated. The breeze whipped his hair back from his forehead, the scent of pine was in his nostrils and he knew that he was excited at the prospect of doing battle with his old enemy.

Sir Philip couldn't touch him now. He was free of his patronage and he had freed his family from the system he had lived under. And he was glad, glad to come back as an invited guest and the old man's equal. He had speculated on the reason for the summons and had come to the conclusion that the old baronet had discovered that he, Oliver, had bought Suttonford land and wanted it back in his possession.

The driver reined back as the horses turned into the sweep of gravel in front of Suttonford Manor and they drew to a sedate halt.

Oliver had never before been inside the house. He had once been into the kitchen, to ask Dolly something but had been shooed away even from there.

Jackson took his hat, without acknowledging by so much as a flicker of the eyelids that he recognised the young man he had on many occasions chastised.

The entrance hall was cool. Marble tiled floors, columns of marble supporting a wide gallery above his head and the great staircase in the same white marble met Oliver's eye. In the shade of the columns, under the gallery, double doors of rosewood led to the formal reception rooms. The distant clicking of a door and the silvery tinkle of crystal water spilling into the Roman bath were the only sounds.

'Please follow me, Mr Wainwright. Sir Philip is expecting you.' Jackson led the way upstairs to the private apartments of the Oldfield family. On the long gallery portraits of ancestors, hunting scenes and landscapes filled the spaces between the doors. Oliver would have liked to look closely at them but a door was being opened for him to the room where Sir Philip waited.

From a high-back chair, surrounded by cushions to support him and covered from the waist down by a cashmere blanket, the old baronet extended a hand.

'Wainwright! Good to see you. Please sit here.'

He pointed to a chair that had been placed opposite his own. Between the chairs a marble and gilt table was set with glasses and cognac on a silver tray. 'Will you join me in a glass of brandy? Jackson!'

Oliver noticed that Sir Philip was paler, probably from being indoors so much, he thought, and thinner than when he had last seen him, but that his eyes were as keen as ever.

Jackson poured, handed the glasses to them and quietly left the room. Oliver's heart beat faster but with anticipation, not fear. His every sense was alert, waiting.

'Well, Wainwright. I don't believe in beating about the bush, like to get straight to the point, you know.' Sir Philip studied Oliver's face. 'I hear you've bought shares in my companies, that you've purchased land on the estate and more mills in the town.'

'Yes. I thought you might guess who the buyer was.' Oliver sipped the brandy slowly. 'Do you want them back? Why sell if they were still of value to the estate?'

Sir Philip looked at him slyly. 'You must be a very rich man by now, young Wainwright.'

'Oh, just "fair to middlin'" as the expression goes!' The old devil had no business to enquire. Oliver smiled broadly.

'How old are you?' Sir Philip demanded.

'Twenty-two.'

'You're very young to have control of so much money. Have you made it all by your own efforts? By honest dealing? No tricks? No gambles?'

'My business dealings are no concern of yours,' Oliver said. 'But, no. No gambling outside the shares market.' He would not give in to the feeling the man always aroused in him, making him defensive and nettled. He was giving nothing away, though he had told him more than he meant to do, annoyed by the implication that his wealth was the result of luck.

There was a moment's pause. Sir Philip looked Oliver over. Then, like a shot from a gun: 'Do you still wish to marry my granddaughter?'

Had he heard right? No words came. Oliver stared. What was the old devil up to now?

'I asked if you'd like to marry Florence!' Sir Philip repeated. 'Good God. I offer you my granddaughter's hand and you've nothing to say.'

This was no trick. Oliver saw that Sir Philip meant it. He tried to appear unperturbed, but he was floored. At last he collected himself enough to reply. 'I hadn't considered it. Not since she was sent away after our headstrong behaviour.'

'Well. Consider it now, Wainwright. Consider and give me your answer in a week's time.' He called Jackson back to refill their brandy glasses. 'Ask for tea to be sent up, Jackson,' he added as the old butler reached the door.

'I'll tell you the reason behind my change of heart, Wainwright. I'm an old man. I don't expect to live for more than another five years and before I go I want to see the estate's future assured.'

So that was it. At last, Oliver thought, we're getting to the truth. 'Carry on!' he said coldly.

'I have a son. He lives in London but he has never married and I see no hope of the title going to his heirs. The title will die out with him but he has no interest in the estate except to support his extravagant lifestyle.' He took a large sip of cognac before continuing.

'So it has been apparent for some time that the estate will go to my granddaughter and her sons.' He appeared to see nothing in Oliver's face to discourage him from going on.

'The Oldfield women are not particularly good breeders. My wife and I had only two children, no infant deaths, nothing like that, and Laura has only the one although she was married for fifteen years. Now I want to see great-grandsons before I die. I can't have the girl marrying some young buck from London and risk losing her to the kind of society my son enjoys.'

'You'll not be considering marrying her off to a poor man, will you, Sir Philip?' Oliver asked cynically.

'No. I have to see her married to someone who can support her comfortably.'

'And help the estate out of its difficulties?' Oliver added. He stood up and looked down on the man he used to despise for a different reason from the one which prompted him to add, 'You're prepared to sell your granddaughter to the highest bidder, aren't you? Do her feelings mean nothing to you? Is this what it means to have privilege and breeding? The morals of the cattle market?' He was angry and it was apparent that his remarks had had no effect on Sir Philip.

'Don't be tiresome, Wainwright. You still have the attitude of the labouring classes, seeing money and the needs of the bedchamber as two separate aspects of your life.' He handed Oliver his empty brandy glass and nodded his head towards the decanter. 'Do you imagine this isn't done … this dealing in marriage … in the very best of circles?' He looked at Oliver quizzically.

Oliver sat down again, after handing the refilled glass to Sir Philip. His anger had gone as quickly as it had arisen. The man was speaking what for him was the truth. 'Your finances are in a sorry state, then, I assume?' Oliver filled his own glass again. 'Leaving aside the question of Florence, her consent or otherwise, you're going to need a deal of help in clearing up the mess you've made of managing your estate, aren't you?'

'Listen, Wainwright.'

Oliver was listening intently.

'When you marry Florence the estate will be as good as yours. It will be in trust for your children but then, what else is land and property for? You'll not be able to dispose of it but for your lifetime it will be yours to run as you wish.'

'You're trying to buy me back! I'll not be in bondage to the estate again,' Oliver said.

Sir Philip looked at him, incomprehension in his eyes. 'Bondage? What are you talking about, Wainwright? We're all bound one way or another to the land we came from. You'll find it a damn sight harder to hold good workers than free them from your imaginary slavery.'

It came to him suddenly, the logic, almost the inevitability of it. Oliver knew what his answer would be. He'd marry Florence and run the estate. He'd be a fool to refuse even if he found Florence unattractive, and he did not. But he'd make the old schemer wait for his answer.

'I'll give you my answer a week from today, Sir Philip,' Oliver told him. 'Does Florence know anything of this? Her mother knows, of course!'

'Her mother told me that, when she was seventeen, Florence wouldn't consider marriage to anyone else but you, Wainwright. You must try to regain her affection if she's lost it. If she hasn't had a change of heart you're a lucky man!'

'Would I have complete control of the estate, right at the start? There'd be no point in anything less,' Oliver asked.

'I'll be happy to see it in your capable hands. Lady Oldfield and I will remain in residence here, but we'll live separately from you.'

On the drive back to Middlefield Oliver considered what might lie ahead for him as master of Suttonford. He would have to study the accounts and balance sheets before any decision could be taken on the future running of it as an enterprise and he winced as he imagined the financial bungling his investigations would uncover.

So it was to Florence that his thoughts turned as he told himself that she must never learn of the contract that lay behind their marriage. Nothing less than a love match would do for her and he must sweep her off her feet, make her believe that his need for her was just as strong as it had once been. And it was not. When Rosie left a part of him had died; a part he did not believe would ever come to life again.

But he would love Florence. Her sweetness had always stirred him and he was determined to please her, to make himself worthy of her love.

He would have to give up his longing for a proper home. Life at Suttonford would never include fireside comforts. He would never be able to tell Florence about Rosie and Edward and he had harboured a faint hope that one day, perhaps, he would live with his son. Florence would not accept a child that was not of her marriage and Sir Philip Oldfield would not contemplate a bastard as part of the deal.

* * *

Tomorrow was 'Balgone Day'. Florence would be there, he was sure. Sir Philip said that she'd have him. Florence had told her mother that she'd have no one else. Oliver laughed softly at her guile. She'd not be able to keep away, in spite of her rebuffing his advances. He smiled at the memory of her putting him in his place when he'd kissed her in public, since her actions belied the look in her eyes. Now he knew, as he had always known, that she was his for the asking.

The next day dawned fair and warm and Oliver found that he was eager to see her, just as he used to be when they first made their secret rendezvous in, what seemed to him, ages past. He dressed with care so that he would not disappoint her and at exactly half-past two o'clock he set out on the first day of his official courtship.

Oliver was shown into the sunlit garden. Florence looked more beautiful than ever today with her blonde hair tied back, its colour outshining the pale apricot of her dress. She and Lucy met him at the entrance to the rose garden. He smiled broadly and put out his elbows, inviting them to take an arm each. 'The two prettiest girls in Cheshire,' he declared. 'What a fortunate man I am, to have them all to myself!'

Lucy recited the names of all the rose bushes, led them round to the shrubbery and must have noticed that Florence and Oliver were looking into each other's eyes more often than they looked at the shrubs, so that finally, when they were within yards of the summer house, she put her hand to her mouth in dismay.

'I have forgotten to order tea, my dears! Please excuse me. I must return to the house. It will be ready in about twenty minutes. Oh, dear!'

Oliver turned to Florence when Lucy had reached the gate. 'I think she means us to be alone, Florence,' he said mischievously. 'Do you think we should? Will you slap my face if I take you into the summer house and try to kiss you?'

He saw with delight that he had made her blush. He felt her hand, unsteady on his arm.

It was cool in the summer house. Potted geraniums were placed along the outside wall and their sharp scent filled the tiny hexagon of a resting place. Their knees touched as they sat on opposite sides of the bench and Oliver leaned across and lifted Florence's chin, making her look into his eyes.

'Why, so shy, fair miss?' he asked softly. 'You have hardly spoken this afternoon and yet I know that you have arranged all this.' It excited him, seeing her wide grey eyes looking into his. She was artless and innocent, and she was longing for him to kiss her. Her lips parted, red and soft.

'If I tell you that I want to kiss you whenever I look at you and that I want to make love to you whenever I think about you what will you have to say?' he whispered.

Florence put her hands in his. 'I will say, "I am glad."'

He lifted her to her feet and drew her to him and as he bent to kiss her he heard the quick, nervous catch of her breath. He drew back for a questioning moment and looked into her eyes. 'Have we waited too long, Florence?' he asked.

Her eyes closed, her lips parted, waiting for his, and Oliver had his answer.

* * *

There was a message for him, from Dolly. He would have to go to Southport and it was the day Sir Philip Oldfield expected his answer. Sir Philip must wait. Oliver sent a letter to him at Suttonford by messenger saying that he had agreed to his proposition and would see him the following day.

Southport was at its prettiest in July with flowers and trees at their best and pretty girls in light summer dresses shopping and taking tea in the Lord Street shops, but Oliver could not take any interest in the scene for wondering what had gone wrong.

He found her in the kitchen, turning out a cupboard. 'What the hell are you doing? And where's Edward?' He had expected to find that she was ill or wringing her hands in despair at some domestic disaster that was beyond her capabilities – and here she was, dressed in mulberry silk on a hot day like today, her arms jangling with trashy jewellery, a scowl on her face, attacking the contents of a kitchen cupboard.

'Edward's all right. The children have gone to the park with Iris. Don't you start bloody well yelling an' all!' She climbed down the step ladder. 'It's Wilf! He turned up last night, demanding to stay. He says he's got a right to live here; that he'll get Lizzie back. He's going to get you, he says.'

She washed her hands at the sink as she spoke. 'You know what I'm like. If I don't know what to do about something I start looking for things I can do. That's why I'm cleaning the cupboards.'

'Where is he now?' Wilf – in his house! Oliver was angry. Rage was boiling in him. 'How dare he come here? Is he coming back? Does he know this is my house?'

'Yes to both. God knows how he found us. He's either asked at the station in Middlefield or he's followed you here.' Dolly opened

243

a cupboard in the dresser and brought out a bottle of tonic wine and two glasses. 'Do you want a drop?'

'No. And I wish you'd stop drinking the stuff. You must get through a bottle a week. You don't need a damned tonic!' He put the kettle on the gas. 'What time will he be back?'

'Tonight. Will you stay?' Dolly drained her glass, then, seeing the look on Oliver's face, put the bottle back in the cupboard and made tea for them.

He walked to the park and found Iris and the children sitting by the edge of the lake. Lizzie was hurling pieces of bread at the ducks, squealing with delight as they dived into the shallow water, tails in the air. She saw Oliver approach and ran towards him, arms outstretched, her hair, the colour of carrots, streaming out behind her. She was an adorable little girl, affectionate and good-natured.

'Oliver!' she came towards him and he lifted her high above his head in the way she loved and she wrapped her arms tight around his neck, clinging to him like a monkey.

Oliver peered into the perambulator. Edward slept peacefully and he didn't wake him. He'd help Iris to put them to bed and play with his son later.

His anger simmered below the surface all afternoon, leaving him only when he put the children to bed. Oliver thought that Edward was very advanced for his six months of age. He held him around the waist while they waited for Iris to fill his little bathtub. Oliver settled himself down on the low nursing chair and already Edward was trying to pull himself up onto his feet.

The baby grasped his hair as his father put his face affectionately towards him and the frown of concentration on his little face was the best thing Oliver had seen in a long time. Strong little feet pushed into Oliver's lap and the baby's wet mouth found his cheek.

'Look at him, Iris! Did you ever see a baby so clever?' Oliver asked the girl. 'I believe he's exceptionally talented. He'll be walking before he's a year old. You mark my words!' He passed the baby to Iris who, aided by an adoring Lizzie, soaped and rinsed the kicking little body.

The house was spotless. Mahogany gleamed, brass and silver shone and the carpets were brushed daily to Dolly's strict instructions. She was not an easy-going employer. Oliver had never found food to compare with Dolly's and now that she was able to buy well they kept what she called 'a proper table'. They dined at the big table in the dining room, both at one end. Tonight Dolly had prepared fillets of sole with shrimp sauce and these were served with green peas and runner beans from the garden, and new potatoes coated in best butter. There was veal and ham in a light golden pastry and dishes of crisp salads. Finally, to please Oliver, she had prepared layered sponge slices with his favourite, strawberries and cream.

It was ten o'clock before Wilf returned. They heard his footsteps echoing hollowly down the side passage and the crash as he slammed the garden gate. 'Dolly. Open this door!' he shouted, beating on the back door. 'Open it before I break it down!'

Oliver wrenched the handle on the inside, making Wilf tumble into the kitchen, off balance. Then he caught him and whirled him around to face him. 'What are you doing in my house?' he snarled. 'Answer me! Who said you could come to my door?'

Wilf threw himself backwards to free himself from Oliver's grip and clenched his fists, challenging Oliver to attack him. 'I don't need your permission to see my own child and her mother,' he spat out. His eyes were bloodshot and his breath was foul with alcohol. 'It might be your house but it's my property as is in it!'

He lashed out at Oliver with his fist, catching him unawares, making Oliver's eyes stream. 'Forgotten how to fight have you, lad?' he jeered. 'You'll not have had so much practice lately.' He punched with the other fist and this time he caught Oliver on the shoulder. 'Been too busy making little bastards, have yer?'

Oliver was spoiling for a fight … He squared up to the foul-mouthed man he detested. His knuckles smashed into Wilf's face, making Wilf reel backwards, sending plates from the dresser shelves crashing to the floor.

It did not silence Wilf. 'Whose is the bastard?' he jeered.

Wild rage surged through Oliver. He dragged Wilf towards him and with a swift left to the ear knocked him against the wall. His right fist came up under Wilf's ribs, making him retch and grab wildly for support. Another blow to the face and Wilf was down, coughing and spluttering on all fours. Oliver pulled him to his feet.

'If you're not gone from this house within five seconds, you'll not live to see morning. I'm not making threats. I'll kill you, Wilf Leach, without a thought if I ever see or hear of you again. It's only for the sake of my household that you're alive to hear me now.' He pulled open the back door and pushed Wilf ahead of him, holding him over the balustrade, making the man grab at his clothes to prevent himself from being thrown on to the slabbed yard below.

'Get yourself away from here. And away from Cheshire. If I discover you within a hundred miles of me I'll have you killed, or take pleasure in doing the job myself.'

Wilf stumbled down the steps, hanging on to the railings, with Oliver only a step above him, until he reached the yard. Then he turned and ran from the house.

* * *

Wilf lifted his face out of the water. He had no recollection of finding his way to the beach but at last the salt water was numbing his bruises. His ribs ached, one eye was closed and his clothes were heavy with seawater. He reached upwards until his hands found the cast iron of the pier supports. The tide was out but there was water in the deep depressions at the base of the piles. He did not know when the tide would turn and bring the sea swirling back around him.

It was an attractive beach, but not a safe one. Three masts protruded from the sand and stories were told by the local fisherfolk of ships being beached and swallowed up in the ever shifting quicksands. The tide came in swiftly on this section of coast, spreading fast and shallow over the sand, giving the unwary the impression that they were safe at the water's edge. The water could be ten feet deep fifty yards ahead and the bather oblivious of the danger.

Wilf dragged himself from the pool and made his way back to the promenade. 'I'll get the bastard. I'll get him in Middlefield soon,' he promised himself, muttering threats as he shivered in his wet clothes. 'Next time I'll end it for him.'

He took a train to Middlefield when it was light enough to see, telling himself that he would be back to live with Dolly when he had killed Oliver. 'There's plenty as'll help me,' he said to himself.

* * *

This time Sir Philip Oldfield was in his office. He was seated in a bath chair beside the bench with a footman in attendance. Sir Philip dismissed the man when Oliver was shown in. 'Take a seat, Wainwright,' he said, looking up at Oliver. 'My sainted aunt! What have you done? It's the blackest eye I've seen in years.'

'I was kicked. By a horse,' Oliver lied. 'Yesterday.'

'Do you hunt?' Sir Philip enquired. 'You should have a bit of steak placed on it.'

'No, and yes,' Oliver said. 'No to the hunting. Yes to the steak.'

'So. You are going to ask Florence to marry you,' Sir Philip said. 'You have made your decision.'

'Yes. I'll ask her to marry,' Oliver answered, then added gravely, 'but there is a condition.'

Sir Philip's face returned the old look Oliver knew well, a look of arrogant disdain. 'You are to be accepted into one of the best families in England, Wainwright. Don't assume too much. You do not make the conditions.'

'Hear me out,' Oliver demanded, curt and impatient.

'Go on. What condition do you think you can ask?'

'You want grandchildren, Sir Philip,' Oliver said quietly. 'And I want children. These children will bear the name of Wainwright, not Oldfield. You have thought of that?'

'It has not escaped me, Wainwright,' Sir Philip replied. 'Wainwright is a good name. Nothing wrong with Wainwright.'

Oliver went to the window and looked out in the direction of the quarry. 'I want my father's body brought out,' he said. 'At whatever cost to the estate. I know it will be considerable. My father will have a proper burial.' He looked hard at Sir Philip. 'My father is to be given a resting place. He is to have a place in the burial ground at Suttonford church.'

'Only Oldfields are buried in that ground, Wainwright,' Sir Philip said.

'My father was all the family I had. He will be remembered and honoured as the grandfather of my children. I will not father Oldfield children unless I can show them where their grandfather Wainwright lies.'

Sir Philip put out his hand. 'Wainwright,' he said, and there was at last respect in his voice, 'I agree. I admire you for that. I hope that when I am gone these children will honour my memory.'

'Then you'll do it?'

'Of course.'

'When?'

Sir Philip smiled. 'As soon as your betrothal is announced I shall have Joe Wainwright's body brought out. Your father will have a place alongside the family graves. What do you want on the headstone?'

Oliver thought hard for a moment. 'All I want is "Joseph Edward Wainwright, Laid to Rest in 1880".'

'That is not the date of his death, Wainwright,' Sir Philip said. 'He was killed when you were a young boy.'

'Nevertheless,' Oliver answered, 'I want this done.'

'It shall be.'

Sir Philip rang for the butler. 'Bring cognac, Jackson,' he said when the man came into the room, 'Oliver Wainwright and I have something to celebrate.'

'I'll have to start calling on Florence officially. We've been kept apart until now, you realise?' Oliver said when the door closed behind Jackson.

Sir Philip put out a still firm hand and the two men shook. 'I shall call you Oliver once she accepts you. Now take a look at these ledgers will you?'

Half an hour later Oliver faced Sir Philip who had patiently watched Oliver's face as he tried to make sense of the estate accounts. 'You're going to have to take drastic measures to save the estate, aren't you?' he said. 'I'll need to spend a lot of time sorting this out, but from here it looks as if you are in trouble. You must have other assets?'

Sir Philip shook his head. 'That's it, I'm afraid, Wainwright. There are a few rents, the farm income, the quarry is making a profit and a few thousand in shipping.'

'You'll have to sell something. You know that, don't you? You must get money coming in. Stop it flowing out all the time.' Oliver closed the big cashbook firmly and faced his future father-in-law.

'I see why you wanted me in the family. You think I can save your estate for you, don't you?' He spoke without rancour. 'What a task!'

'Where will we get the income, Wainwright?'

'Why are you still growing wheat?' Oliver asked him. 'With cheap wheat coming in off the prairies?' He drew up a chair and tapped at the desk thoughtfully. 'You should have been building up a dairy herd with all the people in the towns. Supply them! Grow the stuff they want to buy in the markets and in the shops. The towns are growing by the day, taking your estate workers from your cottages and villages and still you people don't believe what you see before you!'

'There's not time for that sort of thing, Wainwright. We need money now,' Sir Philip said. 'The things you suggest will take a year or two.'

'Sell some land for building houses. Sell one of your sites in Middlefield. Don't start quibbling about who you sell to. Rich people don't get richer by selling to their friends. There's a hell of a lot more poor people about than rich ones and a penny or two from every poor person will make you a rich man!' He saw that this kind of talk was not what Sir Philip had expected but he continued. 'I didn't make my money wondering what the rich were looking for. I see what the poor folk need and sell that. Then I look ahead to see what they'll need next.'

'You don't have any compunction about stepping outside your own class to do it, then, eh, Wainwright?' Sir Philip asked. 'Are you ambitious to move up in the world? Be taken for a gentleman?'

Oliver looked at him shrewdly. 'Not in the way you think. I'd not want to be taken for the kind of ruddy gentlemen I've come across so far. I don't care for fancy manners and living the way you do. I want a good life for myself and my family and I don't feel I ought to pull the whole working class along with me. But I'm not afraid of them, as you are. And I'm not afraid of you, as they are.'

'Big sentiments, Wainwright, but how will you feel when you have all this?' He waved his hand towards the window. 'And you are visited by the kind of gentlemen you despise and you want to be accepted by them?'

Oliver laughed out loud. He could just imagine it and the prospect amused him. 'If they are coming here to see me then it will be they who will be trying to please me, won't it?' he replied. 'It will be the gentlemen, as you call them, who will want to be accepted. I'll not try to please them.'

Chapter Twenty-One

Florence could not decide which dress to wear for Oliver's visit. It was his fourth in a fortnight. Mama had ceased voicing objections and even seemed to be encouraging him.

'Do I look prettier in the scarlet or the blue?' she asked her maid as she looked from one dress to the other. 'I think I'll wear the scarlet satin. It has a daring feel to it. Tonight I'll make Oliver very eager.'

'Be quick with the hooks,' she added impatiently. The girl fastened the last hook and Florence dismissed her quickly and crossed to her window. The heavy nets ensured that she could not be seen. She knew it was so because she had obliged her maid to stand where she herself stood and had gone into the street and looked hard at the windows and not seen so much as a shadow. She stood for five minutes, waiting.

Oliver would turn into the alleyway at the top of Rivergate at any moment. He always came this way, shortening his journey by only about fifty yards, reappearing from an alleyway almost opposite the imposing entrance to number twenty-three. Then it took him precisely to the count of eight with her eyes closed, before the clang of the iron gate and the doorbell sounded almost simultaneously. He leaped up the short flight of steps to their door, hardly giving the gate time to swing back on its hinges before he was tugging at the bell pull.

She saw him and her heart quickened as it always did. She liked to keep him waiting for two minutes. Two minutes seemed an age and she did not want to miss any more of his company than she had to.

She heard Mama greet him as if his call were a pleasant surprise and he had caught them unaware. 'Go up to the drawing room, Oliver. I will tell Florence you are here,' she heard her say.

When she entered the room Oliver had his back to her and he spun round at the sound of the door. She would be startled at the sight of his eye, which was even more obviously bruised than it had been the day before, when he had seen Sir Philip.

'Oliver! Your eye! How did that happen?' Florence was solicitous, fluttery and worried.

'Close the door, sit down and I'll tell you all about it,' Oliver said. He took her hand and led her to the sofa. 'I want to talk to you about my family.'

She sat close to him, holding onto his hand. 'My stepmother, who was a cook at your grandfather's house, has two children. Their father ...' it was not a very big lie, Oliver thought, '... is a violent creature and she's afraid of him. I've bought her a house in Southport and it's there that I go when I'm away at weekends.'

'You've bought a house for her? Oh, Oliver, how good you are.' Her eyes were shining with admiration and relief. Had she imagined that he had another woman?

He had made up his mind to tell her something of his responsibilities. He could not tell all, would not tell all, but Florence would surely agree with what he was able to tell her. He watched her face carefully as he spoke. If she showed anything other than understanding then he would not continue to court her. He would not have her dismiss his family as unworthy or come to think of them as a shameful secret.

'My stepmother and the children's father never married,' he said, his eyes intent on her face. 'My stepmother still holds the name of Wainwright. So the children ... Leach's children ... were registered in my stepmother's name. They are Wainwrights and are not to know anything of their father.'

'They are illegitimate, Oliver. That is what you are telling me, isn't it?'

'Yes.'

There was no scorn or pity on her sweet face so Oliver continued, 'My stepmother and I have broken the law, Florence. We have registered those children as if they were legitimate. Their birth certificates carry the name of my own father who died many years before they were born.'

'Oh, what a lovely thing to do.' Florence's eyes held nothing but clear understanding and love as she held on to his hand. 'I am sure your own father would have been proud of them, Oliver. He would have agreed to so small a deceit, wouldn't he?'

'I know he would,' Oliver said, relief flooding through him at her acceptance of his story. He was suddenly filled with love for her, for this adorable, generous girl whose heart had gone out to the plight of the children and Dolly.

'My stepmother and I have decided that the children must never be told about Wilf Leach. But he discovered her whereabouts. He had me followed, threatened her and the children and I had to go to Southport.' He went on, fingering the bruise wryly. 'I had to tell him to leave my house and to leave my stepmother alone.'

'Have you reported it to the police?' Florence asked. 'I've never in my life come across a man as thoughtful, as protective and as kind as you are, Oliver. I'm so proud of you. When I imagine the vile creature who injured you I could weep,' she added.

'I've given him an even worse set of bruises. He'll not trouble them again,' Oliver boasted.

'Can you be sure he won't return and terrify your poor stepmother?' Florence asked. 'What's his name? Was he a worker at Suttonford?'

'His name's Leach – Wilf Leach. He used to work for your grandfather but I believe he left the estate some time ago.' That was enough. He wanted no more questions. He wanted her in his arms. 'Now, Florence. Let's talk about us – about you and me – and not dwell on unpleasant matters.'

'Oh, what a marvellous person you are! To think you support the woman who brought you up, though she's not your mother! To think that you protect her and her children!' Florence's eyes were brimming. 'I do so admire you for your compassion.'

He was beginning to enjoy her praise and believe he merited it. Then he asked himself how it would be if she knew the whole truth and insisted that they talk no more on the matter.

He was here to court Florence. He wanted to waste no time in bringing about their betrothal ... but how was he to go about it? Girls like Florence were different from those a man could meet every day. It was so long since he had been inexperienced that he found it hard to know what he could do without upsetting her. Rosie and he had fallen into one another's arms like starving tigers and, in the falling, only increased their hunger. Florence was an innocent.

She would have to be wooed and coaxed. She wanted him, he knew that, but on her terms and he had no means of telling if he was making the right approaches. She'd set out her stall. She'd invited him to look, to touch but not to take, though he was impatient with delay. He wanted her now yet he was afraid that his true appetites would repel her. He had known grand passion, his needs had been met and surpassed by his old love and now he was bewildered by Florence's shyness.

He thought of the art of courtship as mere billing and cooing and he was tired of it. She excited him. He put his arm around her waist, letting his hand slide upwards against the swelling of her breast, pressing the side of his thumb into the soft flesh with its covering of scarlet satin. She pulled his head down to hers and wrapped her arms around his neck as he kissed her and he heard again the quick, nervous sound she always made, catching her breath as if she were not quite ready for him; as if passionate response was not natural to her.

Oliver stayed another hour. When Laura left them alone, and she did so often, returning a little more under the influence of drink each time, they took their chances and fell into each other's arms eagerly. These lengthy embraces pleased Florence but frustrated Oliver with delay.

At ten o'clock he took his leave. Florence took him to the door and closed it demurely behind him. Then she flew like the wind, up the wide staircase, along the landing to her room where she could watch him enter the alleyway opposite and wait for him to reappear at the corner of Rivergate. Tonight she was fast enough to catch him closing the iron gate behind him and she sighed with pleasure at the sight of his agile figure crossing the road, swinging easily into the alleyway.

She never closed her eyes when she watched Oliver leaving. It was usually dark and she might miss him. Instead, they were fixed on the spot where he entered Rivergate.

But where was he tonight? He ought to be out by now. It wasn't likely that he'd stopped to talk to someone. It was late for small talk.

Three men ran from the alleyway Oliver, had entered only seconds before ... They looked up and down the street nervously before they entered Churchgate. Two of them passed below her window and Florence saw that one was the drunken market sweeper, notorious for his dirty clothes and loud-mouthed behaviour when he was not cooling off inside the jail on his frequent spells in custody. The third man ran towards Wallgate and disappeared from sight. And still there was no sign of Oliver and suddenly, with a terrible cold fear clutching her, Florence screamed.

'Mama! Mama!' She flew down the stairs and found Laura in the hall. 'Get the maids, the cook, everybody. Something has happened to Oliver.'

Florence lifted the bell and ran towards the servants' quarters. 'Quickly everybody! Come with me. Oliver's been attacked!'

They all obeyed. She would for ever be grateful to them for following her out into the night. She ran across the road, carrying the lamp she had picked up in the hall, crying softly, fearing for him, hoping that her premonition was wrong; that he had reached home safely.

She had only gone twenty yards into the alley when she found him, crumpled, lying on his side in a pool of blood, the handle of a knife protruding from his chest and his fingers locked around it. His moans were terrible to hear but they told her that he lived. 'Oh, thank God you're alive,' Florence sobbed as she dropped to her knees in the mud and filth of the alley. 'Run, Jess. Run to the police office. Bring all the men you can find to carry Oliver home. Mama! You must run too. Bring the doctor. Quickly! All of you!'

Florence cradled his head in her hands, lying alongside Oliver in the gutter, afraid to move him lest his blood drained away and all the while she willed him to live. 'Don't die, Oliver. Do you hear me? Don't die! Help's coming, my love,' she whispered in his ear. 'I'm here beside you. Oh, live. Just live and I'll ask no more of you.'

It seemed an eternity since they had gone for help and now a little crowd had gathered round Florence and the man she was holding in her arms.

'Is he dead, miss?' an old woman asked. 'How can a man live after losing all that blood?'

'He's not dead! Oliver! Oliver, do you hear me? Oh, please say you're not dead.' Florence held him closer, placing her cheek gently against her poor darling's, making her warmth flow into him.

Jess had four police officers with her when she returned. They carried a stretcher and lifted Oliver on to it, leaving the knife in position. 'Let the doctor get that out, Miss Mawdesley,' they advised. 'Hold on to his hands. Don't let him pull it out.'

Florence gripped Oliver's hands, pinning them together, running alongside the stretcher. Her tears had gone; now fear replaced them. 'Carefully!' she ordered as they laid him on the bed in the room next to hers. The doctor was waiting. 'Leave him, Miss Mawdesley, while I remove the knife,' he said.

'No, indeed. I'll stay. I must stay with him,' she said. 'I am not going to lose my head, doctor.'

She stayed with Oliver when they cut off his clothes, leaving the knife protruding through the ragged layers of cloth. She held his hands and forced herself to look and not to flinch while the doctor and his assistant removed the knife and tried to staunch the blood, which oozed relentlessly around the wound. She felt his hands alternately grip and grow weak from the pain and she willed him, silently, not to give up.

And all the time, Oliver groaned. He was awake the whole time, looking at her with pleading eyes. He needed her comfort and strength. The doctors had removed the knife. The blade had missed Oliver's heart by half an inch but the attacker had ripped the blade downwards as it plunged into him, leaving a ragged, six-inch gash to be cleaned and repaired.

'I have to give him chloroform, Miss Mawdesley,' the doctor said. 'Perhaps you'd rather leave us.'

Florence shook her head. 'Not until you have finished. Not yet,' she told him firmly.

The doctor dripped the chloroform on to a gauze pad, which was held, in a little wire cradle, over Oliver's nose and mouth.

The doctor and his assistant worked methodically, dousing with iodine, stitching and bandaging, taking note of Oliver's feeble pulse, his pallor and shallow breathing.

'Go, now,' the doctor said when he had bandaged Oliver's chest. 'He's asleep. The police want to see you.'

Florence went to her room, tore off the scarlet dress and washed at the little washstand. She was calm at last. Now she would dress, go downstairs, and tell the waiting police inspector all she had seen. Oliver's words were coming back to her. The bruise. The man's name was Leach – Wilf Leach. Let the police inspector find him. They'd know where to find the market sweeper. He'd lead them to the attacker, to the man who had meant to kill Oliver.

When she had told the police all she knew she returned to Oliver's bedside.

'If he comes through the night, Miss Mawdesley, then, unless sepsis takes hold, his chances are good,' the old doctor told her. 'He's lost a lot of blood and he'll need to be kept warm but he's young and has a fine constitution. Someone will have to sit with him through the night. I've sent for a nurse and I'll return at eight o'clock in the morning.'

'I shall sit with him myself, doctor,' Florence said. 'I cannot allow anyone else to come near him.'

She called for every restorative the house held. In the event that he should have difficulty in breathing she ordered a bowl of camphorated water to be set at the bedhead and she found comfort in its pungency. She brought rosewater for the linen pad she used to wipe his forehead. Woollen socks had to be found and pulled gently over his cold feet and stone hot-water bottles were wrapped in flannel and placed around his still body.

She ordered beef tea to be prepared and she sent for ale and porter, which she knew would strengthen his blood. Fresh milk was to be available at all times and beaten egg and brandy to hand.

Florence never took her eyes from Oliver's face throughout the night. Had she been an ordinary girl she believed she would have been a nurse. She demanded a white apron from the kitchen maids and she sat, holding his hand, wiping away the flecks of brown that crept to the corners of his mouth, reaching over the fearful bandage that stained her apron red from his blood.

She turned the lamp low and watched him, holding her breath when his own was inaudible; her heart leaping when the sound of it returned. His every movement had her attention. She dared not take her eyes from his face. She prayed, 'Dear Lord, let him live. Dear Lord, let him live,' whispering the words over and over.

As the night wore on his sleep was more fitful. He murmured and Florence stroked his unresponsive hand. He groaned and she bit her lip in terror that he would die. She stayed close so that he would know she was there. As Oliver returned to consciousness his pain increased and he held her hand in a grip that all but crushed her fingers when his pain was at its height.

The morning came and he was alive still. Florence allowed the nurse to have charge of him for a few minutes at a time when she attended to herself, returning to sit beside him, to watch and pray. On the second day he was in high fever and Florence and the nurses sponged his face and chest, pressing cold flannels to the pulses at his wrists, trying to cool him. He was delirious in his fever, sometimes sitting bolt upright and shouting, Florence thought for roses.

'Rosie! Rosie!' he yelled before he sank back on to the soft pillows, sweat in great droplets on his face and neck.

He was growing thinner. Florence saw him grow pale between the bouts of fever. His face was ashen but he could not speak and she held him between times on the bed, letting him rest against her bosom, stroking his head to soothe him as the bouts of fever subsided.

Then suddenly on the fifth day the crisis passed. His pulse became strong. He did not grip her hand and normal colour came into his cheeks leaving him cool, his breathing clear and untroubled. At last he slept a deep, refreshing sleep and Florence, exhausted, slept on the bed beside him.

When she opened her eyes, Oliver was lying on his side stroking her hair. He was well. His eyes were clear. The suffocating heat had gone out of him and he gazed tenderly at her.

'You have compromised yourself, fair miss,' he said tenderly. 'Now I shall have to marry you. Who else would take a girl who'd spent so many nights in bed with a stranger?'

* * *

Oliver could not attend the trial. Albert watched from the public gallery as Wilf Leach was sentenced to life imprisonment for attempted murder. He was led away, bitterly reviling the judge and jury for their conviction of a man who had been so cruelly wronged by the stepson he had loved, he said, like a brother.

Chapter Twenty-Two

Dolly put the finishing touches to the tree, clipping the enamelled candle-holders to its prickly branches, testing them with the twisted candles in place. It wouldn't do if they were too heavy. She couldn't wait to see the faces of the children when they came down in the morning. Edward was not quite a year old but he was walking and beginning to string a few words together. He had clutched his empty stocking with as much eagerness as Lizzie, handing it over to Dolly to tie to the bed knob. He was like his father had been; a clever little fellow, learning to do things much faster than other children.

The clock over the fireplace chimed seven. Oliver would be here soon. Everything was ready. The walls were festooned in red and green swags of artificial stuff, like cats' tails, Dolly thought, looped together every yard or so and held with great bunches of silver bells. They had caught her eye in the shop and she had not been able to resist their glittering cheerfulness. She stepped down from the wooden ladder-stool to admire the room. The scent of pine needles filled the air, increasing her pleasure, giving the room a festive feel.

She had added a mirror since Oliver's last visit; a wide heavy oval of dark mahogany with thin bands of inlaid mother-of-pearl and ebony around the bevelled glass. It made the spacious room appear to double in size, with a glittering tree at each end.

Dolly knew how to celebrate Christmas. She had served the Oldfields all these years; seen their lavish entertaining and never in her wildest dreams had she expected to have a fine house to preside over. She thought with satisfaction of the way the floor manager at Boothroyd and Rimmer greeted her at the shop; of the way a messenger followed her as she carefully, with much frowning and inspecting for quality, made her selections.

She liked to delay her homecoming, so that her purchases would arrive before she did. She liked to think of several vans drawn up outside the house, the drivers hiding their impatience, holding the horses back until it was their turn to unload her parcels.

She had invited the couple who kept the wine shop to have Christmas dinner with them and the ringmaster and trapeze artiste from the circus. It would be good fun, better than spending the whole day watching Oliver play at 'silly-asses' with the children. She had them all day, every day, she reminded herself. A mother needs a change now and again.

She helped herself to 'a nice glass of sherry'. Just a drop to put her in the mood for Christmas. She'd have it drunk in a trice. Oliver was a stick-in-the-mud about a little drop of anything. She had only just put the glass away when she heard a banging on the front door.

It was Oliver, his arms full of parcels.

'You've been spending your money, haven't you?' she said as she helped him off with his heavy overcoat and told Iris to hang it in the kitchen to 'air'. 'There's plenty for the children. I've spent the last two weeks shopping for toys.'

'Wait until you see these, Dolly.' He was as pleased as if he were a child himself. 'There's a clockwork merry-go-round for Edward. All the little figures do something and the whole thing jigs around playing a tune.' He unwrapped the parcel in the hall and demonstrated. 'And the doll I've got for Lizzie! It has a china face, real hair and a dress of red satin.'

'Let's get something to eat,' Dolly said. 'I'm starving!'

She had made a rich brown stew, which she carried to the table. There were golden roast potatoes, crisp at the edges, just as he liked them, steamed winter cabbage chopped into tiny shreds, peppered and turned in butter. Apple Charlotte with cream and apple brandy was next. She prided herself on making simple food into a feast.

'This'll be your last Christmas with us, won't it? Your Florence won't let you out of her sight when you're married,' she prophesied tartly as she dished out the pudding.

He glared at her over the table, as if he was not sure how she had taken the news of his marriage. 'I'm not going to be a prisoner, Dolly. I shall come to Southport as often as I like – though I'll be spending Christmas at Suttonford in future. And this time I have to be back for New Year. They have a big party.'

'I know! I used to be up half the ruddy night cooking their damned breakfasts. Eeh – I wish I could see you, lording it about, giving yer orders!' She snorted with laughter. 'Am I getting a present from you?'

'Yes. It's a surprise. You'll get it in the morning.'

'I hope it's what I think it is,' she said.

'What's that?'

'You know. The deeds. The deeds to the house so I know it's mine like you promised. You said, "Come to Southport and it'll all be yours, Dolly." That's what you said.'

'I know. I haven't done anything about it yet. But I will,' Oliver said. 'Anyway, what difference does it make? It's as good as yours now.'

'"As good as" isn't enough. I want it made legal,' she replied. 'I want it done before you marry, then the Oldfield family won't have any say in my life again. Suppose you drop dead? Do you think Miss ruddy Mawdesley will leave us here in peace? Will she hell-as-like!'

'Pour me a brandy and bring it into the sitting room, will you?' He had risen from the table. Oliver was adept at changing the subject when it suited him.

She followed him, waiting to see his pleasure in the room she had decorated. But he stopped in the doorway and pulled a face. 'What on earth's this?' he asked, touching the silver bells. 'Gaudy strings of glass? God, Dolly. It looks like a blasted toyshop. Have you no taste?'

262

'I like it! And so do the children. What's up with it, anyway? I've spent too long with rubbish round me that's not worth looking at. Now I've got this place I'm not going to have anything ugly in it.'

She was quite put out by his criticism. 'I bet they haven't got anything half as nice at Suttonford. They never used to do the place up much for all their damned money. I never saw a paper-chain in the house.'

'All right. I'm sorry! I was being unkind,' he said. 'Forget it. Show me all the things you've got for the children and I'll wrap them up.'

'I've asked some people over for dinner, tomorrow. There's four of them coming.' She'd tell him now, while he was in an apologising mood. 'There's Mr and Mrs Whitehead from the wine shop and the Great Armani and Miss Ariel ... they're in the circus.'

She sat on the sofa, prinking out the folds in her bright green dress, pretending not to expect any objections from him and all the time slyly watching his face. She pushed a box of chocolates towards him in a conciliatory gesture.

'You'll like my friends,' she assured him as she selected the only liqueur chocolate for herself.

'Where did you meet these people? Circus folk and the like?' He was annoyed with her, she saw. 'To think you've asked people to spend Christmas Day with us and the children!'

'I get talking to people in the Winter Gardens and round the bandstand,' she snapped. 'I'm not looking for a man, if that's what you're thinking! I've had enough of them. I'm making a few friends, that's all!'

* * *

It was the best Christmas Oliver had ever had. Lizzie and Edward threw themselves onto his bed as soon as it was light, bringing the toys he had only hours before placed in their stockings. Lizzie sat, cross-legged in her nightgown, nursing the china doll as if it were

Audrey Reimann

a baby, gently lowering and raising it, enraptured by the clicking of
the eyes as they opened and closed. Lizzie's hair had never been cut
and it fell around her shoulders and face in a soft tangle of bronze.

She adored Edward, treating him as if he were her own real, live
baby, anticipating his every wish, ever at his side. Edward had the
brown eyes he had inherited from Rosie and a mop of dark curls,
uncut like Lizzie's. He looked a little like a girl, until he moved or
spoke when there was no mistaking his boyishness.

He climbed onto Oliver's chest, a wooden soldier doll in one
hand, a toy drum in the other and, evidently delighting in the noise
he could make, he beat the soldier against the tight skin of the
drum, screeching with pleasure when Oliver stuffed his fingers into
his ears in mock distress.

Oliver took them back to the nursery, dressed them in long
woollen gowns and took them to the sitting room where the tree
candles had been lit and more parcels awaited their eager little
hands.

'Did you ever see so many toys?' Oliver asked Dolly. He
was as pleased as the children were, winding up the clockwork
merry-go-round for Edward, pretending amazement when Lizzie's
jack-in-a-box popped out with a squeak for the umpteenth time.

'Do you think we're spoiling them?' he asked anxiously 'I don't
want them to grow up like some we've known.' He knew Dolly
would remember the petulant little monsters, accompanied by a
retinue of servants, who had, all unaware, been the laughing stock
of the village when they had come to Suttonford with their aristocratic parents.

'No. I keep them in order when you're not here. They don't
get all their own way with me,' Dolly assured him. She clapped
her hands smartly together, to demonstrate. 'Come along now!
Upstairs with Iris! Washed and dressed in five minutes! Don't keep
Mammy waiting!'

They scuttled off obediently and Oliver grinned. 'That takes me
back, Dolly. You never went in for gentle persuasion, did you?'
He handed her a bulky parcel, which had been concealed behind

264

the curtains, and watched as she carefully untied the string before removing the paper, smoothing out its creases as she did so.

It was a cape. A cape of grey squirrel with braided silk fastenings and a black grosgrain lining. She draped it around her shoulders, turning this way and that, admiring it in the big mirror. Her fingers ran over the silky fur, stroking it against her arm. She pouted her lips, half-closed her eyes, stood on a chair the better to see its length and finally she pronounced. 'It must be the best fur cape in the whole of bloody Southport! Wait till I walk round the bandstand in this.'

Her present to Oliver was large and flat. He tore at the paper with hasty fingers. It was a picture; he could feel the frame ... but what a strange thing for her to buy for him!

It was a framed photograph of his father. Where had she found this? 'I never knew there was a photograph of Dad. Where did you get it?' he asked.

'There's a photographer's shop in town. I got him to do it from a negative I had. Joe had it taken before we got married. There's one of me an' all,' she told him.

She didn't tell him that she had also bought a photograph of Oliver and a woman in a silk shawl ... a photograph that a 'Mr and Mrs Wainwright' had never collected, the man told her, more than a year ago. She had hidden that one in the attic.

'Thanks, Dolly. I think I'll keep it here, if you don't mind. If Dad's portrait ever hangs on the wall at Suttonford Manor it will be painted in oils.' He held the picture at arm's length. 'We're a good-looking lot, aren't we?' he said proudly. 'Dad, me, Tommy and Edward.'

* * *

Florence dated Mama's decline from Oliver's brush with death. Mama had taken to her room for longer and longer spells; sometimes only appearing in the afternoons or before dinner. She stopped visiting. They did no more calling. Nobody came to the house.

She was not as steady on her legs, not as alert as she used to be. Instead of improving, on hearing of Florence's betrothal – for Oliver first asked Grandfather and received his blessing – Mama had taken a worse turn and physicians had been summoned.

They said that it was a temporary decline, due to Mama's age and prescribed iron tonic for anaemia and brandy for her tremors.

It was time, Florence decided, that Mama regained an interest in life and today, to that end, she would ask Mama to help her choose patterns and fabrics for her trousseau. There were catalogues from silversmiths and designs for upholstery to be considered. Mama would insist on being consulted if she were in the best of health. She should be encouraged to do so now. She went upstairs and tapped on Mama's door.

'Mama,' she called.

'Come in, Florence.'

Mama's speech was slurred but Florence saw, with relief, that her eyes were bright and her cheeks had a healthy colour. She was dressed, too, and it was only two-thirty.

'You're better?' Florence said, crossing to the desk and taking Mama's hands. They were cool; a good sign, surely. 'Are you able to help choose my trousseau? I have no idea what to order without your help.'

Mama took a sip of brandy and stood up. 'I shall enjoy it, dear,' she said. She took Florence's arm and held on tight in a painful grip as they descended the wide stair to the drawing room.

A fire had been lit since early morning and the room was warm and inviting. A Christmas tree had been brought in for Florence to dress. Dozens of cards adorned the mantelshelf. They would be taken to Suttonford tomorrow, Christmas Eve.

Mama sent down for brandy and gave her full attention to the catalogues. Florence was pleased that she seemed to be her old self again, dismissing some – no, most of the designs with a high-handed 'Hideous', 'Ugh', 'Ghastly', as she turned pages quickly. Now and again she'd stop, scrutinise a drawing and ask Florence to pass a bookmark.

Florence beamed. Mama loved the limelight. She behaved like a dowager duchess when she was being deferred to. Her eyebrows were raised high above the droopy eyelids, her lips were pursed, nostrils drawn in. Only her shaking hands betrayed the fact that all was not well.

And this was Florence's chance to ask Mama about marriage. The subject had not been broached. It was a mother's duty to share her knowledge with a daughter whose own wedding date was near.

'There is much I don't know ...' she began shyly. 'What shall I expect, Mama?' Mama had not understood. She merely lifted her eyes from the catalogue, sipped the brandy and said, 'What?'

'Of marriage. I know so little ...' Florence began to twist the engagement ring round her finger in embarrassment. The pairs of diamonds, set between oval cut rubies, caught the light prettily and she concentrated on them so as not to see if Mama, too, was uncomfortable.

'You must lie still, Florence, and let him take his pleasure,' came the drawled reply. Florence was shocked. 'Is it no pleasure for us then, Mama?' she asked quietly.

'It cannot be. Not with a man of that type.'

Florence watched Mama's face for a sign that she was trying to wound, but saw only pity. What must Mama think of Oliver?

'Mama, Oliver is not a type. He is dear and considerate. I cannot tell you how good he is for that would betray a confidence but I promise you Mama that his concern is only for my happiness. I so want to please him.'

Her need to share with Mama the joy that Oliver had brought into her life made her add, 'You and Father were happy. You said so, often. You loved one another. Marriage must have been a pleasure to you.'

'Your father was a gentleman. He understood ...'

Mama's eyes had gone bleary. Florence did not want to hear again the reminiscences of Mama's youth, the masked balls, the endless flirtations; she had heard them too often.

'Understood what?' she asked quickly.

'That love is a sport. A game of skill. That it is not a need.'

'Is that what you believe, Mama? That love is a game? That once the rules are learned there's no more than that?'

Mama's eyes were cold again. 'For the lower classes it is a crude appetite. They are the beasts of the field. And the middle class is sprung from below, Florence.' She sipped her brandy lazily. 'The middle classes are furtive and full of shame. They believe that they are being base. They cannot know the delights we know.'

'Oliver is different,' Florence interrupted her.

'Oliver will already be versed in the ways of his class. He will have had women of no refinement. He will continue to use them.' Mama put up her hand to signal that she was not to be stopped. 'You will be disappointed if you expect married love to come from this misalliance.'

Hurt and rage fought in Florence but she would not let Mama see that her words were wounding her to her very soul. 'I won't be disappointed,' she said. 'Look at Uncle Bill and Aunt Lucy. They were happy. They loved one another.'

'Theirs was a true love match,' Mama answered in a weary tone.

Mama was the worse for drink now. Florence hated it when she began to stumble over her words. She was on her feet, groping for the decanter with one hand, her eyes dull as she tried to focus on Florence's face.

Florence could not help it. She was overcome with the injustice of Mama's words. She snatched the brandy from Mama's hand and held it high, out of reach of Mama's grasping hand. 'And mine is a love match, Mama,' she found herself saying, anger and triumph in her voice. 'Oliver has wanted to marry me since I was fourteen.'

Mama's face turned to stone, as Grandmother's did when she was at her most cutting. 'Grandfather has asked Oliver to marry you, Florence. It is a financial arrangement that suits them both. Love has nothing to do with it.'

It was as if Mama had struck her. Florence felt the blood drain from her face. Her limbs had turned to water. It wasn't true…? Mama was lying. She put down the decanter slowly and sank into the chair.

She put her arms upon the desk and hid her face from Mama. 'Say it isn't true, Mama,' she whispered. 'Please say it isn't true.'

There was silence. Florence lifted her eyes and looked at Mama's face for the truth. And it was there. Mama had not lied.

Mama gave her a look of pity and began to walk towards the door. 'Mama ...' Florence beseeched the retreating figure. 'Please ...'

Mama turned. 'Will you break the engagement, Florence? If I say it is true?' she asked evenly.

A cold, hard little place began to form in Florence's heart. She felt it. She must nurture it. She would not be used in this way, as if she were a malleable piece of clay. She would marry Oliver, even if he had deceived her. She could live without love. She could not live without him.

'No, Mama,' she said firmly. 'I will not give him up.'

* * *

Oliver left for Suttonford on New Year's Eve and found a carriage waiting at the station. Florence was waiting for him in the hall, dressed in violet velvet, her hair a bright torch against the sombre colour of her dress.

They were all present; Lucy and Lady Oldfield, Laura and Sir Philip and Godfrey, the dissipated son. They greeted him warmly, asked if he had eaten and then continued to talk amongst themselves.

Florence took his arm. 'I'm going to show Oliver the house,' she announced. 'It's dreadful that he's not seen over it yet.'

They went from room to room with Florence pointing out family treasures; the Japanese vase presented by an emperor to her great-grandfather; an Egyptian stool from an expedition to the tombs of pharaohs; books handwritten by monks in medieval times; and portraits and tapestries in a never-ending sequence.

After the fourth such splendid apartment Oliver had seen enough to satisfy an avid historian. 'Is anyone about?' he asked, then before she could either reply or protest, took her in his arms in a passionate embrace.

'I've been wanting to do that since I saw you,' he told her. 'The house can wait!' Guests were arriving for the party and Oliver knew that he was going to be assessed by the 'county' set and the relatives who came to Suttonford for the festivities. He had learned a lot about the family and their way of life. He had conceded nothing to the snobbish hangers-on who invaded the great house from time to time, looking down their long noses at the 'upstart' Florence was to marry.

He knew they hoped that the engagement would soon be broken, that Florence would come to her senses and choose someone from their ranks; someone more used to their ways. Once he was in control of the house he'd see that they never crossed the threshold again.

The ballroom was splendid. The fine maplewood floor gleamed from repeated polishing and buffing. At its centre stood the Christmas tree, reaching almost to the ceiling, lit by hundreds of candles in silver holders, heavy with fine crystal ornaments, blown glass swans and tear-drop decorations in jewel colours.

Gold curtains were pulled across the tall windows, making one wall a draped background to the elegance of the guests. Six chandeliers, each holding a hundred long candles, lit the room and giant candelabra lit the platform where the family stood. Around three walls of the ballroom slender columns supported the gallery, where tonight, the orchestra played.

Guests were announced and brought to the platform by liveried footmen, to be welcomed by Sir Philip, from his chair, and Lady Oldfield who stood at his side. Laura, Florence and Oliver were next in the receiving line and for an hour or longer the handshaking, bowing and kissing of soft, rouged cheeks took all their attention.

At last Oliver held Florence in his arms. They took to the floor first, to polite applause from the guests.

'You were wonderful, Oliver,' Florence whispered. 'I thought you might find the introductions a trial. Oh, I'm so happy!'

At midnight the Scottish dancers entered. The girls, sashed in tartan over white dresses, slid on their slippered feet, spun and skipped to the haunting music. Their kilted partners held and turned them, looking proud and handsome in black velvet, lace and silver.

Oliver noticed that Lucy had tears in her eyes. Bill had introduced his Scottish traditions to the clumsy English celebrations. How he would have enjoyed seeing Florence and himself celebrating their betrothal at his favourite festival.

Servants slipped amongst the guests, giving each a glass of whisky to toast the New Year in the old Scottish manner.

The dancers stopped. The great clock struck midnight and skirling pipers circled the ballroom. Then came the kissing of partners and neighbours and hands were joined for the playing of 'Auld Lang Syne' before the party really began.

'A new year and a new life, Oliver.' Florence toasted them, sipping the amber liquid swiftly, laughter in her eyes as she attempted to get the fiery drink down.

Oliver drained his glass in one quick movement. He threw back his head; his eyes were alight with anticipation for the years to come. He placed his strong arms around his beautiful bride-to-be, lifted her high off the ground and kissed her soundly before the eyes of her family and friends.

'Our future!' he said.

PART TWO

The Moses Child

1900

Chapter Twenty-Three

Edward Wainwright, twenty years old, dark-haired and as handsome as his father had been at the same age, straightened his long back and looked up from his desk out over the tree-lined road. Laden branches of flowering peach swayed under the window. Through them he saw, to his great delight and amusement, his mother riding her bicycle.

Dolly Wainwright wore knickerbockers of grey woollen cloth, a frilled blouse of white cotton and a large hat of yellow straw, tied on with a chiffon scarf. She pedalled away from the house, the machine rattling over the setts, disturbing the tranquillity of the summer afternoon. It was her fifty-fifth birthday.

For three hours Edward had been writing, concentrating on the papers he had before him. To study 'The Causes of Non-Obstructive Jaundice' any longer would be useless. There were four weeks until the exams. He shook his pen on to the blotting paper, wiped the nib on a little inky square of felt, placed it in the wooden box and began to work his shoulders to unlock their set.

Then he turned to look at Lizzie. She lay sprawled across the hearth rug of the room she had converted from their old nursery. A drawing board was propped against the steel fender and she jabbed at the paper violently with a stick of colour.

Lizzie was tall and graceful, slim and vibrant, with hair the colour of copper, a fine straight nose and a wide, generous mouth. This afternoon her face was a picture; her mouth pressed into a firm line, clear forehead furrowed and her greenish-blue eyes a mere glint under drawn brows.

Audrey Reimann

She lifted her gaze from the jar of lilac blossom and her expression dissolved into a smile. 'I'm trying to get the effect the Impressionists make,' she told him. 'Have you finished?'

'If I don't know it now I'll never make a doctor,' Edward said. He uncurled his legs, stood up and stretched long arms high above his head. For he was tall. At six feet four he was two inches taller than Oliver but he had his father's features and was unmistakably a Wainwright.

He tugged Lizzie upright. 'Are you having second thoughts?'

She dusted her hands over the crumpled dress of sprigged muslin and pushed back the unruly mop of hair, which had escaped from its tortoiseshell combs. 'You could give it up and work for Oliver,' she added with what Edward knew was a shade of hopefulness.

'I'm going to be a doctor, Lizzie,' he said firmly. 'And I will be one in a few years' time.' It was inconceivable that he would not. But Lizzie and Mother had never really understood his vocation. They had always supposed that one day he would join his brother in the thriving industrial world of the cotton mills.

'Even if I fail my exams I'll not work for Oliver,' he explained. 'He'd want to give me an easy passage and too big a wage. I won't take any more charity from him.' He sat down again on his chair and looked at Lizzie with affection. 'But I don't think I'll fail.'

'You won't fail, Edward,' she said staunchly, 'but you've chosen a difficult path. Oliver would pay for your training. You're doing it the hard way.'

Edward said, 'It's hard on you and Mother.' He reached out and took her hands in his. He wanted her to know how much their support meant to him. 'You sacrifice to help me; you pay for my books and clothes. I'm grateful. You know that. It isn't difficult for me. It's the only thing I want.'

Lizzie's face had a look of devotion. Neither she nor Mother thought their economies were a sacrifice. 'We're proud of you, Edward,' she told him. 'We don't want you to feel any gratitude, though I wish I knew what made you want to take up medicine.'

He let go her hands and smiled as she absent-mindedly tried to catch her loose hair and fasten it, while giving him her attention.

'I'll tell you. Do you remember Iris?' he asked.

'Of course I do.'

'Do you remember Mother taking us to Liverpool to see her after she married?'

'Yes.'

'Do you remember the street, Lizzie? The street Iris lived in. Do you remember all those poor people?' He hoped she would understand. 'Do you remember those children with spindly legs ... and the pretty little blind girl who begged on the corner, turning her head and shaking her money bag when she heard footsteps?' he asked earnestly. 'Do you remember old men stooped from humping great loads at the docks?'

'I remember,' she said gently. 'They used to frighten me. But doctors can't make blind people see or straighten old men's backs.'

'I can help the children,' he told her. 'When I'm a doctor I can improve their lives. Some of those children work in factories. Factories like Oliver's. They're growing; they need good food and fresh air. They don't see daylight from one week to the next. It's wrong.'

'Oliver doesn't think it's wrong,' Lizzie said. 'He had to work hard when he was young. He believes it's the normal thing for poor people to do.'

'He's fair. He doesn't employ children under twelve but Oliver thinks everyone's capable of doing as he's done. And they're not. The strong and healthy have to care for the weak and sick.'

'But he wants to help you, Edward. He wants you to accept his money.'

'I won't take any more from him. Mother's got enough. And Dad left us two hundred pounds each. That was never touched. It's worth over five hundred now. I have the interest off that and the bursary.'

He stood up, touched her cheek tenderly and bent to brush his lips against the riot of copper hair. 'I've enough, Lizzie,' he said.

'Oliver's got his son and a baby daughter to support. I wouldn't want them to think we were sponging; that we were taking anything that was theirs.'

'He's probably got enough problems with James, anyway, without our little worries,' Lizzie said.

Edward had not much interest in Oliver's son. He had met James once when the boy was ten and Oliver brought him to Southport. Lizzie and he had found James to be such an aggressive child that there was no pleasure in his company. 'Is Oliver coming today?' he asked. 'He usually remembers Mother's birthday.'

'Maud's birth was difficult, his letter said. Florence didn't find it easy after all these years. I don't know if he's coming over.' Lizzie pulled at his hand. 'Come on. I've spent the morning making your favourite scones. I like being economical. Let's go down and make our own tea.'

Edward led the way to the big, comfortable kitchen downstairs, past the framed photographs in the hall of Joe Wainwright, their father, and their older brother Tommy, whom they had never met.

Tea was set at the long oak table and Edward picked up a scone and spread butter thickly; too hungry to wait until the tea was made. 'You love all this, don't you, Lizzie?' he said. 'All the making and baking. The household work. What they call "home management"?'

Lizzie filled the teapot from the copper tap on the range, placed it on its tile stand and pulled a knitted tea cosy over it. 'Yes,' she laughed. 'I'll not campaign for Votes for Women or anything. I'm just a simple homebody.'

'You are more than that, my sweet,' said Edward. 'You're beautiful and talented.'

'Edward!' she protested, 'I'm not. I'm a dabbler.'

She was laughing at him now but he knew he spoke the truth. 'Just remember all the things you do, Lizzie. You paint and draw – your pictures are all over the walls – look!'

She put her finger to her lips, making him smile more broadly at her attempts not to let the two old servants in the next-door scullery hear the praise. She was blushing. He loved to give her confidence in herself. Lizzie made light of her achievements. He pointed to the three pictures on the walls. 'Look – we don't even have a cat, yet you've done a wonderful likeness on that one.'

There was one of her still lifes over the door, above the velvet draught-curtain. He held out his buttery knife towards it. 'And there – look at those oranges. You could eat them.'

'Edward – stop it!' She had put her hands over her mouth in the shy way he loved but her eyes were huge and shining.

She needed praise, Edward knew. It was no use her protesting that she merely filled in her idle hours. 'You are very artistic, Lizzie,' he said seriously. 'You love to sew. I bet you made the dress you're wearing – didn't you?'

'Yes.'

'And embroidered the new fire screen?'

'Yes.'

'And whose little sampler do I have on the wall of my London room?'

'You don't! Oh, Edward.' She bumped down on to a chair. 'I'll do you a nice picture for your room. Why didn't you ask?'

He was enjoying himself, making her admit to her talents. 'You get it from Mother,' he pronounced. 'She never had a chance to develop her gifts when she was young, but she had artistic ability.'

'I always thought so, Edward. I wish she'd try something.'

'She does – her cooking! And she buys lovely, outrageous clothes that only a woman with imagination could wear.'

'Yet she thinks she's so down-to-earth.' Lizzie smiled.

He cut a large slice of Mother's fruit cake and let Lizzie fill his teacup again. 'She is. Mother's practical but hasn't she made this house into a home filled with colour? I love coming home – seeing the changes she's made.'

'I know. She's forever changing the rooms around. As soon as I do a picture or she buys so much as an ornament or fills a vase with flowers she rearranges everything to set it off.' Now she was laughing with him. 'And her friends, Edward! Some of those singers and dancers ... !'

'Will she be in for tea?' Edward asked, all at once overcome with the realisation that he had eaten all but three of Lizzie's scones. There were no chicken sandwiches left either and at least a quarter of the fruit cake was gone.

'I expect so. She's out cycling. She says if she does it for half an hour in the morning and the same at night she'll get her tiny waistline back!'

He grinned. 'I saw her, half an hour ago. I've told her that middle-aged women of her build invariably become stout and she could better lose it by keeping to a reducing diet. But she'll have none of it.' He laughed now, remembering. 'She said she'd rather add another pleasure to her life than lose one.'

Lizzie put a hand to her mouth again so that the servants wouldn't hear. Her eyes were full of suppressed laughter. 'If only cycling didn't give her such an appetite,' she said. 'She can't understand where the weight's coming from when she's so active. But she can't resist her own cooking.'

'I suppose half the Variety turns will be here tonight, as it's her birthday,' Edward said, trying in vain to make what was left on the tea table look adequate. 'We'll have to put in an appearance at the table, I expect.'

'I'll cut more sandwiches if Mother wants some,' Lizzie said, brushing his hands away from the plate. 'We'll eat with them tonight, then you can say that you have to work for your exams and I'll make some excuse as well.'

They heard the side gate slam, heard their mother's quick feet on the steps outside before Dolly flung open the back door. 'Put my bicycle in the shed, Edward,' she panted. 'I'm that hot!' She dropped into the rocking chair, limp and red-faced. There was a sprinkling of grey in her hair, taming down the colour, and a few lines around her eyes and mouth but she did not look as old as some women of fifty-five, as she often told them. 'I'm going to the Variety tonight. I'm bringing people back for my birthday supper so I'll go and get ready soon. Top the pot up! Give your poor old mother a cup of tea!'

Edward filled a cup for her and buttered a scone. 'I expect you're hungry, Mother,' he said, avoiding Lizzie's eye. 'Go upstairs to change. I'll put your bicycle away and bring this up to you.'

'Thank you, love,' she said, beaming at him. 'Will you put my combs in when I'm dressed, Lizzie?'

'Are you wearing your pink dress, Mother?' Edward loved to tease her. 'The one all splattered with beads?'

'Yes. It's my favourite. I haven't worn it for weeks.' She pulled herself to her feet and Edward followed her, carrying a tray of tea and scones.

'Don't eat all the fruit cake, Lizzie,' he called. 'I'll be down in a minute.'

* * *

Oliver's hands on the neck of the stallion were as firmly in control of the animal as they were on the cotton empire he ruled. It was a fine May morning and he waited at the top of the moorland path for his son, James, to catch up with him.

High above Suttonford House he watched the sun's first rays flash on to its windows and light the surface of the ornamental lake, rousing a flurry of waterfowl. At forty-one his hair was as thick and black as it had always been; he was fit, the energy in his broad, powerful body had increased with age and he had an outlet for it, hunting in season and riding out alone most summer mornings.

The stallion shook his head, knowing he was within sight of his stable. Oliver held him and looked over his shoulder. 'Come, James!' he said. 'Don't pull on the bit. You're riding like an old woman.'

James, now only a few yards away, had drawn his brow with a look of fierce resentment and Oliver recognised, as he so often did, that their only son had inherited little from Florence, but from his father both looks and temperament.

281

'Don't put that expression on your face,' he ordered. 'I know you didn't want to come out this morning but for God's sake do it with good grace.' As James drew up beside him he added, 'You'll be back at school by tonight. Don't spoil your last few hours.'

'Father?'

'Yes.'

'I don't want to go back.' Hostility clouded James's dark, handsome face.

'Why?'

'I hate it,' James replied. 'I want to stay here. You sent for me.'

'It was your mother who wanted you to come home to see your baby sister, not I.'

'You didn't consider it of sufficient importance then?' James said in the arch tone of voice that so annoyed Oliver.

Oliver tried not to show his exasperation. 'When a man has only two children they are important,' he replied.

James's face was a dark mask of fury. 'Then why not listen to me? I'm your firstborn and I tell you, school's a waste of time – and money.'

Oliver was quickly losing such patience as he had shown. 'I'm the one who decides on the waste, or otherwise, of your time. I pay the bills. Don't tell me what's best for you,' he said brusquely. 'Now go ahead. Stable your horse. I'll see you at breakfast.'

James dug his heels into the bay mare viciously, making the animal throw back her ears before she pulled away in an excited canter. He turned her towards the moor and the road that led upwards into the Pennine Hills.

Oliver's anger was kindled by this show of ill-temper. He'd taught James to ride. He would not allow him to treat a good hunter this way.

'Come back!' he ordered. But James was beyond hearing, twenty or thirty yards ahead, kicking the mare savagely to spur her into action.

Oliver tightened the right rein to turn Comet in the same direction and pressed his heels into the black stallion's flanks. 'Go on,' he yelled, lifting himself out of the saddle, urging the powerful animal into a gallop as he leaned over its strong neck. 'I'll knock some sense into him this time.' He kept his head well down as they chased, gaining ground on James.

James was asking for trouble – he was insolent and this time Oliver's own temper was roused. James would regret his behaviour. 'Stop!' he shouted over the pounding of hooves. 'Pull up!'

The path ahead divided, the left-hand fork going up to the hills, the right going down through the forest to the house. At the last moment Oliver saw James pull the mare on to the homeward track.

Oliver reined in. He heard his son's wild laughter ring out over the moor; he watched James slow his pace and turn to look up at his father. He would not follow him. He did not hear what James said – perhaps he was meant not to hear. But the mutiny was over. James would return to school.

Oliver watched him go and wondered, not for the first time, on the different temperaments of his two sons. Edward, twenty years of age, who had been brought up without a father's influence, believing Oliver to be his older brother, was clever and sensitive. He'd won a bursary to study medicine and was the finest son a father could hope to have.

James, on the other hand, had had his father's influence, love and attention, the best of education and a devoted mother and grandmother to sustain him. James had cultured manners, fine clothes and was indulged by the women of Oliver's household in every whim. Yet he was wilful and arrogant and nobody, except Oliver himself, appeared to be aware of the fact.

He saw James, riding easily now, cross to the coach-yard and stables. Oliver remained where he was for a little while longer. He liked to be alone, to think without distractions and often he rode or walked in the hills, finding answers to questions that troubled him.

Today he pondered on the feeling of dissatisfaction that had become a part of his life. He saw it as his own ingratitude, for life had given him much more than he had a right to expect. And yet . . .

He had imagined himself, in his youth, as head of a large family, taking his children with him, teaching them to ride and to swim, walking, working and at night seeing them around his supper table, all under his roof, surrounding him, filling his hours with their talk and their joy. He never imagined that the only son of his marriage would be so difficult to understand.

Oliver tried to be rational about James's character. He knew that he and his son would have to learn to work together if James was to run the estate in his turn. But then, he thought, the boy is only fifteen. Perhaps he was expecting too much of him.

The horse trampled impatiently and all at once Oliver was angry with himself. Providence had given him so much. 'Hell,' he said out loud. 'He's just like I was – resentful of restriction and ready to fight the world. He'll be all right when he's older.'

Oliver leaned forward again over the stallion's neck. Comet's hooves beat against the trodden earth of the path. The air was fast and cool against his cheek, and the speed and strength of his favourite mount exhilarated him, clearing his mind of everything but the age-old challenge of man in control of a spirited animal.

He slowed the horse and rode into the yard, dismounted and led Comet to his loose box before handing the saddle and bridle to a waiting groom, then he strode across the cobblestone yard, his boots ringing in the morning stillness, to the back entrance of Suttonford.

Water had been brought and his valet had laid out his business clothes. He washed and dressed and made his way downstairs. Wilkins would have left the morning post in the side room. He'd sort out his letters before he went to see Florence.

Laura and James were talking at the table. They had not seen him cross the hall to the anteroom that adjoined the dining room but since there was no door between the rooms he could hear their conversation clearly.

Laura's voice was as strong as it had ever been but the drawling, languid tone was now at odds with her appearance. She was past sixty and her haughty demeanour had gone. Time and alcohol had taken their toll on Florence's mother. The girlish figure and youthful looks were no more. She was a gaunt, waspish woman, dressed always in grey or black, with a face excessively lined and suspicious.

She had never wavered in her dislike of him. He knew that she thought of him still as a rough character; as one who could easily revert to type.

'Mason!' Laura's voice held a note of complaint as she spoke to her foolish companion woman. 'Ring the servants' bell and ask for my restorative.'

Oliver heard her tapping with her silver-tipped cane on the table. 'You'll soon learn all there is to know, Mason. Don't be upset if I speak sharply. I'm a sick woman, you know.'

'Do you need brandy even at breakfast, Gran?' James asked in a tone Oliver recognised as sarcastic, but which Laura would understand to be one of concern.

'I have to take a pint each day, James. For medicinal reasons. It must be taken every hour to prevent my suffering another seizure,' Laura replied. 'What did you say earlier, darling? You want to stay at home with your new sister and your mother?'

'Father won't allow it,' James replied shortly.

'Oh, the celebrations we had when you were born, James. My father had the house filled with guests. We had a grand ball and fireworks display. The servants were given a week's pay and a party in the village hall ...'

'... And by the time I was old enough to enjoy a carnival,' James said caustically, '... I had ceased to be a novelty, I suppose. When did the rot set in, Gran? When did Father decide I should be sent away?'

'When you were young your father wanted to keep you here,' Laura drawled. 'It was the last time your dear great-grandfather imposed his will. It was he – Sir Philip Oldfield – who insisted you go to his old school. Your father would have treated you like a common labourer's child, making you attend the village school.'

'Can't you speak for me, Gran?' James interrupted. 'Or ask Mother to send for me? I hate school.'

'What will you do, darling? If you come home? Will you go to the Transvaal to fight the Boers? Your grandfather was an army man.'

Laura was becoming maudlin. Soon she would be reminiscing about the husband she had lost when Florence was a child, thought Oliver.

James answered. 'I'll run the estate. Father prefers his cotton mills. I'm going to inherit one day and I want to have charge of it.'

'Oh, my darling,' Laura drawled. 'You are so like your dear great-grandfather was. Life at Suttonford was so much more pleasant when my dear parents were alive.'

Oliver decided to leave the remaining letters until he'd seen Florence. He could not concentrate with Laura's inane outpourings ringing in his ears. He could have tolerated her, had she spent more time in the considerable comfort of Balgone, which she'd inherited from Lucy Grandison after her death from a stroke a few years ago. Instead, as ever, she spent her days at Florence's side, arriving by carriage at nine o'clock and not leaving until dark, her proud boast being that she had hardly spent a day of her life away from her daughter.

Before baby Maud's birth Laura had taken up residence. She had a suite of two bedrooms and small sitting room for herself and her companion. Oliver now decided to tell her to return to Balgone every night, as before. He knew that Florence often found her mother's company tiring and wondered at his wife's forbearance. He left the anteroom, unobserved.

Dr Russell, a youngish man, one of the best doctors in the county, was being shown into the hall as Oliver crossed the upper landing. Oliver ran down the marble stairs. 'I understand that you wanted to speak to me?' he said. He held out his hand. 'Follow me. We'll talk in my study.'

Since the death of Sir Philip, Oliver had transferred all the books and records into this pleasant panelled room, which overlooked the front of the house and the lake. 'Come in, Dr Russell. Please be seated.'

The doctor remained standing, stroking his chin. 'I've bad news for you, Wainwright,' he began. 'You know that the baby had adopted a difficult position in your wife's womb?'

He must have seen Oliver's look of disquiet for he said reassuringly, 'She was never in danger. She was delivered safely.' There was a moment's pause before he added, 'There must be no more children. A third pregnancy would kill her.'

'Does she know this?' Oliver's voice was steady.

'Yes. She was naturally upset but I must ask you to comfort her all you can.' Oliver nodded and waited for him to continue. Obviously the man did not flinch from speaking plainly.

'You understand what this means? There are no precautions you can take, which are certain to prevent conception. There are ways and we all know about them, but the only safe thing is total absence of sexual contact until her childbearing years are over. And that, I'm afraid, is what you face.'

'How long must we wait?'

'If the menses recommence then it could be ten years. If they do not you must wait until a year has elapsed.'

'Are you certain she's in no danger now?' Oliver demanded.

'There's always a possibility of something unforeseen but every skill known to medicine was brought to bear on this delivery.'

'I shall take great care of her, doctor,' Oliver told him.

'If Mrs Wainwright has complete rest, freedom from anxiety and young company to look forward to I believe she will make a quick recovery,' the doctor added.

Oliver looked at him keenly. 'And you think that she is being denied them?' he asked in a sharper tone.

'I think that the constant presence of her mother at her side will not aid her recovery,' the doctor answered, evidently not inhibited by Oliver's apparent rebuke. 'My concern is for my patient's welfare.'

Oliver smiled and extended his hand. 'Thank you for your advice,' he said. 'I shall see that Mrs Wainwright has the best of care.' He walked to the door of the study and turned before opening it. 'There will be no more children,' he told the doctor solemnly.

Oliver ran up the stairs to Florence's apartments and found her at the window of her sitting room, a tiny figure in a white silk kimono, gazing out over the lawn and lake of Suttonford.

'I was looking for you, darling,' she said. 'Did you come in the back way?'

Oliver put his arms around her and bent forward to kiss her lightly on her nose. 'I did. You should be in bed, my love,' he said. 'Doctor Russell says that your lying-in must be spent at complete rest.'

'I'll be all right, Oliver. Don't worry so. I was only twenty-four when James was born. At thirty-nine I could not expect to have so easy a time.'

He led her to her bedroom, beyond the sitting room she had decorated in the modern style, lifted her as if she were a doll and placed her in the high bed. 'I've spoken to the doctor,' he said.

'Has he told you?' Florence's eyes were troubled and he knew that she had been worrying about his reaction to the doctor's injunction. 'I'll risk it, Oliver. I don't care, darling.' She held tight onto his hand. 'You're only forty-one. Can you contemplate abstinence? It might be years before ...'

'Your life's more important than children,' he told her, smiling at his darling, stroking her hand, watching intently as the relief she was trying so hard to conceal flooded into her sweet face. 'I love you so.'

It was true. Oliver loved her dearly though it had never been a marriage of passion. Florence, from the start, had shied from deep displays of emotion. Something had held her back, some hidden reserve had prevented her from releasing herself, from abandoning herself to the love he wanted her to share. He smiled when he thought of her pretences, her feigning of pleasure in his advances. Long, long ago he had known that she wanted to please him, wanted his attentions, but could not respond to them. He loved her though he had seen through her artfulness.

But there would be no more children. He could not allow her to risk another pregnancy. He would remain in his own separate suite. Florence would protest for the sake of his vanity, he knew, but in her heart she would be glad that her duties were over.

They must both endure this separation for they had so much else. They laughed together, they understood one another, shared friends and pleasures and, most gratifying, Florence still delighted in being his wife.

He fussed over her now, arranging the sheets and the silk coverlet around her. 'I'm going to Manchester today,' he announced when she was propped up on her pillows. 'I'm meeting Albert to look over the site of a new factory. Then I must go to Southport. It's Dolly's birthday.'

Florence looked exactly the same as she always had. Her hair was unfaded, her beauty unimpaired. But the strain of the pregnancy had exhausted her.

Oliver brushed her hair from her face with great tenderness. 'Your little grey shadow is having breakfast, Florence,' he said, warning her of Laura's impending arrival. 'I'm going to tell her that she and her companion must return to Balgone today. They must go home.'

'But, Oliver,' Florence said, 'you know that Mama is only happy here, at Suttonford.'

'I know,' he told her, but the tender tone had gone. Command came easily to him now. 'Suttonford is not her home. She was born here and I understand her attachment to the place. But she has a companion. She will come to Suttonford daily. It's for your sake that I allow her to come here every day. She has a home of her own and she must return to it.'

Florence gave him an understanding smile. 'I'll speak to her, Oliver. It will be better for her – kinder – if I say that I would prefer to be left alone.'

'As you wish.' Oliver stood at the bedside. 'I'll walk with James to the station. He is going to ask you to allow him to remain here when he comes to say farewell. Don't encourage him.'

'Oliver,' Florence said, pulling herself into an upright position. 'Why don't you spend a few days with your stepmother and her children?'

'Don't you need me?' he said.

'No. I'll recover all the faster if I do nothing but rest.' She leaned back against the pillows. 'And, Oliver ...' She smiled.

'Yes?'

'Ask Elizabeth if she'd like to spend a summer here. I've never met those young people. And you've talked about them so much. Perhaps your stepmother will agree to let her join us. It will be fun to have someone young to entertain.'

Oliver was startled by her request. 'You know that I have always insisted on their remaining in Southport?' he said.

'Yes, I've known but I never understood why.'

He sat down on the bed and took her hand in his. It had been a weight on his shoulders all these years, concealing his paternity of Edward. Often he had wondered if he should confide in Florence. She would have understood, and forgiven him. But he could not reveal the deception to Edward and Lizzie. They were happy, confident young people who had no reason to believe themselves anything other than Wainwrights and he their half-brother.

He stroked Florence's little hand. 'You know that Edward and Lizzie are registered as Wainwrights?'

'Yes, but Leach was their true father,' she answered.

'You remember that I told you we, Dolly and I, registered them in my own father's name?' He watched her face closely.

'Yes, darling, of course I do,' she replied.

'I have always been afraid that they might hear something ... that someone at Suttonford would remember Wilf Leach.'

'Who could? There is no one, Oliver.' Florence spoke gently.

'I have never told them about Wilf Leach,' he went on. 'He is dead now. He died in prison five years ago.'

'Well?'

'Don't forget that they came from the estate,' he reminded her.

'You are protecting them, Oliver, aren't you, my darling? All these years you have supported and protected them. And now you are afraid they will discover who their father was.' Florence leaned forward again, a sweet smile of understanding spreading over her tired little face. 'You are afraid that if Elizabeth comes here I might let slip the truth?'

He knew that she would never do that but he let her go on.

'Oh, Oliver, I'd never do that. I never think of them as anything but Wainwrights – as anything other than they know themselves to be.' She gripped his fingers with her own now, to emphasise her words. 'I swear to you, darling, I'd cut out my tongue if I thought there was any danger.'

'I know, my angel,' he said. 'But if they came here they could see Joe Wainwright's grave. They would see for themselves.'

'Truly, Oliver, I had forgotten the details. James knows the grave as that of his grandfather. Edward and Elizabeth should see it.'

He was afraid that she was tiring.

'Even Mama thinks of them as Wainwrights. She couldn't bear James to have a grandparent that she could not boast about. She talks about Joe Wainwright as if he were of distinguished – oh, sorry, darling.'

Perhaps he had been unnecessarily cautious. 'Edward will not come,' he said at last. 'He has to return to London and his studies.'

'I know. Perhaps one day. But Elizabeth? Do ask her, Oliver.'

'In a few weeks' time I will. When you are on your feet again.' Oliver kissed her cheek. 'I'll be back in a few days,' he said, then added impulsively, 'I'll ask Lizzie if she'd like to come.'

Chapter Twenty-Four

James and Laura had left the dining room by the time he returned and Oliver helped himself to scrambled eggs and cold ham. The post had been brought to the table and he made two neat stacks of the envelopes, one of tradesmen's accounts and one of personal letters.

He kept until last the one written in unfamiliar handwriting. As he read, his face drained of colour. He went to the dining-room door and closed it and found that his hands were shaking with fury. He took the letter to the window and read it again:

Dear Oliver Wainwright,

It has come to my notice that you have committed the very serious offence of falsifying a birth registration.

I have in my possession four items that would reveal to the world your duplicity and callous disregard of your dear wife's finer feelings. One of these items is a photograph, taken in 1879, of yourself and Mrs Rosalind Hadfield, the mother of your son. This alone is not sufficient evidence of infidelity but I also have three exercise books in her handwriting containing a confession of guilt from your paramour.

It is plain, from the content of these books, that Mrs Hadfield is the mother of the young man who knows himself to be Edward Cromwell Wainwright and who was registered under that name as the child of Dorothea Wainwright and your own father, Joseph Wainwright.

The writer is not greedy, and although the temptation to offer to you the aforementioned for a larger sum was considered, it was overruled in favour of a monthly fee, guaranteeing my silence, of ten pounds. Two five-pound notes must be sent to the above address, in an envelope addressed to A. King, Esq.

Unless this modest amount is received on the first day of every month the incriminating documents and photograph will be delivered into your wife's hands at Suttonford.

You could try to discover my identity but that would ultimately mean the revelation of your deception to your wife and to both your sons. I am sure that you will consider the price of silence to be worthwhile.

Underneath was a scrawl. The letter had been carefully written in childish print to conceal the handwriting. The money was to be posted to an address in a poor part of London.

With shaking hands and burning with anger Oliver put the letter back in its envelope and pushed it deep into his pocket. His appetite had gone. He went to the fireplace and rang the servants' bell. 'Tell Master James that we shall be leaving in five minutes' time,' he told the footman. He returned to his room and hurriedly packed a leather bag. Perhaps his anger would cool on the walk to the station.

James was waiting for him in the marble hall but he had no patience with James's sullen manner as they walked to the village station. 'I thought we'd have taken the trap, Father,' James began.

'You'll walk,' Oliver spoke angrily. 'Don't annoy me again today, James.'

They boarded the train and travelled in silence, James glaring out of the window until they reached Middlefield, where Oliver took him to the London platform and, in a sudden need for conciliation, gave his son a five-pound note.

'Here,' he said. 'I know I make you keep to your allowance, but I'm sure you'll find a use for it.'

James, though an inch shorter than him, managed to look down his nose with disdain as he took the money. 'Thanks,' he drawled. 'I'm overcome by your generosity.' He turned on his heel and moved swiftly to the open compartment door of his train before Oliver could succumb to the wild temptation he had to hit him.

When he was seated, alone, in a first-class compartment, Oliver took the letter out of his pocket and re-read it, though he had understood it perfectly on the first reading.

He was in the blackmailer's hands. He would have to pay. He would have this King watched, but that left the difficulty of recovering the books. The only other course was to report the matter to the police ... and exposure of the truth.

Oliver folded the letter and put it in his pocket and grimly asked himself, as he had so many times, if the truth would hurt, and he knew that it would be a cruel blow to Edward.

It had always been a burden, this pretending to his eldest son of brotherly interest. At the beginning he thought that the hardest part in the deception would be when his son asked for his father. It had been easy though, for Oliver to tell him about Joe Wainwright, sharing with his son his remembrance of his own father. The difficulty was now, when every impulse in him wanted to guide and steer him and have his complete trust, to stand aside, to watch his son struggle through life without the comfort of a father's hand.

And Oliver knew that he had denied himself the satisfaction of owning to two fine sons, for he was fiercely proud of Edward. No, he couldn't tell him. He'd have to pay the blackmailer. Even if Florence could accept the truth ... and how could he ask her to, now, when less than two hours ago he had compounded the lies. Their married life was finished ... how could he tell her of an affair that he'd conducted so long ago and lied about for so long? And if he did, Lizzie would have to be told about her murderous father.

'Damn. Damn!' He beat his fist against the upholstered seat. 'I must pay the blackguard. Pay him enough to keep a household going.' He would not notice the loss but the knowledge did not lessen his frustration.

When the train pulled in at Manchester he walked down the station approach road and caught an electric tram to Deansgate. If he walked he would have to think and he liked the trams; the clanging bell the driver rang at a stamp of his foot, the dynamo whining as the speed increased, the sparking of overhead wires, the wooden seats with their reversible back rests and the noise and chatter of the passengers inside. The tram ride took his thoughts, for the moment, away from the letter.

He alighted and walked to the grassy site where Albert and the architect were deep in conversation. 'What do you think of it?' he asked his partner. 'Do you think we should take the whole site?'

'No, but I know we will,' Albert said, 'and no doubt we'll ask ourselves how we managed without it twelve months after it's working.'

'Let's take the plans back to the hotel.'

Oliver took the parchments from the architect and together he and Albert made their way to Piccadilly on foot.

'You're looking down in the mouth, Oliver. You've hardly spoken a word. What's up?' Albert asked.

'Blackmail. That's what's up.' Oliver kept pace with Albert through the crowded street. He couldn't even confide in Albert for he'd never told even his closest friend that Edward was his son.

'What have you done to give anyone a hold over you?' his friend demanded. 'Is it another woman?'

'No. I've never been unfaithful to Florence,' he replied.

Oliver knew that Albert, despite a happy marriage and a large brood of children, had not been able to resist the charms of a succession of women.

'I've never been tempted,' he added, as if to apologise for his fidelity, smiling in spite of himself at the expression on Albert's face; half-envying, half-pitying. 'Unlike you I never could take my pleasures lightly.'

But even as he spoke Oliver knew that soon he would have to find a woman. He'd look for a discreet liaison with a sensible mistress, under the new circumstances of his marriage. There were such women. He was not innocent of their existence. But he would not look for real passion. For the twenty years of their marriage he had made do with affection and tenderness, and had denied what he thought of as his baser appetites. Florence and he had come together quickly and infrequently and it had been enough. When he took a mistress satisfaction of his physical needs would suffice.

They reached the hotel, newly built and splendid. They crossed the circular entrance lobby, magnificent in pink marble, to the deeply polished mahogany desk where they were met by the hotel manager and led to a reserved place in the dining room.

'We can talk in private here,' Oliver said as they were shown to one of the plush-seated and high-backed cubicles. He lowered his voice across the narrow dining table as a waiter brought them the menu. Oliver quickly returned to the business that was uppermost in his mind. 'I can't tell you why I'm being blackmailed but it's over the Southport connection.'

'Your stepmother's family? Leach?' Albert asked.

'You're near enough,' Oliver said. 'Do you know of anyone who'd trace the blackmailer?'

'Yes. I'll give you his address.' Albert ordered wine for them. 'Do you have to pay? Have you told Florence?'

'I can't.' Oliver answered. 'She'd never agree to pay a black-mailer. You know what Florence is like for "doing right".'

'Yes. She'd want to meet him and convert him to her ways,' Albert said, making Oliver smile. 'She never sees bad in anyone, does she?'

'No. Not even when it stares her in the ruddy face.' Albert would know he was speaking about Laura Mawdesley.

'Is the old woman still the same?' Albert asked.

'Worse. Florence believes that "poor Mama" is not well. She even supplies brandy to strengthen her.' Oliver helped himself from the dish of hors d'oeuvres, catching Albert's eye over the silver tray and grinning broadly for the first time that day.

'It'd be funny if it weren't true,' he added. 'It seems to have strengthened her all right. She's got the power of ten men when she resists being steered to her carriage.'

* * *

Edward and Lizzie had been sitting in the kitchen for an hour when Mother came downstairs corseted and cloaked for the theatre, wearing a fuchsia pink evening dress, with bugle beads and pearls on the tight bodice.

'You'll be mistaken for one of the actresses, Mother,' Edward said, knowing she would consider it a compliment.

'Make sure Nellie has everything ready, won't you?' Dolly fussed. 'There'll be at least ten coming back and it's all ready to dish up. Eeh, I wish you'd come with me.'

Edward took her arm and escorted her to the front door where he kissed her cheek soundly and squeezed her arm. 'Don't worry, Mother,' he said. 'Everything will be done. Enjoy yourself.'

At last she'd gone. The house was quiet again, save for the clicking of cups and plates in the kitchen where Nellie and Bertha busied themselves preparing supper.

'Shall we sit in the garden while it's light?' Lizzie asked.

'Yes. Let's go into the orchard.' It had been a favourite hidey-hole since childhood, the little group of apple and plum trees, out of sight of the house, behind a thick wall of overgrown damsons and raspberry canes.

Lizzie went ahead, slender as a willow, and leaned against a tree that was hanging with blossom.

He took her hand and pulled her on to the cool, silky grass where she lay. He watched her, blinking at the bright sky between leaves overhead. 'Shall we play at Think Dream?' Edward spoke softly. It was their secret game from childhood, when they used to creep into one another's rooms at night when sleep wouldn't come, and hold hands, eyes tight shut, letting their thoughts and dreams merge.

'All right. But we should stop this. It's silly playing games at our age,' Lizzie answered, letting go his hand. They closed their eyes, drifted into the Think Dream state and ...

'Summer,' whispered Lizzie.

'Dark,' Edward answered.

'Hair.'

'Beautiful.'

'Love,' Lizzie added after a second's hesitation.

'You.'

'Kiss me.'

'Someone's coming! Damn!'

Edward leaped to his feet, angry that the game was spoiled. Lizzie knew, she must know, that this was no longer a game they had played as children and that it would lead them down a path they both longed to tread.

He dared not speak of it, but he believed she knew as surely as he did that what he felt for her was no longer brotherly love. And he knew his passion was returned but that neither he nor Lizzie dared take the step that would make outcasts of them.

And why should we be outcasts, he thought angrily.

His anger evaporated when he saw Oliver striding down the garden path towards the orchard. Oliver, at forty-one, was so youthful it was hard to imagine the age difference between his brother and himself.

Edward loved and respected Oliver, wanted to please him by his efforts, to have his brother's respect and love. He would one day deserve it. For wasn't this the man who had sacrificed so much of his time and money on helping their mother after Joe Wainwright had died? Wasn't this the man who wanted to give more, who had to be told that he'd done enough – that the love they bore him didn't depend on what he could give to them – that now Edward was adult he must make his way unaided?

'Hello. Good to see you, Edward. I thought there was nobody at home. Is your mother out? Hello, Lizzie. What are you doing down there messing up your pretty dress?' Oliver gave Lizzie his hand. 'Let's go inside.'

They followed him to the kitchen.

'How's the studying?' Oliver asked as soon as they were inside the cosy kitchen and he had seated himself at the still-laid table.

'Not too bad,' Edward answered. 'There's only Chemistry to put some more work into.'

'When do you go back to London?'

'Next month. Will you be down there on business soon?' Edward handed the teapot to Lizzie who filled it for him.

'Yes,' Oliver replied. 'Where's Dolly?'

'Mother's at the theatre,' Edward said. 'Did you remember her birthday?'

'Yes. I remembered. I've bought her a present.' Oliver had begun to help himself to Lizzie's scones. 'These are delicious,' he said. 'Has your mother been teaching you to cook?'

Lizzie, Edward saw, was blushing.

'Have you found a young man yet, Lizzie?' Oliver continued. 'You don't spend all your time cooking and sewing, do you?'

Lizzie smiled. 'I prefer it. I'm not much of a girl for parties.'

'Dolly ought to take you around with her. She must know plenty of people with eligible young sons. How old are you now?'

'Twenty-two. Don't worry about me, Oliver. I'll probably be swept off my feet one of these days.'

Lizzie glanced over to Edward and pulled a face – a help-me-out-of-this face. Edward made one back.

Oliver took his bag upstairs and unpacked in the bedroom that was always kept ready for him. It was not the room he and Rosie had shared. Dolly slept there. This room overlooked the garden. He went to the window and looked out on to the calm suburban scene, reflecting on the unchanging way of life of this prosperous town, wondering whether the red brick walls of the houses he saw around him hid deceptions from the world, as these walls concealed theirs.

He had not been able to take his mind off the letter all day and he was anxious to talk to Dolly about it. Now it seemed that he was to be frustrated again. Dolly was at the theatre and would be bringing her friends home for supper. He would have to wait until tomorrow to speak to her. He went to the washstand and poured cold water into the bowl, puzzling again over the letter-writer's knowledge.

The exercise books had been kept here, in Southport. Had he really been so careless as to leave them in the house all these years? And why hadn't Dolly burned them? He had left them here when

Rosie disappeared. They should have been destroyed at the time. And the photograph the blackmailer spoke of – he remembered going with Rosie to the studio but had no recollection of ever seeing the photograph itself.

The cold water refreshed him. He cupped some in his hands and splashed it over his face. It was strange too, so long afterwards, to be reminded of the love affair with Rosie and the reason for the double life he had been forced to lead to keep his two families apart. Once only had he brought James to Southport but seeing the two boys together, seeing the strong family likeness, he had known that regular contact between them was out of the question. Nor had he been able to take Edward to Suttonford. Florence would not have gone on believing that Wilf Leach had fathered both children. Edward was so obviously a Wainwright.

He went again to the window, drying his face on a snow-white towel. For twenty years he had believed that only he and Dolly knew of the deception. Yet somewhere, a man who called himself King had uncovered the truth and threatened to expose the lie that his Southport family was founded on.

He saw Edward and Lizzie walking in the garden below, hand in hand, perfect companions, secure in the world of lies their security was based upon and he knew he could not allow it to be destroyed.

'Damn,' he muttered at last. 'I've had enough of these thoughts.' He tapped on the window and saw Edward and Lizzie, startled, drop hands and look up. He motioned them to come indoors and he ran down the stairs to meet them in the hall.

'Let's join your mother at the theatre,' he said. 'We'll take the tramcar and watch the show ourselves, shall we? Who's on tonight?'

'Celia Bellman,' Edward told him. 'The singer. You've met her. She's been to the house with Mother and her friends.'

'I don't remember her,' Oliver said, 'but Dolly knows so many theatre people I don't try.'

There was a tram stop around the corner from their road and ten minutes later they were aboard a noisy car that would take them right to the door of the theatre. There were posters all along the route, advertising tonight's programme and Lizzie excitedly pointed them out to him, usually too late for him to be able to read the names of the performers.

They were in luck. There had been a cancellation. A box remained unsold and they were ushered in to the tiny room of plush and gilt that overhung the stage. Dolly was on the front row. She waved exuberantly, opening her eyes wide in surprise at seeing them. The houselights went down as enthusiastic cheering greeted the conductor.

Oliver knew what attracted Dolly to the Variety shows. There was an eagerness in the crowd, a willingness to be entertained, that with the ascending waves of music reaching the box was a palpable feeling in the smoky air.

He began to enjoy himself, forgetting for a while the black-mailer's threat. He laughed with Lizzie and Edward at the comedy turn, where a man, dressed as a dandy, with tails and top hat, kept tripping over his feet and tangling his legs with his walking stick as he attempted to persuade a pretty girl to dance with him.

This was followed by an animal act, then a juggler. Edward and Lizzie, sitting either side of him, made Oliver's evening even more enjoyable as they whispered to him, telling him of the off-stage exploits of the actors Dolly had befriended.

Tea and biscuits were brought to the box at the interval, when they were joined by Dolly. 'Happy birthday, Dolly.' Oliver rose from his seat and gave her a peck on the cheek.

'Are you staying for the party?' she asked. 'You're not going back afterwards, are you?'

'No. I'm going to spend a few days with you,' he replied.

She returned to her seat before the houselights went out for the second half of the show, when the star turn, billed outside as Celia Bellman, was the last name on the programme. The lights dimmed, the master of ceremonies came forward and announced her.

'At last, ladies and gentlemen ... the little lady we've all been waiting for, a star of the London theatre, a sensation in New York and Paris, our very own North Country lass ... Miss Celia Bellman.'

There was wild applause. The velvet curtains rolled slowly back and Celia Bellman, the star of the show, flung wide her arms in an inviting gesture and stepped towards the footlights.

She wore a dress of scarlet satin, low cut and daring at the front, trimmed with black frills, which swooped down the centre of her bodice and were caught into a high bustle at the back of her small waist. She revealed at least six inches of neatly turned ankle where the hem lifted at the front of her dress and was, Oliver thought, the most provocative little baggage he had ever seen.

Her hair, black and glossy, was held on top of her head with a scarlet confection of ribbon and flowers and her eyes, dark like a gipsy's, were outlined in charcoal. Oliver saw every detail clearly. He was only feet away from her, so close he could have leaned out and touched her. Her cherry-red lips parted to reveal teeth that were very slightly crossed in the front, giving a hint of imperfection in the perfect, pointed face.

He expected to hear saucy songs but she began with a popular sentimental ballad he'd heard Lizzie play many times. And she was spellbinding. It seemed that the audience held its breath. She bowed to the storm of clapping that broke at the last notes and flashed a smile towards Oliver. Then, it seemed to him deliberately, she gave them a song which demanded some wriggling and turning, making the men roar their approval.

Oliver was loud in his enthusiasm but he knew that it was not her looks but the power and quality of her voice that had brought her to the top of the bill. Finally she sang 'The Londonderry Air'. The theatre was hushed: even Oliver had a lump in his throat when she ended to rapturous applause, and bowed and curtseyed for a full three minutes.

She turned towards the box and blew kisses to Oliver, Lizzie and Edward while they clapped, leaning over the padded edge of the box in their enthusiasm.

'Mother goes backstage after the show,' Edward said when the final curtain came down. 'Shall we go ahead, to the house?'

'Yes,' Oliver replied. 'Walk or tram?'

'Let's walk,' Lizzie answered.

Oliver felt a strange elation tonight. It was a long time since he had been so relaxed. Twice his problems had surfaced briefly and twice he had easily pushed them to the back of his mind. He intended to enjoy Dolly's party.

They had been home for half an hour when they heard the noisy arrivals at the front door.

The stage manager and the master of ceremonies were the first to enter the house, the comedian the youngsters had found so funny and who, offstage, was a rather solemn character, followed, some girls from the chorus, excited still from their performance and, lastly, now dressed in a high-necked dress of black silk, jet-beaded and buttoned, came Celia Bellman.

Whisky was being handed to the men and wine and champagne to the ladies, and the company followed Dolly to the dining room and the mountain of salads and cold dishes that had been prepared for them. In the centre of the table was a huge cake, in three tiers with, on the top tier, more candles than most would ever admit to.

Oliver sat across the wide table from Celia Bellman, a chorus girl on one side of him and the juggler at the other, hearing little of what was said, conscious as he was of the dark-haired singer. She was captivating and full of life and her interest in him was evident. Her bold, flashing eyes met his and held them, making him aware of an excitement that he had not known since his youth.

Lizzie and Edward, he noticed, slipped away from the table and the guests as soon as they could without arousing comment from Dolly, preferring each other's company to that of the merrymaking crowd.

When supper was over and Dolly had been acclaimed a wonderful hostess she led them to the drawing room and begged Celia to sing for them.

Oliver positioned himself at the other side of the room, facing the piano. He tilted his head and leaned back in the plush armchair, long legs outstretched, pleasantly cheerful from the two glasses of whisky, watching her as she placed a hand demurely on the side of the piano and sang 'Speed, Bonny Boat'.

When she finished she smiled at their applause, crossed her hands in front of her skirt and began to sing 'Drink to Me Only, With Thine Eyes'.

Oliver wondered if he were deceiving himself. But, no! He was sure! The minx was singing it for him. How anyone can make 'Drink to Me Only' sound like an invitation, I'll never know, he thought, but there was no mistaking her intention and now his body was charged with the current that was flowing between them. She bowed a second time, held up her hand in protest at requests for more and came to his side.

She stood by the arm of his chair, smiling meanwhile at the others of her party as she bent her head towards his.

'Take me to my hotel, will you?' Her voice was low and husky and she spoke softly, so that only he would hear, but she ran her fingers slowly along his arm.

In reply he took her arm and pressed it hard against his side, not looking at her. 'When I'm sure we'll not be missed,' he said, almost under his breath, smiling towards Dolly who looked at him enquiringly.

'I think I'll get a breath of fresh air, Dolly. It's too warm in here.'

Celia halted as soon as they rounded the corner. Her dark eyes held his and Oliver kissed her with a fierce insistence. He could see the need in her; knew immediately that her desire was as great as his. It inflamed him, drew him to her with an overwhelming force.

They were behaving like young eager lovers who had only the street corners. They could not wait. Every few yards they stopped, looked and embraced, their kisses growing wilder and deeper, leaving them breathless. They did not speak. They were oblivious of the warm, starlit night, the gentle sighing of the breeze through the sycamores overhead. They ran the last fifty yards to her hotel. There was no night porter; no need for courtesies before Oliver followed her light footsteps up the deeply carpeted stairs to the sanctuary of her bedroom.

She leaned against the door, her breath coming fast, her dark head lifted, eyes closed as he slid the bolt and began to undress her in the moonlit room. She helped him, running her hands with lightning speed over the jet beads of her bodice. The dress fell away. She was naked.

Oliver gave a low cry and lifted her to the bed. To think that she wore nothing beneath her dress – no slip – no stays – no drawers. His own shirt was being stripped from his back by her quick, expert hands. His clothes were dropping to the floor and her hands were skimming over his body while his mouth was upon hers, loving the movement in her own.

She was exotic and exciting and he was on fire for her. He put up his hand to pull the gas-mantle chain and fill the room with its soft light. He wanted to see her before he made love to her.

She was narrow, narrow and strong with small, hard breasts with rigid, dark nipples. She was slightly tanned, taut and smooth with a sheen that paler women do not have. He buried his face in her silken body, tasting the scented oil she used to keep her skin supple.

He ran his hands inside her thighs and found her warm and moist and she moved upwards towards him, towards his mouth as it fastened on her breast, towards his hands where they held her hips, and when he entered, thrusting deep into her, she cried out and dug her nails into his shoulders.

Harder and harder he went, not caring if he hurt her. She cried out again, but it was a cry of pleasure as she came to a crescendo at his final thrust into her deep, narrow body.

It had been so long … so long since he had felt a woman respond in this way.

He kissed her eyes, her mouth, her breasts, feeling them firm against his mouth, and, still inside her, he began to harden, feeling her writhing beneath him, bringing him into her again.

Afterwards, as he lay limp and relaxed against the sheets, she began to stroke him. Her hands moved swiftly over him, making demands he thought he was past fulfilling. He closed his eyes, enjoying her ministrations, drifting along with her. He felt a stir within him as his body began to obey her touch and she moved sinuously, giving him the exquisite, new sensation of being helpless in a woman's hands.

Now she was doing things he had read about, had heard about, but never thought to experience. She would not allow him to take her quickly this time but made him learn delay; made him linger until he could bear it no longer and even then she held him back until she too was ready for him and at last he took her in the way she wanted him and she was unlike anyone he had known before.

And this was what he had been seeking. This was the mistress he would take, if she would consent. He knew that he would want more of her; knew that he would come back to her again and again.

She was spent. She lay face down, outstretched across the bed, her hands clasped loosely together above her head, the black shining hair strewn over the pillow.

Oliver turned her over and looked into her face. 'And now, Celia Bellman,' he said. 'Shall we get to know one another?'

She smiled, cat-like, satisfied. 'I've known you for a long time,' she told him. 'I met you once at Dolly's, but you didn't notice me.'

'I can't imagine who else could have been occupying my attention, that I didn't notice you.' He smiled.

Her hair lay about the pillow and Oliver played with the shining looseness of it as he looked into her dark, passionate eyes.

'I wanted you to make love to me the first time,' she said without a trace of coyness. 'And tonight, when I saw you from the stage, I knew that you would.'

'Are you always so sure of yourself?' Oliver asked. 'Do you always take what you want and ask afterwards?'

She smiled.

'You make me think I've been seduced,' he teased, giving the black hair a gentle tug.

'You have,' she said, 'and you loved it.'

Oliver laughed quietly. 'You talk like a scarlet woman, Celia Bellman.' He kissed her throat. 'And where did you learn these – these seductive wiles?'

'In Paris.' She laughed too, a soft inviting sound. 'They are wise in these ways, the French.'

'And tell me about our first meeting,' he cajoled. 'For I am sure I would have remembered, if I'd met you before.'

'I'd heard of you before I even met Dolly or was invited to the house,' she said.

'Tell me.'

'I'll have to tell you the background story first,' Celia said. 'Do you want to hear it all?'

'Yes. I want to know all about you,' Oliver told her. 'I'm not in the habit of making love to total strangers.' He smiled and began to run his fingers over her smooth, shiny skin.

'I was brought up in Bradford by my granny. I never knew my parents – and my granny was a very devout chapelgoer,' Celia began.

Funny how, even now, he could not hear the name of Bradford without remembering Rosie. Oliver pulled himself up and leaned against the pillows. 'Religious fervour's very common over there,' he said. 'Did you share your granny's faith?'

'When I was very young, I did.' Celia's dark eyes were serious. 'You aren't laughing at me, are you?'

'No.' Oliver put an arm out and she lay against him, running her fingers along the line of his jaw. 'Carry on.'

'I was friendly with a girl called Annie Hadfield. She and her sisters lived with their grandparents.' Celia stopped speaking for a moment. 'Does the name of Hadfield mean anything to you?'

Oliver sat, stock-still, his face no longer relaxed and amused.

'Did you know her mother?' he asked.

'Yes. Their mother lived with them only until their father died. She didn't like the grandparents; they treated her badly.' Celia hesitated again, as if she were reluctant to tell him more. 'They used to call her the fallen woman and say she was mad.'

'And …?' Oliver's mouth was set in a grim line.

'She was mad,' Celia said quietly. 'She used to talk to herself all the time. She was very beautiful … but she was mad.' She pulled herself into a sitting position beside him and added, 'The grandfather used to sneer at her and say she was the

Mrs Wainwright of Suttonford, in a patronising way, and she'd walk away, muttering.'

'What happened to her when her husband died?' Oliver asked in a voice that had turned to ice.

'She left the girls with their grandparents. They were happier with them than with their mother. I believe she remarried and went to live in London.' She smiled at Oliver. 'So that's how I knew of you.'

'Is this why you sought me out? To satisfy your curiosity?' he asked coldly.

'No. I knew that a man called Wainwright must have had a love affair with Mrs Hadfield. Years later I met Dolly in Southport but I never connected the two Wainwrights until she spoke of her stepson who lives at Suttonford. Then I realised that it was the same family.'

'What else do you know?' Oliver demanded.

Celia pulled a dressing gown around herself and stood up. 'You'd better leave,' she said. 'I didn't know you'd be so angry, so long after your affair with her.'

Oliver looked at her steadily. 'I want to know whether you asked me here tonight to satisfy some perverse kind of curiosity about me and Rosie Hadfield.'

It was her turn to be cold.

'No,' she said. 'In fact I thought, until a few moments ago, that your father was the man Mrs Hadfield knew. You look too young to have been her lover twenty years ago.' She drew the cord tight around her waist, picked up his clothes from the floor and held them out to him.

'I actually believed,' she said as she looked at him with a direct gaze, 'that it was love at first sight for me and at second sight for you. How silly of me. Please dress yourself and go.'

Oliver's face relaxed. There was no subterfuge about this girl. She was completely open and truthful. He dropped his clothes at the side of the bed and held out his arms to her.

'Come back to bed with me, Celia Bellman. Please ... I need you.'

Chapter Twenty-Five

Oliver stayed with her until late the following afternoon when she left for the theatre. He made his way to the house with some trepidation. He knew that Dolly would have much to say about his disappearance and wondered what her attitude would be now that it was he, and not she, who was the transgressor.

He was childishly glad to find that Edward and Lizzie were in their sitting room and unaware of his arrival.

There was a man sitting in the kitchen with Dolly. A little fellow, beaming at her, hanging on to every word she uttered. He was seated in the rocking chair, rolled cloth cap in one hand and a glass of wine in the other. His legs, swinging like a child's, did not reach the floor.

'Hello, Oliver,' Dolly greeted him as he opened the back door. 'This is Bert. He's come to give me a price for some work I want done.'

'Do you normally do business at six o'clock at night, Bert?' he asked pointedly. 'And what sort of work is it, pray?'

Bert scrambled out of the chair, leaving it swinging loud and vigorously behind him. He placed the empty wine glass on the table and unrolled his cap. He was tiny, only about two inches taller than Dolly, Oliver guessed, and he grinned at Dolly with a great deal of affection in his smile.

'Eeh. I'm a builder, Mr Wainwright. Dolly here wants me to put a new fireplace in for her.' He made a move towards the back door as Dolly opened it for him. 'Ta-ra, then, Doll. I'll see yer soon.'

Dolly saw him out before turning to speak. 'What do you have to go upsetting folk for?' she asked in an exasperated voice. 'Poor Bert!'

'Never mind "Poor Bert" – take a look at this.' Oliver pushed the letter into her hand and poured himself a glass of her tonic wine.

She reached for a pair of spectacles from the mantelshelf and stretched the wires over her ears before smoothing the paper flat on the kitchen table and reading slowly.

'My God!' she said, when she took the glasses off. 'Who is A. King? Have you ever met him?'

'Don't be a fool, Dolly. That's not the real name. Whoever is blackmailing me his name's certainly not King.' He would have to spell it out to her. 'Somebody has taken the photograph and the writings out of this house, and is using them to get money from me.' He waited for the effect of his words to sink in. 'Somebody you have invited to the house. One of your friends!'

'It must be that Celia Bellman,' Dolly declared triumphantly. 'I thought she had something on her mind. She asked when you'd be coming to Southport again.'

She had not taken last night's goings-on lightly, Oliver could see. 'I hope this isn't the start of you and her carrying on,' she added. 'I'll not put up with it.'

'It's not Celia.'

'She'll want to marry you now. She'll want Florence to divorce you. Mark my words!' Dolly squinted up at him, looking shrewd, waiting for his reaction. 'You don't know much about women, do you?'

'I don't think you're right. If I pay blackmail money then it proves that I'm going to protect my wife, not desert her,' Oliver replied.

'You're not going to pay?' Dolly was aghast. 'You'll never pay that kind of money will you?'

'I'll have to pay.'

'Oh, Oliver!' She sat down quickly. 'I am sorry. I should have thrown the damned books out. I don't know why I kept them. Edward or Lizzie could have got hold of them.'

'I'll get a man to watch the house in London, to find out who this Mr King is. But what do I do when I know? I still have to get hold of the things. Have you no idea who took them? How long they've been missing? Try to remember when you last saw them.' Oliver lifted lids over dishes on the side-table. He was hungry. He could do justice to one of his stepmother's suppers.

'We'll have something to eat in a minute. It's the maids' night off so we'll eat in here if that's all right.' Dolly pushed his hands away from the dishes. 'Stop poking about, will yer? Help me lay the table.'

She still treated him like a child at times. He smiled at her as she busied herself, pulling a cloth from the dresser drawer and flapping it smartly to release the folds. 'You're doing your "second cook at Suttonford" act now, Dolly,' he told her.

'I haven't seen those things from the attic for ages. I remember putting them away under the spare blankets in the big chest and after that I never saw them again. They could have been missing for years.' She spoke furiously, as if annoyed with herself for her carelessness, banging down the mats, knives and forks. 'I've made a Lancashire hotpot. It's in the oven. Will that do?'

'Yes. I haven't had one for years.' Oliver said. 'I don't think the things have been missing all that long or they'd have been trying to get money before now.'

'Well, let's hope your investigator finds out who it is for you.' Dolly took plates from the steel rack above the oven and carried them to the table, holding them in a thick cloth. 'There's red cabbage pickle to go with it and apricot snow for pudding. I was going to ask Bert to stay for some supper,' she said. 'His wife died last year and I think he's lonely.'

'If you give him his supper he'll never be off your doorstep,' Oliver told her, glad that the talk was no longer about himself and Celia.

She ladled a plateful of hotpot for him and Oliver heaped red cabbage pickle on to his potatoes, watching the purple juice soak through them before closing his eyes with pleasure as the half-forgotten taste of vinegar-crisp cabbage nipped his tongue.

'I was going to ask you if you'd let Lizzie come to Suttonford for a few weeks once Florence is on her feet again,' he said. 'It's time she met more people of her own age.'

'Get her married off, do you mean,' Dolly said, 'to someone from Suttonford?'

'No. I don't mean that. But tell me, Dolly, why have you never let her go to work? Many young women work. There are nurses and teachers ...'

'... Aye, there might well be. I was a cook, remember? But I vowed I'd never put her time and her talent at anyone else's disposal. Never give anyone the right to say "Do this or do that" and her have to obey them.'

She sat down opposite him and placed her elbows on the table in the battling attitude that he remembered. 'She wanted to go to art school! I ask you. Art school? I said, "Look here, Lizzie, any drawing and painting you do, you'll do for us."' Now a look of doubt crossed her face. 'You think I was right, don't you?' she asked. 'She never pestered me or anything. They've been good children ... just grand.'

'I don't think you're right,' he told her, but kindly. 'I believe everyone should work. Though I know some girls would rather stop at home and help their mothers.'

'Do you know, Oliver, those two have never needed outsiders. They seemed to have found all they wanted in each other. They have never made bosom friends with anyone.' She began to fill a pudding dish with a frothy concoction of apricots and cream, waiting for him to indicate to her when she should stop. When he nodded to stop her she continued. 'It was me as was always the outsider with them. They didn't need me.'

She laughed as she said it, obviously not in the least hurt at their apparent neglect. Oliver smiled in agreement with her. 'Well, you've never been one to pine away unnoticed, Dolly. Would you miss her if I took her to Suttonford?'

'Are you trying to marry her off, then?'

'No. She should be having more fun than she does. She and Edward spend all their time together when he's home and he'll be going back to London soon.'

'Edward won't like it. Lizzie getting married. He's a bit possessive about her,' Dolly replied. She helped him to more pudding. 'But he'll maybe find himself a girl in London.'

'Who said anything about Lizzie marrying? Don't go saying that to her,' Oliver told her sharply, 'and Edward's far too young to be thinking about settling down. He's got years of study ahead of him.'

'You were married at twenty-two! And you'd had your moments before then,' Dolly said, leaping to Edward's defence.

'I know. But I was no good at playing a cautious game.' He wiped his mouth on the starched white napkin, pushed his chair back from the table and stood up. 'But I've got to be careful this time,' he added.

'You're seeing her again, are you?' Her mood had changed. She snapped the words out, rose from the table quickly and stood, head to one side, looking at him with narrowed eyes. 'Can't you wait until your wife's finished lying-in? Have you no decency? Can't you contain yourself?'

'My marriage, in the proper sense of it, is over,' he told her, without emotion. 'Florence and I will have separate apartments until she is past childbearing.' He leaned against the mantelshelf and looked his stepmother in the face. 'And by that time I don't imagine we'll start again.'

'Get yourself a woman with a bit of sense, then,' Dolly said tartly. 'Don't get tangled up with Celia Bellman. You're not the first you know!'

'I thought you'd have understood,' he said quickly and added, with a trace of sarcasm, 'you weren't content with a lonely life after Dad died.'

'My life's always been lonely,' she retorted quickly. 'Just because I've kept my side of the bargain and not looked for a man doesn't mean I've not wanted one. I've been happy and I've been secure but I've been lonely, too.'

'I kept my side of the bargain as well, Dolly,' Oliver reminded her. 'You were to have everything you needed as long as you brought my son up.'

'I know,' she replied. 'I've never regretted it. I've never wanted a man more than I wanted this.' She waved a plump arm, indicating the house and all her responsibilities. 'I've loved every minute of my life since I came here.' Her voice dropped as she added, 'All except the lies, Oliver. I've never felt right, deceiving them. They should know who they are.'

She took cigarettes and matches out of her handbag and put a cigarette to her lips, sucking at the end to make it light, eyes narrowed in concentration.

'Good God, Dolly! Don't tell me you're smoking now?' Oliver tried to get her on the defensive. He'd had enough of her haranguing.

'Never mind what I'm doing! It's what you and Celia Bellman are doing that I'm talking about. What about Edward and Lizzie? Do you think they won't notice? You just start being a bit more careful if you want to come here to see them.' She blew a great stream of smoke into the room.

'If I want to come here? What are you talking about, woman? I'll come here whenever I want to. I bought the house. I pay for everything! You're getting above yourself.'

'The deeds are mine! Remember?' she hurled the words at him. 'I knew I'd need to say that, one day. You signed them over to me!'

She looked at him with the same scowling expression he had seen so many times before. 'And don't think we need your money any longer. I could marry Bert. I can take in lodgers. There's plenty'd come for my cooking alone!'

Now she was being ridiculous. Oliver tried to calm her. 'I'll not stop your money,' he said. 'I'll be more discreet.'

'Edward thinks you're the most upright and honest man in the world. He looks up to you, Oliver. He tolerates me, he knows my failings. But he doesn't think you have any,' Dolly said, but now her tone became sorrowful. 'He's had to grow up without a father, not like James, and he's not sure how men should behave since he's only lived with women. What's he going to think of you if he finds out?' She dropped on to a chair and put her head in her hands.

'I can't keep up all the lies,' she said wearily. 'I've told too many. Sometimes I've a job to remember what the truth really is.'

She began to cry. 'We're doing wrong by them, not telling them who they are. They ought to be told. But we've woven such a web of lies that there's no way out of it,' she said.

Oliver took her hand. 'Keep going, Dolly. There's no need for them to know. They've got birth certificates and they've never questioned their parentage.'

'They have,' Dolly whispered. 'Oh, but they have.'

'What?'

'Edward asked me how it was that a quarryman, even a quarry-master, could have left us enough to live on.'

A chill went through Oliver. 'What did you say?' he asked.

'I told him you'd been clever. I reminded him that you were grown up when he was born and I said you'd invested it to give us an income.'

'Did that satisfy him?'

'He said, "Five barley loaves and two small fishes?" and when I asked him what he meant he said, "If Dad had left only a few pounds it would have taken a miracle to invest it to bring that sort of return."'

'How did you answer that?'

'I said I didn't know how you did it. All I knew was that when their father died you took control and that we moved to Southport. I told them that my allowance is paid into the bank once a year and that's all I know.'

'So he thinks I'm supporting you from my own money?'

'Yes. At the expense of your family. And he doesn't like the idea. He wants to look after us himself. He says he'll keep us when he's in practice.'

'Oh God! Poor Edward. He must resent me.'

'No. He doesn't, Oliver. He loves you. He wants you to respect him.' Dolly wiped her eyes with the corner of a table napkin. 'He's a wonderful son, Oliver. If he'd been my own I couldn't have loved him more.'

'It would do no good, Dolly. Telling them.' Oliver sat down beside her and spoke earnestly. 'Don't you think I want him to know I'm his father? It's not for my sake, now, that I want the secret kept. We can't burden them with the truth – with the truth that they are illegitimate. Not when they're happy to be who they are.'

'Suppose they find out for themselves. What do we tell them then? That we were protecting them?' Dolly asked.

'They can't find out,' Oliver told her. 'Who knows the truth?'

'Iris knew.'

'It's fifteen years since Iris left. They've had no contact with her.'

'Wilf knew.'

'He's dead.'

Dolly looked bewildered. 'Has nobody asked at Suttonford?' she said.

'No. It's twenty years since you left there. There's nobody but you and me who knows the truth.'

'And your blackmailer,' Dolly said.

'And the blackmailer,' Oliver echoed and it seemed that the threat of exposure was gathering force. He pulled himself together quickly. 'No more of this talk,' he said. 'I'll find out who it is before long.' He lifted his jacket from the back of the chair and pushed his arms into the sleeves. 'I'll be leaving in a few minutes, Dolly,' he said briskly. 'I'll go upstairs and say farewell to Edward and Lizzie.' He would have to keep it from her, the fact that he intended to return to Celia tonight.

* * *

It was a hot July morning, the last day of Edward's summer leave. They had gone early to the beach and paddled in the shallow water.

Lizzie felt the sun burning into her arms through the fine cotton sleeves of her white blouse. She shifted her position where she lay on the sand and turned her head to look at Edward.

He was staring out to sea, lost in his thoughts, his strong profile outlined against the blue expanse of sky. He had taken off his jacket and unfastened the top button of his stiff-necked shirt. His sleeves were folded back to his elbows and his slender brown fingers idly lifted and sifted handfuls of trickling sand.

'What are you thinking?' she said.

'You know exactly what I'm thinking.' Edward continued to stare at the waterline.

'It's impossible.' Lizzie sat up quickly. 'You know I can't go with you to London.'

'Yet you can go to Suttonford!' Edward's hands were clenched now. 'It will be months before I see you.'

'You know why I have to go,' Lizzie spoke softly. She could not bear to hurt him.

'Because I love you?' Edward turned to look at her and she saw hurt and pain in his eyes. 'Going away won't make me love you less,' he said.

'We have to try.' Tears had begun to well up behind her eyes and she made a determined effort to hold them back. 'Other girls don't feel this way about their brothers, Edward,' she said softly. 'All the girls I know think their brothers are hell.'

'I don't care, Lizzie. I don't care tuppence for other girls and their feelings. Only you.'

'I know,' Lizzie pleaded. 'Please help me, and yourself. We've got to learn to live apart. What we feel is infatuation. It can't be love. It will die if we will it.'

Edward put both hands on her shoulders and shook her gently until her head came up and their eyes met.

'I love you, Lizzie. Can't you accept what we feel for one another?' His warm brown eyes searched her face for an answer. 'There will never, never be another girl in this world for me.' He paused for a moment. 'You are all I want and I know you love me too. You won't say it but I'm certain that you do.'

Tears sprang to her eyes. Lizzie pulled herself from Edward's hold. 'I must go to Suttonford,' she said, 'and stay until Christmas as Oliver suggests. We have to spend time apart.'

Edward stared out to sea again. 'We already do,' he said. 'I spend months at a time in London and it hasn't cured me of loving you.'

'Then you must only think of me as your sister,' Lizzie whispered, 'and I of you as my brother. We must. We must, Edward.'

There were children on the sands, playing at the water's edge, splashing and jumping just as they used to do when they were children. There was a strong, salty smell of cockleshells in her nostrils as Lizzie tried to concentrate on the children's antics, tried not to think of anything.

'Have you ever thought that we might not be?' Edward was saying quietly.

'Not be what?' she answered.

'Brother and sister.'

'Don't be silly, Edward,' she replied. 'What else could we be?'

'Listen, Lizzie,' Edward said and the anxious note had returned to his voice. He propped himself on an elbow and faced her again. 'We've known for years that there is something hidden from us, haven't we?'

'Yes, but that ...' Lizzie began to say.

'We've known there was something strange about our births,' Edward went on insistently. 'Mother and Oliver won't answer reasonable questions. You can see panic in Mother's eyes when we ask for information.'

'I know that. But haven't you thought that the memories might be painful for them?' Lizzie asked.

'No.' Edward began to push his hands into the sand, to feel its resistance. 'I've never thought that. Mother and Oliver aren't the kind of people who refuse to face painful things. They are hiding something; hiding it from us; hiding it intentionally – and I mean to find out what it is.'

'What makes you think so?' Lizzie said. 'How can you say, "There is some mystery"? What makes you suspicious?'

'A hundred little things, Lizzie, that I sense rather than know.' He turned his face to her. She knew that she could not hide her feelings from him, that he would see that his talk was upsetting her, but she let him go on.

'It's in Oliver's manner. He's far too protective and I don't know who he's protecting. Himself, us or Mother? And Mother ... you can see her flinch when we ask questions. Flinch as if she'd been struck. We're afraid to question her in case she dies of fright.'

'Perhaps all women who've been left widows, so young, are like Mother. Maybe they don't want to be reminded.'

'No, no, Lizzie. There is a whole area of their lives – Oliver's and Mother's – that they don't want to talk about. There are missing years, Lizzie. They talk freely about Joe Wainwright until Oliver was about ten. Then – there is nothing. There is a whole chunk missing.'

'Perhaps – perhaps they just led normal, quiet lives, Edward.'

'People don't marry, have two children, then have fifteen or so childless years, leading normal, quiet lives, Lizzie. There are no memories – nothing. Then suddenly, just before the man dies, this busy couple go on and have two more children.'

'What do you think happened?' she asked him.

'I think they separated. I think Mother left. Perhaps Joe Wainwright was not a good man. Perhaps Mother was not a faithful wife.'

'I don't want to know if there's anything dreadful hidden,' Lizzie told him fearfully. 'I couldn't bear it.'

'I'm sorry, Liz.' He reached for her hand and held it firmly. 'It's too important to me not to ask for the truth. I don't believe I would want you so much. I don't think I could feel so passionately about you if I felt it was unnatural. I'm going to ask Oliver to tell me everything. I'll choose my moment. I'll wait until I see him in London, away from Mother.'

'You're not going to tell him that you – that we – that we want to—?' she asked.

'No.' He touched her face tenderly. 'I promise I won't let him suspect. And, Liz ...?'

'Yes?'

'See what you can find out when you're at Suttonford. There must be someone who knows what happened. Someone must remember a rich quarryman called Joe Wainwright. It's only twenty years since he died.'

Lizzie stood up and began to beat the sand out of the folds of her linen skirt. 'We'll take a tram back, shall we?' she said. 'Oliver and I have to catch the two o'clock to Manchester.'

Edward shook his legs to release the sand from his turned-up trousers. He reached for his jacket and slung it across his shoulder before putting out a hand to drag her up the steep, cobble-sided slope of the beach wall.

Lizzie glanced quickly at him. The brooding look had gone from his face and he was grinning broadly now, making her long to give way to the surging feeling of love that so often overcame her. 'It might be a test of endurance, Lizzie – living under the same roof as James,' he reminded her. 'Do you remember what a rude little beast he was? He flaunted his wealth and possessions in front of his poor relations from Lancashire when he was only ten years old. I hope time has improved him.'

'So do I,' Lizzie said. 'Florence sounds nice. It was a lovely invitation. She says she's always wanted to meet us and can't wait until I join them.'

'And I can't wait until I see you again,' Edward told her, but he had laughter in his face and would not make her feel distress again.

* * *

Dolly was angry. Oliver had not seen her so angry for years. Hands on hips, head cocked to one side, she faced him in the drawing room.

'I don't give a damn what excuses you make! You can lie till you're blue in the face but don't tell me you aren't seeing Celia Bellman.' She paused for breath for a second and lowered her voice. 'The girl's been on at the Variety three weeks on the trot and you've been to every bloody weekend performance.'

Oliver answered her. 'I'm not making excuses. I'll not explain myself to you.'

'You've fallen for her, haven't you?' Dolly demanded. 'Hook, line and bloody sinker. She's got you dangling on the end of her line.'

'I'm not here to talk about Celia. Where's Lizzie?'

'She's gone for a walk with Edward. They'll be back before lunch.'

He watched as she went to the long sash windows and snatched at the cretonne curtains, pulling them quickly across the windows so that the sunlight wouldn't fade the velvet chairs. She had not lost the mannerisms of her younger days. She still took the battle to the enemy.

Oliver decided to divert her attention. 'When does Edward go back?' he asked.

'Tomorrow.' She drummed her fingers on the lacquered table and narrowed her eyes. 'Wouldn't a decent sort of woman have given you what you wanted? Do you have to make a fool of yourself and of us?' she snapped. 'Don't you have any feelings left for your wife?'

'I love Florence. I always have,' he flashed back at her. 'But a marriage is not simply affection. I'm a normal, healthy man, with appetites. Have no fear. You, Edward and Lizzie won't suffer in any way.' He was in danger of losing his temper. She had no right to question him.

Dolly had not finished though, he could see. She would, as ever, have the last word. 'Don't get too involved with that girl. She had no interest in you at all the first time she saw you. It wasn't until I told her all about Suttonford and the estate that she set her cap for you,' she said.

'That's enough!' There was anger in his voice now. 'Hold your tongue.'

They were spared from further argument by the sound of footsteps on the path under the window. Dolly tugged at the curtains again. 'Here they are,' she said. 'I'll say no more. I'll go and see to the lunch.'

Oliver opened the door to Edward and Lizzie. 'Run upstairs and pack your bags,' he told Lizzie. 'We'll be leaving after lunch.

Come into the drawing room, Edward. We'll have a drink together before we eat.'

Lizzie prostrated herself on the bed, clenching and unclenching her hands around the floral counterpane, trying to muffle the sound of her sobs in the pillow.

Had they guessed? Did Mother and Oliver know about her and Edward? Was Oliver's thunderous face a sign that he suspected? They'd not done anything wrong. Not yet. But soon it would happen, she knew. Was it written on their faces for all to see? Other young women didn't feel this way about their brothers, they despised them, wanted to be free. But she had tried to put her feelings for Edward aside. And she had failed. Her brother loved her with a single-minded intensity. He had begged her to go to London with him, saying he'd rent a house there and they would be together. And she longed to go, longed never to suffer his absence again. Her days were full. She did all the things that gave her satisfaction, yet inside there was always a gnawing emptiness without Edward.

Her neck was tight from trying to stifle her tears. She buried her face in the bedcover and bit the cloth to gain control. She must be strong. Oliver had shown her a way out. At his house she'd forget Edward; she would put him out of her mind whenever she started to think about him. They would get over it if they were apart. They would meet new friends, maybe even marry when time had cured them, she told herself.

She sat up. There was no time left. She had already packed everything she had, dresses, underwear, winter and summer clothes, her knitting and embroidery and paints and pencils. She got to her feet and put down the lids of the two great trunks that were full to bursting.

Edward's footsteps sounded outside on the landing. He wanted to be alone with her, he'd said, just for a few minutes before she left. She began to tremble as he entered the room and stood with his back to the door, preventing her from passing. His face was a white mask of pain at their parting. It was always this way when he returned to medical school.

'Shall I see you before we meet at Christmas?' he asked her.

'No. Leave me, Edward. I have to learn to live without you. We both have to.' She was trying to be brave and calm, not looking into his face.

He towered above her, and for all her height and the two years by which she was older, she felt small and disadvantaged.

'Will you write to me?' he asked.

She nodded.

'Oh, Lizzie!' He held out his arms and she went to him. Her tears rolled gently down her face and he kissed them away, making her melt as his lips found hers.

* * *

Lizzie's worst fears were realised when James returned to Suttonford from four weeks' holiday in Scotland. She found him little changed from the boastful boy she had only once met.

He seemed to fill the great house with noise and loud demands for attention from family and servants alike. She noticed that when Oliver was near he was more subdued but whenever he found her alone his behaviour was impossible.

She sat in the conservatory, working on an embroidery. It was pleasant in there, hidden from view behind the hanging purple flowers whose name she did not know. She thought that James would not find her so easily here. But after only ten minutes the door from the house clicked and she heard his footsteps approaching.

'There you are!' He had an unpleasant way of tipping back his head, as though he was looking down his nose at her. 'Father told me to find you, Elizabeth. He wants to see you.' He had the same dark hair as his father, the grey eyes of his mother and, at fifteen, was tall and well made.

Lizzie had never seen him smiling. His mouth curled into a sneer when he thought he was being clever but she had not seen warmth or genuine amusement in him. 'Where is he? Does he want to see me now?' Lizzie asked. She folded her embroidery.

'He wants to take you to Middlefield. He sees his partner, Albert Billington, every week. You are to have the honour of meeting his wife and family.' James leaned against the wrought-iron seat, with the smile that was a sneer on his handsome face. 'I expect he wants to show you round the slums,' he added in his drawling tone. 'For some reason he is enormously proud of his wretched little factories. Perhaps they will strike a sympathetic chord in your soul, Elizabeth. They bore me to death!'

'I expect I shall enjoy it then, if it bores you!' Lizzie swept past him, furious at his disparagement of Oliver's achievements. 'It's a pity for your father that his son has nothing to be proud of.'

She reddened as she heard his guffaws ringing in her ears. How had the boy grown so despicable? He had had everything. Oliver had talked, often, about the privileged way in which his son was being brought up in comparison with his own early life. From birth he had been pampered and petted, been given everything he could want, yet he had never lifted a finger to help himself, let alone others. Perhaps that's why he's so vile, she thought.

Oliver was in his office, scribbling figures onto a sheet of paper, which he folded and placed in his breast pocket at Lizzie's approach. 'Do you want to put your bonnet on, Lizzie, and come visiting with me?' he asked. 'I'm going to see my partner at the factory and then we'll go to his house for lunch. You'll like the Billingtons. They have hundreds of children and they're a jolly lot.'

'I'd love to go with you,' she said. She always enjoyed Oliver's company and had longed, for years, to see inside his factories. He had always been generous, bringing her lengths of cloth to sew. Her earliest memories were of sorting through bags of pieces of cotton, placing matching lengths into little piles all over the dining-room table, planning her dolls' wardrobes.

When she got there she found the mill fascinating. She lingered beside the looms, making Oliver smile at her stream of questions. Even the factory girls, not known for their good manners, took to her, answering her questions in a friendly way. Normally, Oliver told her afterwards, they gave onlookers a rough ride, especially the well-dressed ones, whom they derided with a coarse humour that was a language in itself, sending gales of loud laughter down the lines behind the disconcerted visitors.

'You reminded me of myself on my first visit, Lizzie,' he told her when he had torn her away from the mill and they were walking to his partner's house. 'I found the whole process absorbing.'

'How are the printed cottons made, Oliver?' she asked. 'I'd love to meet the people who draw the patterns.'

'Middlefield's known for its silks as well as cottons,' he told her. 'There are some gifted artists working in the silk mills. I'll take you round to Partington's next time – if you'd like to come again.'

'Oh, please,' she answered, praying that he would not forget.

Late in the afternoon they took the train back to Suttonford and found a first-class compartment to themselves. 'Are you enjoying your stay with us, Lizzie?' Oliver asked her. 'Do you miss Edward and your mother?'

'I miss them but I'm happy with you and Florence,' she replied. 'Did you see Edward when you were in London last week?'

'Yes. We had dinner at my hotel and talked half the night away,' Oliver told her. 'He speaks about you all the time. He misses you.'

'Mother has been to London to see him, hasn't she? I wonder why she won't come to Suttonford to see me. Surely there are no hard feelings after all this time? It's years since she worked here.'

'Your mother will never return as a guest in the house in which she once served. She'll never set foot in Suttonford again. There are too many painful memories for her here. Dad being killed. All that,' Oliver answered.

He usually avoided mention of their past life. Lizzie took her opportunity to probe into the family history. 'Edward and I know little of our father. We only have the photograph. Is there anyone who still remembers him?'

'No. They've all gone. I'd know if anyone was left. You saw the grave. He was my father too, you know.'

Lizzie knew that he would not say more. But why should seeing the grave be significant? What an odd thing for Oliver to say. Graves don't tell you anything.

Even innocent-sounding questions alarmed him and Mother. He was staring out of the carriage window as if absorbed in looking at the familiar landscape as they approached Suttonford station. It was useless to question him.

And Oliver hoped that she'd be satisfied; hoped she'd ask no more questions. He reassured himself that there truly was nobody who remembered Joe and Dolly Wainwright when they'd been employed by the Oldfield family. Even his mother-in-law Laura, who had lived in London with Florence until she was widowed, did not remember. But then she had never bothered to learn the names of the servants. She was no threat; she could hardly recall the big events in her own life, let alone his.

They were slowing down as the train passed the village. The school he had attended was as it had always been. The cottage he'd lived in stood empty now, not fit for habitation.

He glanced at Lizzie as she gazed at the place she could so easily have known well. He saw for a moment the Lizzie she might have become with Wilf Leach for a father and he saw a Lizzie grown old prematurely with poverty and toil. He was glad he had spared her.

Chapter Twenty-Six

The lecture on transmission of infectious diseases was being followed by a tour of the fever ward. Edward enjoyed working in the fever hospital. He knew that he was the only student who actually liked the smell of carbolic. He watched Dr Hart's careful examination of the patients, finding himself anticipating the diagnosis in some of the cases. This was the branch of medicine that interested him and he did not mean to miss a second of the great man's teaching.

Already he felt a bond of understanding growing between him and the specialist. He knew Dr Hart had noticed his absorption in the speciality and had begun to follow his progress, encouraging Edward to come forward with his own attempts at diagnosis.

'Would you like to see the laboratory findings before you try this one?' Dr Hart asked, at the bedside of a young man who lay, incoherent, limbs jerking.

'Where's he from?' Edward asked, noting the patient's extreme thinness and his ragged, dirty fingernails.

'He's a vagrant,' Dr Hart replied, looking at the faces of the four students. Edward waited for one of the others to speak but it seemed no one else wanted to give an opinion.

'I'd like to see the laboratory report, sir,' he said, 'but ...'

'Go on then.' Dr Hart's thin, intelligent face showed a quick flash of humour. 'Have a guess. The poor patient's not going to be any the worse if you get it wrong.'

'Relapsing fever?' Edward ventured.

A smile broke across Dr Hart's face.

'Good!' he said. He turned his attention fully to Edward now.

'Occurrence?' he asked quickly.

'Mostly the poorer classes,' Edward replied. 'Tramps, hawkers—'

'Incubation?'

'One to sixteen days, but often under nine.'

'Symptoms, Wainwright?'

'Pyrexia – nausea – vomiting ...'

'And?'

'Tenderness in the hepatic region,' Edward told him confidently.

'Rash?'

'Not always, sir.'

'Good,' Dr Hart said. 'Well, gentlemen. That's all for today.' He looked directly at Edward. 'Can you be at the laboratory at nine in the morning, Wainwright? We can examine the samples under the microscope.'

'Thank you, sir.' Edward felt a warm glow, the satisfying feeling of having been worthy of Dr Hart's attention.

The feeling lasted until he had left the ward and contemplated the evening ahead of him. He was hungry and there was nothing to eat in his rooms. Outside the hospital he could easily become dispirited, missing Lizzie, allowing himself to dwell on the bleakness of his life without her.

It was a raw, foggy night and he dug his hands deep into the pockets of his thin overcoat as he crossed the darkened quadrangle and reached the gates.

'There's a message for you, Mr Wainwright.' A porter put his head out of the lodge door and waved a piece of paper.

Edward stepped inside the little waiting room. There was a telephone at the lodge that the students could use, and usually a queue of them waiting their turn. Tonight he was the only person there. 'What does it say?' he asked, as the porter thumbed through a sheaf of memoranda for the message.

'It says, "Your brother is in London. Can you join him at his Bond Street hotel tonight?"'

Edward gave a broad smile of relief. 'Thank you. Sure it's for tonight?'

'Have I ever been wrong?' The porter gave him a wounded look.

'Once, you were,' Edward laughed. 'You sent me on the wrong night the last time.'

'I'm right about tonight,' the man assured him. 'Shall I call a cab for you?'

'No. I'll walk,' Edward said. It was not far to Bond Street and when the roads were busy it was quicker on foot.

Horses, carriages and omnibuses moved slowly through the dense November fog. Many shop windows were illuminated now that electricity was commonplace and Edward made his way from one island of light to another as they first glimmered then blazed into the gloom.

He lingered in front of a jewellery display. A necklace caught his attention and he decided to buy it for Lizzie for Christmas. It was a gold chain with amethysts suspended at the front in a delicate cascade of gold and lilac. He could picture it against her creamy skin, the stones settling into the hollow at her throat. He would draw the money out of his savings account. It would give him a bit less to live on but there was a little more, Mother said another hundred pounds, to come from their father's estate when he was twenty-one in January.

Tonight he would ask Oliver again for information about their father, quarryman Joseph Wainwright. Oliver seemed to be adept at changing the course of the conversation whenever he or Lizzie broached the subject but he must know more than he was prepared to tell.

The hotel lobby, mirrored and smelling of polished wood, was warm and quiet in contrast to the bustle outside. Through the etched glass doors it was an ordered corner of London. Trolley wheels ran silently as a waiter crossed to the lift. He was expected, the frock-coated manager told him, in suite six on the second floor.

Edward stood at the back of the lift, fascinated by the porter's handling of the iron- and brass-hinged gates as the man closed the

Audrey Reimann

second pair. The heavy ropes of metal, which ran down each side of the well, began to vibrate, taking the strain of raising it. After the endless stairs at the hospital a lift was a decadent luxury. He tipped the man extravagantly with a shilling he could ill afford and knocked at the door of Oliver's suite.

'Hello, Edward. Come in and warm yourself.' Oliver beamed a welcome, ushering Edward into the carpeted sitting room where a coal fire burned brightly and plush chairs were placed before it with decanters and glasses on the heavy side-table.

'It's foggy out there. I didn't keep you waiting, did I?' Edward warmed his hands and stood with his back to the fire as his brother poured whiskies.

Tonight both wore boiled shirts with hard wing collars and dark suits. Their resemblance to one another was striking. Edward, taller and thinner than Oliver, did not have the look of watchfulness that characterised Oliver; nor Oliver's quick anger. Rather he had a reserve, an impression of held-back energy and tightly reined emotions, until he relaxed and his features broke into the same disarming smile that Oliver had used to such unconscious effect at the age of twenty.

'What brings you to London again?' Edward asked. 'You were here only a month ago. Business?'

'That and a summons from James's headmaster,' Oliver replied. 'I'm sure it's nothing serious, just a prank, but the school wants to talk about it. The boy doesn't fully exercise his energies. James isn't keen on sport and there is no provision for young men who don't play games.'

'How long will he remain there?' Edward asked, though he was only being polite, not really interested in James's education.

'James isn't clever like you, Edward. You are fortunate in having a good brain. I think perhaps he's already learned as much as he ever will,' Oliver replied.

'He doesn't really need brains, does he?' Edward said, not unkindly, merely giving comfort to his older brother. 'He'll never need to earn his living as I shall.'

330

It was a knife twisting in Oliver's heart; Edward's acceptance of the natural order of things under which James would benefit from all that his father's life work would bring. It was a growing burden, when every instinct told him to help Edward as a father would, to hold back and watch him make his way alone. Edward was so like himself. He saw the boy's progress following the same pattern; fatherless and being brought up by Dolly; making his way unaided through life.

'Was Father a clever man, Oliver?' Edward asked. Edward often dropped such questions into the conversation.

'Yes.' Oliver picked up a newspaper. 'Would you like to go to a theatre tonight, Edward, or will we just dine here and talk?' He did not want to be questioned again about Dad.

'Let's eat in the restaurant. How's Lizzie?' Edward asked eagerly.

'Grand,' Oliver replied. 'Come then. We'll eat in the dining room. Unless you'd rather we had it sent up?' he asked.

'No. I'd rather go down,' Edward said.

A table, heavy with silver and crystal, was set for them in the corner of the dining room. Oliver ordered turbot to start with, followed by roast beef. He saw, with paternal anxiety, that Edward was hungry. His son said little until the first pangs of his hunger were satisfied.

'Nobody does it as well as your mother, do they, Edward?' he said. 'But it's almost as good.'

They finished with ices, cheese and salad and Oliver watched with pleasure Edward trying to give the impression of a delicate eater while consuming twice as much as he did. Port was brought to the table.

'Lizzie has learned to ride. She goes out every morning with one of the grooms. She shows promise of becoming a fine horsewoman,' Oliver reported when Edward asked about his sister again. 'Florence has taught her to drive the pony and trap and she comes down to the station for me when I've been to Middlefield.'

He leaned back and smiled at the recollection of Lizzie, her lively hair netted into a chignon and pinned under a brown velvet hat, clad in Donegal tweed, concentration in every muscle of her hands and face as she shortened and loosened reins, steering the trap back to the house along the empty drive. The pony she used could have done the trip blindfolded with nothing but a bit of string around its neck, but Lizzie did not know that.

'Florence is very fond of her. Takes her everywhere. They spend hours at the dressmaker's. Florence has promised to take Lizzie to Paris in the spring to order gowns from Monsieur Worth. Florence and her mother go every year.' Oliver offered Edward a cigar and a waiter came forward to clip off the ends for them.

'Florence has introduced her to a farmer whose land lies next to ours. The man's quite besotted, Florence tells me. He contrives to meet her whenever she's out riding.' Had Oliver been watching Edward's face he would not have missed the leap of consternation his words had aroused, but he was not looking and he exhaled the fragrant cigar smoke before continuing. 'He must bribe Lizzie's groom to lead her across his path every day.'

He smiled benignly at Edward. 'Lizzie finds more amusement than excitement in it I'm afraid. Florence's little matchmaking attempt looks like coming to naught.'

They talked on into the night, perfect companions. Oliver wished that his son had a little less pride for he longed to help Edward with money. The boy's cuffs were frayed, his suit was thin and shiny at the elbows and seat, and he was certain that Edward was frugal in his eating. The money Oliver had put into trust for the two children brought only an inadequate income. But no matter how he approached the subject Edward was firm about not accepting help. Others managed on as little as he had, he told Oliver, and he considered himself fortunate in having a good home to return to during his holidays, where his mother cared for him so well.

Oliver looked forward to these evenings, these times alone with his son. They were oases of relaxation and enjoyment in a world of business that grew ever more demanding.

* * *

Oliver walked through the town to the gates of the school. The fog had lifted overnight and the sun shone on the mellow stones. He would have enjoyed this when he was young; the chance to learn, the opportunity to row and ride and bat. A group of tail-suited young men raised their hats to him as he reached the entrance and one stepped ahead of him to hold open the doors.

Dr McCormack's large, comfortable study overlooked the playing fields beyond the hedge that secluded the staff wing from the ancient, sprawling school buildings. He was a tall, gaunt man, a wise academic, dedicated to honouring the traditions of his school. He rose from his desk as Oliver was shown in.

Oliver had taken to the man when they first met. He reached out to shake hands with him and they seated themselves before the headmaster spoke.

'Mr Wainwright. There has been trouble in the school for some time. We instil into our pupils respect for teamwork and consideration for others. Individuality is encouraged but only insofar as it benefits the rest of the community. I am afraid that your son has flouted the authority of his housemaster, has demonstrated a lack of willingness to co-operate and rejected all of the principles the school is founded upon.' He paused for a moment, anticipating some response from the man who sat silent and intent before him.

'Go on,' Oliver said evenly.

'James has gathered around himself what can only be likened to a bunch of thugs and bullies. We are expert at detecting this kind of thing and weeding out individuals who wish to practise their own brand of despotism, but your son has deceived the most hardened cynics amongst the staff.'

'What has he done?' Oliver asked in a cold voice.

'He has extorted money from younger boys with threats of reprisals. He has beaten boys who do not belong to his nasty little gang and he has tried to escape retribution; using force to extract false confessions from the boys he intimidates.'

'What do you propose?' Oliver tried to sound calm and reasoned but he knew with awful certainty that James was guilty of these crimes. He had seen in his son an arrogance and viciousness he had chosen not to acknowledge, hoping James was passing through a rebellious period; that soon his behaviour would moderate. He had taken the easy way out and left it to men he believed were better equipped than he was to deal with undesirable traits. He should have brought the boy up his own way, given him a respect for others and pride in the work of his hands.

Now he must deal with James himself, in his own way; a way that knew nothing of kid gloves or subtlety.

'We will warn him in your presence,' the headmaster continued, 'that his behaviour is intolerable. We will separate the individuals he has gathered around himself and, if necessary, we'll send him down for the rest of term.'

Dr McCormack rang a bell on his desk to summon a messenger. 'I'll have him brought to the study, Mr Wainwright. Are you an Old Boy?'

'No. I didn't have the advantages I've given to James. As a matter of fact I believe that I've benefited from their absence.' He walked to the window and gazed out.

The fires of his anger had been stoked. He had not felt this way for years. His mind went back to Tommy and his cheating ways. He had put a stop to Tommy's nonsense and his younger brother was a prosperous sheep farmer in Australia now. Drastic measures were called for again, though he didn't contemplate banishment for James. There was silence for a moment before he turned to face the headmaster.

'I'll deal with my boy in my own way. I'm grateful for your assessment of his character but I don't believe your punishment will go anything like far enough to check him. I'll set him upon a proper course myself.'

The door opened and James sauntered insolently into the study. Surprise registered on his face when he saw Oliver and his eyes flew from him to the headmaster enquiringly.

'I've heard all about it. You needn't start explaining,' Oliver said before James had a chance to speak.

James appeared to recover his composure. He walked the few paces to Oliver's side and slapped him on the shoulder. 'I'm sure you don't believe all the rubbish that's being talked about me, Father,' he drawled.

Oliver's hand caught him a blow across the side of his head, sending him to the floor, stunned by its force.

Dr McCormack had not expected this. His reaction was a quick intake of breath and a hand gripped on to the desk to steady himself against the shock of seeing such swift retaliation.

James sprang to his feet. 'Father! What do you think you're doing? You are in school, not one of your back-street factories.' He got no further. He was felled again with Oliver's other hand.

'Get your things.' Oliver's voice had a grating edge that he had never used on James before. 'Go to your room. Pack an overnight bag and be back here in ten minutes.'

James stood before him, white-faced but trying to show some bravado.

'Move!' Oliver went towards him and he retreated through the open door. He would hasten to pack now, Oliver knew, before he was disgraced any more.

'The fees will be paid. He'll not be back,' Oliver told Dr McCormack. 'Have his belongings sent to Suttonford.'

James was back in seven minutes, carrying a leather case.

'Goodbye.' Oliver shook hands with the headmaster and led James from the school.

Outside the gates he turned once more to face James who was dragging his feet. 'Get moving,' he growled. 'Walk behind me. I don't want to see your face or hear your voice until I've decided what to do with you.'

James stopped and faced Oliver. 'I'll not be treated like a naughty child,' he began. Oliver made a move towards him that told the boy that indignation was of no benefit and strode ahead, to the station.

James hung back in the press of passengers while Oliver booked a whole compartment. He slunk behind as they went to the train.

He made no attempt to help as Oliver swung their cases on to the rope-net luggage rack.

Oliver slammed the door and hauled on the window strap to close it. 'Right. Now you want to know what I'm going to do with you, don't you?' he said.

The train heaved forward, heading north. There was no humour or warmth behind Oliver's dry smile as he spoke. 'You've had all the lessons you are going to get, James. I never wanted this kind of education for you, you know. My father died when I was young and I missed him so much that I promised myself I'd never deprive my own children of a proper home life. But they were all against me; Sir Philip, your grandmother Mawdesley, even your mother. They felt you'd be better for a public-school education.'

James sat, silent and sullen, but Oliver knew that he was listening to every word. 'Well you've had your chance to learn. From now on you are going to make your own way in the world. You'll maybe not find it so easy to be top dog in the real world as you did at school, especially when you've done a hard day's work. But this is life, lad. For most people it's not all about learning and playing. It's about earning and paying.' He started to smile at his own joke and the expression of disbelief on James's face. 'You'll enjoy it. There's no better feeling, my boy, than knowing that what you've got is what you've worked for.' He leaned back against the seat, loosened his jacket and, hands in pockets, began to outline his son's future.

'James. I think you are a leader. You need to get down to some proper work. Use your ingenuity. I'm going to have you apprenticed to a textile manufacturer. You'll start at the bottom – learn everything – see how the whole business works; spinning, weaving, dyeing, printing.' He smiled broadly at his son. 'One day you'll run Suttonford. The house and your livelihood depend totally on my factories. It's better you know exactly what you've got.'

James stared at him now. 'All right, Father,' he drawled, 'I'll do as you say but—'

'You will, my boy. You certainly will!' Oliver agreed.

'. . . but I'll start after Christmas. The second of January perhaps?'

James's confidence appeared to be growing by the minute, sufficiently encouraged by the smile on Oliver's face to try to set a few of the conditions.

'You'll start tomorrow, boy.' Oliver's voice was stern. 'As soon as we reach Middlefield we'll find lodgings for you near to the factory. Not one of my factories, of course. It wouldn't please the workers to have the boss's son put amongst them.' They would give him a hard enough time at one of the other mills, Oliver knew.

Oliver raised the window blind and looked out into the blackness. 'We'll stretch our legs at Crewe; find something to eat on the station. This is a treat for me, having company on the journey home.' Oliver was enjoying himself. It would be a new challenge, supervising the boy's education. For that was how he saw it. It was a wonderful chance for James to put his spoiled childhood behind him and learn to act like a man.

It was nine o'clock when they reached Middlefield and walked up the Wallgate to the home of one of the mill managers. The man was delighted to accept James as an apprentice. He admired the boy, he said, for wanting to learn the business properly.

Oliver knew that the wife of one of his own foremen took in lodgers at their house in Rivergate and next he and James walked down the steep slope of the gaslit street to the lodging house directly opposite The Pheasant. Oliver pointed out to James the yard behind the tavern where he had first lived as a stable lad. 'It was my first job, James and I was very proud to do it. I hope you'll be as happy as I was.'

The Smallwoods' house was narrow, squeezed in between The Crown and a dry-salter's but it was inviting, warm and homely with scents of rising bread dough and baking coming from the kitchen. James would be all right here.

The bedroom they were shown was clean and there were plenty of blankets on the bed. The boy would be warm enough and Mrs Ellen Smallwood seemed a good sort. Oliver paid her a week's rent in advance.

'After this you pay your own rent, out of your wages on a Friday. I expect to see you at church on Sunday morning. It's very important to your mother. You can come for lunch at Suttonford afterwards. It will be a pleasure for your mother to have her working son at the lunch table, once a week. Good luck.'

He squeezed James's shoulder affectionately and left for Suttonford.

He softened the story a little for Florence, telling her that James was not really bad, just young and impulsive. Young men need an opportunity to exercise their talents, he assured her. After all, her own father and her grandfather had been army men. They had been through a testing time and it was wrong to deny James a chance to prove himself.

Florence snuggled up to him in front of a glowing fire in her bedroom. He put his arm around her shoulders as they sat together on her little satin-covered sofa. 'You're a wonderful father, Oliver darling. I hope James knows how lucky he is,' she sighed contentedly.

Oliver tossed and turned in bed in his room. He would not be able to sleep tonight. He tried to focus his thoughts on the events of the day but an image of Celia kept intruding and the need for her, which was growing from, not being assuaged by, their weekly meetings rose to torment him.

He pictured her face, the dark, flashing eyes and her deceptively prim mouth, her eager, supple limbs wrapped around him, her cries of pleasure when he ...

'Oh, God,' he said to himself. 'I can't live like this!' He rose and pulled on riding breeches and boots, tucking in his nightshirt. He brought out a stalking jacket and pushed his arms quickly into the sleeves before slipping, unseen, from the great house to walk in the cold night.

He walked quickly at first, in a fury of frustration, away from the house, towards the woodland path. What should he do? The more he saw of Celia, the more he wanted her. He had tried to think of her as an instrument; an instrument of his release from the tyranny of his appetites but had only succeeded in increasing those appetites. He had told himself that she was of no consequence – a mere circus act who could be replaced if he so chose – he would soon tire of her and find a more acquiescent, undemanding mistress. He thought of all these things … and he knew that they were not true.

He trod the wet leaves beneath the elms and leaned against their rough trunks and filled his lungs with sharp night air. The moon shone silver and brilliant between the trees. He listened to the sounds of the night creatures; an owl's strange sustained call – a scuffling in the undergrowth and the wailing of the stable cats as they courted their chosen mates.

Then he walked five miles over the heather-clad moors before returning, with the dawn, to Suttonford.

He would confide in Albert. Albert was more experienced in these matters than he was. Perhaps Albert would tell him how he kept his feelings under control; for Albert had always had a weakness for the fair sex yet never allowed the weakness to dominate his other life, the life of contentment Oliver so desperately wanted to regain.

He went slowly back into the house, no nearer to understanding his own dilemma. Tomorrow he would go to Manchester to see Celia.

Chapter Twenty-Seven

James opened one eye. He was not a young man prone to 'Where am I?' thoughts when he awoke to unfamiliar surroundings. A match was struck and the room swelled with light as the girl who had carried hot water to his room lit the gas. From the back she was such a pretty creature. She wore a long white cambric apron tied firmly around her neat waist and her hair, blonde like his mother's, was tied just as firmly at the back of her head with a large black bow. The sleeves of her grey woollen dress were pushed back, revealing milky-white forearms with a downy covering of fine silver hairs. James closed his eyes tight as she turned towards him.

'Mr Wainwright. Time to get up.' Her voice was not that of an ordinary maidservant. It had the Middlefield accent quite strongly, James heard, but lacked the whining tone he found so unpleasant on most of the locals. In fact he rather liked the way she pronounced his name … Mister Wayn-wright … he wondered how she would say James … Jay-ms … probably. He pretended to be asleep.

'Mister Wainwright!' she raised her voice and tapped the patch-work counterpane above his shoulder. 'Wake up. Mr Wainwright!' She shook his shoulder firmly.

James's hand darted out from beneath the covers and he snatched her slender wrist. The girl lost her balance and pitched on to the bed. James opened his eyes and looked into the blue, startled gaze of the prettiest girl he had ever seen.

For all her pale skin and hair her eyes were fringed with dark lashes and she had finely arched eyebrows above eyes of corn-flower blue. Her nose had the faintest bump in it, adding, in James's

340

opinion, to her charm, and her mouth, when she opened it to catch her shocked breath, was small and firm.

Her teeth were white and even, so level that he could have ruled a line under them and not one would have been out of true, save where the eye teeth turned very slightly outwards, revealing their edges. And her mouth was inches from his own, her breath sweet and warm. He could kiss her if he dared. James saw all this in the seconds after he had pulled her down onto the bed.

The girl sprang back on to her feet, twisted her arm from his grasp and delivered a stinging slap across his cheek. He grinned up at her from the pillow.

'Breakfast in five minutes,' she told him. 'First left at the foot of the stairs.' She rubbed her reddened wrist and was gone, snapping the door to behind her and he heard her, sure-footed and quick, skipping down the wooden stair.

'Oh, hell! I wonder if I'll be thrown out of here as well,' he muttered. But he was fairly certain that the young woman would take it in her stride. She probably had to slap a good few faces, working in a lodging house.

He had slept soundly and he stretched before he slipped his feet out of bed onto the cold boards and reached for the clothes he had worn the day before. It was still dark outside and when he opened the curtains he saw that the window was frosted prettily on its inside. He placed the palms of his hands against the glass until the warm imprint melted the ice but there was a film of grime on the outside of the window from the belching railway smoke and the foggy pall which often lay over this part of the town.

He cupped his hands around the melted space and pressed his eyes to them, obliterating the reflected light from inside the room. He could make out the chimneys of the mills, already disgorging smoke into the heavy air and saw faintly the alleys where clogged feet rumbled downhill towards the mills.

A mirror above a plain washstand reflected his image back at him and he tried to assess his looks and his attractiveness to girls. He had dark hair, and some girls liked tall, dark-haired men, he had heard, and often blonde girls preferred them to fairer men. That was a good start – he liked blonde girls. His eyes were grey, like his mother's, and he had what he thought of as pretty ordinary features – a straight, long nose and a plain, biggish mouth. He did not know whether or not he was handsome. Nobody had ever mentioned his looks.

Girls had long had a fascination for him but he had had little opportunity, so far, to test his charms on them. There were young maids at Suttonford, of course, but Mother made a point of knowing them all by name, having overseen their progress at the village Sunday school. They would have been sure to report to her if he'd laid a hand on them.

School was a masculine environment and though the boys there experimented with town girls when they got the chance, and with one another when they didn't, that kind of public sexual activity did not appeal to James. He was not averse to using the boys' weaknesses against them though, and many a boy had prayed to God that James Wainwright would not discover his dreadful secrets.

He washed his face, using a new piece of yellow common soap the girl had left on the soap dish, dressed quickly and went downstairs, remembering that she'd said, 'first left ...'

Three men were at the breakfast table when he took his seat. Two, merchants of some kind he guessed, were much older than himself, the other was a hearty-looking young man of around eighteen. A newly lit fire crackled in the grate and a place was set for him.

'Good morning!' James greeted the seated men. 'I'm James Wainwright. Please introduce yourselves.'

The young man reached a hand out to him. 'Nathaniel Cooper. Pleased to meet yer, James. This is Mr Brocklebank, an auctioneer from Chester. He'll be selling cattle in the market this morning.'

The man had a grip of iron. 'And this 'ere is Mr Sefton, his partner. It is him as'll be taking the money.' Nathaniel laughed heartily at his own joke. 'I am just a farmer's lad. Looking for a few good cows.'

'You don't live here then?' James's voice, with its cultured tones, used normally to great effect when dealing with people he considered to be of a lower order than himself, did not command more than a quick glance from the two older men. They looked at him with barely concealed impatience before returning to study the sheaves of papers they had laid out on the tablecloth.

'No. Me father farms seventy acres up at the Clough and I work with him. I allus come 'ere for me breakfast. You get a good plateful and it's clean and cheap.'

It was the first time that James had not had the trappings of wealth to indicate his social position and he was surprised to find himself being judged simply as another lodger.

'I'm the son of Oliver Wainwright. Wainwright and Billington, the cotton weavers,' he ventured. This drew another glance from the auctioneers but Nathaniel appeared to have lost interest in James's family history at the sound of a footfall outside the room.

'Mornin', Mrs Smallwood.' Nathaniel leaped from the table and held open the door to the woman James had seen the night before. She carried a steaming tureen of porridge to the table. 'Is your Alice late for school this morning? She allus fetches us breakfasts.'

'No. She's not late. Something's annoyed her this morning. It wasn't you, was it, Nat?' Mrs Smallwood asked. 'There's ham and eggs to follow. Our Sarah's fetchin' the teapot.'

'It weren't me. Eeh, your Alice is a grand lass,' Nathaniel beamed as he ladled porridge into his bowl. 'Is she still set on her education then?'

'Yes. She wants to be a teacher. Dad and I encourage her,' the woman answered with a trace of defiance in her voice. 'It's bad enough that Sam and I have to fight for Alice's education without having to justify it to all and sundry.'

She took a big brown teapot from her daughter and set it in the centre of the table. 'You'd better eat up as quick as you can, Mr Wainwright. Your father said he's sending someone for you at seven o'clock sharp.'

James curled his lip at the mention of his father's orders. 'I'm sure they'll wait, Mrs Smallwood, until I'm ready.' He was hungry. The ham and eggs were just as he liked them and he had barely finished before she returned to announce that, 'A Mister Hunt is waiting for you.'

'Tell him I'll join him in about half an hour.' James would not be rushed. If the wretched woman insisted on chivvying him, he decided, he'd put her in her place. He smiled expansively round at his companions but they were busily spreading Dundee marmalade on crusty bread and noisily drinking sweet tea.

James sat at the table after the three men had finished, drinking tea slowly. He waved flamboyantly at the auctioneers as they left the table for the kitchen, to pay Mrs Smallwood, and he smiled when he heard their lowered voices, believing them to be discussing him. Well, he'd show them as well as his father that James Wainwright would not be ordered around.

He studied the long case clock and made a mental note of the time of the next full moon from the movements of the heavens across its face and turned his attentions to the painting of a young girl who drooped beside a lily pond.

He would make it clear, right from the start, that he had no intention of soiling his hands or of spending the whole day in a filthy factory. If it turned out as insufferable as he thought it would he'd take the next train to Suttonford and complain to Mother about it. If it were not for the look of disgust that would spread across his father's face, and the prospect of an even worse fate, he'd go now.

'Wainwright?' A purple-faced man of about thirty years pushed open the door, apparently not in the mood to wait any longer for his charge. 'Coom on! You were meant to be at work half an hour since. You'll lose money for bad timekeeping. Are yer coming like that?'

James gave him a withering look. 'When I am ready, my man, we'll leave for your dismal little workplace.' He pulled on his alpaca overcoat and kid gloves. 'Lead the way,' he commanded.

Through the crowded back alley behind Rivergate they had to push against the crush of workers who jostled and elbowed James, forcing him to hurry to keep pace with Mr Hunt. He had begun to feel rather foolish and a little apprehensive when they reached the mill and the gatekeeper's iron gates clashed together behind them.

'We was expecting you a while back. See as yer get here on time tomorrer,' a wheezy old man told him sharply. James took off his coat and held it out to the old man. The man wiped the back of his hand over his mouth, threw the coat over a dusty chair and nodded towards a door at the top of a flight of stairs.

He was in a long room with lines of close-packed looms. It was deafening, the huge machines clattering and groaning and over all the choking air from hot metal and cotton dust. James winced as he took in the scene before him.

The women, young and old, who tended the machines were staring at him in open curiosity. They wore scarves, tied tightly over their hair to keep it away from the machinery. They wore drab dresses and pinafores but they were neither drab nor dowdy by nature. Rather, they displayed a coarse liveliness James had not come across before.

'Here,' an old woman called out to him. She had no teeth and her mouth sank in alarmingly at every word she spoke. 'I'll show you how to do it.' She dragged him, unwilling, to her side and placed her large red hands over his, guiding them on to the front bar of the machine. The vibrations throbbed through him, making his teeth chatter until he clenched his jaws and pulled himself free.

'Let go of me, you disgusting old devil!' He spat the words at her.

His words and the outraged expression on his face, far from reducing her to tears as he had hoped, sent her into near convulsions. She placed her hands on her great belly and laughed so loudly that two more women left their machines in the charge of apprentices and came over, begging her to tell them what she had found so funny. The old woman could hardly speak for cackling.

'I've half a mind to have you sent home. I'm not one of your common mill workers.' James was so angry that he found he was shouting. He brushed one hand against the other, to remove the feel of the hateful creature's hand on his. How dared these low women ridicule him?

'Ooh. Look at 'im! Arf parst me garter and twice round me leg!' the younger woman teased, pointing her nose to the ceiling, a finger outstretched beneath her nostrils. The others began to giggle.

'Be quiet, you stupid girl,' James snarled at her as she pirouetted before him, tears of laughter pouring down her thin cheeks.

Her clogs enabled her to whirl fast and she lifted the hem of her skirt, showing a grimy petticoat, black-edged from the dusty floor. Beneath the petticoat her thin legs in wrinkled and darned grey stockings were poked into heavy wooden-soled clogs.

'Mister Wainwright is it?' Another woman had joined the group. This one was hard-faced and had a nasty set to her mouth. 'Not "The Mister-bloody-Wainwright" of Wainwright and Billington's? Surely not?' Her spittle hit him. It was unintentional; she always sprayed as she spoke but it was the action that inflamed him. He grabbed her about the shoulders and pushed her to the floor but the girl was a match for him. 'Gerrim, girls,' she yelled, 'before he tries his bloody nonsense!'

At least six women had joined the original three and one pulled at his sleeve. She had thin, mousy hair, wispy over her forehead with rats' tails hanging limply under her headscarf.

'Good lookin', inn't he?' she jeered. 'Coom on, girls. Let's show 'im that he can't push Mavis about even if he is Mister Wainwright.'

Before James could run for his life he was on the floor, one girl astride his chest while two others held his arms outstretched and another tugged at his trousers. He kicked and heaved but the odds were too heavily against him. A minute later they smeared his naked flesh with thick brown grease from a deep tin, each girl rubbing it in gleefully when her turn came. Then they pulled up his trousers but kept him pinned to the floor and he felt the horrible mess sliding inside his clothes while his nostrils were filled with the grey, clogging dust of the floor.

'You bloody wretches!' he yelled, but his words were drowned in the hilarity.

'Give 'im a kiss, Polly,' one of the girls screeched as the toothless creature he had first spoken to knelt clumsily beside him, saliva dripping from her sucked-in bottom lip.

'Oh, God. No!' he shouted.

'I don't care for him. He's too thin for me,' the old woman said, wrinkling her bulbous nose and reaching out for the skinny girl who crouched beside her. 'Here. You 'ave him.'

One by one they approached and knelt over him. Some kissed him, urged on by the encouraging shrieks from the crowd of girls around him, others merely puckering their lips before collapsing into peals of giggles and when they had all had their turn they left him alone.

James sat on the floor of the hateful room with his head in his hands, wondering how he would avenge himself. The women probably did this to every new man who came into the mill. He knew all about humiliation; he was not in the least embarrassed by an initiation ceremony that was no worse than he had suffered or meted out at school but he saw that if he were to survive in the mills he would have to have things running his way. He could not go home to Suttonford and tell his father that the girls had frightened him. He even managed a wry smile at the thought.

He stood up and went to one of the looms where the old woman stood. 'All right,' he said. 'Let's get on with it.'

The work was tiring and much more difficult than he thought it would be. The old crone showed him how to 'set up', then pronounced on his poor attempt, pulled his work apart and made him practise over and over again until he got the feel of the machine.

'Didn't yer bring no food?' the skinny girl asked at twelve o'clock.

'I thought I'd be given something here,' James replied in as neutral a tone as he could muster.

'You should've asked yer landlady to make yer up some butties,' she said kindly. 'Have one of mine.'

She handed him a thick slice of bread and margarine and he ate gratefully before putting his head under the tap in the corner of the room and gulping the ice-cold water to quench his thirst.

At seven o'clock when he returned to his lodgings he was tired and dirty and it had grown dark again without his once having been aware of the light of day. His shoulders sagged and he appeared to have become one of the crowd. The skinny girl tucked her arm into his for a few minutes before their ways parted.

'Mind and don't forget to bring yer food tomorrer!' she called after him as he went up into Rivergate and the lodging house.

Mr Smallwood brought hot water to his room. Sam Smallwood looked a kindly man; fatherly but not a man to be disobeyed. 'Had a rough day, young Wainwright?' he asked. 'You look done in.'

'I'll be all right,' James replied.

'Supper's nearly ready. You can eat with us at night when there's no one else staying,' Mr Smallwood told him. 'A parcel of clothes came for you this morning. I'll bring them up.'

James had to ask for a second lot of hot water before he was clean, then he cut his chin while trying to shave. He had only done it once for himself. There were barbers at school for the older boys and Father's valet obliged at Suttonford.

Finally he bundled his greasy clothes up and pushed them beneath the bedstead where, he supposed, they would be collected.

There was a big coal fire in the homely living room, chairs before it and a table laid for the family. In a corner sat the girl who had come to his room that morning. She was reading her schoolbooks. She looked up and smiled at him. 'Hello, Mr Wainwright. I'm Alice Smallwood. Did you have an enjoyable day at work?'

James gave her a startled look. Had she heard? No. The look on her face told him that it was just a polite question. There was laughter in her eyes but that was because of their little tussle this morning, he guessed.

'It was interesting. Hard work but interesting,' he told her pompously. 'How was school? You must be the little bluestocking.'

'I wouldn't say I was a bluestocking, but it's important for me to do well at school,' she said, pursing her lips in amusement. 'I'm going to be a teacher.'

The aroma of cooking wafted through the half-open door of the kitchen and Ellen Smallwood and Sarah followed the kitchen maid into the room, carrying and helping her to load dishes on to the table. They placed a rib of beef for Mr Smallwood to carve and they set down plates and dishes of roast potatoes, boiled carrots mashed with turnip, chopped and peppered green cabbage and a small mountain of light-as-air batter puddings.

James had a healthy appetite and he ate everything they put before him and as he ate he felt himself to be quite at home with these people. He was overwhelmed with the amount of talk at the table. Everyone had something to tell and they pronounced seriously and volubly on every topic, interrupting one another at will. This was so different from Suttonford, where conversation, he had been taught, never disturbed, was kept on a light and polite level and where, had he dared to interrupt or venture a different opinion from his parents, he would have been banished from their company until he had learned better manners.

At Suttonford, Mother was always in control at the table. Mother, so tiny and pretty, held them all in check. Mother, who would not allow contentious talk; Mother, who could change the subject adroitly if it were leading in a direction she did not wish to follow; Mother, who appeared not to notice the gross drunkenness of grandmother Mawdesley; Mother who went her own sweet way, loving and adoring everybody, refusing to acknowledge problems in the lives of those around her; Mother would be shocked and distressed at the way the Smallwoods lived, James believed.

The lively talk continued through the clearing away of the dishes and the setting of teacups. Mrs Smallwood even raised her voice, to be heard from the kitchen, if she wanted to say something. Whenever James was addressed with a 'What do you have to say, James?', he only managed to reply, 'I've never really thought about it.'

'Time you did, lad,' Mr Smallwood said after a lengthy discourse on exploitation and low wages. 'One day you'll be in a position to improve the lot of the workers.'

'No mill-owner's going to pay out more than he has to do, is he?' James ventured. 'You are not going to get high wages until there is more demand for skilled workers than there is for cloth.'

'Not unless we strike,' Mr Smallwood said.

James knew that Mr Smallwood was a foreman at Wainwright and Billington's. 'And will you?' he asked. He was becoming more confident now and talk of strikes and trouble interested him more than the talk about the failing Queen Victoria.

'If we do, we'll concert our efforts and shut the whole of Lancashire and Cheshire down.' Mr Smallwood warmed to his subject.

James felt the excitement that a conflict roused began to stir. Here was a way he could get his own back against Father. Father had no sympathy with unions so James would join. If there was to be trouble he'd be right in the centre of it – and serve the old man right.

* * *

Oliver reached Middlefield at nine o'clock and hurried to the mill. Wainwright and Billington's stood on the banks of the Hollin; still the original building but much increased in size over the years. They had four mills in the town but this was the only one that bore their name. After all the years it still gave him satisfaction seeing 'Wainwright and Billington' built into the front, high above the top storey.

On this morning, though, he was too angry to think of anything but the news he had received. He pounded up the stairs, not even glancing through the glass panels of the doors into the weaving sheds as he passed them on the three flights to the office.

Albert was giving instructions to one of the overlookers from the first floor and Oliver waited impatiently until the man was ready to leave.

'Tell Sam Smallwood to come up here before you do anything else,' he ordered as the overlooker reached the door.

'What's up?' Albert asked. 'Sam Smallwood's not done anything, has he?'

'Not him. No,' Oliver replied. 'But I heard this morning that he's been taking James to the union meetings.'

Albert smiled. 'You're not afraid of the unions are you?' he asked.

'You know I'm not. But I know James. He's not interested in it. He's doing it to annoy me.'

'He's succeeding, by the look of it,' Albert said as they heard Sam Smallwood's knock at the door.

'Come in,' Oliver said.

Sam Smallwood was a big man, a reliable foreman and he had always been on good terms with him, but Oliver's face was dark with annoyance and his speech was unceremonious. 'How's James's work?' he asked.

'He's doing grand, they tell me, sir,' Sam Smallwood replied.

'He's learning all right?'

'Aye.'

'No complaints from the factory?'

'No, sir.'

'And yourselves? Is he fitting in? Making himself at home?' Oliver asked.

Sam Smallwood seemed to hesitate before answering, then it seemed that he took a deep breath and summoned up the courage to speak out. 'He's a fine lad, Mr Wainwright. We like him very much. He's come with me to a couple of union meetings.'

'I didn't know you were a member, Smallwood,' Oliver said.

'I've always been in it, Mr Wainwright. I've never hidden the fact,' Sam Smallwood said gruffly.

'All right! All right!' Oliver banged the desk with the flat of his hand. 'I've no reason to think you want to make trouble. But I'll not have my son going against me. See he doesn't go to any more meetings.'

He dismissed the foreman with a curt nod and when he heard the man's feet on the stairs Oliver turned to Albert again.

'I've heard from the investigator,' he told him.

'What does he say?'

Oliver took an envelope from his breast pocket and withdrew a sheet of paper. He went to the window and read:

Dear Mr Wainwright,

I have, after much searching, discovered the identity of your 'correspondent'. When you are next in Manchester I will give you my latest report and hope that we find ourselves nearer to a resolution of your problem.

Archie Wilson

'I'm seeing him this afternoon,' Oliver said, putting the letter back in his pocket. 'You don't need me here do you?'

'No.' Albert gave him a worried look. 'Is your little actress in Manchester this week?' he asked.

Oliver sat down abruptly on the corner of the big oak desk and looked up at Albert, where he stood with his back to the roaring fire. 'She means more to me than that,' he said. 'I am seeing her tonight – and the next.' He began absent-mindedly to close and open the lid of the inkstand as he spoke.

'I want her all the time now,' he confided in a low voice. 'The days when I can't see her are torment. I can't sleep. I can't think of anything but the next time,' he added. 'I don't even know what my feelings for Florence are any longer.' He could see that this revelation had shocked Albert.

'You've always overvalued them, haven't you?' Albert said.

'Who?'

'Women,' Albert told him in an exasperated manner. 'You still can't gallivant. Can't love 'em and leave 'em, can you?'

'I've never been one for philandering, if that's what you mean,' Oliver answered.

'Well. If you're not . . . what the hell are you doing with an actress half your age?' Albert asked. He was not smiling. 'You know what you're like. If you can't keep 'em at arm's length you shouldn't be playing the game.'

Oliver was surprised at Albert's taking this outraged attitude. Albert had never hidden from him his own propensity for dalliance and flirtation. 'I don't see why you're so worried,' he replied shortly. 'You've never been a faithful husband.'

'No,' Albert answered. 'But I love my wife. I've never thought of my other bits of nonsense as anything more than a game.'

'Well then,' Oliver said. 'Perhaps I'll start to see Celia in that light.'

'You're not that type, Oliver.' Albert shook his head. 'You never were. You're bloody well obsessed with the woman. You're useless for anything else.'

'I know,' Oliver agreed. 'I know what you mean. But what you don't understand is that Celia ...'

'Oh, come on!' Albert interrupted him sharply. 'Your little actress is not unique. They're all the same. There's hundreds like her. She's probably just a bit more obvious than most.'

'What makes you say that?' Oliver asked. He'd be glad to believe that Celia was replaceable. His possessive need of her was worrying to him. He wanted to be back loving Florence and not troubled by this imagining of the girl, which never left him.

'I know how you work, Oliver,' Albert said dismissively.

'How?'

Albert grinned at him. 'I've known you since we were sixteen, don't forget,' he said. 'I remember your efforts when we were lads ...'

Oliver began to smile, remembering his clumsy attempts to charm the rough girls who frequented The Crown. 'Well?'

'You either do nothing – or fall on top of 'em,' Albert said. 'You don't waste time courting them, do you? I bet you've never even tried.'

Oliver let him continue. Albert evidently saw no annoyance in his partner's face for he added gleefully, 'The only two occasions when you've had a woman outside marriage they've fallen into your arms as eager as yourself. I bet it was the actress who seduced you, if the truth was known.'

Oliver could not keep the laughter back now. He held his sides as Albert went on, taunting him, so near to the truth that it was even funnier than his partner knew.

'You're a ruffian, Oliver. Where women are concerned you've about as much delicacy as a bloody rhinoceros. I don't know how your poor wife has put up with you for twenty years.'

'I'd like to think you're right.' Oliver was cheered by Albert's analysis. 'She's not a shrinking violet. Not Celia. Not by a long way.'

'I wouldn't worry, then,' Albert answered. 'You'll wear one another out before long.'

Oliver got to his feet and put his overcoat on. 'I'll go now. I'll look over the new mill while I'm there,' he said.

He left the factory and walked, behind the mills, along the river path to the cattle market. He could almost feel the throbbing machinery as he passed the immense brick back walls of the buildings. He saw the river water gushing from discharge pipes, back into the Hollin, warmed and foaming where it dropped back into the cold clean water that came from the hills. Further along the river was stained red from the used water of the dye works.

He reached the bridge that took him to the station and stood for a few minutes watching the busy town; the industrious northern people going about their business. He was a part of all this – he shared with them their plain-speaking manner, their solid, dependable strength of character and their innate distaste for being made fools of by outsiders. Was he making a fool of himself? Oliver believed he was and he pondered, as he did at every spare moment, on the predicament his obsession with this girl was leading him into.

He caught the train and sat, silent and thoughtful, looking out of the window, trying to put from his mind the exciting prospect of the evening ahead and to begin to wonder about his coming meeting with the investigator.

He went immediately to the address at the top of the letter from Archie Wilson. It was a small room in a long, monotonous back street and he had difficulty in finding it, having talked with Archie in a hotel on the first two occasions they'd met.

Archie invited him in. Archie looked like a clerk and a timid one at that. He was under average height and thin, with sleeked-back hair of an unnatural-looking black colour, centre-parted. His hooked nose was set below small, dark eyes, which were as observant as a bird's, shiny and button black.

'Your Mr King is one Gregory King, Mr Wainwright. He keeps a lodging house in Elison Road and is an altogether nasty piece of work. The lodgers are all women.'

He offered Oliver a mug of beer and carried on talking in his quiet, high-pitched voice. 'They are not fast women or anything, just ordinary working women who have respectable jobs in London. They leave after a few weeks, when they find rooms nearer to their work and I think Mr King comes from the north of England since many of his lodgers are from this part of the country.'

Archie opened an attaché case and took out a newspaper. 'He's been in prison once. For blackmail. He was in the habit of going through the papers of his lodgers when they were at work and he uncovered something about the husband of one of them. The woman in question didn't know that her landlord was blackmailing her husband. It all came out when the police arrested the husband. King was jailed for blackmail and for not disclosing information of criminal activity to the police.'

'You've done well,' Oliver told him. 'Have you a list of names of his lodgers, going back a year, at least?'

'I've got some, but none that tally with the ones you gave me. There have been no women from Middlefield or from Southport as far as I can tell. But I'll keep on delving, Mr Wainwright. We'll get there soon.'

Oliver left Archie and returned to his hotel. She'd be there by now, bathing and scenting herself for him. If he hurried then they would have a few hours before she left for the theatre. He ran.

Chapter Twenty-Eight

It was good to be home, to be with Mother and Lizzie for Christmas. Mother insisted on having the biggest Christmas tree the house would hold and yet she was too small to reach the top, even on a stepladder. Edward secured the tree, wedging bricks firmly around the trunk in the brass-banded oak barrel and set it in the bay window of the downstairs sitting room where Mother stood back to admire its shape.

'The candle-holders are in the attic. I'll buy new sets of candles when I'm out,' she said as she pulled gloves over her plump, ringed fingers and tied her fur cape under her chin.

'Did you know that the Queen lit her tree with electric lights last year?' Dolly said. 'You'd think the tree would go up in flames, wouldn't you? Or make the ornaments electrified. It can give you a shock, can electricity.'

Edward roared with laughter. 'You are funny, Mother. You have to have a negative and a positive – you have to send the current to earth – you have to …'

'… And see if you can find the big Father Christmas. The one that goes on the table with presents in it. We'll not go in for electrics. I don't want to know all that.'

'All right, Mother. Off you go. The shops will be full and you'll tire yourself if you rush,' Edward said at last.

He took Mother to the door and closed it behind her, then he turned to look at Lizzie who was standing in the hall.

She was wearing a sage-green velvet dress that reflected the colour of her eyes. It had tiny, covered buttons down the bodice, a cream collar of ruched lace and was held at the throat by a cameo brooch, giving her the air of a demure governess, were it not for the glorious warm bronze of her unruly hair. She seemed lovelier than when he had last seen her and he wanted to have her reassure him of her love.

He followed her into the sitting room. 'Is Oliver coming today?' he asked.

'He was here yesterday,' she answered him. 'He brought me home but had to go back before your train got in. He says he'll see you in London in January.'

'Let's ask Nellie to sweep this floor, shall we?' Edward said, 'and we'll go up to the attic and find the stuff for the tree.'

'All right. You go ahead. It's in the tin trunk on top of the old toy cupboard,' Lizzie said. 'I'll speak to the maids.'

Edward ran up the two carpeted flights of stairs to the attic and lifted down the boxes and chests they would need, listening for her quick footfall on the stairs.

He found a box of silver tinsel and brightly painted fir cones, blown-glass decorations and candle-holders. Also in the trunk and on top of the cupboards were toys from their childhood: a forlorn-looking rocking horse, Lizzie's dolls' house and his boxes of soldiers.

Lizzie came into the room and he turned to her. 'Look at this.' He held up a tattered golliwog.

'Look at this!' She picked up his clockwork merry-go-round. 'Do you remember this?'

'Yes. Here's your doll as well. We had these when Iris looked after us. This room brings it all back.'

He stooped to lift the lid of an old tin chest where the photographs were kept and they looked at stiff, old-fashioned portraits, remembering how they had had to sit still for them, without flinching or blinking.

'Fancy you remembering Iris. She left when you were four, didn't she? We were taken to see her a couple of times in Liverpool after she'd gone. You surely don't remember her

357

looking after us,' Lizzie said as she stared at a photograph of herself, Edward and Iris.

'I do. I can see her now, sitting at the nursery table, writing the endless letters she sent to her friend in Bradford. She chewed the end of the pencil when she was thinking hard,' he said. 'I remember Iris asking you how to spell and thinking that a big girl like Iris shouldn't have to ask.'

Lizzie looked so lovely, so animated, that he was overcome with desire for her. 'How do you like living at Suttonford,' he said, 'and who's this farmer chap who chases you all over the county?' He tried not to let his jealousy show but it was impossible to hide his feelings for her.

'I'm not living there permanently, but yes, I'm enjoying it. Florence is very kind and baby Maud is an angel.'

She had not answered his question about the farmer. 'Are they trying to find a husband for you?' he demanded.

She turned her face up to his and put her hands on his shoulders. 'Look, Edward,' she said. 'We can never, never let anyone know we love one another. It's wrong. It's against natural law and it's against the church law. Don't make it harder for us.'

But her eyes belied her words; they were alight and he felt the tremor in her hands. He had waited so long to see her. He pulled her towards him and held her hard against his chest.

'I love you. It doesn't feel wrong to me. I'll never love another woman as long as I live.' His eyes were closed and his voice sounded harsh in his ears as his lips brushed against her brow.

Lizzie began to cry. 'I love you too. Too much. I've missed you, Edward.'

'Come to London with me, then. There are students there who live with their families. Some of them live with brothers and sisters. You could keep house for me and nobody would think any wrong of it.' His mouth was against her hair.

Lizzie looked up and he saw her tears.

'Lizzie! Oh, God, Lizzie!' His mouth found hers and she clung to him, answering his kisses with a fire that matched his own. There was no hesitation in her and he pulled her down on to the old nursery rug, his hands caressing her as she began to unbutton her dress. He could not stop now for he knew that she wanted him to love her.

Her eyes were liquid with longing for him as he gently took her, feeling her moving under his hands until he knew she was ready for him.

She drew in her breath sharply at the first quick stab of pain and he held back until he found that she was pulling him in to her. He felt her curling around him, inside her, and she was whispering his name and telling him that she loved and wanted him. And there was nothing in him but delight in her pleasure and urgent desire that only she could release in him.

And he found such joy in her and she in him and their loving was so complete that they believed they were the first lovers in the world to have discovered the secret of life.

And nobody guessed their secret. Edward thought it would be written on their faces for all to see; that their very presence together would speak of their love, but it was not so. He came to her bed every night, when the household slept, and he left before dawn, tiptoeing down the carpeted landing, climbing into his own cold bed and their love was so right that he could not feel ashamed.

On the night before he left the house to return to London they sat downstairs in the warm kitchen when the servants and Mother were asleep. Edward made the fire bright and she sat opposite him, rocking in the big carved chair, while he sat on the fender stool.

'Will you come to London after the New Year Ball?' he asked. 'We'll celebrate my twenty-first birthday. Oliver is going to hold a party for me in his hotel. You could come with him and stay down there with me.'

'I can't promise. It might not be possible,' she whispered. 'Mother will object, you know. And I'm so afraid. I need to think about all this.'

He looked anxiously at her. He had been waiting to tell her about his hours spent at Somerset House, searching the registers. Would it upset her to hear? They had always wanted to know. At last he spoke. 'There's something I ought to tell you. Something about us. I made a discovery last term and I'm not sure if I should say anything until I know more.'

'Go on! You can't start to tell me something and change your mind before you finish. What is it?' Lizzie seemed to have picked up his anxiety. The gentle rocking of her chair stopped; poised in centre swing. Her hair was loose, a flowing gold mane on her narrow shoulders. He saw her tighten her grip on the padded arms. 'Tell me, Edward!'

'Joseph Wainwright was not our father. He died seven years before you were born; nine years before I was.' He paused, waiting to see her reaction.

'What are you saying, Edward? If not Joe Wainwright, then who ...?' She was groping for words. 'Whose children were we?'

'I don't have the answer. I went to Somerset House, out of curiosity. You know how evasive Mother and Oliver are? Well, I decided to find out for myself. I wanted to know if he was a quarryman, if that was on the certificate, as we've never understood how a quarryman had enough money to leave Mother comfortably off. And I wanted to know the cause of death.' He paused again, wondering how Lizzie had taken the truth. 'Only part of what we've been told is true.'

He raked the fire thoughtfully and stared into its depths. 'Joseph Wainwright was Oliver's father; that part's true. He was also Tommy's father; that's true as well. But Joseph Wainwright died when Tommy was a child, eight years before you were born.'

'No,' Lizzie said. 'I've seen the grave, Edward. Joseph Wainwright's grave is at Suttonford. It says he died in 1880.'

'His death certificate was issued in 1870, Lizzie. I've seen the record.'

'But – I've seen the grave.'

'I expect Oliver made sure you saw it, did he?'

'He did.' Lizzie dropped against the back of the chair, whitefaced. 'Oh, Edward. What are we to think? Are we adopted?'

Lizzie still seemed not to grasp the obvious explanation. 'Did Mother adopt us, Edward?' she said in a small, frightened voice.

'No.' This was going to be hurtful and he could not bear to upset her.

He stopped raking the coals and turned to look at her steadily. 'It means we are probably bastards – Mother's bastards.' He saw shock in Lizzie's eyes but he had to go on. 'It would explain a lot. The secrecy and prevarication are all because they don't want us to know the truth.'

'We must be Wainwrights. You look like the others. You know you do.' Lizzie lifted her hands to her face and began to sob.

'If people expect a likeness they'll see one. Just because I'm tall and dark-haired doesn't mean I'm related to anyone who looks the same.' Edward stood up and placed his arm around her shoulders. 'Don't cry, Lizzie. You'll be able to accept it after a time. I have.'

'Have you asked Mother?' Lizzie said, trying to control her tears.

'No. I couldn't. I don't know if it's cowardice or if I don't want my suspicions confirmed,' he said. 'But I know I don't want to upset her. I'm sure she wants to keep it from us. I'm going to make Oliver give me the answer. We've nothing to go on. No names. Even Mother's maiden name revealed nothing. It's impossible to do anything more at Somerset House without a name. We are both registered as the children of Dorothea Wainwright and Joseph Wainwright. But we're not and now I don't believe that we ever had the same father.'

He had said these last words carefully, hoping that she would understand their significance but she seemed afraid and bewildered. 'Do you see what this means, Lizzie?' he asked gently. 'We may only be half-sister and half-brother.'

Lizzie pulled herself out of the chair. 'Leave me alone tonight, Edward. I need to think.' She went towards the door. 'Do you think you could get the truth from Oliver,' she asked bitterly, 'or is he another bastard?'

Lizzie could not bear it. If she was a bastard then did it matter about her own wrongdoing? Wasn't she born in sin and an outcast anyway? No wonder Mother wouldn't talk about it. She could have felt pity for a woman who made a mistake and had one child out of wedlock ... but two? She lay wakeful and shocked throughout the night. Had her life up to now been a sham? How could those few words change her life for ever? No wonder Mother and Oliver were unable to tell them the truth. 'We are Mother's bastards.' She had clung to childhood too long.

Had Mother, Edward and she been an unwanted responsibility for Oliver? It must have been Oliver who had kept them all these years. She saw that now. Had Edward suspected? Was that why he was determined to pay for his own medical training? And what could she do to put a stop to this – the life of a parasite?

* * *

The train pulled across the flat plain of Lancashire, through fields overlaid with a thin fall of snow. Lizzie held her hat in her hands and closed her eyes as she rested her head against the back of the seat.

She felt worthless; not because of her love for Edward, for that was the most wonderful thing that had ever happened to her. The terrible events of yesterday crowded into her thoughts. She would never forget last night's scene with Mother.

They had seen Edward off at the station and returned home. Mother was sad that they would not have him at home for another few months, but pleased at the prospect of the grand party they would share with him in London, soon.

For herself she had felt numb and dazed, unable to reassure Edward with a word or a look that he had been right to tell her what he knew. Edward had tried to find her alone but she had stayed at Mother's side until they left to take him to the train.

When they returned she spent the afternoon packing for her return to Cheshire, unable to drive the question from her mind, the question that would hang over her, tormenting her for ever unless she steeled herself to demand from Mother the facts she had to know.

And at last, after supper, she insisted that Mother sit with her in the drawing room and listen. 'Edward has not been occupied with his studies the whole time, Mother,' she began.

'Oh! What's he up to then? Got a lady friend, has he?' Mother settled herself into the armchair opposite. 'It's lovely having a daughter; someone to chat to, cosy-like by the fire. A woman doesn't always feel like making the effort; always "primping" to go to the theatre,' she said.

Lizzie watched her take a cigarette from the green-enamelled box she kept on the lacquered table, strike a match to it and idly follow with her eyes the curls of grey smoke. Mother stabbed at the air with the cigarette, making circles follow one another upwards towards the ceiling.

'You should try one, Lizzie. A lot of young women are taking it up.' She offered the box to Lizzie.

'Edward's been doing a bit of investigating, Mother,' Lizzie persisted, waving away the cigarette box.

'Investigating what? Diseases and that?' Mother asked incuriously, closing her eyes as she inhaled the hot smoke, holding her breath for a second before sending it out in a quick, blue stream.

'He went to Somerset House.' Now she felt herself to be close to tears. She knew that she sounded nervous but she had to go on.

'Where's that then?' Mother asked encouragingly.

'It's where the registers are kept.'

Mother looked at her quickly, uncomprehending. 'You look pale, Lizzie,' she said. 'I hope there's nothing was wrong with you. I've no time for feminine "vapours" and all that nonsense.' She said nothing for a moment then looked at her sharply. 'What do you mean – registers?'

'He was looking for Dad's death certificate. In Somerset House, where the big registers are; births, marriages, death registers. Registers of everybody, Mother.' Her heart was racing. She saw the blood drain from her mother's face.

'Births and deaths? Yours? Edward's?' Mother asked in a whisper. Lizzie watched her press the cigarette out against the side of the china ash dish, extinguishing it in a little shower of sparks.

'Yes. Edward found Dad's death certificate. Only he wasn't our dad, was he? Joe Wainwright died seven years before I was born. Nine years before you had Edward.' She started to cry and mop her eyes with the lace cuff of her dress. 'You must tell. Whose children are we?'

'I can't. I can't tell you,' Mother said dully. She dropped her eyes from Lizzie's pleading face and put her trembling hands on the arms of her chair. 'This is dreadful. Why couldn't you have said all this when Oliver was here? Oliver would have known what to say to you,' she cried. 'I must get out of this room. It's too stuffy. It's the smell of Christmas ... candlewax and tangerines and everything.'

She ran to the door and kicked the draught roll away with her foot.

'Don't you see what it means, Mother? Edward and I are nobodies. We are bastards, Mother. Bastards!' Lizzie found herself shouting in her distress. Then she watched in horror as Mother crumpled up in a dead faint in the open doorway.

'Nellie, Bertha, quickly!' Lizzie ran along the narrow passageway to the kitchen. 'Mother's ill. Help me get her into bed. Bring the smelling salts. Nellie – run for the doctor.'

They propped Dolly up in bed and passed the bottle of sal volatile backwards and forwards under her nostrils until her eyes opened. But she did not speak.

'Mother? Are you all right?' Lizzie put her arm around her mother's shoulders, holding her as she would a child. 'The doctor's coming.'

Mother made a croaking noise at the back of her throat, as if she wanted to tell her something. Tears were rolling down her cheeks and she clutched at Lizzie's hand.

Lizzie wished she had never spoken; wished she could put the clock back. God alone knew what poor Mother had gone through already. Perhaps their father was a madman and Mother had fled from him. Why would they have left Suttonford, unless to escape? She must not do this to Mother; question her about the past. Mother never spoke about her life before they came to Southport.

It seemed an eternity until the doctor arrived and was shown into the room. He patted Lizzie's hand. 'Will you help me to examine your mother, Miss Wainwright?'

Lizzie's hands, normally so deft, were clumsy lumps of clay as she unbuttoned Mother's dress. She had to bite her lip and avoid looking into Mother's face as she unthreaded laces, released hooks and buttons on the succession of chemises, petticoats and stays her mother wore.

The old doctor warmed his hands at the fire as Lizzie worked silently and at last Mother lay, oddly childlike, beneath the sheet. Lizzie studied his face anxiously as he worked, prodding and pressing, eyes on the ceiling so not to offend his patient while he made his examination.

'Thank you, Miss Wainwright. You may dress your mother now. I will give you my diagnosis downstairs,' he told her.

Lizzie tucked Mother up and kissed her cheek. 'I'll be back in a minute. I'm sorry, Mother. Sorry I did this to you.'

The old physician told her, 'Your mother has had a stroke. It has taken away her power of speech. There is nothing wrong with her systems. She has a fine constitution but she'll need medical attention if she's to make a complete recovery. I'll take her to the new hospital immediately.'

'I can look after her,' she said. 'She'll get well if you leave her here.'

'No. She needs to be in trained hands. We have very advanced methods now, my dear.' He looked at her over his spectacles. 'Don't worry, Miss Wainwright. The galvanising baths are particularly beneficial in these cases. I shall see that your mother has the best of treatment.'

'Can I go with her?' Lizzie pleaded.

'No. I shall lift her into my carriage and take her to the hospital. There are to be no visits for a month. She must have a month of complete rest. A daily bulletin will be posted in the hospital foyer and flowers and fruit can be left for her.'

She helped him carry Mother to the carriage and settled her on to the seat, piling pillows and cushions around her. And Mother was conscious all the time, Lizzie knew. Mother's eyes were frightened and pleading, as if she were trying silently to beg Lizzie not to send her away.

When the carriage, with the doctor at the reins, disappeared round the corner, Lizzie ran into the house and flew to her room. She did not want to speak to anybody. She wanted to die. But she lay on her bed, her thoughts in turmoil.

What had she done? She and Edward had gone beyond the boundaries of morality – of decent human behaviour. Even if Edward was right and she was his half-sister they had committed one of the gravest sins. And in seeking to find excuses for it she had broken Mother's heart.

What if Mother died? If Mother died then she would blame herself for the rest of her life. Mother hadn't wanted them to know the truth. Why had she spoken to Mother as she had? She turned her face into the pillow so that Nellie and Bertha would not hear her cries.

'Mother,' she sobbed, far into the night. 'Please forgive me. Only get well. That is all I want. I'll give him up. I'll never see Edward again. It's my fault. Not Edward's. I'm older than Edward. I ought to have known. Have I kept Edward to myself? He would have been better without me. Oh, Mother. You must wish you had never had me. I ought never to have been born. Oh, Mother, please, please get well.'

Dawn came and she had not slept. She got up and went to her washstand. There was not a scrap of colour in her face. But she knew what she must do.

She would atone. She would write to Edward and tell him to forget her. If she told him of her fears he would try to find her. She would tell him that she did not love him. She would go to Suttonford and ask Florence and Oliver's help in finding work. For she would accept no more charity from Oliver. She would find rooms – perhaps rent a little house in Middlefield where Edward would not find her.

She could not live here, in Southport, a reminder and temptation to Edward. And she could not continue to live at Suttonford. She would earn her own living. But how? What could she do? Oliver would help her.

There was a month to go before Mother was allowed visitors. Mother would then tell her everything, Lizzie knew. All the things she no longer wanted to hear.

* * *

It was late afternoon, dry underfoot but with a sky full of unshed snow, when the train reached Suttonford. The trap was waiting for her. The journey only took a few minutes at a fair trot along the gravel road and Lizzie watched the carriage lantern swinging ahead as they approached the house.

'I'll go in the back way,' she told the groom. 'Drive into the stable yard, will you?'

She did not like making a fuss of her return. She'd send a message to Florence and rest in her room before she went to speak to Oliver. A servant would take her bags up, as there were plenty of servants, here at the back of the house.

The lamps were being lit in the old kitchen, ranged along the side cupboards and neatly, in rows, on the big deal table. It was hard to imagine what it must have been like in her mother's day. The new kitchen next door was tiled and held a modern range and had shallow sinks with brass taps for hot and cold water. The servants lined up, waiting for the lamp man to hand lamps to them to carry to every corner of the house.

The smell of lamps would for ever remind Lizzie of this house. Life was easier in Southport, where gas lights were there for the pull of a mantle-chain but she liked the mystery and softness that the oil lamps gave to a room.

* * *

Oliver looked at the calendar on his study desk. Below the little window showing nineteen hundred years was another and he turned the brass wheel at the side of the wooden frame to today's date, the twenty-ninth of December. Upstairs, at her own little desk, Florence was carefully writing out the invitations to his birthday dinner early in the new year. Oliver's birthday was only days before Edward's twenty-first.

How strange, he thought, that he would then be exactly twice Edward's age. He looked up and glanced through the window before he pulled the heavy tapestry curtain. There was no snow yet but the lake was frozen. He could just make out the trees at the water's edge. If the ice held no doubt Florence would soon be arranging skating parties. He smiled to himself as he realised how much happiness the presence of Lizzie had brought into Florence's life. Now she had an outlet for her ingenuity for she was trying so hard to make a match.

He set a lamp on the desk. In the drawer was a book of telephone numbers and he searched through the pages for that of the army barracks at Chester. Florence said he was to invite the officers newly returned from South Africa to attend the New Year Ball. There might also be some about to leave for the war with the Boers who would be glad of a night's diversion.

Thank God that James was too young for the army. He hoped James would be present at the ball for he had returned to Middlefield on Boxing Day, to Florence's annoyance. Oliver lifted the telephone from its cradle and called the operator. It had cost him a pretty penny to have a line brought to Suttonford but now he could speak to his stockbroker and to his partner in the comfort of his study. He could also, secretly, make assignations.

He asked the lady operator to connect him to the number he knew by heart, that of the stage doorkeeper at the London theatre, and left a message for Celia. 'This is Mr Wainwright. I shall be in London on Thursday. Thursday the third of January. I'll order dinner, tell my friend. Keep my seat. Yes, second row of the stalls. Thank you. Good day.'

It was almost a code they used. He dared not mention the name of his friend since the Middlefield telephone operators' chief enjoyment came from eavesdropping on conversations and speculating on the secret lives of the subscribers. He did not enjoy deception. Cheating had never been part of his nature. It made him feel like a thief in the night, having to conduct his love affair in this furtive way. When he had called the barracks and replaced the telephone he was aware of a light tapping at the door.

'Come in,' he called and was surprised to see Lizzie put her face timidly around the study door. He had not heard her arrival.

He stood up to greet her. 'Did you have a good Christmas, Lizzie?' he asked. She was wearing a costume of lilac cloth in a severe cut, which combination made her appear pale, very pale … as if she had not slept.

Oliver went around the desk and took her hands in his. 'Are you all right?' he asked. 'Come to the fire and warm yourself.'

'It's Mother,' she began hesitantly, 'she's been taken to hospital.'

'Dolly? In hospital? Whatever …'

'The doctor says she'll be all right. He says she needs complete rest … for a month. We're not to visit.' She had turned her face away and was wringing her hands.

'What happened? Was Edward there?' Oliver asked.

'No. It happened last night – after Edward had gone back to London.' Tears were falling now and her voice was light and frightened. 'She fainted. I called the doctor. He took her away.'

It was a fainting spell, Oliver thought, relieved. 'She'll soon be all right, Lizzie. Your mother's as strong as a horse. Dolly's never ill. I expect she's exhausted herself. She makes a tremendous occasion of Christmas, doesn't she?'

'She couldn't speak, Oliver. Her voice has gone.'

'I'll go to see her as soon as the New Year celebrations are over,' Oliver reassured her.

'They won't let you in, Oliver. They … they are keeping her locked away,' she whispered.

Oliver tried to calm her. 'I shall see her, Lizzie. They will not keep me away. You are not to worry. Walk in the fresh air. Get the roses back into your cheeks.'

She sat in the leather armchair and Oliver saw that her knuckles were white, she was gripping the arms so hard. 'Can I have a serious talk with you, Oliver? Now?' she said.

'Of course. What do you want?'

Her tears stopped. 'I want to work. Can you help me? I want to find lodgings, maybe a house, in the town.'

'What?' She had surprised him. Lizzie – a working woman?

'Please, Oliver.'

Her eyes were filling with tears again. He would have to be tactful. 'But, Lizzie – what can you do? You are overwrought with the worry. You know that you mother doesn't want you to work. And Florence – she hopes to make you a match.' It had been the wrong approach. She put her hands over her face and began to sob, her shoulders lifting and shuddering. He felt helpless, clumsy, completely out of his depth. Should he send for Florence? No, he must try to help Lizzie. After all, she had approached him: but he had never known what to do when faced with a distressed woman.

He placed a hand on her heaving shoulder and spoke gently. 'You shall have whatever you want, Lizzie. Come. Dry your tears. We'll talk sensibly. What is it?'

She raised a tear-stained face. 'Let me go, Oliver. I need to stand alone. I need to work. I need to do something for myself – by my own efforts. Didn't you ever feel this way?'

'I did. I did, Lizzie. I understand,' he told her. So that was it. The girl had wanted independence all along. 'What do you want to do?'

'Will you let me learn to be a pattern-maker? I could become apprenticed, couldn't I?'

He was relieved to see that her face was losing a little of its frightened look. The strain of her mother's being taken ill had overwhelmed her.

'And, Oliver ...?'

'Yes?'

'Find a house for me. Near to the mills. I have money. I have nearly five hundred pounds. That will buy a house, won't it?'

'It will buy two houses, Lizzie, if you so wish.'

'I'll buy a house and furnish it and work for my living if you help me.'

'If you're sure it's what you want. I'll do all I can. I'll speak to young John Partington. They print cloth. He'll tell you how to go about it.' He was about to ask her to take time, to think the matter over, but she had jumped from the armchair and taken to her heels.

'Thank you.' She flew from the study, as if afraid she'd dissolve into tears again.

Oliver closed the door behind her. It seemed to him that nothing was going the way he'd hoped it would. His children, and he thought of Lizzie as one of his children, were turning their backs on him. He'd wanted a family – wanted them all around him. How had this happened? Edward, of course, was not rejecting his paternal affection – but he was not here. James had walked out. James had coldly walked out on Boxing Day. He'd walked all the miles to Middlefield, evidently preferring his new-found family to being here with himself and Florence.

And now? Now Lizzie was not content here. He sat by the fire, smoking a cigar and sipping his brandy, at a loss to know why his every action seemed to be making his family disaffected.

* * *

The ballroom was filled with sparkling light from the chandeliers. The crystal drops seemed to splinter its brilliance, sending tiny points of silver dancing above the heads of Oliver and Florence where they stood at the head of the reception line.

Lizzie had refused their invitation to stand with them and sat watching them from the far side of the room where little gilt chairs had been set between the columns. She knew she ought to be enjoying herself, that the nervousness that plagued her had been an anxiety to Florence since her return from Southport.

Florence looked lovely, gracious and outgoing, in a dress of silver thread on palest grey chiffon, her sweet face alive with the happiness of the occasion; shaking hands and laughing with the guests as they were introduced. Two farmers' wives, corseted, rouged and overdressed, sitting next to Lizzie were bewailing the fact that dance cards were no longer in fashion.

'It makes the evening so much less formal. Don't you agree, Miss Wainwright?' one of them said.

'Oh, but my dear,' her companion cut in before Lizzie could think of a reply, 'one gains so much excitement from the – the unexpectedness.'

Oliver, his face serious and interested, was being spoken to by one of the scarlet-jacketed officers whom Florence had invited in the hope that perhaps one might take the heart of the girl she referred to as 'my darling sister, Lizzie'. And Lizzie could not help but be aware of it; she could not help but feel unworthy of Florence's good intentions.

The women's voices, high-pitched and eager, were making no sense. The scent of pine from the great tree that stood in the centre of the floor was sickening to her and the dancing music, played by the little orchestra in the gallery, was a cacophony in her ears.

'Why, anyone could ask simply anyone and nobody would know ...'

'Know what?'

'How it will all turn out. Don't you agree, Miss Wainwright?'

James, next to his grandmother, still had the arrogant habit of looking down his nose at the person he was speaking to but at dinner Lizzie had found him quieter than of old and much improved in manner. Laura, in black, leaning on her stick for support, looked bewildered. Lizzie murmured in agreement with both the ladies who had now launched into discussion on modern etiquette.

For herself, she felt shamed and worthless. She should not be sitting here amongst decent, God-fearing people who would be horrified if they knew her secret. But she could not believe that what she and Edward had done was wrong. She did not feel like Edward's sister. She had never felt that they were cast in the same mould, or even from the same metal. How could the love they had shared be wrong? Had they never met until now they would have instantly been drawn to one another.

And suppose they had not been brought up together? What then? Suppose they had never known they were brother and sister? Or suppose they were not brother and sister? She must stop these thoughts from tormenting her. She could not even eat. Daily she saw her face in the glass grow more pinched and shadowed.

James had left the line now and was coming towards her across the floor. Perhaps Florence had asked him to dance with her. But Florence would not have asked if she knew, Lizzie imagined; if she knew that her 'darling sister' was a fallen woman. Oliver was going to visit her mother the day after tomorrow. They would not be able to prevent Oliver from seeing her. And Mother would tell all. Mother would tell Oliver that her own daughter had turned against her in disgust. Mother would never dream that she, Lizzie, had defied the very laws of nature and was beneath contempt.

She had to get away.

'You look lovely tonight, Lizzie,' James said as he stood before her, hand outstretched to help her from her seat. 'Will you dance with me?'

She heard her own voice, remote yet sounding quite normal, reply, 'Thank you, James. Are you enjoying yourself?' She followed him to the dance floor.

'Yes. But I am going to return to Middlefield before morning.'

'Does your father know? Doesn't Oliver insist that you stay?'

'He can insist until he's blue in the face, Lizzie, I have long since ceased to care.' He smiled at her. Perhaps he was teasing. Lizzie could no longer tell. To her surprise she heard herself laughing in response to the look on his face. They had reached the edge of the floor and James was holding her hand. 'Will you waltz with me or shall I leave you to the army and the local farmers?'

'We'll dance,' she replied. 'And afterwards, will you take me to meet John Partington? I heard his name announced but I've not been introduced.'

He was holding her around the waist now and she found that her feet were following his. It was such a pity that he and Oliver spent so much of their time at loggerheads. The music stopped for a few moments and they waited on the floor for the second waltz, for the dances were always repeated.

'I'll take you meet John Partington now, if you wish. But promise to dance with me again,' James said.

'Stay with me, James. I want to ask Mr Partington for work,' she heard herself, as bold as anyone, telling James. The shocked yet interested look on James's face made her laugh out loud again.

'Good for you, Lizzie. What on earth makes you want to break free ...?'

'I can't tell you, James. But I need to find a house and a job of work.' They were walking towards a corner of the room, where under the columns the Partington family sat, but James was going slowly, saying, 'There's a house in Rivergate to let. The owners have gone abroad. They've asked my – my landlady, Mrs Smallwood, to find them a tenant. It should suit you well if you are in a hurry.'

'I'll take it, James,' she said in deadly earnest.

'Come.' James led her towards the Partington group. 'I'll make the introductions. By gum, Lizzie.'

She laughed again; laughed at James's imitating the local accent. 'You're a right one! You are that! I didn't know you 'ad it in yer,' he said, a great smile of delight on his face.

Chapter Twenty-Nine

There had been a heavy fall of snow overnight and the park was beautiful, deep-mantled in white, before the early sun could melt the heavy layers on the branches of the cypresses and pines. There was no wind and the lake had thawed, navy blue under the early January sky.

Breakfast was being served in the dining room as some of the guests from old year's night were staying at Suttonford. Florence had woken Oliver at seven so that they could eat together before he went to Middlefield.

'I'll have to go to Southport, Florence. I must see Dolly and speak to her doctors. Then I will have to tell Edward about his mother's illness. It's his birthday soon and I'm going to give him a party in London. Dolly and Lizzie were to travel to London for it. He doesn't know yet that his mother's ill.' They were seated at the long walnut table, nearest the fire.

'Very well, darling. Will you go today?' Florence asked as she fussed over him, filling his plate with scrambled eggs and kidney while he sat back a little way from the table, waiting for her to hand him a napkin.

'That's enough, love. Now help yourself.' Oliver enjoyed her attention. She treated him as she would a young child. She filled his cup from the silver samovar they used in the dining room.

'Drink your tea, darling.'

'Will you give my apologies to our guests, Florence? Tell them I had to attend to urgent business.' He warmed his hands at the fire. Even though the sun streamed into the dining room it was cold in winter in the big rooms.

375

'Is James enjoying work? He said very little over the holiday, didn't he?' Florence said. 'Mother thinks he should come home to Suttonford, of course.'

'Of course. She would,' Oliver replied. If anything was calculated to turn him against a proposition it was that Laura had suggested it. 'She's always treated him as if he were her own little heir apparent. But her own little heir has turned against me,' he told her gravely.

'What do you mean, darling?' Florence was all concern now.

'One of the mill-owners – young Partington – told me at the ball that James has joined the union,' he said.

'Silly boy!' Relief flashed into Florence face. She evidently did not see any significance in James's behaviour. He would not try to explain it to her. Two of their guests entered the room and she went to welcome them.

A path wide enough for the trap had been cleared down to the village but Oliver liked to walk, to stretch his legs and breathe deeply of the clean, cold air. Sometimes, like today, he wanted to run, to throw himself into the banked snow at the side of the path and roll and flail about in its freshness.

He waited until he was out of sight of the house before breaking into a run, grabbing handfuls of snow as he went, cold and compressible, perfect for snowballs. He made one and bowled it overarm at the trees. He'd see Albert first then go on to Southport and find out how Dolly was, then tomorrow ... Tomorrow he'd be with Celia in London. He'd see Edward on the following day.

'Mornin', sir,' the stationmaster greeted him. 'Fine mornin'. Half the estate are up and doin' today.'

The man had too much to say for himself. Oliver bristled and nodded curtly to him before stamping his feet on the unbrushed platform.

'Miss Wainwright was out on the early train,' the man continued.

'Lizzie? Miss Elizabeth Wainwright?'

'Yes, sir. She caught the seven o'clock.'

What on earth was going on? Did nobody tell him anything these days?

'She'd a lot of bags with her, any road,' the stationmaster added.

The train was delayed and a noisy little crowd waited on the platform. When it came even the first-class was full and Oliver had to stand, lurching against other passengers' knees. His early good humour was beginning to evaporate and by the time he walked up the packed snow of Wallgate, sliding and slithering backwards with every step, it had turned to plain ill-temper.

Twenty-three Churchgate, Florence's old house, had been used as the head office of Wainwright and Billington since Laura had vacated it in favour of Balgone, on her aunt's death. The chief clerk, sitting at his high desk in the front office, greeted him with little enthusiasm. Oliver knew that when the clerk saw him at the office outside his normal thrice-weekly routine it usually meant trouble.

'Is Mr Billington upstairs?' Oliver asked.

'Yes, sir.'

'I'll go up. You needn't ring.' Oliver ran up the polished staircase to the two big rooms he and Albert occupied.

'What's James up to now? Have you heard?' he asked Albert. 'The young bugger's been rousing our workers as well as the ones at his place, I'm told.' He clasped his hands behind his back and went to the window. The sky, filled with more snow, lowered over the slushy, manure-laden street where cartwheels were slipping into gutters, spraying passing feet on the dirty pavements.

'Aye. There's to be a meeting tomorrow night in the mill yard. I'm told James is leading it; agitating for more pay and shorter hours,' Albert said. 'Come away from the window, will you? Sit down and talk about it.'

'I'll not take it from him, Albert.' Oliver went to the fireplace and kicked a lump of coal, sending flames and sparks up the chimney. 'I can't have my son against me. The young devil won't see sense. What's he trying to do?'

'Get his own back, I shouldn't wonder,' Albert said. 'You've pushed him into a corner and he's got to fight his way out.'

'How do you keep your lot in order then, Albert? You and Edith seem to have them all doing what you want them to,' Oliver asked.

'We spend a bit of time with them. That's all,' Albert answered.

'What do you mean? That I don't?'

'You've never spent time with James. You handed over him to nannies and tutors when he was little. Then you bundled him off to boarding school,' Albert said. 'In fact, Oliver, you've spent a damn sight more time with your stepmother's children … what's their names? Edward and Lizzie … than you have with James. The lad hardly knows you.'

'That's enough, Albert,' Oliver cut in sharply.

'Look, Oliver. Take James in with you. It's the only way. He's not going to learn about mills and how to run them when he's working against you. Bring him in. Let him get his teeth into a job; get the rebellion out of him.'

'I'll put a stop to this union nonsense first. Have a word with the mill hands, will you? Tell them not to go. Send someone down there tomorrow night to get the names of any of our workers who go to the blasted meeting.' Oliver's face was like thunder.

'All right. But it's a mistake, in my opinion. Where will you be?'

'I'll be in Southport. Dolly's ill. Then I'm going to London for a couple of days. I'll be back the day after that.'

The hospital was a two-penny tram ride from Lord Street and stood back from the road, facing the sand hills and sea on the high ground above Southport. Oliver was agreeably surprised by its size and the well-kept grounds. It was as big as Suttonford with an entrance that could have graced a palace.

Four tiled corridors led off from the central waiting room, oak doors with brass hinges and handles gleamed as did the big brass-framed bulletin board where Dolly's name was written near the foot of the list.

'Mrs D. Wainwright. Satisfactory,' it said.

A system of hot-water pipes kept the place warm, running the length of the corridors and round the lofty waiting room. The room was deserted so Oliver tapped with his cane against the pipes.

A nurse came out of one of the rooms, evidently annoyed by his arrogant summons. She was tall and wore a navy blue dress under a stiff white apron, which went down to her ankles. A wide triangle of starched linen was pinned on to her head. It came down low above her eyebrows and jutted out alarmingly in sharp points above her ears. Oliver took an instant dislike to her.

'Where's Mrs Wainwright?' he demanded.

'Women's ward. At the end of the corridor,' she said as she pointed hesitantly in a northward direction. 'But you'll not be allowed in. She is not to have visitors for another three weeks.'

Oliver would not be told when he could see his own stepmother.

'Out of my way, woman. I pay the bills. I'll see whoever I like!' His voice brooked no argument and the nurse retreated as he strode past her to the place she'd indicated.

The ward was long and dim. Iron bedsteads ranged down either side and a double bank, head to head, was placed down the centre, making two aisles in the airless room. The room smelled of carbolic and had a strong undertone of sickness and unwashed bodies. The tall, narrow windows were tightly closed and the heat and silence oppressive.

Oliver strode down the rows, peering at the faces on the pillows but could not see Dolly. He reached the door on his second turn around the room and called to her.

'Dolly! Dolly Wainwright! Are you there?' Footsteps scuttled along the corridor outside. The nurse must have gone for reinforcements, he thought.

He saw a hand waving weakly from a bed at the far end of the ward and he heard Dolly's familiar voice. 'Over here, Oliver.'

He had a chance to recover from his initial shock as he covered the fifteen yards to her bedside. This couldn't be Dolly ... this thin, white-haired old lady.

'Dolly. What have they done to you? Are you all right? Your hair?' He tried to lower his voice, not to upset her.

'It went white, Oliver. Overnight.' She would not let go of his hand and her thin fingers, ringless now, were like the claws of a bird.

'Take me home, love,' she pleaded. 'I've got to get home. Thank God you've come. I'll never be right here. I spend half me life asleep. I don't know what they give me but it tastes horrible, bitter!'

Oliver set his mouth in a grim line. 'Where are your things? Are your clothes here? In a cupboard? You're coming home with me. Now.'

He went, angry, to the head of the ward where more nurses and a doctor waited for him. 'Bring Mrs Wainwright's clothes and send for a cab. She's leaving,' he ordered.

'She is not fully recovered,' the young doctor began.

'And she never will be, here,' Oliver told him. 'Don't try to obstruct me. I am removing my stepmother to her own home and I'll not tolerate any delay. Her clothes. If you please!'

They brought a paper sack from the office, containing Dolly's dressing gown, a shawl and a pair of silver dancing slippers. He saw that they had taken her away in a hurry. They dressed her and wheeled her to the big doors and lifted her into the horse-drawn ambulance.

She went silent, leaning against him on the journey but she wept when he carried her into her own home again and he held her up as she went, unsteadily, from room to room. 'To make sure,' she said.

He and Nellie brought her bed downstairs to the sitting room where, unseen behind her lace curtains, she could see the street. And Dolly felt better already, she assured them. Nellie and Bertha fussed and coddled her. Her tonic wine was brought to her bedside and Bertha hurried off to steam a 'nice bit of halibut' and a custard cream for her tea.

'Eeh, you are good to me!' she whispered tearfully, a hundred times.

'I can't remember,' she said, when Oliver asked her how it came about; her collapse. 'I seem to think I was having a nice evening with Lizzie. We were sitting in here, talking. The next thing I remember is waking up in hospital. Ooh! It was just horrible in there, Oliver.'

Oliver stayed overnight and left for London the next day. At the stationmaster's office he telephoned Florence who sounded out of breath and indistinct over the miles.

'Hello. Hello. Is that you, darling?' he said.

'Oliver!' She was shouting now.

'Steady yourself!' There was a little silence before she began again.

'Lizzie's run away. She went yesterday. She's taken all her things. She left a note. Wait a minute. Here it is.'

'"I am going to live in Middlefield. I am going to work at John Partington's mill. There is a house in Middlefield I can rent. They will apprentice me to their artist. I didn't want a fuss with Mother ill. Hope you understand. See you on Oliver's birthday, Lizzie."'

Florence was upset. 'Isn't it alarming, darling? I'm worried about her. She has been so prickly since she came back.'

Oliver could scarcely get a word in. 'I think she'll be all right, Florence. Though it's a bit hasty for my liking.'

'Don't be cross with her, Oliver. You won't, will you? Be sweet to her when you see her.' There was a pause, a clicking on the line and Oliver shook the receiver in irritation.

'How is your stepmother, Oliver?' Florence's voice came back to him.

'She's home. Much improved. Tell Lizzie if you see her before I do.'

On the London train he had time to think. And he was no clearer about what was going wrong with his children by the time the train drew into Euston station.

He rang the hospital lodge when he reached his Bond Street hotel and left a message for Edward. 'Tell him that his brother is in London,' he told the porter, 'and would like to give him dinner tomorrow evening. There is no need for him to contact me. I'll be expecting him.'

The old excitement gripped him. Tonight Celia would be in his bed. He called the head waiter. 'Champagne and a cold supper. Have it left in the suite. I'm entertaining a guest this evening.'

They were a more worldly lot in London. Not an eyebrow was raised when, instead of the brother he often invited, a well-known singer spent the night with him. When Celia was in Manchester or Liverpool they had to find a different hotel each time. The discretion of the staff could not be guaranteed in the north.

* * *

Edward awoke early in his dingy little room. He pushed his feet into the slippers at his bedside and went to the sink where he filled a kettle and put it to boil on the gas ring. There might be a letter from Lizzie downstairs. It was late arriving. He shaved at the speckled mirror above the sink and dressed while his tea brewed. His only suit was a bit shiny but it was dark and he looked good in it, despite his thinness, with the stiff white collar stark against the black jacket.

Today he was one of the six students chosen to be at the fever wing when Dr Hart did his round. There was no food in his room but his eagerness for the day to start had diminished his appetite. He'd get something to eat at lunchtime. He hastened downstairs to the dark hallway. No letters for him, though the postman had been. It might come by the afternoon post.

His room was on a long, bleak street and he'd be glad to leave it, if Lizzie would only join him. They'd find a place near the park. It was cold; greatcoat weather really, but he'd soon be indoors. Trams passed the hospital gates every five minutes. He banged his hands together and paced the length of the stops until his tram came.

Edward was pleased he'd been selected for the fever lectures and visits. He hoped to follow in Dr Hart's footsteps when he qualified. He had read everything the man had written and tried to go to all his lectures. Dr Hart, full of enthusiasm for his subject, was in the habit of throwing questions at the students without warning, punctuating his lecture with checks on their knowledge.

They assembled in front of the rostrum in the lecture room and waited for the great man to arrive. He arrived exactly on time. 'Pull your chairs into a semicircle,' he ordered and without preamble went straight into the lecture. 'Our subject is delirium.'

'In a delirious patient accurate diagnosis is vital,' Dr Hart began. 'The state of delirium can result from – what, Wainwright?'

'Infection.'

'Yes. Anything else, Wainwright?' he asked Edward.

'Head injury.'

'Yes. Anything else, Wainwright?'

'Mental derangement.'

'Just so, Wainwright!' he said.

The questions were always addressed to him. Edward would love to work for this man. Edward absorbed every word.

When the lecture was over Dr Hart led the small group of students to the main fever ward. The beds were spaced far apart to keep down the spread of infection. Some of the patients had gone since Edward's last visit. Some had recovered and been returned to their homes; others had died; and a few had been certified as insane and taken to the asylum.

They followed from bed to bed, the specialist making his diagnoses only after they had ventured their own. Dr Hart discussed with them the case notes before they moved from one patient to the next. An old lady, breathing with gurgling sounds, was dying from a fever of the lungs. She could not hear them, Dr Hart said, it was only a matter of hours.

In the next bed a young girl lay, blue-lipped, teeth chattering, under the blankets. They watched a nurse sponge her face. 'Milk fever. Her baby died at birth. She'll recover,' the specialist said.

A middle-aged woman sat on the next bed, wringing her hands, as if despairing. She had the features of one who had been beautiful in youth, but her hair was lank and had been tied severely back with a piece of tape, the straggling ends lying damp, brown and grey across the woollen shawl that covered her fine-boned shoulders.

As they grouped themselves around her bed she lifted her head and tried to smile at each in turn, until her eyes met Edward's and held them. She appeared to recognise him, and she stretched her hands out towards him and had to be restrained by the nurse.

'Oliver! Oliver!' she cried in a strong North Country accent. 'You've found me.'

Edward was startled. 'Do you know Oliver?' he asked.

'Yes! Oh, Oliver,' she said, searching his face as if, he thought, she was trying to compare him with someone she knew.

He leaned across the bed, the better to let her see him. 'What's your name?' he asked. 'I'll ask my brother if he knows you.'

She shook herself free of the nurse's hold and held on to Edward's arm. 'Rosie. Rosie King ...' She was about to say more but the nurse pulled her arm sharply back to her side and the woman called out with the pain. Some of the nurses used force too freely for Edward's liking but he dared not tell the nurse to stop. That was for Dr Hart to do.

'Mania,' Dr Hart pronounced. 'She was found wandering in the streets of the city. Nobody has come to claim her.' He put his hand on the woman's arm and bent over her, speaking kindly. 'We are going to send you away, Mrs King. You are going to another hospital where you will be able to rest and recover in peace.'

He turned to the nurse. 'Take Mrs King into a side ward until the magistrate arrives to sign the certificate. Don't be rough with her. She is not dangerous.'

They passed on to the remaining patients but Edward could not put from his mind the sight of the poor woman who had spoken Oliver's name. There was something familiar in the set of her head and her soft brown eyes.

At lunch he mentioned her to the student who sat beside him. 'Can you remember the name of the woman who was about to be certified?' he asked. 'The one who mistook me for Oliver? I have a brother called Oliver. She may know him. She may not be mad.'

'King, wasn't it?'

'Yes. I'll make enquiries the next time I'm here,' Edward said. 'I could study her for my case history. I'll ask sister for her notes.'

He'd ask Oliver when he saw him, if he knew of a Mrs Rosie King.

He went to the lodge at teatime, to collect a parcel of books. 'There's a message for you, Mr Wainwright,' the lodge porter said, 'from you brother. I wrote it down.' He handed the paper to Edward.

'May I use the phone?' Edward asked, when he'd read the note. 'I can't see my brother tomorrow evening. If he's in town already I'll have supper with him tonight, instead.'

The operator put him through quickly and he spoke to the lady clerk.

'Is Mr Oliver Wainwright at the hotel tonight?' he asked.

'Yes,' the clerk answered. 'He's booked the suite for two nights.'

'This is Mr Edward Wainwright,' he said. 'My brother has invited me to join him for dinner tomorrow. Will you tell him that I'll see him tonight instead as I have an appointment tomorrow.'

He heard the lady clerk speaking to the manager. 'That was a call from Mr Wainwright. His brother is going to join him for dinner in the suite tonight.'

'That's all right. Mr Wainwright told me he was inviting a guest. I'll see that everything is ordered.'

If there was no word from Oliver, telling him not to go, then he'd go to the hotel straight from the hospital, Edward decided. He'd be lucky to be there before eight o'clock. He had a lot to ask Oliver too. He would insist on his brother telling what he knew about his and Lizzie's birth.

Chapter Thirty

Oliver bathed and shaved and, satisfied with his appearance and with excitement growing like a pain in him, set off for the theatre. He had his usual seat on the second row and he waited impatiently for her performance, applauding the other acts only feebly. She saw him as soon as she stepped on to the stage and when she sang, she sang to him, giving him their secret looks, making him long to have her to himself.

At last the final curtain fell and he made his way backstage. Her popularity was growing and he had to push through a crush of people in her dressing room, but as soon as he reached her side she took his hand and held it against her cheek while she chattered excitedly with the admirers who clamoured around her.

'Have you ordered supper,' she asked as soon as the others had left them, 'or shall we go somewhere?'

'We'll dine in my suite. I can't waste time in a restaurant,' he said.

She let him watch her as she changed into a dress of black lace, pinned up her hair and slipped her arms into the coat of Russian sable that he had bought for her. She would not allow him to touch her in the theatre, but she tantalised him with glimpses of her body until he could barely contain his ardour. He called a cab and they went speedily to the hotel.

The lift took them up to Oliver's rooms and he opened the doors into the little hallway. The hall was unlit and he held her with her back to the door, hungrily seeking her mouth, unable to wait. Alone at last. 'Oh, Celia. It's been so long. I've needed you so often, love,' he said urgently.

But Celia's eyes were wide and frightened, looking over his shoulder and not holding his own. Oliver whirled round and found himself looking into the shocked, disbelieving face of Edward.

'I'm sorry!' Edward tried to hide his embarrassment. He had never imagined ... had never suspected that Oliver and Celia were lovers. He must leave, as quickly as possible. He felt sick. 'I thought the supper table was set for us. I'm so sorry. I'm afraid I helped myself to your food.'

Oliver appeared to be regaining his composure. 'Will you stay and have supper with us, Edward? You've met Celia Bellman before, haven't you?'

'You were a guest of my mother's, weren't you?' Edward found that an edge of reproof was coming into his voice. He felt embarrassed, foolish and unwanted. He had to get out. 'I'll not stay. Thank you,' he stammered, wondering, even as he spoke the words, why on earth he was thanking them.

'You'll be here tomorrow night, will you Edward?' Oliver said. 'There's a lot to talk about.'

'I'm sure there is. Don't worry. You needn't tell me anything. It's all quite clear.'

Edward left the suite and made swiftly for the stairs, wanting the relief of the open street, not able to stand or face others in the lift.

The streets were wet. Rain fell steadily as he made his way back to his room. What an idiot he'd been! Why had he been outraged, like a silly girl, at Oliver's bringing that music-hall woman back to the hotel? Was it because she had been there before? 'It's been so long,' Oliver had said. How long? A year? Two? And how many more women were there?

It happens, he tried to tell himself. It has happened to me. But if I had Lizzie I'd never want another woman. Did Lizzie know about it? Could she befriend Florence if she knew? What went on at Suttonford?

The light in the hallway was dim but Edward saw that there was a letter for him, from Lizzie. He'd read it in bed. His bare little room was cold and there was nothing to eat. He drew the faded curtains, placed his good clothes carefully over the back of a chair for tomorrow and climbed between the icy sheets.

He tore at the envelope. She usually wrote pages of news to him and this was a single sheet.

Dearest Edward,

What we have done is wicked and evil. It would be the death of our mother if she were to discover our shameful secret. You must know that we can never be alone together again. The guilt is mine alone and I pray that you will not blame yourself for our wrongdoing. I cannot see you until I have recovered my self-respect. I am ill, Edward. I am sick at heart and so ashamed.

I am going away. When you receive this letter I shall not be living at Suttonford. I do not love you, Edward. I want to be free of you.

This is the most difficult letter I have ever written.
Try to forgive me,

Lizzie

Edward leaned his head back against the pillow and let his tears roll down his face unchecked. His world was crumbling around him. The two people he loved most were gone from him.

Lizzie said she did not love him. She was trying to tell herself that their love was shameful and wrong. Did she really believe it? Was it really making her ill? He knew in his heart that she'd known what she had written was not true. But he knew she would not have written it unless she meant him to believe it. Their love was no lie.

And Oliver? Oliver had been living a lie for years. 'I've needed you so often, love,' he'd said to the singer. Oliver didn't even know what the word meant. Had he never known love, that he mistook a romp with an actress for love? And what of the story Mother had always told them, of Oliver and Florence meeting and falling in love so young and of their having to wait until the Oldfields approved. Was that all lies?

And what was the truth to Oliver? He and Lizzie had been lied to by Oliver for years. They did not know who their father was. And nobody cared to tell them. Truth was unimportant to Oliver.

Well, it didn't matter now. None of it mattered. They could keep their cheap flirtations, their disgusting little secrets. They could keep their stinking way of life. Heaven alone knew what went on at Suttonford. They probably don't even know themselves who fathered whom, he thought bitterly. He'd not speak to Oliver again, nor would he go to the house in Southport where his stepbrother could walk in at any time. Mother would come down here to visit him and they could go to a theatre on his twenty-first birthday. He'd write to her.

Tomorrow he'd move to new rooms, in case Oliver came looking for him. He'd find somewhere where he'd get peace of mind. Nothing mattered now, except that he become a doctor.

* * *

Oliver tried to comfort Celia. 'I'm sorry. They must have given Edward the wrong message at the lodge. Don't worry about it. I'll see him tomorrow and explain.'

'There's no point in explaining. Edward understood it all,' Celia said. She went ahead of him into the sittingroom and looked down at the table. 'Pour me a whisky, will you? The poor boy must have been hungry. He's eaten most of the supper.'

Oliver poured whiskies for them both. He needed one. Edward's finding them together was shocking. He had seen the hurt, the shock in Edward's face and would have given anything to wipe it away. The boy was an idealist and would take it badly.

'I'll send for more food,' he said as he looked at the pathetic remains of their supper. Edward had tried to be strictly fair, he saw, not taking more than half of anything. He could picture him, ravenous as he always was, not wanting to appear greedy; trying to hold back his appetite until Oliver joined him and, finally, having to eat.

'I don't want anything,' Celia said and Oliver saw that she, too, had been shaken by the encounter. Straight-backed and rigid, she drank the neat spirit down fast and held out her glass for more.

Oliver refilled it and sat beside her on the sofa. 'We're both upset about this,' he said. 'I'll take you back to your hotel and we can eat there.' He put an arm around her shoulders but she did not respond to the pressure. 'Try to forget it.' He spoke gently, to console her.

'Oliver, I'm sorry, but I can't forget something like this. It has made everything clear to me. You ... Me ... And seeing Edward like that. I felt cheap.' She pulled away from him and stood with her back to the fire. 'I don't want to see you any more.'

Oliver rose and took her hands in his but she withdrew them sharply and he saw that her black eyes held a warning. 'Because of Edward? His finding us together?'

'Partly that. Mainly because I can't take our affair lightly any longer.'

'I don't take it lightly. I never have. You know that,' Oliver said softly. 'I told you from the start that I was not a philanderer. The only thing I can't ask you to do is to marry me.'

'I know.' She spoke in a calm tone and averted her eyes. 'The thing is – I don't want anything less now. And I can't go on like this.'

'Then live as my mistress,' he said. 'I'll find a place for us here, in London.'

'No.' Celia went to the hall where she picked up her fur coat. 'Help me on with this, will you?'

Oliver held out the fur and picked up his own coat. Then he held her wrist; made her look at him; made her see that he could not give her up easily. 'You can't go out of my life like this. If you say you take it seriously, you must give me an explanation. A better one than having Edward stumble upon us.'

'Oliver, let me tell you something.' She went back into the room and sat at the fire, motioning to him to sit opposite. She leaned forward and he saw that the flames from the fire reflected, sparkling and glinting in her dark, passionate eyes.

'I love you and I want to be married. And these facts can't be reconciled. I don't mean to perform on a stage for ever. I want to make enough money in a few years of singing that will keep me for the rest of my life.' She poured herself a glass of wine from Edward's leftovers.

'I want children, my dear Oliver, and I want a home. And I mean to have them. And I mean to be there, in my home, with my husband and children, not in a pretty parlour with a man who calls when he's in town.'

She had always been forthright. There was nothing of the coquette in Celia. 'Would you ...?' he started to say.

She shook her head and went on. 'I won't settle for less, Oliver. I've wanted it for too long; the ordinary home life I never had. I must try to remember you as a diversion, an aberration. I should have run when I met you, not fallen into your lap.'

Oliver looked at her with affection. 'I wanted all that, too,' he said. 'I wanted exactly what you do. It's not easy. It takes two to want it.'

'It couldn't have been so important or you'd have seen that you got it,' she said, an edge of impatience in her voice. 'You couldn't have wanted a normal family life. You'd never have married Florence and abandoned your son to Dolly, if you had.'

Oliver felt ice running in his veins. 'Abandon my son?' he said. 'What the devil are you talking about?'

'Edward. Your son, Edward!' she snapped. 'Your son by Rosie Hadfield.'

'How long have you known this?'

'For God's sake,' Celia said in exasperation. 'It's as plain as if you'd written it on the wall in letters of fire. Edward is your son. You don't behave towards him like the brother you claim to be. If he were your younger brother you'd have a different attitude towards him.'

'Is it so obvious?' He was stunned by her perception.

'Not to anyone else,' she told him. 'I see things, I don't need to be told. If what I see and what I'm told don't coincide, then I believe my eyes.'

The secret he'd kept for twenty-one years was out. She'd seen through it. There was no point in denying it. 'What else have you seen?'

'Edward and Lizzie are lovers,' she replied.

She was sincere. She wasn't trying to make him angry. But she had to be wrong. This time her powers had deserted her. Please, God, she had to be wrong. If she was right? The closeness of Lizzie and Edward – the time he'd found them in the garden, lying on the grass, hand in hand. The hours they spent in their sitting room. Their endless questions to him about one another when they were apart. And now Lizzie had run away. Why? Why unless she and Edward ...? Celia was wrong. 'You are wrong, Celia,' he said.

'Oh. Poor, poor Edward,' Celia said. 'Let me ask you something, Oliver. If you wanted your family life why didn't you share with Edward the roof you'd put over his head?'

'It was impossible.'

'Because you wanted to marry Florence?'

'Yes.'

'Then you didn't want your home life enough, for Florence and her sort wouldn't know what it is.'

'And do you? You were brought up by your grandparents. Do you know how to make a home?'

'Yes. Your way isn't mine. I couldn't hand my children to governesses, tutors and schools to have them knocked into shape. I could make a better job of it myself. When my children need a helping hand, I want that hand to be mine. I need to live close to those I love, to reach out and touch them.'

Oliver held her hand to comfort her. She had wanted him. She had wanted him to marry her and he must disappoint her. 'I hope you get what you want, Celia. I can't give it to you. And I can't think where I went wrong. Those were my dreams, as well.'

'You sold yourself, Oliver. You wanted the other things too much. You wanted Suttonford and to get it you sold yourself at a bargain price. You made a loss.'

'That's not true.' Oliver smiled at her, at her anger against him; he knew now that it wasn't true, that he had always loved Florence. 'I had to take Suttonford to get Florence. Not the other way round. Where will you find the husband to share your dream, Celia?' he asked her.

'I don't know. I'm not short of admirers,' she replied in her unabashed way. 'When I've rid myself of affection for you I'll accept invitations.'

'Can you do that? Rid yourself of affection for me?'

'Yes. In time I shall.' She pulled on her gloves. 'I'm going to America soon and I'll not be back in London until September. That will give me a good start.'

He took her back to her hotel and they exchanged polite, respectful kisses at the door before Oliver returned to his suite.

He no longer needed her. It had gone. In her very presence it had left him. And it had left him feeling empty and strangely clear-headed. Perhaps he would desire her from time to time but he'd know the desire for what it was. But he would never have another affair. This time it was the girl who had been hurt the most. He'd try to establish a proper understanding between himself and his sons and put all thoughts of passion behind him.

There was a note from Edward at the desk. The boy must have paid a messenger to bring it round for him. It did not even commence with Dear Oliver; it simply said, '*I shall not be able to see you tomorrow evening. I am moving to another area of the city and will send the new address to Mother where you can find it if you need to contact me on any urgent matter.*'

Oliver knew that he must let Edward alone for the time being. After time had dulled the shock, he'd understand and come back to him. He left the hotel the following morning and took the early train to Middlefield. He meant to take Albert's advice and bring James into the business.

* * *

The Smallwood family was gathered in the living-room. Ellen Smallwood put her head round the open kitchen door. 'Put your books away, Alice. Lay the supper table, there's a girl,' she called. 'Supper's nearly ready. Call James.'

Alice stacked her schoolbooks quickly and placed them on the dresser, opened a drawer and brought out a starched waist apron of calico, which she tied firmly around her tiny waist over the brown school dress.

'Sarah. You do the fire and help Mum,' she said to her young sister who was frowning, in the gaslight, over an embroidery. 'I'll call James.'

'Dad,' Mrs Smallwood called again, 'will you go over to The Pheasant for a jug of beer for you and James?'

Sam Smallwood roused himself and reached for the overcoat he'd pegged behind the back door ten minutes ago when he came home from work. 'Aye. All right, Ellen. I'll get enough for us all, shall I?'

Alice spread a tablecloth over the big table and quickly laid cork mats, knives and forks, spoons and tankards. She took a peep at her reflection in the sideboard mirror when Sarah's back was turned, and bit her lips with her small, even teeth, making them shine redder before she opened the door at the back of the room and called up the stairs.

'Jay-ms! Supper's nearly ready. Coom on down.' She lingered at the foot of the polished staircase, her hand on the turned post. She'd practised the pose before the long mirror in the room she shared with her sister and she knew it set off her waist.

James came slowly down the stairs. He'd washed and shaved; he always shaved in the evening, to look his best at supper, when Alice sat opposite. She'd taken the pins out of her hair again; she'd done so every evening since he told her it was 'fetching'. James kept his bold, admiring eyes on her until she blushed and looked away.

He ran down the last few stairs, snatched at her apron tie and tugged. It came loose and he hid it behind his back. Now she must wait there until he chose to give it back to her.

'Give it to me,' she laughed as she tried to retrieve it, blushes forgotten, bobbing this way and that, blonde hair dancing around at the level of his chest.

He bent at the knees, bringing his face to a level with hers. 'Give me a kiss for it,' he teased as he stroked her hair with his free hand.

'Someone might see—' she whispered.

He puckered his lips, and Alice planted a kiss on them, but the palms of her hands were flat against his chest, pushing him away so he could not pull her close.

'Do you miss me when I go out at night, Alice?' he asked, real anxiety giving the lie to the carefree look on his face.

'You know I do,' she told him.

'Will you come down tonight when they're all in bed?' he said.

'I'll try,' she said, putting her fingers to her lips as if to tell him not to let Sarah overhear. Then she added in a louder tone, 'I'm going to lay the table now. Are you ready?'

She held out her hand for the apron and he gave an exaggerated sigh as he handed it over and let her go ahead of him into the living room. He stepped down into the warm, busy kitchen, familiar now with the family routines. 'What's for supper, Mrs Smallwood?' he said.

'Vegetable broth, lamb chops with peas and mash and a lemon sponge,' Mrs Smallwood replied. 'Get out of the kitchen, James, you're in my way, love.' She gave the soup tureen to him. 'Carry that in, there's a good lad.'

'Good,' he said. 'I'm starving. I've done a lot of work today.'

'Have you? What have you been doing?' Alice asked.

'I'm out of the weaving shed now. I've been helping the engineers set up machines all day,' he told them proudly. He loved the evenings around the table. He had eaten with the family from the very first, after he'd arrived back from the day he could now smile about; his disastrous first day at the mill.

He felt like one of the family. They treated him as such, never making him dine with the other guests, though none but Sarah had an inkling of the growing passion he and Alice had for one another.

He had grown up, he knew he had. He liked working for a living; liked being treated as an equal by Sam Smallwood and he wanted, above all, to please Alice.

He found that he could not look at her without wanting to kiss her. He dared not think about her at work or his concentration went. And when he was with her he felt easy and very, extraordinarily, happy.

Even last night's fiasco couldn't dampen his spirits. The meeting in the mill yard had broken up when they'd noticed the man sitting on the wall, taking down names in a little blue-bound notebook.

The back door opened, letting in a draught of cold air as Sam Smallwood entered, carrying two tall china jugs of ale, which he placed on the sideboard. James took his overcoat from him and hung it behind the door while Alice's father warmed his cold hands at the blazing fire.

'It was one of Wainwright and Billington's men taking names last night, James. There's been an informer at the last three meetings. This one had his cap pulled down so we wouldn't recognise him but I heard it from Mr Billington this morning. Two union men were arrested.' Sam Smallwood's face was stern. 'They'll have to let them go. They arrested them for criminal damage but there was nothing broken.'

'What will happen to their jobs, Sam? Can Wainwright and Billington sack them without causing trouble?' James asked. He felt responsible. His father must be behind this.

'They might get the sack. They could get it for less than that but I don't think they will. They'll lay them off until after the case is heard, if it goes to court, of course,' Sam said. 'They'll want to make an example of them. They'll be saying, "Look what happens if you join the union; loss of pay, no promotion." Most of them are family men and the poor devils will be too scared to risk their jobs, not knowing whose name is in the book.'

'I'm sorry. I feel as if it's my fault,' James said.

'It's not your fault. I'll have a word with your father when he comes back. I'll see if we can settle it between us.' Sam smiled at him. 'Forget it for now. Wainwright and Billington aren't unreasonable.'

James took his usual place, opposite Alice, and tried to catch her looking across at him. There was the usual rush of talk with everyone giving what Mrs Smallwood called 'their two-pennoth of opinion on everything'.

He loved to watch Alice. She didn't pick at her food as the ladies of Suttonford did; pushing it around their plates, occasionally lifting a morsel to their lips. Alice had a good appetite.

She never protested at his stealing a kiss lately. She no longer rushed away when there was a chance of a few moments alone with him. In fact she seemed to be as eager as he was for them to be alone. She woke him every morning and dawdled at his bedside until he pulled her down for a kiss. Perhaps tonight she'd come back into the living room after they'd all gone to bed and find him, sitting by the fire, waiting for her.

There was a knock at the front door. Sam rose from the table and went to the Rivergate door, at the front of the house. James heard his father's voice. What the deuce did the old man want? His father wouldn't be here to see how his son was enjoying life, that much was certain.

His father came into the room, filling it, making the place seem overcrowded. James stood up.

'Will you have supper with us, Mr Wainwright?' Mrs Smallwood asked.

'I will if it's no trouble,' his father replied. 'Thank you. Sit down, James.'

Alice set a place for him quickly, beside James, and the table chatter became more subdued. 'It's more fitting for visitors,' Ellen Smallwood always said, 'if we keep our opinions to ourselves.' Talk was general. Alice was congratulated on her studies and Ellen on her cooking and little of significance passed between the men. James wondered if his father had come to see Sam or himself. Whichever one it was, he thought, it'll probably be about the union meeting.

At last supper was over. 'Can I talk to James in private, somewhere?' Oliver asked Mrs Smallwood.

'Take your father into the dining room, James. It'll be cold in there though. Shall I light the fire?' Ellen said.

'No, Mrs Smallwood. It won't take me long,' Oliver assured her. Ellen Smallwood went ahead and lit the gas. 'How's work going, James?' his father asked cheerfully as they followed her. But as soon as the door closed behind her he asked, 'Are you still in the union?'

'Work's all right, and yes, I'm still in the union,' he told his father, unsmiling. He never knew what the old man had in mind until he actually said it. It's got something to do with work though, he thought, since Father's put on his strong accent.

'Do you like the work?'

'Yes,' he answered. 'I didn't at first, but I like it well enough now.'

There was a pause as James waited for his father to speak. 'I want you to come home, James; back to Suttonford. It's time you and I saw eye to eye. Time we stopped doing battle. Time we worked together.'

He hadn't expected this; his father speaking to him as if he ought to be grateful for the few crumbs of his charity. What did the old man think he'd do? Drop down on his knees and say, thank you, Papa? He was in for a disappointment. 'I am home, Father. This is home now,' he said.

'What do you mean by "This is home" …?' His father's voice rose in annoyance.

'I can't go back to Suttonford. I mean to stay here,' James answered, pleased at the angry expression on his father's face.

Father pulled forward one of the dining chairs and sat with his long legs outstretched, feet apart, head back; looking at him as if trying to guess what lay behind his son's refusal to do as he was told.

James was enjoying himself. They hadn't had a confrontation since he was brought here from school. Let the old man stew for a bit, he told himself.

'It's the girl, isn't it?' Oliver said. 'The pretty daughter? Alice? You've fallen for her.'

'I want to marry her,' James replied. That'd show him.

'Sixteen, are you?'

'Yes.'

'And how do you think you can support a wife, at only sixteen?'

'I'm working. Earning money ...' There was a smirk on his father's face. 'One day I'll have plenty,' James added.

'When I'm dead you'll have Suttonford,' his father said, 'but no girl's going to wait that long. Have you asked her?'

'No.'

'Spoken to her father?'

'No.'

'You haven't taken advantage of her, have you?'

'No. She's not that sort of girl,' James said. His father could see for himself that Alice was a decent girl. The imputation was levelled at him.

'Sure?'

'Sure.' James was losing his grip on the exchange and wished to change the subject. He was not prepared to talk about Alice.

'What have you done then?'

'Kissed her.'

'Where?'

'Father! Where do you think? On her mouth, of course.' His father was laughing at him. James saw it in his eyes, though his lips hadn't moved. How he hated him. Now he'd have to ask him to keep quiet about it. He hadn't even told Alice about his plans to marry her.

'I haven't said anything about marriage to Alice, yet, so don't say anything outside,' he said.

'I see. You'll need time to give her a proper courtship, James. I take it you're going to wait until she's a teacher?'

James thought he detected a note of sarcasm in his father's tone but the old man's face gave nothing away. 'Yes,' he said.

'Does she have any plans of her own? For afterwards? For when she is a teacher?'

'She says she wants to teach at her old school.'

'You're going to have a long wait, then.'

'I suppose so.'

'And you want to stay here?'

'Yes.'

'Is that wise? Is it fair to the girl to distract her from her studies?'

'I don't distract her. I'm out a lot.'

'Union meetings?'

'What if it is?' Now, at last, James thought, we're getting to the real reason he came.

'I want you to leave the union, lad. Come and work for me. You can't have a foot in both camps. You've got to be on one side or the other.' His father stood up, as if he was ready to depart. 'Unfortunately, James, for your position in this house, your side is the same as the owners.'

'I'm only a mill hand at present, remember?' James told him.

'You were.' A look of triumph was on Father's face. 'I spoke to your boss before I came here. I told him I didn't want you to work for them any longer. I told him you were setting up union meetings and I told him that I've got a list of names, some of his men included.'

'You bloody ... bastard!' James made a move towards his father, raised his fist; but Father was too fast for him.

He pushed James against the wall and held his shoulders against it, pinning his arms to his sides. Their faces were only inches apart and James saw the anger his father had been holding in check.

'You'll not make a fool of me, James. I can't have my son going behind my back, setting my workers against me. You'll be at my office in Churchgate on Monday morning. I'll find you a job in Wainwright and Billington's. On the same side of the fence as me. And I'll pay you what you're worth. No concessions.' He released him and James did not try to attack his father again.

'You can live here for as long as it suits you,' Oliver told him. 'You're a free man. Think it over tonight. Talk to your friends about it. But if you want independence you'll work for it, the same as everyone else does.'

James closed the front door behind his father before returning to the dining room and sitting alone at one of the tables, elbows resting on the table top, chin on hands that no longer shook with rage. He had to get out of this somehow, with his pride intact. He would not turn up at Churchgate on Monday like the prodigal son. His father should have known better.

Alice slipped into the room beside him, carrying his tankard of ale. 'Here you are. Has he gone?' she whispered and she tucked her hand into the crook of his arm.

James tightened his elbow, fastening her hand against his side. He turned around to face her. 'Alice,' he said. 'Will you marry me?' She blushed and looked at him as if to make sure he wasn't teasing her.

'I love you, James,' she said softly.

James stood up and closed the door, keeping hold of her arm all the while. Then he took her in his arms, properly, and kissed her hard and long. 'Will you run away with me, to Scotland?' he said. 'I'll be a good husband to you, Alice. I'll never desert you.'

Alice cast trusting eyes upon him. 'Yes. Yes, I'll do it. But how?'

'I'll go to see my grandmother tonight. She goes home to Balgone at six every evening. She'll be there now. She'll give me money. She hates Father and I know she's going to leave everything she has to me. I'll ask her for enough to see us through.'

Urgency was making him think fast. It could be done if Grandmother helped him with money. James studied her face. 'Do you think your mother will let you come to Balgone with me? I'd like grandmother Mawdesley to meet you.'

'They'll let me go, if I take Sarah with me. How far is it?'

'About two miles. We'll have to walk.'

'All right. I'll go and ask. And get Sarah. Put your coat on.'

James heard her asking Sam Smallwood. 'Aye,' Sam said. 'I'm going out. Come with me. I'll wait at the corner for you at ten o'clock and walk there and back with you.'

* * *

When she and Mason arrived at Balgone Laura felt better than she had for weeks. She and Florence had had a wonderful time, looking at samples of silks for Florence's autumn wardrobe, sent over from Paris by Monsieur Worth. They had chosen three and dear Florence had even persuaded her to order a gown in an irresistible shade of lavender. When they travelled to Paris later in the spring, to see the new collection, their clothes would be ready to bring home.

They had played for hours with baby Maud, taking her from the nursery more often than Nanny liked to release her, but as Laura confided in Mason on the wearisome journey home, 'I never let a single day of Florence's life go by without having her by my side for at least two hours. I believe that mothers should be with their children, Mason; for at least two hours a day.'

Laura always dined with Mason in the morning room. It was a more inviting room in winter when the fire was alight, as tonight, and the oval, wheeled table set before it. They dined at eight and it was seven already and she had not changed. 'Bring brandy to the dressing room for me, Mason,' she said as she ascended the stairs.

Tonight she would wear her black taffeta. Sometimes she thought it seemed hardly worth the effort of dressing but the servants expected it. They would think it odd if she remained in her afternoon dress.

'There are visitors to see you downstairs, ma'm,' Mason announced when she brought the tray to Laura's room, 'Master James and a young girl.'

'James? Darling James? Here to see me? Show them into the morning room, Mason. Say I'll be down directly.' Laura drained the brandy glass. Her hands were shaking but the cognac would soon settle that. She had little use for her looking glass, these days, mainly leaving it to one of the maids to arrange her hair, but she looked tonight, and powdered her face lavishly to hide the paleness and wrinkles. She applied rouge from a small, enamelled box she kept beside her scent, rubbing it well in until her cheeks looked young and rosy again.

Laura stood, riveted to the spot, thrown quite out of true by the couple who waited in the morning room. 'I am sorry, my darling,' she said to James. 'So sorry I stared. You look so like your father, standing there with the young lady at your side. It gave me quite a shock.'

Twenty years rolled back in an instant. Florence and Oliver stood before her again, vowing everlasting love. She knew that James was on the same errand. She saw it in his posture, in his eyes, and on the face of the pretty little blonde girl whose hand he held so protectively. This time she would not refuse them.

'This is Alice Smallwood, Grandmother. My future wife.' James had such beautiful manners. What a handsome boy he was, so dark and tall against the tiny girl.

Alice bobbed a little curtsey to her and reached for James's hand again.

'Sit down, my dears. Tell me all about it,' Laura drawled. 'You may leave us, Mason.'

* * *

James had known it would be easy; Grandmother had always indulged him but he had not anticipated her being so pleased at the prospect of his elopement. He could see that she had taken to Alice. She led them to her dressing room and opened her jewellery box. They were to have Aunt Lucy's wedding ring, she told them. Aunt Lucy had eloped to Scotland. James had never known that. She gave Alice a string of good pearls and a brooch set with tiny rubies and diamonds.

She hugged them. James thought it embarrassing in front of Alice, to be treated like a little boy, but he had warned Alice that Grandmother was peculiar. Tonight, thankfully, she did not appear to be sodden with drink.

'Do you need money, James? Have you enough of your own?' she demanded.

'I've no money, Grandmother. None that I can get to, that is. I understand there's money in trust, from my great-grandfather, but I can't touch that until I'm twenty-five.'

'That is quite shameful, James. Your father has no right to make you earn every penny. When I think of you, living with the poor creatures in Rivergate, I could cry.'

Grandmother managed a good flow of tears as she spoke and James had to tell her that he did not live in abject poverty. 'Alice is the daughter of the family I live with. I think you can see that she is not a poor creature,' he said.

'Of course. How dreadfully rude of me. Forgive me, child. How much do you need, James? I have about a hundred sovereigns in my safebox. Will that be enough?'

'Half of that should be enough,' James said. 'We'll return to Middlefield when we're married. I thought we might live with you for a time.'

'Would you? Oh, how wonderful. I'll be very happy to have you here.'

Grandmother was nearly insensible with the excitement of their presence. 'Will you make use of my carriage to go to the station?' she asked. Of course he wouldn't use the carriage. One didn't elope by carriage. James told her of his plan. 'We'll leave the house, as normal, and make our separate ways to the station. With any luck we'll be far away by the time we're missed.' He caught Alice's hand and held it tight. 'We'll be married before they can come after us and stop us.'

He'd ask her the other favour too. 'There's something else, Grandmother. Father has got a small, blue-bound notebook holding the names of the union men who were at the meetings I attended. I don't want to be thought of as a traitor. Can you find the book and destroy it? He'll leave it in his office; he puts the really important papers in the second drawer from the window.'

'I will do that for you, James. Naturally I will. Of course you can't be branded as a traitor. Whoever heard of such a wicked thing? I'll destroy it for you.'

Chapter Thirty-One

Edward found a medical student who was prepared to share a small flat with him and he moved his things. He could not bear the loneliness any longer and in Charlie's company he'd be able to forget. He would give all his attention now to his studies and, more immediately, to the patient he'd seen at the fever ward.

'There's not much on Mrs King,' the sister said, when he went back. 'Just the information she gave us and doctors' reports.'

The notes were scanty. Mrs Rosalind King. Age: Forty-nine years. Married to Gregory A. King. Born Bradford 1851. Worked in weaving mills until 1880. Lung infections intermittent. Periods of mania from the age of twenty-nine. The manic illness was becoming more pronounced and the patient, it was thought, would end her days in an asylum when found unfit to care for herself. She had already been transferred to the new mental hospital.

Should he follow up this patient? Was his interest simply curiosity? He did not want either to think or talk about Oliver. But suppose the woman was suffering from a fever and was not being treated for her condition? She'd be in a desperate state by now if she needed medication. It was this last thought that made him decide to visit her on Saturday afternoon.

He dressed in his dark suit. 'Where are you off to?' Charlie asked. 'Are you meeting a girl?'

Edward knotted his tie at the mirror and called through the open door. 'I'm visiting a patient, Charlie, the woman we saw at the fever hospital. I thought I'd do her for my case study. I think Dr Hart's got it wrong this time. I had a feeling the woman was in a fever.' He ran a hand along his jaw to check that it was smooth and, using his finger, tidied up his moustache with water from his washing jug.

'I remember her – the one who thought she knew you. Come back in time to go to the theatre. I've got a couple of extra tickets for the Alhambra. Margaret and her sister would be willing, I think.'

'I'm not looking for a girl, Charlie,' Edward said as he went into the study they shared. 'But if it means you'll have to waste them, I'll go,' he added when he saw the crestfallen look on his companion's face, 'but I don't want to give the girl ideas.'

'She's not so short of men's company,' Charlie teased, 'that she'd throw herself off the bridge for you, old thing.'

'I didn't mean …' Edward answered.

'All right. I'll tell her you'll come but she's not to go swooning all over the place, when she sees your smouldering brown eyes … your sensual mouth, your …' Charlie laughed.

'Fool!' Edward cuffed his friend across the ears. He was glad he'd moved out of the rooms. It was easier to stop thinking about Lizzie when he was surrounded by lively idiots like Charlie. 'Shall I give her flowers? The patient, I mean.'

'It's probably enough for her to see a dashing young doctor. You don't want her passing out at the sight of you, as well as Margaret's sister,' Charlie replied.

It was no use trying to be serious, not in Charlie's company. Edward grinned at him, picked up his overcoat and left the hostel to look for a flower-seller.

There was one on the corner of the street and he bought a posy, made from bright yellow mimosa heads and tiny lily-of-the-valley. Nearer the hospital he found a chocolate shop and bought a brown-ribboned box of soft-centre chocolates, which he asked the shop girl to wrap.

He was directed to the ward and found it big and noisy. Beds were crammed tightly together round the walls, leaving a wide open area in the centre and the cacophony was such that he had to bend his ear to the little nurse at his side to catch what she said.

'Mrs King has given us her address. We've written to her husband. He's coming to see her this afternoon at three o'clock, doctor.'

'I'm only a medical student.'

She hadn't heard him. There were women singing in loud, shrieking tones. One kept up a wail like a dog and others shuffled up and down the room, moaning or laughing wildly. All of them had had their hair cut in a hideous pudding-basin crop with short fringes. He knew there was good reason for it. Some of the women's heads were infested with lice when they were admitted and the nurses didn't have time for dressing hair, brushing and combing. All the same, he believed it was wrong and demoralising to treat them so.

The women wore shapeless grey dresses, tied with tapes at the open back, revealing underclothes on the more sensible and bare backsides on those with crazed minds. There were no bedside tables and the women who lay in bed kept their heads well down, some with frightened eyes above the drawn-up blankets, others, expressionless, howled in a formless, unemotional way, without grief, without tears.

'Mrs King. Here's Dr Wainwright to see you,' the nurse said, giving him a look of quick invitation. 'If you have any trouble with her, come for me,' she said. 'I'll be in the side room. You can have a cup of tea with me before you go, if you like.'

Edward leaned over the bed. 'How are you, Mrs King? Are you feeling better?' he asked.

She turned her head at the sound of his voice and put out a hand to him, not clutching or wild this time. He took it and helped her pull herself to a sitting position. She drew the sheets up to her chest with a modest, nervous gesture. Her hands were dry and hot. He took one and held it in his, so that he could feel the pulse at her wrist.

'You came. You came to see me, Oliver.' The woman's voice was slightly hoarse and she coughed after she had spoken, the deep-seated cough of chest disease.

'I brought you some flowers,' he said and handed her the posy. She was calmer than when he'd first seen her, but much, much sicker and a feeling of unbearable sadness came to Edward as he looked into her warm, brown eyes. He knew he had been right to come and a need, a compelling need to help her, overcame him. He looked around him at the patients who did not know where they were and, sad though they were, they didn't need his help, as the woman whose hand he held did.

He unfastened her fingers gently. 'I'll be back in a minute,' he said.

'Don't leave me, son,' she said. 'Please don't go.' She began to cough again, putting the sheet up to her mouth.

He smiled to reassure her and spoke gently in her ear. 'I'm going to have you moved, Mrs King; to a quiet room where your cough will get better.'

Fancy her calling him son. Some women did speak like that, he knew, but oddly enough even his own mother had never called him son. Always Edward. The nurse gave him a flirtatious look. 'She's rambling. Mrs King's been rambling since she was admitted. It's worse in the night when she can't get to sleep,' she told him.

'Send for Dr Hart, will you, nurse? I think he should come and examine her again,' Edward said, not responding to her smile. 'It's urgent. Go quickly. Go to the office and have them send a messenger or telephone his home.'

She returned in minutes, flustered and pink. 'Dr Hart will be here in half an hour. He says I'm to assist you until he arrives.' She smoothed her apron and pulled back her shoulders.

'I want her moved to a small ward,' he said. 'There must be a quiet room somewhere.'

They lifted Rosie into a wheelchair and covered her with a counterpane and took her to a little warm room near to the office, where a bed had been made ready. There were pictures on the wall and a high shine on the polished floor.

She was light, frightening in her weightlessness, and yet she held on to his hand tightly and would not let go when the nurse arranged the covers over her.

'I'll sit with her until Dr Hart comes,' Edward said and saw that his words brought relief into the eyes of his patient.

They had cut her hair, too, into the fringe the other women had, but already it was beginning to curl and it gave her a young, girlish look. She still had hold of his hand and lay, smiling at him, her head resting against the heap of white pillows.

'You look like him,' she said. 'You'll be about his age. About his age when I knew him.'

'Oliver?' Edward asked, suddenly afraid to hear more, yet wanting to know.

'Yes. Oliver Wainwright. I loved him. I loved him so much, son. You're like him. So alike.' She closed her eyes and drifted off into a sleep and Edward had to hold himself back from waking her, from asking more. He knew now that she held the key to the mystery of his birth. And he knew that when she had rested she would tell him all he wanted to know. He was normally calm, in control of his feelings yet now, he looked at his watch, and prayed that Dr Hart would come.

He sat for half an hour, holding his slumbering patient's hand, until the specialist arrived.

'I don't take kindly to being disturbed on my day off, Wainwright,' Dr Hart said, but there was a smile in his eyes as he added kindly, 'I knew you'd not call me unless it was important. Is this the patient?' He moved Rosie's hand where it lay, loose on Edward's, and took his place at the head of the bed.

'Is this the patient we saw at the fever hospital?' he asked. 'Did I send her here?'

'Yes. She has a history of mania, but I think she has a fever as well,' Edward said. 'I hope you don't think it presumptuous of me, sir, to question the diagnosis?'

'You were right to do so, Wainright. She has a fever.' Dr Hart took him aside after he had examined Rosie. 'It's far advanced though. It's an industrial disease. We can only ease her symptoms. We can't cure her.'

'Her husband's coming to visit her later,' Edward said. 'We should be able to get more information then.'

409

'Keep her here. She's not in any condition to be moved if Mr King wants her home,' Dr Hart said.

'You don't mind if I come in and take notes, do you, sir? I thought I'd write up a case history on her for my exams,' he asked. He would visit her anyway, even if he was not to be involved in her care. He wanted to know more about her.

'You can work with me, Wainwright. Though she won't recover,' he added quietly. 'Poor soul. She's been a beautiful woman in her day.'

'She knows my brother, sir. She keeps confusing me with him, I think.'

'She'll have periods of mental confusion, even if the fever does predominate her mental disorder,' Dr Hart said.

A nursing sister came to them. 'Mr King's waiting in my office, doctor,' she said. 'Will you see him?'

'Come along, Wainwright. We'll talk to her husband.'

Edward did not like the look of Gregory King. He looked a nasty bit of work; slimy and untrustworthy. He cared nothing for his wife, or why had he left her to wander, unknown, in the streets of London? There was a woman with him, a brown-haired woman who looked like Mrs King.

'My wife's a strange woman, doctor,' he began, as if apologising.

'Your wife is a sick woman, Mr King,' Dr Hart was curt. 'She won't live to the end of the week.'

The woman by Gregory King's side began to cry but there was no compassion in the man who swiftly turned on her. 'Don't you start, Agnes. It's bad enough hearing your sister snivel without you starting.'

'This is Dr Wainwright. He'll be working with me in the treatment of your wife.'

Edward felt a glow spread through him as the great man said, 'Dr Wainwright'. He hoped he'd deserve the title one day.

'If I'm not here and you have questions you can speak to him,' Dr Hart said. 'Don't upset the patient. Stay only a short time. You may go in now.'

Edward and Dr Hart walked down the corridor together.

'You should be at my lecture on Monday, shouldn't you, Wainwright?' Dr Hart said.

'Yes, sir.'

'You're excused. Sit with Mrs King. Listen and observe. You'll learn more about industrial lung disease and psychological sickness at her bedside than I can teach you in a month of lectures.'

'You don't think it's true mania, then, sir?'

'No. Something happened to her, something that took her reason. Some women have no balance, Wainwright. They need a quiet life without too much emotional shock.' He smiled at Edward. 'They have to have it, you see. Security, stability. If they don't ...' He threw his hands in the air in an explosive gesture. 'They sacrifice a lot for it, too.'

Edward thought of Lizzie. Did she need this same security, the stability that would prevent her from losing her reason? Had she gone away to find peace of mind?

'I think I'll call back tonight, sir. I'm going to the theatre first but I'll see the patient afterwards,' he said.

'Good man!' Dr Hart replied. 'Call me if you need to.'

The music hall performances took Edward's mind off the woman who waited for him, but only for a few minutes at a time. As soon as he courteously could, he bade goodnight to Charlie and the two pretty girls who had failed to distract him and returned, through the now-quiet, icy and moonlit streets to the hospital.

He closed the doors quietly behind him and made his way along the dimly lit, silent corridor to her room. She was asleep, breathing with a light sighing sound. He took his place at her side and regarded the pale features of the woman who had recognised him the minute she set eyes on him as a Wainwright. And yet he was not the son of Joe Wainwright, so from where did her conviction spring?

She opened her eyes and smiled at him. 'I knew you'd come back,' she said. 'Did you go for Oliver?'

'No. Oliver's in Middlefield with his wife and family,' he told her.

She seemed to be searching his face and he held his breath, fearful of what he might hear. He lifted her high on the pillows to relieve the deep, troubling cough and waited for her to speak.

'They called you Edward, didn't they, after I left? Iris kept in touch with me for years, you know. She sent me the photograph and the diaries.' Her voice was not much above a whisper. 'I've still got them. They are here. I asked Agnes to bring them here for you. You'll understand; you'll forgive me, son, when you've read them.'

Her eyes never left his face as she spoke. She was not rambling. There was truth and love in her face and he knew she felt this love for him. His hand closed on hers and a feeling he had never known before came over him, there in that dim little room, lit only by three nightlights.

It was as if a veil had silently been drawn back; not a dark, heavy veil but a light-as-air, gossamer thing and he knew in that blinding moment that he was looking into the eyes of his mother. In a second revelation, which came without shock but with a sense of happiness and gratitude that swelled in his heart, he knew that Oliver was his father.

He leaned over and gently kissed her and saw a flush of warmth return, momentarily, to her cheek.

'Tell me,' he said. 'Tell me all about it.'

They talked in whispers. He did not want to tire her but her time was running out and he knew that she must tell him why she had deserted him, before it was too late.

She told him of her torment, of her need to return to the three sisters he must one day get to know, of her fear that if she had waited until Oliver returned after his birth she would not have had the will to leave them both.

She told him of the fierce, protective love that Oliver had had for him before he was born and of the fear of losing him that had driven him to bring his own stepmother to take her place.

And finally, amid tears, she asked him to pass her the hand-bag that lay in her bedside drawer. He handed it to her and held a nightlight up so that she could find the vellum envelope, sealed and ribbon-tied, that, she told him, had never left her possession for twenty-one years. She smiled with relief as he opened it carefully and read that he had been registered, all those years ago, as Oliver Hadfield.

And when she had told him all, and he had told her that he loved her, she sank back upon the pillow and fell into the quiet sleep from which she never awoke.

He held her hand long after she had gone, until it was cold. Then he picked up the parcel she had brought and returned to the hostel.

It was five o'clock. Edward switched on the light in his room and looked at the photograph of Rosie Hadfield, for he could not think of her as Mother – that title was sacred to the woman who had brought him up as her own. Rosie had been a beautiful woman and, beside her, younger and very like himself, Oliver.

He opened the first of the three exercise books and read of her thoughts and her fears over the months before his birth and he saw, quite clearly, that she had been a tortured soul and that the decision she had made was the only possible one for her. And he silently thanked her for not taking him with her, for leaving him with Oliver and Mother and Lizzie.

It was not until he had read her words and wondered what the new knowledge would mean to him that he thought again of Lizzie. It had not been his first thought when he learned that they were not brother and sister; that they could be married. His only consideration had been the story that had unfolded before him and pity of the doomed love affair between Oliver and his mother. Now he wondered how he would reveal the facts of his birth to Lizzie.

When dawn came he walked around the quiet London streets, trying to understand his new emotions. For now he felt himself to be a different person, not merely because he knew his true identity but rather, he thought, he was a wiser man. He forgave Oliver and Mother for what they had done to him. He found that, instead of the resentment he had been harbouring against Oliver, he could admire him again and feel, not gratitude, but respect for his father.

There was no bitterness in him now. He saw that there was no other way in which Oliver could have given him the life of contentment that he'd had. He knew now that he would have to reveal his love for Lizzie and that he must face them all with the truth.

He waited until nine o'clock on Monday morning before going to a telephone and asking the operator to call Wainwright and Billington. His hand was shaking and his pulse was racing as he spoke. 'May I speak to Mr Oliver Wainwright, please?' he asked the old clerk.

'Who is calling?' the old voice crackled across the miles.

'Tell him it's his son,' he said.

He heard footsteps and a jumble of sounds, then the receiver being lifted and Oliver's voice.

'Hello, hello,' Oliver said. 'Who's there?'

Edward's voice was unsteady. 'Hello, Father,' he said, 'Edward here.'

There was a silence and Edward held his breath in case he had been mistaken and Oliver did not want to recognise him as his son.

'Edward?'

'Yes, Father?'

'You know ... who told you?' There was another silence and after it, in a voice that was hesitant as well as proud, Edward heard his father say, 'I love you, son. Can you forgive me?'

There was a knot in Edward's throat. 'I love you, too, Father.'

'Have you met her? Your mother?' Oliver said.

'She died. I was with her,' he replied.

'I'm sorry.'

'It's all right. Mrs King – my real mother – she was a lovely woman. I'm glad I found her,' Edward said, and his words sounded strangled to his ears. 'I'll go to the funeral and then travel straight up to Southport. Will you be there?'

'Oh, yes. I'll be there,' Oliver assured him. 'I've a lot to tell you. And, thank you, Edward.'

'Oliver?'

414

'Yes.'

'Let me tell Lizzie.'

* * *

'When James comes in I want him shown the office work. I'm bringing him in, Albert. He's an awkward devil but – you were right – he must learn the work here at my side,' Oliver told Albert before he left twenty-three Churchgate to return to Florence and tell her, at last, about his years of deception.

Friday's confrontation with James appeared, after two nights' sleep and the events of the morning, to be an inconsequential event. He should have been more tactful, more sensitive to James's predicament. He'd give him his head a little when they worked together, show the lad that he had not meant to curb his spirit, just point him in the right direction. He grinned as he recalled the scene.

'It was like looking in a mirror, Albert,' he said. 'I saw myself all over again. If you'd seen him ... The boy's in love.'

'What are you going to do about his other activities, Oliver? Is he still in the union?' Albert asked.

'He can't be on both sides. I've told him that. You can tell him I'll not take any action against the men on the list. I'll not make it harder for him. He must deal with the union himself – tell them he's dropping out but that he can look after their interests just as well from the management side.'

'And now,' Oliver said. 'I'm going home.'

The Wallgate had been swept clear of slush and Oliver ran down it. He raced through the cattle market, between the empty, iron-railed pens and caught the ten o'clock train that would take him back to Suttonford.

He looked with unseeing eyes at the familiar scenes that rolled past the window; the rows of workers' cottages whose damp roofs were level with the railway line, the winter stretches of ploughed land beyond the town, the withered grass, dull brown and grey on the embankment, the blackened places where sparks from the engines had ignited the banks in the autumn.

In time with the rushing wheels his thoughts came together in the question that repeated itself, that rhymed with the sound of the train, 'How shall I tell her ... how shall I tell her ...?' For the future of his marriage depended on Florence's response to the truth. He'd have no reproaches once the tale was told. She must accept it.

From the station he ran along the gravel road. One of the grooms and the trap from Suttonford was in the station yard. The groom showed no surprise when Oliver waved him away. All the servants thought of him as unpredictable, he knew. Laura must be late, this morning.

He ran up the marble stairs calling for Florence. She came to the door of her sitting room, looking startled at his reappearance so soon after his departure for Middlefield. 'Whatever's the matter, darling?' she said. 'Mama isn't here yet. What brings you home?'

'Florence, come with me to the study. I don't want to talk in the sitting room. It's quiet in my room and I've something important to tell you. Order coffee and biscuits for us and tell the servants not to disturb us,' Oliver said. He called for the fire to be lit in the study and waited there until she came. He was shaking slightly, whether from excitement or anxiety he could not say, but he knew that all he wanted now was Florence's love and understanding.

She had changed into a maroon dress in the new Russian style, braided around the hips and hem and she had re-done her hair. Oliver looked intently at her, his brows drawn in concentration.

'You said it was important, Oliver, so I changed into something ponderous,' she explained.

He closed the door firmly and led her to the fireside where he stood before her. 'I can't tell you the whole story immediately, Florence,' he began. 'Some parts will have to be told later when I explain the facts behind my confession.'

'Confession?' Florence looked worried. 'Please don't unburden yourself of anything I'd prefer not to know, Oliver.'

'Dear Florence.' Oliver took her hand and let it lie on his. 'I know you have an exceptional ability to turn your mind from unpleasantness and I know that having done so you refuse to see the truth or choose to ignore it, but this time – this time you must sit and listen,' he said. He kept her hand as she obediently lowered herself into the fireside chair.

Oliver studied her face for a moment before continuing. 'A long time ago, before we were married, I met and fell in love with a woman who worked at the mill.' He saw Florence wince at his words but she did not try to stop him. 'Edward was the result of that liaison, Florence. I never saw his mother after the child was born. She left him and me, and she returned to her husband and children.' His eyes never left her face.

'I've deceived you all these years and I would have continued to do so; I would have continued to keep the truth from you and Edward but …' He saw shock and disbelief in her expression, but he thought that he saw pity too and he paused for a moment to give her time to collect her thoughts before continuing.

'Two days ago the woman died and by chance, or fate, or even by intervention of the divine, if you'd have it that way, Edward was at her bedside, as her doctor.'

Florence's eyes were bright but she looked at him steadily as she pressed her fingers into the palm of his hand very hard, so that he could feel the line of her sharp little nails marking him. 'I had told no one; not you, not Edward, not Albert; only Dolly who registered him as her own and brought him up for me.'

There was no sound from Florence, nothing to tell him if he had shaken her belief in him.

'Can you imagine that, Florence? Can you imagine bringing up your own son and never letting him know that you were his mother? I did it. I had to stop myself a hundred times from taking him in my arms like a father would. And I did it because I was afraid that the woman who had given him life might take him away from me.'

Florence dug her nails harder into his palm and spoke. 'Miriam's mother did it, you know,' she said.

'Miriam?'

'Yes. She did it with the Moses child. Pharaoh's daughter found the baby and brought him up as her own. His sister, Miriam, was told to search for a nurse and she brought Moses's own mother to Pharaoh's daughter.'

'I wasn't the first, then?' Relief flooded him; relief that reproach had not entered her mind. He remembered that his own thoughts had been exactly hers, all those years ago. His features relaxed into a smile at her serious face and her elevation of an ordinary little story to something mystical.

'No. But ... but I wish you'd told me at the start,' Florence said and she let go his hand. 'It would have made so much difference, to know.' Her eyes were full of tears as she looked up into his. 'Did Edward know she was his mother? Did he recognise her as soon as he saw her?'

'I only know what I've told you. Edward rang me at the office and called me Father. I can't tell you how I felt. I'm so glad he knows, so glad he's pleased and ...' He pulled her to her feet and held her tight to his chest. 'I love you, Florence,' he said.

There was a catch in his throat and he buried his face in her shining silk hair. 'This is the second time today that I've been near to tears.' He released her and they stood, side by side, he so tall and powerful and she, whom he'd thought of as tiny and fearful, he now saw had the greater strength.

'You'll see Edward soon, darling, won't you?' she said.

'I'll go to Southport at the weekend. Edward is coming on Friday,' he replied.

'Will you tell Dolly?' she asked.

'Yes. She'll be relieved that he knows. She always wanted him told. She's not a possessive mother. I think you'd like her.'

'How do you think Lizzie will take the news, Oliver? Does she have to know that Edward is not her brother after all?' Florence asked.

He hadn't thought about it. Lizzie – would she be upset? Or would she rejoice? 'Edward wants to tell her himself. It's not for us to do,' he replied.

Florence left him sitting by himself in the study, to think of all he'd say to Edward when they met. Outside he heard the trap arrive and deposit Laura and her companion at the door. He heard her talking excitedly to Florence as they ascended the stairs and wondered if she were not aware of his presence and if she normally held forth at such length when he wasn't there.

Laura wore her customary detached look, adding little to the talk at lunch, which, since Oliver was present, they took in the dining room. Dessert was finished when Wilkins announced that a Mr Smallwood had been shown into the study and waited to see Mr Wainwright. Though this in itself was unusual and Oliver knew well that it could only be Sam Smallwood, it was Laura's reaction to the news that gave cause for alarm. She held on to the edge of the table and in a state of severe agitation, ashen-faced, as if struck down with a dreadful disease, said, 'I'm going to expire. Will somebody please help me to bed?'

Her companion pushed back her chair and stood behind her mistress, evidently at a loss to know how to proceed.

Florence jumped to her feet and rang for help. 'Take Mrs Mawdesley to her bedroom and send for a doctor this instant,' she said to the housemaid.

'No! I won't see a doctor. I'll be all right, Florence,' Laura said, gulping for breath, making it appear that the words were being forced from her. 'Just let me lie down for an hour.'

'I'll go and see Sam Smallwood, Florence,' Oliver said quickly. He was used to grandmother Mawdesley's performances. They were precipitated by the least thing and it made him angry, watching her. She would, he knew, now declare that she was unable to return to Balgone until her health was improved.

'Take the brandy flask along, Mason. She may suffer one of her seizures without it,' he added, keeping an even countenance so that Florence would be unaware that the suggestion was not well meant.

Sam Smallwood was not in his working clothes. He wore a suit of navy serge, high-buttoned and tight across his burly chest. In his hand he held his bowler hat and over his arm a heavy overcoat. He put out his hand to Oliver then withdrew it as if he thought better of it.

'Sit down, Sam.' Oliver motioned towards one of the leather armchairs at the fireside. He knew that only a serious problem would have brought his senior foreman to the house.

'I can't do that. I'm here on a difficult errand, Mr Wainwright,' Sam said. His words rapped out, staccato fashion, as if he had no time for pleasantries.

'Speak up then.' Oliver reverted to his blunt accent when he dealt with the workers. He knew he did it; there was no inverted snobbery about it; it reassured the men that he was approachable.

'It's James. He and Alice have tried to run away. They were making for Scotland. To wed,' he told Oliver. 'I found them at the station, this morning.' Sam's face was a mask of controlled anger. The man was not overawed by having to confront his boss.

'How did you discover them, Sam?' said Oliver.

'They'd sworn our Sarah to secrecy but she told us, just in time,' Sam answered. 'And half the town was watching when I fetched 'em back.'

'Where are they now?'

'They are with Mrs Smallwood – my wife.' Sam stood rigidly to attention. 'I want justice,' he declared. 'I want my daughter's honour respected.'

'Do you think my son had defiled her?'

A look of anguish came into Sam Smallwood's face for a moment. 'No,' he said. 'I don't think that.'

'Sit down, Sam. We'll have to talk.' Oliver rang for Wilkins and told him to bring brandy.

'I'm sorry, Sam. I could kick myself for not thinking of this. I should have guessed,' he said. 'You wanted something better for her, didn't you?'

'It's not that, Mr Wainwright. We like James. I'm sure you're very proud of him. It's been a pleasure having him in the house, but ...' Sam seated himself on the edge of the leather chair and placed his coat and hat carefully on the floor beside him, 'but he can't have Alice.'

Oliver stepped forward and took the outdoor clothes, handing them to Wilkins who had returned with the tray. He nodded to Wilkins and when the man had left the room, poured two large

420

glasses of cognac for himself and Sam Smallwood, before seating himself at the other side of the polished oak fender.

'You wanted an education for Alice, didn't you, Sam?' he asked. 'Are you disappointed with her for wasting her good brain?'

'No, Mr Wainwright. You don't understand. Ellen and I only want what's best for her. If she wants an education then she'll have it. If she wants marriage she'll have it . . . but not like this,' Sam protested, as if he could not understand Oliver's lack of comprehension.

'You don't want her seduced, violated, by my son, do you, Sam?' Oliver said as he passed over the brandy to the angry father, watching the man's face as he flinched at the words.

'He'll not do that,' Oliver assured him. 'He'll not cast her aside or anything like that. If he's like the rest of us, if he's a true Wainwright he'll have made up his mind; made it up a bit sooner than most and he won't change it. It was a good thing you found out.'

'Sarah, that's our youngest one, told us. Alice wrote a letter to us. We weren't to get it until teatime but Sarah was frightened to keep it till then.' Sam slid his broad hand into the tight slit of his breast pocket, brought out a piece of paper and handed it to Oliver.

He seemed calmer, happier now that he had been assured that Oliver was not treating the matter of his daughter's virtue flippantly. Oliver unfolded the note and read.

Dear Mum and Dad,

James and I love one another and we want to be married. We can't wait until James has a better job, or a house or anything so we are doing the only thing we can. We are going by train to Scotland. We can't tell you where, but you won't be able to find us until we are married. Don't be angry with James. He wants you to go on liking him and he says he'll take care of me, you mustn't worry. We have got some money. James asked his grandmother for enough to see us through.

Alice

Oliver read it again and smiled. He couldn't stop himself from feeling pleased. He looked at Sam's worried face and knew that he would have to convince the man of his son's good intentions.

'I think we'll let them marry, Sam. But properly, after a year of courtship. James couldn't find a better girl than Alice in a long day's march. Marriage is what James needs. I'm glad for them. Really, very glad.'

Sam Smallwood was starting to relax. He sipped the brandy and placed it on the side-table before settling himself back into the chair.

'And how do you think young James will propose keeping a wife, Mr Wainwright?' he asked. 'Has he got much to offer her?'

Oliver made a great effort to control the laughter that was bubbling up in him. Sam Smallwood! Acting the stern father! Well he'd let the man have his hour of glory, if he could keep his face straight. He managed a sincere, concerned expression and leaned towards the big foreman.

'I think we'll have to help them, Sam,' he announced. 'We'll both have to dip deep and set 'em up. You won't send Alice out empty-handed, will you?'

Sam, Oliver knew, was not blessed with a sense of humour. He was a good, plain-spoken man, serious and thoughtful. He frowned as he pondered the question.

'I mean to say, Sam,' Oliver couldn't help himself, it was a little devil that made him draw the man along, 'the parents of the bride provide the linen and the trousseau. You'll not want to be shown up if anyone asks to see the wedding chest, will you?'

'Oh, no. No. Of course! Me and Ellen'll set them up with what's right. The linen, you say?'

Oliver frowned. 'I think it's the pots and pans an' all, Sam,' he added, trying to get the right note of mournful apology into his words.

'We'll do what's necessary, Mr Wainwright,' Sam told him. 'They'll get their portion from us. What about you and Mrs Wainwright?'

'Mrs Wainwright? My God, Sam. I'd forgotten her,' Oliver cried, leaping off his seat. 'We'll have to tell her now. I'll go and fetch her.'

He ran up the marble stairs, two at a time and halted when Florence came again to the door of her sitting room. 'Your son's tried to elope, Florence,' he called out to her. 'James has tried to run away to Scotland with a pretty little girl.'

Her face was a study in outrage, making him want to laugh. 'What is going on, Oliver?' she said. 'Mother's talking about letting me marry you after all this time. She says she'll not stand in our way. And you say that James has tried to elope! I think you are both out of your minds.'

'It's true, love.' He reached the top step and rested, panting for breath, all the while laughing at her face and the expressions crossing it. 'And that's the servants told as well. They'll be talking about it in the kitchen before you believe it yourself.'

He reached her side and tucked her arm in his. 'Poor Florence,' he said. 'What a morning! Come downstairs. Meet James's future father-in-law. And don't laugh, for heavens' sake. He's sure his daughter is marrying beneath herself. It's up to you now to allay his fears.'

Chapter Thirty-Two

Oliver travelled to Middlefield soon after Sam Smallwood had left and made for the house in Rivergate. Ellen Smallwood let him in. She looked worried and drawn and Oliver patted her arm quietly in a gesture of understanding. 'Where is he?' he asked.

'Upstairs, Mr Wainwright. In his room. Top of the stairs on your right.'

'Where's Alice?'

Ellen gave a wan smile, as if glad Oliver had thought to concern himself about her daughter. 'She's in the parlour. She says she's glad they were caught but I don't know if it's true, or if they'll try it again.' She put her hand on his arm now. 'They are far too young, Mr Wainwright.'

'I know. I'll speak to James.'

He bounded up the stairs and opened the bedroom door. James was lying on his back, his hands behind his neck. He did not look at Oliver.

'Hello, James,' Oliver said.

James pretended to ignore him and Oliver made a move towards the end of the bed where James would have to acknowledge him. 'You can't stay here, James,' he began. 'Not now.'

'Get out!' James snarled, looking at him at last, with such resentment and anger that Oliver had to hold himself back from taking his son by force and removing him.

He made an effort to show the understanding he had truly felt before he'd entered the room, and sat down on the bed. 'James. I've talked it over with Sam Smallwood. He's going to allow you to marry Alice. In a year's time. I think it's good, James. I like the girl.'

James looked at him with eyes full of hatred. 'So you and Sam Smallwood have sorted it out, have you? You've ordered my future?'

He rose from the bed and began to pull open drawers and throw their contents on to the counterpane. Then he turned to face Oliver. 'Well, Mr Wainwright. Let me tell you something. I don't think I shall want to marry in a year's time. I don't think I'll be here, being a good little boy, buckling down to a bit of hard work.'

Oliver knew exactly what James was suffering. 'Oh, son,' he said. 'You're angry. I know. I was the same. Your problem is nothing more than just being sixteen. That's all it is. We want to help you. Really we do.'

'You can best help by leaving me alone,' James answered through gritted teeth. 'Go on. Get out before I hit you.'

'What will you do?'

'I'll not be beholden to you. I'll not answer to you.'

'Where will you live?'

'At Balgone. With Grandmother. Or with Lizzie.'

'Come home, James.'

'Tell Mother I'll be all right, will you?'

'James ...?'

'I don't want to talk to you, Father. And I don't want to work for you. I'm going to join the army.'

Oliver left the house. There was nothing to be gained for either himself or James if he forced the boy to return to Suttonford. James needed to be alone, to think; to decide where his future lay. And Oliver said a silent prayer that James would come back to him, and that they could build a future together, father and son working in harmony.

He went to the office, ran up the stairs and spoke to Albert. 'Come with me for a drink, Albert. I need to talk to you,' he said.

They crossed the market square. There were no stalls on Mondays but it was still hazardous with horses, carts and cabs.

A flock of starlings beat their wings as one, swooped and turned, silver and black like a sheet of patterned silk above the churchyard, then settled for the night in chattering lines on the belfry sills.

'We'll have storms before the week's out!' Oliver prophesied.

'Country bumpkin, are you, lad?' Albert grinned, reminding Oliver of their first meeting.

'Aye. At heart I am. But I've come a long way since then, Albert,' Oliver said. 'And I'm going to tell you about it.'

They seated themselves in the back room of The Bull where Oliver ordered a decanter of whisky and poured drinks for them both. He regarded his friend carefully. 'You didn't know I had two sons, did you?' he said, waiting for Albert's reaction, wondering if his friend had ever guessed at the outcome of what Edith and he only ever referred to as 'that early business'.

'Edward?' Albert asked, surprise in his voice.

'Yes. Edward's mine,' he told him solemnly. 'Did you guess?'

'Not until this very minute. It was the way you said it,' Albert said. 'Why are you telling me now?'

'You haven't seen him?' Oliver pulled a wallet carefully from his inside pocket, took out a photograph and handed it to Albert.

'Good God!' Albert looked up from the portrait. 'He's you, James and your Tommy all rolled into one,' he said. 'How did you keep it secret?'

'I told him I was his brother – his half-brother.' Oliver put the photograph back in his wallet. 'Edward was with his mother when she died. She was a patient in the hospital. It was her husband who was blackmailing me. She can't have known. I guessed when Edward told me he had a patient called Mrs King.' He smiled now. The whisky was having its effect. 'I'll not tell Edward about the blackmail though.'

He took another gulp of the fiery liquid. 'She recognised him, Albert. She must have known as soon as she saw him. She told him everything. I'm grateful to her.'

'Have you told Florence?'

426

'Aye. She was wonderful about it,' he said. The whisky was loosening his tongue. 'To Florence!' he said as he drained the glass.

'You still love her, don't you?' Albert asked. 'I take it that the actress affair is over?'

'We've never been close, you know,' Oliver said slowly, considering every word. 'Me and Florence.'

He'd tell him everything, he decided, now that he knew about Edward. 'It was never like it was with – with the other one. That was all good physical stuff. Florence seemed to pull back at the last minute. She never took the brakes off.'

'There's a lot like that,' Albert said. 'They usually come round to it eventually. Then there's no stopping them.'

Oliver reached for the decanter and filled his glass again. 'And now it's too late,' he said in a mournful voice. 'The doctor said it could be years.'

'You'll maybe have learned a bit of patience by then,' Albert said. 'Anyway, let's drink to Edward.'

* * *

Oliver went early to Southport on the day he was to meet Edward, for the first time as his father. He had to break the news to Dolly, give her time to compose herself before she, too, learned how Edward had taken the truth of their years of deception.

He was not confident that Edward would be forgiving, for now he realised how he had wronged his son. All that had been revealed to him, all his memories of Edward's young life, now pointed inexorably to the conclusion that it would have been in his son's interests to have known, from the start, of his parentage.

He had asked himself, in the days that had passed since he had spoken to Edward, what his own reaction would have been, had his father not acknowledged him, and he knew that his nature was such that he would have struck back at those who had denied him. Edward's nature was one that grew strong on truth and courage. Edward had needed a proper father and he had denied him this, and, lastly and even more regrettably, Oliver knew that his own insistence on secrecy had denied his son the freedom to court the girl he loved.

Only Dolly had given without reserve. Only Dolly had seen so long ago that they were doing wrong and even she, with her sharpness and unsophisticated insight, had not seen that what her children felt for one another went beyond affection.

Dolly was fully recovered, and in high spirits when he arrived on Friday afternoon.

'There's a nice fire in the drawing room. Let's go in there,' she said after he'd congratulated her on the hennaed hair and her slender figure. 'Bert's just gone. He has his lunch here, on Fridays.'

She went ahead of him to the front of the house. 'All my clothes have had to be taken in, Oliver,' she said. 'I'm that pleased! Bert liked me when I was fat but I like it much better being thin.'

She was her old self again, full of chatter, full of plans. 'And Edward's coming home tonight. I miss him. And I miss Lizzie. I've had a letter from Lizzie. She's coming home soon.' She was almost dancing with excitement. 'And do you know what I'm going to do? I'm going to go to Australia to visit our Tommy and his wife. I'm that glad to be alive.'

He stood with his back to the window of the sitting room, waiting for her to finish and at last she stopped and cocked her head on one side.

'You're quiet,' she said. 'What's up?'

'Nothing's up. Edward knows I'm his father,' Oliver answered baldly, then wished he had been more tactful as he saw colour drain from her face.

'How did it happen?' she said in a whisper.

'He was with his mother. In London, when she died,' he said. 'He rang me up and called me Father.'

Dolly dropped on to the settee and looked at him with frightened eyes. 'So he knows I've lied to him,' she said. 'What did he say?'

'He said he'd be home on Friday. That's all,' he answered. He went to her and sat beside her. 'Don't take on,' he said. 'You know

428

as much as I do, now. We'll both have been looked at in a different light by Edward. We won't know what he thinks of us until he's home.'

'Oh, Oliver.' She leaned her head against his shoulder. 'My hands are shaking. My knees have gone to water. Will he hate us?'

'No,' he comforted her. 'I'm sure he won't.'

'I can't just wait here until he comes,' she said. 'I'm too agitated. Let's meet him at the station.'

She went into the hall and reached for her brown velour coat with the astrakhan collar and her wide-brimmed hat.

'He used to stand at the gate, Oliver, when he was little, and as soon as he could pick me out he'd fly up the road and throw himself at me,' she said, remembering the little boy he had been. 'You used to do that an' all,' she added. 'Only it wasn't in the streets. You used to hide behind trees near the big house, waiting for me.'

'I never knew that,' Oliver replied.

The Southport streets were always brushed clear of snow. It was piled in the gutters, a knee-high gritty barrier, with slabs of yellowed and straw-laden ice beside the tramlines with gaps cut through for the pedestrians to reach the trams. There was a strong wind, with the smell of snow to come and Dolly had to hold on to her hat with one hand and Oliver's arm with the other.

'You wait outside, will you?' she said to Oliver when they reached the station. 'I want to see him on me own, first. Because I'll know, Oliver. I'll know the minute he looks at me what he thinks of it all.'

Tonight, even the power of the train, the piercing thrust of steam hitting the glass roof and rebounding in enveloping clouds around the passengers, the noise and the fumes of sulphur, could not take Dolly's attention from the coming meeting with Edward.

Would he be nervous too? Was Edward, even now, as the brakes ground on to the iron wheels, preparing to accuse her of playing false with him? She could not make out a single face in the crush of people who approached and passed by. Had Edward missed the train?

There was an arm around her shoulders, a well-known cheek against her own, the warm, familiar sound of his voice and it was all right. 'Mother! Hello, little Mother. Look at you! Your hat's all crooked,' Edward was saying. He straightened her hat and held her shoulders as he looked into her face. He looked at her, held her at arm's length for a moment while his big brown eyes looked at her, from her head to her feet, and he smiled the broad, happy smile she knew so well.

There was no need for him to tell her. It was written all over his face that he was happy to be her son. A glow spread through her, right down to her toes. She wondered why she'd ever imagined that Edward might hate her; might think she'd betrayed him. She took his arm, as she'd always done, proudly, with not a little touch of vanity at being seen with so tall, so dark, so handsome a son.

'Come on, love,' she said. 'Oliver's outside. Best not keep yer dad waiting.'

Dolly stood back a few yards as the two Wainwrights, father and son, whom she had brought up as her own children, clasped one another's hands and did not let go. They were finding it difficult, here in the street, to hold back the dam of their feelings.

'Let's get home and sort ourselves out,' Dolly said as she took an arm of each of them, placing herself between them. Soon they would not even notice her presence when the talking began in earnest but just for these few moments they needed her.

Dolly had made their favourite food for their 'little private party' as she called it, saying it was a twenty-first and a christening party in one, making them laugh at her.

Nellie and Bertha had laid the table with the best china and silver on a handmade lace tablecloth. The wines were ready, the red uncorked, the white in a silver bucket of broken ice, brought from the icemaker that morning. A fire burned in the dining room and the curtains were pulled when they reached the house.

They were hungry from their walk in the cold. She had made an onion soup, and to follow it an open lobster tart in thin, flaky pastry filled with mushrooms and sieved tomato in a thick cream sauce.

They were laughing together, she saw with satisfaction, now at ease with one another, filling each other's glasses. She brought in the fillet steaks and watched as they heaped vegetables upon their plates. It's funny, she thought, how men will remember what they've eaten long after they've forgotten what was said at the most important times of their lives. She'd opened a jar of her best apricots in brandy and served them with cream until they declared that they could not eat a single morsel more. They would, they said, leave the fruit and cheeses until later.

She left them, talking by the drawing-room fire and made her contented but light-headed way to her bedroom.

* * *

It was over a week since dear James and the pretty little girl had gone to Scotland and still Laura had not been able to search the study for the blue notebook James wanted. There were too many servants around, following her and watching. Soon Oliver would tell her to return to Balgone, saying she was recovered from her seizure.

'When do you expect to see James?' she asked Florence on the eve of Oliver's birthday. She had drunk nearly all her medicinal brandy and it was only three o'clock. It would not be too wrong of her to open another bottle. At times of strain it was permissible, she was sure, to drink two bottles in a day. It was bitterly cold in the blue sitting room too. It had been a mistake to use blue to decorate it.

'Tomorrow. He'll be here for his father's birthday. He is being rather a trial to us, Mama. I can't tell you how upset Oliver is at James's behaviour.'

'Isn't James married, then?' Laura faltered. 'I thought he had run away. He said he was going to elope with the pretty child.'

'They were stopped, Mama! How often must I tell you?'

Florence appeared to be annoyed with her. Laura frowned and searched her mind for something to say. 'I did not stop them, Florence. They had my blessing.'

'Oh, Mama. I am sorry. I didn't mean to be short with you.' Florence took her arm. It was such a comfort. 'But James has not married. And Oliver wants James to come home.'

'Oliver hates James. You know he does,' Laura said.

'Mama! Oliver does not hate James. He wants to make a man of him, that's all,' Florence replied crossly. 'James says he is going to join the army. I shall speak to James myself, tomorrow – Oliver's birthday – when James comes home. Do you understand, Mama?'

Laura's hands shook noticeably. Tomorrow! What would darling James think of her if the book was still in Oliver's study? 'Ask the servant to bring brandy, Florence,' she said. 'I've had only a single drink today and my nerves are unsteady.'

Florence rang for a maid before continuing. 'Lizzie is coming to Suttonford tonight, Mama. She will be here for dinner. I so want to hear all about her apprenticeship.'

Florence poured the cognac for her and Laura drank quickly, feeling the warmth spread through her. Now her thoughts clarified. It was essential that she destroy the notebook today. Oliver would be late this evening; he had told Florence so. They would not dine until half-past eight: an hour later than normal. He would not go to his office, much less miss the notebook, when he was late for dinner.

Laura couldn't bear to imagine what might happen if Oliver discovered the loss before dinner. The memory of his disgraceful behaviour, in front of the servants, on the day Mr Smallwood broke the news of the elopement to him still sent shudders of horror through her. She had been made ill by it and had been unable to leave Suttonford. The medicinal brandy did not calm her until Florence ordered the increased dose. She had told Florence, time after time, that one pint daily would not suffice under such desperate circumstances.

'Do you think James and Alice are married by now?' she asked and was rewarded with a sigh of irritation from Florence.

Lighted lamps were being brought into the drawing room and placed on the side and centre tables. Lowering clouds had taken the last shreds of daylight from the long windows and servants were drawing the heavy curtains and refilling the coal box. Florence drew her brows together in a warning frown, so she would not speak too freely until they were alone. Laura's eyelids drooped ostentatiously when the door closed behind the butler and two maids. 'Sometimes, my darling, I feel it would be better to dispense with servants completely,' she said. 'It becomes a strain, having to be aware all the time of their gossiping habits.' Laura's slurring words were coming slower. 'Have you rung for tea?'

Florence nodded. 'Nanny Gibson will bring Maud down after we've taken tea and then I'll go and change. What will you wear tonight, Mama?'

'My purple velvet.'

'I'll wear the plum silk,' Florence said. 'Oliver likes me in that colour.'

'I won't see baby, today, Florence. I shall rest after tea,' Laura said. She wouldn't take a lamp to Oliver's study. That would be foolish. It might be missed. She would take candles and matches. As the brandy cleared her head so her plan simplified. She would go down when the servants were absent, bring back the notebook and give it to darling James tomorrow, when he returned.

As soon as she entered her bedroom Laura saw that Mason had ordered the extra bottle of brandy. Mason was proving a most loyal and helpful companion. 'Did you ask a maid to brush and iron my purple velvet, Mason?' she called through to the little sitting room that lay between their two bedrooms. 'And did you ask the girl to bring candles and matches for me to use in the night?'

She poured herself a large measure and swallowed it greedily before pouring a still bigger one, which she sipped rapidly at first, then slower until the level was down to a respectably low point in the bulbous goblet.

Her bedroom faced the eastern side of the drive where it curved round the front of the house. This was the quiet wing of Suttonford; the side furthest from the servants' quarters and kitchens. Suttonford was not noisy but footmen, servants or Wilkins seemed constantly to be present in the large rooms or the hall.

There would be fewer people about at half-past six. 'That's when I'll do it,' she told herself. 'The servants have their supper then. Oliver insists on strict observance of his rules. We must not expect service, except for personal maids, between the hours of six and seven.' Laura's hands shook as she recited these points to herself like a litany. She drank quickly to steady them. She heard Nanny outside her door, talking quite loudly to the maid.

'What's that strange smell, miss?' the woman asked.

'I've been cleaning Mrs Mawdesley's dress, Nanny, with petroleum spirit,' the girl replied. 'It should be hung in the air to freshen afterwards but I couldn't put good velvet out in this damp weather.'

'I hope the smell goes away, miss.'

Really! Laura thought. What airs Nanny Gibson gives herself. She'd have a word with Florence about her. It was a good thing that she was here to supervise Florence's handling of the staff. Oliver had been far too tolerant, so much so that soon, she believed, the servants would be allowed to voice their own opinions in front of the family.

The nursery suite was beyond the three doors she and Mason had and its four doors opened on to the east landing. It was well staffed with Nanny and two nursery maids but the maids would join the other servants at six and Nanny would be busy bathing Maud and settling her down before her own meal was served to her at seven.

Laura must dress immediately and be ready to go as soon as Nanny returned. Florence would be in her dressing room with her maid and she, Laura, would give the nursery maids five minutes to reach the kitchen quarters before she began her journey to the study. She would order Mason to rest before dinner.

Mason helped her into the purple velvet. 'If you had asked a little earlier, ma'm, the dress could have been cleaned and aired,' she said. 'Are you sure you want to wear this one? The black taffeta and your grey silk dresses are both here.'

'Do you dare to tell me, Mason, what I should wear?' Laura attempted her haughty look as of old, but being a little unsteady on her feet had to cling to her companion's arm as she spoke and the effect was lost.

'No, ma'm. I'm sure your choice is the right one. The odour is growing fainter. It will have left the garment by the time you go down to dinner.'

'Mason! Do not answer back.' Laura planted her feet firmly a little apart, the better to balance. The full skirt concealed her inelegant posture. 'I'll go to the servants' hall to ask for candles and matches and, while I'm there, shall complain about the excessive use of cleaning fluid.'

'Oh, ma'm, I don't mean to be impertinent, but Mr Wainwright told us that on no account must we go into the servants' quarters in this house.'

Mason looked distressed but although the Laura of old might have dismissed her on the spot she did not want to alert the woman to the danger of letting her mistress wander the house alone. 'Very well, Mason. I shall rest in my room until dinner. Please do likewise.'

'Thank you, ma'm.' Mason clipped the last fastener on the bodice of the purple velvet and steered Laura to the door of her bedroom.

Laura waited until the sound of Mason's mattress creaking told her that the woman was resting, then steadied herself with a generous half-glass of cognac before she quietly turned the big china handle of her door.

The landing was deserted but faintly lit by a lamp at the furthest, nursery end and Laura walked with ungainly steps, lurching silently from panelled wall to window wall of the corridor. The marble hall, where Oliver would not allow oil lamps to discolour the pale, veined stone, was illuminated by five heavy brass candelabra. In an hour's time more light would be brought but at this hour, early on a winter's evening, it was not considered necessary to provide more than the faintest illumination.

Laura knew she must move quickly and silently through the marble hall and gain the shadow of the ground floor corridor behind the Roman bath where the study was. She dared not look up in case anyone was leaning on the marble banister. Her heart was beating wildly but she did it, and looking over her shoulder when she reached the safe haven of the corridor, saw that she had been unobserved.

She could feel the pain of her heart in her ears and throat and she snatched at one of the candle-holders before venturing on, running and stumbling, breath now rasping in fright. Past the antlered heads and glass-encased stuffed owl, past the door that led to the stairs and lamp room, until, opposite the door that opened directly into the servants' corridor, she wrenched madly at the door of Oliver's study.

She was in. Her hands shook so much that two of the candles had gone out and she fumbled for her brandy flask before relighting them. She put the narrow bottle neck to her mouth and drained the contents.

That was better. Her hands were under her control again and Laura placed the candle-holder on the top of the desk. What had James said? The second drawer from the window? Oh why hadn't she asked him to be more specific? There were two davenports, one in each window, and each had two columns of drawers.

A blue-bound notebook with names. That was what he'd said. Laura began on the davenport nearest to her, pulling out the drawers and rummaging feverishly but after five minutes she still had not found the book.

There was a tray, set with brandy and glasses. She needed more, to give her a calm head.

Chapter Thirty-Three

Lizzie stood in the station yard, hugging her crimson coat to her body, hands inside her fur muff, chin deep into the black fur collar, watching the groom place her box into the Suttonford trap that had been sent to fetch her from the station. It was almost half-past six. She would have to be quick if she were to wash and dress in time for dinner at eight-thirty.

She would have been nervous of returning but Oliver had been so kind to her, reassuring her that Florence was not angry about her hasty departure. They approached Suttonford in pitch-blackness, their carriage lanterns making small impression on the road ahead. 'It's the servants' hour,' Lizzie said to herself. 'Suttonford looks so forbidding before the lamps are brought in.' She held on to her seat as the trap rolled round the curve of the east wing, past the gloomy, unlit front windows.

Then she leaned forward in her seat and called to the groom.

'There's someone in my brother's study. Look! I can see some-one looking through the desk.'

'It's maybe the master,' the groom called back.

'Mr Wainwright is in Middlefield, I saw him before I caught the train. Pass the house and then stop,' she ordered.

'I'll go in, miss,' he answered. 'I'll put you off round the back, by the stables.'

He seemed to have seen immediately, as she had, that whoever was in the study was up to no good. He was a young groom, eager to make his mark, for he turned into the yard sharply and pulled the protesting horses to a halt.

'Go the back way, miss. Tell the men to bring heavy weapons in case there's more than one intruder. I'll go in by the big door. I'll surprise him.'

Lizzie watched him take a carriage lantern from the side of the trap and hold it low, so that he would not be seen from the window as he ran swiftly and noiselessly along the grassy border. Her legs were trembling when she made her way to the back door of the kitchen area and she tried to control herself, blaming herself for lack of courage.

Why did she always want to run from trouble? Why was she so full of fear? Her mother would have risen to any challenge that came her way. Why couldn't she be like her mother instead of the clinging, whimpering creature she was? Why did she always imagine the worst that could happen and take evasive action and why, oh why did she suddenly have this awful foreboding; this chilling feeling of catastrophe?

She reached the door of the kitchen area. There was more light at the back of the house, coming from the well-lit kitchen and lamp room but the door was locked and these rooms empty. She could hear the servants, in their room beyond, chattering, scraping chairs, chinking cups and saucers.

She banged on the door with the palms of her gloved hands. 'Open up! Open up, for God's sake,' she shouted.

They had not heard but another groom was coming. He had fastened the driving pony to a post and was running towards her.

The groom turned the brass handle of the study door quietly and cautiously pushed it forward. The intruder was still there and – his eyes adjusted to the flickering light – it was a woman. He lifted the carriage lamp high to see her face.

'Mrs Mawdesley,' he said. 'What is it? I thought that a burglar ...'

Laura whirled round, her face frenzied with rage. 'Close the door,' she snarled. 'The servants will hear.'

The groom pushed the door to behind him and approached her with a hand outstretched. He had driven Mrs Mawdesley to

Balgone on many an occasion. He knew about the crazed woman's drunkenness and saw that he would have to calm her before she would allow herself to be led away from whatever mad intention she was set upon.

Laura backed away from him, as if afraid, then suddenly darted across the study and stood, breathing noisily, with her back to the door. Her fingers were on the key and the groom saw them turn the key and remove it.

'You will not stop me from finding the book,' she told him in a blurred but strong voice. 'I'll not have James branded a traitor.'

The groom tried to be persuasive. 'I know nothing about a book, Mrs Mawdesley, but do you think you should be here, at night, alone?' He began to move cautiously towards the door. 'Give me the key and I'll have you taken back to your room,' he said gently.

Laura threw the key defiantly across the room and he heard it drop to the polished floor beyond the carpet's edge. She lunged towards him and the groom felt her fingers clawing at his face. He had never hit a woman in his life but he would have to subdue her. He was hampered by the lantern, which could be carried by the spoke below it or the handle on top but could not be set upright. He thrust his free hand under her chin, forcing her head back.

Laura kicked him. She had enormous, unnatural strength. They both went down. The lantern rolled jerkily across the carpet and went out, its glass door breaking, spilling the paraffin oil as it went, soaking the Persian carpet.

The groom used both hands to pull her fingers from his throat. He grasped her hair when he was free. He held on to her, forcing her to her feet, making her stand with her back to him. But she struggled and now began to scream in the most horrific way, swaying her head from side to side, trying to free it. She evidently felt no pain and he tried to edge her towards the part of the room where the key must lie.

With another wrench of her head she had broken loose and she snatched at the candle-holder on Oliver's desk and brought it down with a cry of triumph across his head.

He knew he was going, his head full of light when the heavy brass column hit him, and then he knew black emptiness as the second blow fell.

Laura had found the book, just before the man came into the study. She could hear voices in the corridor. A hand was on the doorknob. They would not be able to open it from the outside. They would have to break it down, she thought with satisfaction. And then it would be too late. The notebook would have been destroyed. One candle was still alight on the brass candelabrum. She opened the leaves of the book, fanning them out as she lifted the candle-stick and set the pretty little yellow flame to the dry pages. She would set it on the carpet to burn: it was well alight now. She lifted it from the desk and the flames leaped upwards towards her hand, making her drop the burning book.

It fell against her skirt. A sheet of flame encircled her. She roared with laughter as the flames reached the oil-soaked carpet and spread rapidly across the floor. That was the beauty of brandy. It gave one such courage and took away all pain.

Lizzie and the groom knew they would not be heard. The servants were shouting to one another, raising the alarm. The groom made for the laundry door and Lizzie ran around the back, alongside the unoccupied west wing, and on flying feet reached the front of Suttonford. The study was alight: a wall of fire behind the long, high window. Nobody could possibly be alive in that inferno and as she reached the front she heard glass exploding outwards behind her.

She was in the marble hall, running towards the study.

'Florence!' she screamed. 'Are you all right?'

Three footmen were kicking at the study door and she watched the door give way, falling back into the blazing room, sending the men reeling from the blast of heat.

'It's too late, Miss Lizzie. Nobody can be alive in there,' Wilkins shouted to her. 'Get out, miss. Go outside. I'm going to get Mrs Wainwright down. She's upstairs.'

Lizzie found she was calm. 'I'm all right, Wilkins,' she heard her own voice, as if it came from someone else. 'You get Mrs Wainwright. I'll go to the nursery and get the staff to come down.'

'Be quick, miss,' Wilkins shouted above the roar of the flames. 'The marble will hold the fire back. The place will go up like a haystack when the fire reaches the lamp room.'

Lizzie ran up the stairs behind Wilkins and flew along the east landing. She could feel the heat from the study on her back as she heard Wilkins shout to Florence and the maid.

'Nanny! Fire!' she yelled at the top of her voice and to her relief Nanny appeared at the nursery door with Maud in her arms. 'Go down the back stairs. Don't take anything with you. There's no time. Go now!'

Nanny Gibson's face was grey with fear. Baby Maud began to cry. 'Mason's in her room, Miss Wainwright! She's next door.'

'Get out, Nanny. Go!' Lizzie's voice was commanding and Nanny appeared to take courage from her.

She found the first door to Laura's suite locked but the sitting room door gave and she tumbled into the dark room, calling out to Mason.

'Fire! Mason! Leave the room this minute. Come as you are!'

There was no reply and little time to spare. There was a deafening series of explosions as the lamp room went up in flames and a cracking sound from the burning of the old roof timbers above the marble hall.

She heard Mason but could not see her. 'Where are you, Mason?' she called, and had to do so again before she heard the woman crying and the sound of her crying coming from a wardrobe.

Lizzie wrenched open the door and saw Mason, crouched, with her back to the door. She hauled her to her feet. 'You stupid creature! Move! Follow me to the back stairs at the end of the landing.'

Mason stood motionless; frozen with fear. Lizzie pushed the woman ahead of her but as soon as she saw the flames the companion woman fainted.

Lizzie grabbed Mason's arms and with a strength she didn't know she possessed lifted her again, taking the dead weight across her shoulders.

The landing was filling with choking black smoke and Mason was heavy. Lizzie's eyes streamed with tears as she bent almost double under the weight of the companion woman.

She reached the stair door and found herself falling through it, rolling with Mason, heads cracking against the cast-iron banisters, clothes tearing as they caught on the iron scrollwork.

* * *

Oliver saw the flames from the train, half a mile before it reached Suttonford station. The sky was aglow above the house and gigantic tongues of fire split the night sky above the trees, hurling showers of charred and splintered timber upwards.

There was no one at the station but he did not need to be told that the fire was at Suttonford. He could see it through the trees, alight from end to end, the most awful thing he had ever seen. He raced from the platform, through the yard, his legs heavy, not covering the distance fast enough and at last his feet pounded the last few yards of gravel drive before the house came into view. The sound of the fire was like thunder and in his nostrils were the acrid, burning fumes.

He saw a huddle of people, well back from the fire, and he ran towards them. 'Mrs Wainwright?' he yelled. 'Is she all right?'

'Aye. She's in the coachman's house with Miss Lizzie and the baby,' Wilkins said, reverting to his local dialect now that the formality of his occupation was no longer required. 'We've lost a young groom and Mrs Mawdesley, though, sir,' he said. 'I'll come along with you. There's nowt we can do for the house now.'

'Did everyone else get out?' Oliver had to shout above the roar of the flames.

'Yes. We've had a count. They're all here. Miss Lizzie's in a bad way, sir,' he said. 'She carried the companion lady out of her room. The woman passed out with fright and Miss Lizzie got her out. The doctor's on his way. One of the grooms rode over for him. We think she's broken a few bones, sir. They fell down the back stairs.'

The estate workers had abandoned their first futile attempts to douse the flames. The fire cart, which was always kept ready filled from the lake, could not be taken near enough to the fire to be of any use and there was nothing for it but to let the inferno burn itself out. The flames had spread so rapidly, they told him, that it had taken under ten minutes for the house to be ablaze from end to end.

He found Florence seated beside the bed where Lizzie lay. Florence looked up at him as he entered the little bedroom and her face was a mask of fear and pain. Oliver knelt beside her and placed his arm around her shoulders. 'I'm sorry, Florence. Your mother! The groom! What happened? Do you know how it started?'

'No. Nobody knows,' she replied in a small, painful voice. 'Mama was in the study. I don't know why. Perhaps she was searching for brandy. I should have given her all she wanted, not kept it from her. The groom and Lizzie were passing and the young man went in to investigate. That's all we know.'

'How's Lizzie?' he asked.

'She's in terrible pain, Oliver. She's unconscious now but when she comes round it's dreadful to hear her,' Florence sobbed, turning her face into his sleeve.

'The doctor's on his way, love,' Oliver said. 'We'll have to move to Balgone if Lizzie can be taken there safely.'

Dr Russell arrived on horseback from his home between Suttonford and Middlefield. He asked Florence to assist him while Oliver waited in the living room of his head stableman's house.

'I've strapped up her ribs and treated the grazes,' the doctor said. 'No bones are broken but there is extensive bruising. I don't believe she has internal injuries.'

'Can we move her?' Oliver asked.

'Yes. Tomorrow, if care is taken. She'll need to spend two or three weeks in bed but she's young and healthy. She should make a good recovery.'

'I'll stay with her, Oliver,' Florence said, 'until tomorrow. Will you go to Balgone tonight? Take Maud and Nanny Gibson? They will have to improvise for a lot of things.'

'Will you be all right by yourself?' he asked.

'No,' she said. 'Come back to me. I want you back.'

It was not necessary to go to Balgone that night. Servants were taken in by the estate families. Nanny Gibson and Maud were placed with a footman's family and Oliver and Florence were offered a bed in almost every house on the estate. They had no idea that they would be welcomed, that they were liked by their workers and Oliver found their kindnesses and generosity touching.

The coach house was far enough from the fire to be out of danger, yet near enough to keep watch and they accepted the head stableman's offer of their best bedroom, next door to Lizzie's room where the stableman's wife kept watch through the last hours of the night.

The men did not pause in their work until the flames had consumed all there was to burn. The pines were winter-wet and had repelled the showering fire. The elms were badly burned; they might have to be felled but the stables and cart sheds, coach houses and tack rooms were spared. Oliver and the grooms led the frightened horses to a field two miles distant and at last it was safe to rest.

Oliver held Florence in his arms until she slept. Since her tearful outburst she had been restrained, trying to control the grief that he knew must come to the surface soon. He did not sleep. He lay still, listening to the intermittent crackling as the fire died away.

Oliver slipped from the house as soon as day broke over the Pennines. There was no wind, no cloud, and as the first rays of the sun lit upon it, revealing the blackened remains of window and door frames and the roof open to the sky, it seemed to him that the place had always been a consuming monster.

It had taken so many people's sweat and toil to support and maintain it; so many generations had struggled against ruin to hand it on to their children, and what was it now? It was a shell, an eyeless, toothless, smouldering skeleton.

Crows circled above the smoking ruin, clacking and calling, their ragged wings beating lazily, eyes scanning the broad acres of Suttonford for food. The burned-out mansion meant nothing to them, their only concern to replace nests that the fire had destroyed in the elms nearest the fire's devastation and they would not be impelled to do that until spring.

Oliver knew that he would never build another nest here.

'Father?'

Oliver turned. It was James.

'I'm sorry, Father,' James said.

'You're back, son,' Oliver said. He put an arm around James's shoulders.

'I came on the late train from Middlefield. You could see the fire from the town,' James said. He did not pull away from his father's arm but raised his hand to grasp Oliver's.

'What a homecoming,' Oliver said. 'This was your inheritance, my boy.' He was thankful for James's presence. He knew that they would be together now; a proper team at last.

'Will we rebuild?' James asked.

'It was under-insured, James,' he said. 'There won't be enough to put it back. Do you want to work for it? Do you want to restore Suttonford?'

'There's enough coming in, isn't there, Father? The mills and everything,' James asked. 'I'll work for it. I've always loved the place.'

'Have you, son? How little we know one another,' Oliver said, regret in his voice for the lost years of James's childhood. 'Let's walk, James,' he said. 'Walk down with me to the old cottages at Hollinbank. I have a story to tell you – a confession to make. I'll find it easier to tell you down there, where it all started for me.'

* * *

They were buried, the following Wednesday, in the little grave-yard at Suttonford. Florence was deathly pale and silently held on to Oliver's arm as her mother's coffin was lowered into the grave that now held her mother and father. The workers on the estate were there and the party moved from Laura's graveside to that of the young groom. There was to be a funeral tea in the village hall but the family were not expected to attend since young Miss Wainwright was still recovering from her injuries.

The church was full. Servants and estate workers packed the aisle and pews in respectful silence. Oliver had made provision for them. None of them would lose their homes. Florence was still holding herself back and Oliver knew that she must soon give way to grief.

* * *

It was over. A compartment had been reserved for Oliver and Florence and they returned to Middlefield by train. They were to be joined, later that day, by Dolly and Edward.

Dolly had responded to the summons to Balgone without pro-test. She would not mourn the passing of Suttonford but she was needed at Lizzie's side, Oliver told her.

'Where will we put everyone?' Oliver asked Florence. 'We only have six bedrooms, apart from the servants' rooms.'

He had been amazed by an unexpected streak of practicality in her. She had risen to the challenge of running a household with only five servants and Nanny. The wheels of domesticity were turn-ing effortlessly but Florence had not let up for a moment and he wanted her to cry, to shout and scream if she had to do it; to be like Dolly and let the world know when things were wrong for her.

'James, Dolly, Lizzie, Edward, Maud and Nanny and you and me,' she had replied. 'That's six.'

They had slept separately since before Maud was born. On the night of the fire they had lain together but the bed had been a place to rest, a place in a stranger's house.

'Lizzie hasn't been told about Edward. He wants to tell her himself. You haven't said a word, have you, Florence?' Oliver asked anxiously.

'No. I've said nothing. Do you think she'll be upset by it?' she said. 'She was so fond of her brother that she may be hurt to think they are not even related.'

'I think she'll be happy for him,' Oliver said.

Chapter Thirty-Four

Edward helped his mother from the train and held her arm as they walked to the station entrance in the cattle market where the Balgone carriage was waiting for them.

So this was Middlefield; this funny, winding little town set on an escarpment at the foot of the Pennines. There was real poverty here, as in Liverpool and London. This was not a town built for the wealthy, as Southport was. There were no tree-lined streets, no wide boulevards and splendid shops, no easy flat walks on an endless plain. Middlefield was noisy and untidy with sharp corners and hilly streets.

The Balgone carriage picked them up and Dolly spoke to the driver. 'Drive us round the town first. I was born here, you know.'

Edward looked at Mother in the black outfit she'd bought. He thought how well the severe style suited her. Her coat and dress were braided around the hem and collar and Mother wore a black hat, a shaped felt affair that hugged her head but lifted becomingly on top, giving her height, its small black veil of lace softening the outline, giving her a flirtatious look.

He also knew that she was nervous. Mother was at her best when she was in charge; when she was needed. She was not a background sort of woman; she liked to be seen and heard. It was going to be an ordeal for her. Even though she hardly remembered Florence from her days at Suttonford, they had both lived there and had lived at opposite ends of the social scale. Mother felt inequality keenly.

He took his eyes from the carriage window and looked down at his long legs, which reached right across the carriage. He wore a new suit, bought with his birthday money; a dark, serviceable suit that would be worn for work and social occasions. His fine slender hands, his own mother's hands, he now knew, lay loosely across his thighs and he stared past them, unseeing, nervous himself at the prospect of coming face to face with Lizzie. He would have to tell her that they were not brother and sister and he must do it quickly, before Mother found she could hold back no longer and he suddenly wanted it over and done with. He had thought about it for too long.

He felt Mother stiffen at his side as they drove in at the gates of Balgone. The house was hidden from the road, behind a high beech hedge, still coppery-leaved in January.

'What on earth was Suttonford like, Mother, if this is the little place?' he asked as they pulled into the short drive. The turrets glittered as the last rays of the afternoon sunshine sparkled on granite coping stones. The long windows were in perfect proportion to the limestone facade and the heavy oak door glowed warm honey at the house's centre.

'This is a beautiful house, Edward. Much nicer than Suttonford,' Dolly whispered before the driver handed them down to where Florence and Oliver waited to greet them.

Edward had never seen Oliver – he must try to think of him as Father – so eager to please. When Oliver visited them in Southport he was always relaxed, easy-going, a carefree sort, and here he was, clucking like a mother hen; watching faces, trying to gauge their reactions from the expressions of his just-introduced family.

They seemed to fill the large hall with their nervous chatter. Mother and Florence were going to like one another, Edward saw, when they had stopped being formal. James shook his hand and introduced the pretty little girl at his side as his betrothed.

'This is my brother, Edward,' he said to her, pride in his voice. 'And his mother, Mrs Wainwright.'

James seemed a little nervous, too, as if he wanted to be liked by Edward. The years had made a difference to James. 'How many

Wainwrights does that make?' Edward said. 'There must be a houseful of us here now.'

The ice was breaking, expressions were softening. Oliver carried Mother's case up the wide staircase, going ahead of Mother and Florence, who were beginning to talk easily to one another.

Edward turned to James. 'Will you take me to Lizzie's room?' he asked. 'I'll unpack later.'

She was sitting up in bed, stiffly bound. Her hair was loose about her shoulders, against the prim white cotton of her nightdress. He stood for a moment in the doorway, drinking in every detail of the girl he loved, and as James's footsteps receded down the stairs he closed the door and went to her outstretched arms.

He kissed her tenderly on her mouth, her eyes, her neck, and her eyes were wet with tears as she wound her arms around his neck, careless of the pain she must feel.

'Do you forgive me?' she asked softly, her mouth close to his ear. 'I never want to be away from you again.'

'I love you,' he told her as his hands caressed her shoulders. 'I never stopped loving you.'

Her tears were falling onto the white sheet and she made no attempt to stem them as he lifted her face to his and kissed her, a gentle, loving kiss to tell her that he understood. 'I know what you've suffered, Lizzie,' he said. 'You don't need to explain. I'm sorry, really I am.'

'I couldn't have come to you, Edward.' She held tight on to him. Her eyes were swimming in tears and he felt the shaking, slender shoulders heave under his hands as she fought to control them. 'But – but I only ever wanted you,' she sobbed. 'I do love you, Edward.'

'Lizzie,' he said quietly. 'Listen to me. I have something to tell you. Can you stand any more shocks?'

'Tell me,' she said.

'We're not brother and sister, Lizzie.' He found that he was saying the words baldly and he took her hands in his and began again.

'We are not brother and sister. Mother brought me up for Oliver. I'm Oliver's son by another woman. I was with my real mother when she died in a London hospital.'

'What?'

'You are the daughter of Mother and a man she met at Suttonford. He was a farm manager, Lizzie. Nothing to be ashamed of. He died a few years ago. I've seen his death certificate.'

Lizzie looked at him as if he were talking like a madman and he smiled as he continued. 'Oliver knows we love one another. And I've told Mother, too. They'd never guessed.'

He saw that she was starting to believe him. Her eyes were wide and she gripped his hands as if to reassure herself that what was happening was not a dream. 'We'll wait a year before we marry,' he said tenderly. 'But we'll never be apart again.'

'Is this true?' Lizzie fell back against the pillows on the high, ornately carved bed. She placed her hands over her tear-streaked face, the gesture he loved, then opened them to look at him. 'You haven't made it up, have you?' she asked.

He pulled the vellum envelope from his inside jacket pocket and handed it to her. Her hands were shaking, he noticed, as she unfolded the birth certificate and read out loud, 'Oliver Hadfield. Is that you, Edward?'

'Yes. I haven't decided which name I'll keep. I thought I'd ask you which you'd rather be,' he said.

She was laughing and crying at the same time now and he covered her face with his own, kissing her, tasting her salty tears until she pushed him away.

'No you didn't,' she said. 'You are making that part up.'

'All right. But which would you prefer to be, Lizzie? Mrs Wainwright or Mrs Hadfield?'

'I think I'll stick to Wainwright,' she answered.

'That will make four of you,' he said, smiling at her.

'Four?'

'Yes. When James marries there will be four – four Mrs Wainwrights.'

'Will you help me downstairs at dinnertime? I'd like to sit at the table tonight with everybody.' She pulled him towards herself and kissed his mouth softly. 'Go now,' she said. 'Ask Mother to come to me. I can't believe it. She'll tell me the whole story.'

He went to the door, turned and smiled at her before he went down the stairs to talk to the family.

* * *

When he went upstairs to change for dinner Oliver saw that Florence had moved his things into her room. She had ordered a fire to be lit and its warm glow against the black fireplace in its blue-and-white-tiled surround made the spacious bedroom warm and relaxing.

He took off his suit, lay on the oyster-silk quilt of the bed in his dressing gown and thought about the events of the day. It was going to be all right, he told himself. Once Florence had recovered from the loss of her mother she would enjoy having less responsibility. She had been quite like her younger self at tea, chattering to Dolly in the drawing room, showing her around the house, following Dolly to the kitchen as his stepmother did a tour of inspection.

And at dinner tonight she would sit opposite him with the whole family gathered together and there would be talk and laughter around his table. It was all he ever dreamed of.

'Oliver? Are you asleep?'

He opened his eyes. Florence held out a cup and saucer to him.

'What is it?' he said.

'I've made you a cup of tea,' she said. 'Try it.'

'Is this the first time you've made tea?' He grinned as he raised himself on one elbow and pulled the paisley silk around his nakedness.

'Dolly showed me how to do it,' she said. 'I like her very much.'

'I'm glad.' He sipped appreciatively. 'Just right!' he pronounced.

452

She took off the bustled black dress and drew on a loose gown of blue wool. Oliver put the cup down and patted the quilt, inviting her to rest. He placed an arm around her shoulders as she came to him.

He heard her sigh and there was resignation as well as weariness in the sound. 'What is it, Florence?' he said gently. 'What's up?'

'What do you mean?' she said.

'Why haven't you cried? You've lost your mother.' He would have to encourage her tears. She must not keep them in any longer. There was a moment's silence before she answered him, whispering her reply, not looking at him.

'I'm afraid,' she said.

'Afraid of what?'

'Afraid of losing you.'

'You aren't going to lose me, my darling. I'll live for a long time yet. You have lost the mother you've had for nearly forty years.'

If he repeated it to her, he reasoned, she would come to accept it; she would not be afraid of facing life without the woman who had seldom left her side. He propped himself up and looked into her face. 'Come on, Florence. Let yourself go. The loss will be easier if you can shed tears.'

Florence closed her eyes and spoke slowly, choosing her words carefully. The words were forced, as if she had held them back for too long. 'I'm not sorry she's dead,' she began. 'I hated her. You'll never know how much I hated her.'

She paused for a second or two but did not look at him and Oliver was silent. 'I hated her until I thought my hatred would eat me up. I tried to change. I tried to be good. I have never told a soul before.'

She opened her eyes and sat, looking at him steadily, but there was a burning in their grey calmness that he had never seen before. 'You think I am a sweet, good soul, don't you, Oliver? There were times when I wanted to kill her, to give her more and more of her foul brandy, to push it down her throat until it choked her.'

Her hands were tight, clenched fists and she pulled herself bolt upright against the backrest, as far away from him as it was possible to be. 'She told me, you know. Before my wedding day, before we even announced our engagement, that you had married me to get Suttonford. She told me that my grandfather had offered you the estate if you would marry me and put your money behind him ...'

He was angry but he did not stop her but listened with growing horror to the revelation of inhumanity that his darling wife had bottled up for all these years.

'On my wedding eve she told me that you had other women. She told me you didn't love me and she said that if ever Suttonford went, you'd leave me.'

He was still shocked and silent but Florence put a hand out in warning and stood up. She was shaking with anger and courage and her voice was high-pitched. 'She told me that if I had sons you would stay with me when Grandfather died. She said I must woo you, entice you, seduce you, to get you away from your mistresses.'

She stopped for breath for a moment before continuing in her normal, even tone. 'It was not until you told me about Edward that I suspected she had been lying, for if she'd known the truth about Edward she would never have kept it from me.'

Florence clasped her hands and turned her face away from his, towards the fire. He could hear the sorrow in her voice. 'Every time you touched me, Oliver, I felt that she was watching me, goading me, telling me to respond, to encourage what she called your base instincts, to submit to your gross desires. And a feeling grew in me, grew and took me over; a feeling that you despised me, that all you wanted was the estate and what the Bible calls "issue".'

She turned around and looked at him. 'So you can go if you wish, my darling. There can be no more "issue". Dr Russell says it is finished. I shall never conceive again.' She took a deep breath. 'If you want to leave, go now, Oliver. I don't think I can live with you, without love, any longer.' Tears were pouring down her face now and she made no attempt to check them.

Oliver took her hands and pulled her so that she stood before him where he sat on the bed. The Oldfield family used to raise these feelings of growing anger in him but now the Oldfields were gone and he had to convince Florence of his love for her; of the love that had won the battle against them.

The bedroom clock sounded unnaturally loud as he began to speak. 'I have never heard such a tale of cruelty,' he said as he held her gaze steadily. 'I had no idea you had been told all those lies.'

She looked young and fragile, her skin translucent against the deep pearl collar that encircled her slender neck. She had a heart-stopping loveliness still and Oliver marvelled at her continuing devotion to him.

'From the moment I saw you, Florence,' he said, not taking his eyes from hers, 'I have loved you. I had one affair when you were taken away to London and that affair resulted in Edward, and I cannot regret it. There was another, and recently, but she was of no consequence. It was brief and loveless and it resulted in nothing but a revelation of the truth, that each of us was looking for something the other could not provide.'

He felt a shudder go through Florence's hands and he held them still. 'When your grandfather spoke to me all those years ago I was astounded. I had already made little approaches to you, to see if you still cared for me. When Sir Philip told me that I had his approval I could not believe my ears. After the years of waiting; after the years of hoping ... you were to be mine for the asking.'

He pulled her close and put his lips to her cheek. 'What a fool I would have been not to take you before you or your family changed your minds.'

She relaxed against him and he could feel in her chest the jerkiness of the tears that were so near the surface. 'I never wanted Suttonford,' he continued, 'I never even liked the place. I wanted you. All I ever wanted, all I still want, is to have a proper home; a home I can return to at night and find everyone waiting for me. My wife – you, Florence – happy to see me. I want to see my children – little Maud glad that Papa is home.'

'I only ever wanted the ordinary precious things that the poorest people take for granted. And I have never had it. Never. Not in my childhood, nor with all my money.'

Her tears were coming now, falling onto his shoulder, rolling down his chest as he held her sobbing, shaking body close to his. He spoke gently. 'Now at last I think there is a chance that we may achieve it.'

She was still, listening.

'Now tell me, Florence. What were your dreams?'

She buried her wet face in his neck and told him in a small, choking voice. 'They were ordinary, romantic dreams.'

'I used to lie in bed at night and imagine you wanting me. I saw myself as desirable, romantic. I wanted you to tell me you loved me. I wanted us to go beyond passion. I wanted us to be as one. I wanted to be needed, I suppose. And I never got beyond the wanting.'

'Did you want me to ravish you, Florence?' he asked and he could not keep himself from smiling as he held her at arm's length and studied her lovely, frightened face.

'Oh, yes,' she said. 'I still want you to.'

'Can I convince you that it's you I want?' he said.

'I want you back,' she said. 'I want you back in my bed and in my arms. I think I could learn to be a proper wife to you.'

'You are a proper wife,' he told her. 'I want no other.'

'Can you teach me to be your mistress as well?' she asked timidly. 'You have always been so restrained with me.'

'I? Restrained?' He could not help but smile at her words. 'If I was restrained then it was because I was afraid of hurting you – afraid you would be repelled by me.'

It was her turn to smile. 'You never gave me a chance to be anything other than I was,' she said.

Now he saw in her eyes a look that he had always longed to see there and as he put his arms around her and answered that look with his mouth upon hers, and felt in her response her need of him, he knew with a quickening sense of desire that a new beginning for them both lay ahead. She wanted to give herself to him and in her arms he would find the joy she had withheld from him so long.

Distantly they heard a clock striking the hour, summoning them to join the family at its first gathering.

Oliver disentangled himself from her. 'We'll keep that for later, Mrs Wainwright,' he said softly. 'Tonight our family is waiting for us, in its first proper home. Come!'